THE HIT

Nadia Dalbuono has spent the last sixteen years working as a documentary director and consultant for Channel 4, ITV, Discovery, and *National Geographic* in various countries. *The Hit* is the third of her Leone Scamarcio novels, following *The Few* and *The American*. She divides her time between the UK and northern Italy.

To JR, AB, and all my friends in Rome.

the hit

NADIA DALBUONO

SCRIBE
Melbourne • London

Scribe Publications
18–20 Edward St, Brunswick, Victoria 3056, Australia
2 John St, Clerkenwell, London, WC1N 2ES, United Kingdom

First published by Scribe 2016
This edition published in 2017

Typeset in Dante MT by the publisher

Printed and bound in the UK by CPI Group (UK) Ltd, Croydon CR0 4YY

Scribe Publications is committed to the sustainable use of natural resources
and the use of paper products made responsibly from those resources.

9781925321609 (Australian edition)
9781925228960 (UK edition)
9781925307832 (e-book)

CiP records for this title are available from the British Library and
the National Library of Australia.

scribepublications.com.au
scribepublications.co.uk

1

LILA SAT CRYING ON THE SOFA, her eye make-up running down her cheeks. The camera panned right to reveal Fernando standing in the doorway, half in shadow. The music was building to a slow crescendo.

Micky Proietti sighed and uncrossed his legs. He'd told them 'no piano'. He'd made it perfectly clear, he'd said it several times and had even set it down in an email, but there was piano everywhere—it was practically wall to wall.

Fernando approached from the doorway and stood behind Lila, placing a shaky hand on her shoulder.

Fernando had a memorable face, but his performance was weak. Right now, he looked like someone had run over his pet canary. Why hadn't the director done a retake? The problem with the old guard was that they were scared of the talent; they didn't ride them hard. The young guns didn't care; they'd do whatever it took, commit their actors to an asylum if necessary. He should have got the Caselli Brothers on this. Why the hell had he listened to Giacometti when he'd insisted on Andrea? Andrea was 65—he was past it. TV was a young man's game.

Yet again, Micky Proietti considered the fact that he turned 43 next month. Would *he* be able to stay in the game until retirement? Would he be squeezed out, forced to take up a new career? *Focus, Micky*, he told himself. *You will be pushed aside if you don't turn this sow's ear into a silk purse.*

Fernando was sitting next to Lila on the sofa now. He was taking her hand gently in his. 'Darling, I have something to tell you ...'

The dreadful piano music resumed, and the screen faded to black …

Micky Proietti cleared his throat, remembering the basic lessons from his management training: start with the positives before moving to the negatives; be constructive; build confidence. Problem was, right now he couldn't think of any positives. Lila was OK-ish. She just about carried it, but it was hardly a stellar performance. As for Fernando, Micky could write the reviews already: 'a limp effort'; 'lacks passion,' etc, etc.

Proietti cleared his throat again. He could murder a line. Maybe he should pop over to the bathroom before addressing the team. *No*, he told himself. *Just get it over with — duty first, pleasure later.*

He shifted in his seat and surveyed the room. The editor was chewing down on a nail, staring at him impassively, quietly defiant. Micky hated that rebellious streak in editors; they always seemed determined to let whoever was higher up the hierarchy know that they wouldn't be intimidated, couldn't be pushed around. Actually, if he was honest, he'd always been a bit scared of them. Andrea, the director, was looking down at something on his notepad, doodling nervous circles with his biro, crossing and uncrossing his feet. Did he already realise it was a disaster? Didi, the producer, was subtly shifting her skirt higher up her magnificent legs. Poor Didi wouldn't be able to screw her way out of this one.

He recalled his management training once more, then thought, *Fuck it*. He needed to be in Parioli in an hour, and then there was that trip to the bathroom …

'Guys,' he said. 'Guys …' He opened his arms as if he wanted to enfold them all in a group hug. 'Guys, what can I say? It's shit.'

Andrea looked up sharply from his notepad. Didi sat straighter in her chair, and pushed her ridiculous glasses higher up her perfect nose.

'What, Micky?' She narrowed her eyes and then sniffed.

'It's not working, is it? You don't need me to tell you that.'

Andrea set down his pen and sat back in his chair, barring his arms across his chest. 'What's not working, Micky? You need to elaborate.'

'Where do I start? Fernando is weak, he's not carrying it. The lighting is off — there's way too much shadow all the time, it's dingy — it looks like a British drama. And as for the music, I thought I made it clear that I didn't want piano.'

'You said, "Go easy on the piano." You didn't say you didn't want *any*.'

Micky shook his head. 'Now, Andrea, you know that's not true. I sent you an email.'

'Well, I didn't see it.'

Didi held up a hand, but Micky ignored her. 'Who did the music?'

'D'Angelo.'

'He's usually good.'

'So you don't like the music?'

'No.'

'As for the shadow,' said Andrea, colour rising up his neck, 'we discussed the lighting plan. You said you liked it.'

The old guy was infuriating. 'How can I like something I haven't seen? You've gone overboard. It's a turn-off. It looks like you shot the entire thing in the dark.'

The wave of red crept further up Andrea's neck before reaching his jaw. His eyes narrowed, then he suddenly kicked back his chair and stormed out. The editor raised a languid eyebrow and extracted a packet of Fortuna from his top pocket. Micky would have to stop him if he went to light up. Didi had shut her eyes and was running a manicured finger across her closed lids.

'Micky,' she said with that smoker's growl of hers that had turned so many men to mush.

'Didi.'

3

'Micky. We discussed the lighting, we discussed the talent, we discussed the music. You can't turn around now and throw it all back in our faces.'

'It's not the choices, it's the direction. Andrea hasn't brought this one to life.'

'Andrea has decades of experience, strings of awards ...'

'Well, this time he's fucked up, and that's very bad news for me, because I've spent over two million on this. We're talking about six prime-time slots, Didi—don't forget that.'

She sighed and pushed a loose strand of blonde hair behind her ear. 'Well, if you give us your notes, I'm sure we can all make this work.'

'No, Didi. From what I've seen today, I'm considering this one an emergency.'

She was shaking her head slowly now, screwing up her face again in distaste. She needed to show him more respect in front of her team.

'I want Andrea out. I'm bringing in the Caselli brothers,' he said, staring her out.

'*What?*'

'You heard me. This show has to work. It has cost way too much to bomb.'

'But you can't do that to Andrea.'

'I can do what the bloody hell I like, Didi. I'm head of drama on the nation's most popular channel.'

He gathered up his things and headed for the bathroom. He didn't have time for this bleeding-heart crap.

Micky Proietti climbed into the passenger seat of the silver Mercedes AMG, pulled down the mirror, and checked his nose. His driver for the day stared ahead, his expression inscrutable. Micky never made conversation with the drivers—he wasn't interested, and he didn't have the time. Out of the corner of his

4

eye, he saw the red light of his iPhone blinking, and realised that he must have left it in the car. There were two missed calls from Fiammetta—it seemed like she couldn't get enough of him. The critics reckoned that she was the next big thing, that she'd run Belene out of town. Micky found the thought both troubling and exciting. Would she grow bored of him the more famous she became? Would she move onto someone younger, hipper? He checked himself in the mirror once more, and made a pistol with his fingers and fired, blowing the imaginary smoke away. No, he still had it. The way women responded to him told him that much.

Fiammetta could wait; besides, it was wise to keep her keen. He dialled his new secretary, trying to imagine what she might be wearing today. When he'd hired her, she'd told him that she was desperate to make it onto *The Inheritance* as a dancer. He'd said he'd do what he could, but she would need to do what *she* could in return. Lola had got it straightaway—she was nobody's fool. He wondered if he had time now to swing by the office for a quick one. He checked his watch. Not really. He had to pick up his wife and son in an hour—Antonio wanted them to head out to Sperlonga for the afternoon.

'We need to stop at my place in Parioli before the beach,' he told the driver.

The man just nodded like an automaton, adjusted the mirror, and fired up the ignition.

Micky jiggled his knee with impatience as the line rang out a few more times before his secretary finally picked up. He was about to berate her for the wait, then decided there wasn't time: 'Lola, I want you to get me the Casellis' agent on the phone ASAP.'

'Of course, Micky. Will you hold, or should I have him call you back?'

'I'll hold.'

The line buzzed for a few moments, and then the rasping

walrus grunt of Marco Bonanni came on—the greedy, obese, pederast fucker.

'Marco, how are you? How's the wife? How are those lovely girls of yours?'

'Micky, what a pleasant surprise! We're all good, thanks. You?'

'Couldn't be better, Marco. Listen, my friend, I need a favour—I won't beat about the bush.'

'Name it, Micky.'

'I know the Casellis are very much in demand at the moment …'

'I found them, you know.'

'Yes, Marco. That's what earns you the title *super agent*.'

'I think they'll make it to Hollywood. Interest is stirring.'

'I'm not surprised to hear that.'

'So, this favour?'

'I've got a prime-time series that needs rescuing. Cancer and infidelity threaten to destroy a marriage; can they keep the love alive? Dinosaur director has made a hash of it.'

'The Casellis don't pick up other people's leftovers, Micky. You should know that.'

'I *do*, Marco, but this is an emergency. I'm convinced they can turn it around. And I'd give them full credit—the old guy will be expunged from the record.'

'Yeah, but what kind of creative freedom will they have? How much is already in the can?'

'We've just started,' he lied. 'I didn't like what I saw.'

'And you couldn't talk the dinosaur round?'

Shit, doesn't Bonanni want to win his clients some business? 'Didn't like what I saw, old guy didn't want to listen.'

'*I* hear you,' said Bonanni, coughing and then wheezing a bit. Word was, he smoked 40 a day. 'I'll run it past them. Obviously, you'll pay full wack?'

'What is full wack now?'

Bonanni laughed. 'Yeah, you wouldn't know, would you, you tight-fisted bastard.'

Micky wanted to tell him to go fuck himself, but he swallowed it and managed to muster a casual laugh instead.

'Full wack for the brothers is 40,000 an episode,' grunted the walrus.

Micky's mouth dropped open. They were already charging Hollywood wages, the cunts. Where the hell was he going to find that kind of money? But this series had to make it …

He took a long breath. 'No problem, Marco. Run it past them. They're free, I take it?'

'Actually, they've just walked off something, didn't like the way it was going.'

Micky's mind flipped over. Had they walked, or were they pushed? Were they still hot, or was their star waning? No, they'd probably walked. They knew they could pick and choose.

'Great. Let me know ASAP, Marco. I need to get the ball rolling—schedule's tight.'

'Isn't it always?' Bonanni hung up, and the line went dead.

Where was the respect?

The driver pulled up outside the apartment block in Parioli where Micky's wife and son were waiting at the kerb. Maia looked good in her long, white sundress, and Micky felt a twinge of guilt; guilt had been plaguing him a lot lately. Why wasn't this magnificent woman enough? What was wrong with him? Or was he just a normal middle-aged man with normal urges? He sighed and felt suddenly low, but then his son beamed and ran to the car, and he forgot the sadness for a moment.

They took the Autostrada out of the city towards Sperlonga, the grey concrete jungles of social housing gradually paling into sunbleached fields of corn and wheat. So far, so good: Micky reckoned they'd got ahead of the traffic by at least two hours.

Maia placed her hand on the back of his neck, and he turned and smiled, imagining that the two of them must look like something out of a commercial. But then, uninvited, an image of Fiammetta came into his mind: an image from their lovemaking the night before. Would he ever be able to walk away from a woman like that, let her go, only for someone else to capture her heart? Somehow, he doubted it.

'My God,' Maia cried out. The synchronicity of it made him fear that she'd been granted a momentary glimpse inside his mind; that, for some inexplicable reason, she knew. But then his stomach flipped when he understood the real reason for her screams: a black BMW was hurtling towards them, doing way more than 160. The car was in *their* lane, heading right at them, bearing down on them fast. In an instant, Micky realised that whoever was behind the wheel wanted to destroy them; there would be no last-minute manoeuvre, no swerve to avoid.

The chauffeur spun the Mercedes to the right. There was no time to know what they were driving into — whether there was a hard shoulder, whether there was anything beyond. The seconds felt like minutes, sound and vision seemed to fade, and when finally the driver's knuckles had turned white and the wheel would turn no more, he threw himself across Micky, forcing his right shoulder hard into the window. But the impact didn't register, because Micky's mind was too busy processing what was happening on the other side of the car: an ear-shattering explosion was sucking in the air around them, dragging them down into a vortex, deeper and deeper until there was nothing but darkness and silence. Then suddenly a blast of light was pulling them all back to the surface, where the airbags mushroomed like bombs and the driver's door began buckling inwards. Time seemed to slow as Micky watched mangled metal rip through leather, smoke particles collide with dust, crystal embed itself in skin. Sound had become liquid, pooling and oozing, but then the driver's window

8

ruptured, and a sharp volley of broken glass brought Micky to his senses.

'Antonio! Antonio!' he screamed, pushing the driver off him. What side of the car had his son been sitting? He couldn't remember now.

He heard muffled sobs from the back seat, and experienced a wave of relief so intense that he thought he might pass out. But then an image from countless films snapped him into action.

'Get out the car, get out the car,' he yelled. He opened the handle and shoved the driver out, then fell onto the gravel behind him. Immediately, the driver scrambled to his feet and tore open the door for Antonio. Micky leant in and wrestled his son free. The boy tottered on the gravel for a moment before finding his balance. 'I think I broke my arm, Daddy, I think I broke my arm,' he cried.

'Let's just get to safety, and then I'll take a look. Quick, come on.'

The driver had already helped Maia from the back seat, and the four of them now limped and stumbled to the top of the hard shoulder, as far away from the smoking Mercedes as was possible before hitting the road. *Thank God there was a hard shoulder*, thought Micky, *thank God*. He really didn't deserve that kind of luck.

'Are you guys OK?' Someone was shouting. 'Jesus, are you all OK?'

Micky turned, and saw movement up ahead to his left. A stranger was sprinting towards them. He had brown curly hair, and was wearing red exercise gear. 'I saw the whole thing,' he panted as he crossed the road. 'Jesus, what was that arsehole thinking?'

'Where is he? Did you see where he went?' asked Micky.

'He just drove off,' said the man, incredulous. 'There was no time to read his plates.'

Antonio was sobbing now, his little legs shaking.

'Your son? Is he OK?'

Micky bent down and tried to take Antonio's arm, but he was holding it at a strange angle, and screamed when Micky tried to touch it. Maia was kissing Antonio's head, whispering that everything was going to be all right.

'I think he's broken it,' said Micky. 'I swear I'll kill that maniac son of a bitch, I'll fucking kill him.'

The stranger pulled a mobile from his pocket. 'I'm calling an ambulance.'

Micky nodded. Antonio was crying in a way he'd never heard before. It was a kind of keening—a primitive, animal sound of groans rather than sobs. Micky was struggling to keep it together: his heart was racing, and his palms were sweating. He couldn't stand hearing his son like this; he felt so helpless, so totally and utterly useless. Maia was trembling, and he could hear someone's teeth chattering. Then, after a moment, he realised that they were his own—it was 22 degrees, and he was freezing. He noticed that the driver was sitting in the dirt, his head between his knees. He looked as if he were about to throw up. Micky made a mental note to thank him for his quick thinking. But now didn't feel like the right time.

He wasn't sure how long they'd been standing there before the sudden shriek of sirens made them all look up. The ambulance had been much faster than he'd expected. It came to a screeching halt on the gravel in front of them, and then the paramedics were out of the vehicle and surrounding Antonio in seconds. They laid him on a stretcher and checked his arms and legs; then they were bending over him, shining a small light in his eyes. When they were satisfied, they moved on to Maia, who was shaking her head, insisting she was fine. Now they were helping the driver to his knees. Micky briefed them on what had happened, as clearly as he could manage. He still didn't really understand it.

'Does your son have any allergies?' one of the paramedics was asking.

'Not to any medicines, just to dog and cat hair,' said Maia.

They started loading Antonio into the ambulance, Maia right behind them. For the first time, Micky noticed that she had a smear of blood across her forehead. Was it hers or Antonio's?

A paramedic was trying to check Micky's pupils now, but he just batted the torch away.

'I'll go to the hospital,' Maia was saying. 'What do you want to do? Will the police be coming?'

'I just called them — they're on their way,' said the helpful stranger.

The second paramedic was helping the driver into the ambulance.

'Does he have to go?' Micky asked.

'There are signs of concussion. He needs to see a doctor,' the man replied calmly.

'You stay with the car then, Micky. You'll need to tell them what happened,' said Maia, her voice cracking.

'What hospital are you taking them to?' Micky asked the paramedic, who now had his hand on the back door, ready to close it.

'Policlinico Gemelli.'

Micky grabbed his wife's hand and kissed it before the doors slammed shut.

'The Policlinico is a good hospital. They'll see them right,' said the stranger as the ambulance disappeared from view, its siren dying away slowly to nothing.

2

THE SQUADROOM WAS EMPTY, Via San Vitale was empty — it was if some apocalyptic virus had claimed the planet, and Scamarcio had been the last to find out. How would he feel if he were the only man left on earth? Not much different from how he felt now, really. He sank back in his chair and took a sip of the insipid coffee. Maybe he should donate a machine to the office: one of those high-end ones that did everything? But that would just be drawing attention to himself — some smartarse would raise questions about how he had financed it.

He scratched his head and surveyed the street once more. Not even the stray from recent months was around. Had someone taken pity on him and given him a home, or had he been knocked down by a car? Scamarcio felt the need to know. That decrepit mongrel had been the focus of his attention for the past weeks.

He returned his gaze to the pile of paperwork on his desk, wishing it was an illusion, that he could just snap his fingers and make it disappear. But then he looked up again, sensing that someone was watching: Garramone was standing in his office doorway, one hand on the filthy squadroom wall. He was motioning him in with the other, his expression solemn.

Scamarcio got up slowly and made a final effort with the dire coffee before tossing it into the trash. He was late in filing a case report. Was that the reason for the boss's frown?

As he stepped into his office, he was reminded that Garramone had just had it redecorated — he had seen them removing the gear the other night. The place was now a calming oatmeal colour, and the battered chairs had been replaced with expensive brown-leather ones. Who had footed the bill? Scamarcio wondered. Everywhere else, the budget cuts were still biting.

Garramone sat down and yawned, running his plump fingers across his eyebrows. He looked beaten.

'You OK?' asked Scamarcio.

'My wife's made me give up caffeine.'

'I couldn't function.'

'I'm not.' The boss yawned again and then sat up straighter in his smart new chair. 'Anyway, I didn't call you in here to talk about me. I wanted to know how *you* were doing?'

'Me?'

'I see you're off your game.'

'Off my game?'

'Are you just going to repeat everything I say?'

Scamarcio looked down at the floor, trying to invent an appropriate response.

'So?'

Was he off his game? The answer was that he really didn't know: some days he thought he was making progress, keeping it all together, but then there were others when the huge dark clouds returned, and the weight of them pressed him into his mattress and pinned him there. On workdays he'd eventually fight back and struggle his way to the surface, find the space to breathe again, but on weekends he could languish for hours until day drifted into the pale sodium of night, and a cavernous grey emptiness echoed out along his street. He couldn't actually remember the last time he had socialised. His ex-girlfriend Aurelia had left for Munich four months ago after a brutal assault, and since then his life had simply ground to a halt. He had no desire to trade small talk, drink overpriced wine, join the absurd dance that was human existence. He worked, he ate, he slept; he washed—occasionally.

And then there was the Piocosta problem: with every call

13

telling Scamarcio that Aurelia was safe, the old man's python chokehold tightened.

Scamarcio realised that he still hadn't supplied Garramone with an answer. 'OK, Sir. I think I'm doing OK.'

Garramone screwed up his eyes so that they almost disappeared into the folds of his wrinkles. 'I know I'm your boss, but I also want you to see me as a friend. I've been through tough times; I know what it's like.'

The comment wrong-footed Scamarcio; he wished they could delete it and return to the default setting. He didn't want to know about Garramone's hard times; he didn't want to talk about his.

Scamarcio's mind was still a blank, so he just nodded and smiled—probably the most meagre of smiles. When Garramone continued to stare at him, he scratched at the back of his neck and silently willed him to move on.

The boss sighed and then glanced down at a scrawled scrap of paper on his desk. 'We've just received a very strange call. I think this might be right up your street.'

Scamarcio felt the faintest bristle of something that might have been excitement. He wanted a challenge; he had been soft-pedalling lately. Perhaps that had been part of the problem.

Garramone tapped the piece of paper. 'So this guy says he's been involved in an RTA on the E45. Some idiot takes the corner at high speed on the wrong side of the road and ploughs straight into him, ripping out the entire left side of the guy's Mercedes. If it hadn't been for the quick thinking of his chauffeur, they'd all be dead.'

Scamarcio wanted to ask why the flying squad should be concerning itself with an RTA, but figured that he should allow Garramone a little longer to explain himself.

'A helpful stranger who happens to be passing calls an ambulance. The guy had his wife and son in the car, and it looks like the little boy has broken his arm.'

Scamarcio still didn't understand why they were discussing this.

'The wife and son are loaded into the ambulance, along with the driver, while the husband waits for the police to arrive. The paramedics tell him they're taking his family to the Policlinico.'

'Good hospital,' said Scamarcio, baffled.

'That doesn't mean much to our guy right now.'

'Why?'

'Cos they never arrived.'

'What?'

'When our guy shows up at the hospital, there's no trace of them. The hospital tells him they've never been alerted to expect them.'

Scamarcio leant forward in his chair. Garramone had his interest now.

'Our guy then does a trawl of the other major hospitals — there's no sign of them there either. Right now he's trying the smaller ones, but it's starting to smell like a kidnap job.'

'Anyone been on to the traffic police who attended? The ambulance service?'

Garramone scratched his forehead with his thumb. 'I've only just put the phone down to our guy.'

'You took the call yourself?'

'They passed it up from downstairs — he's a VIP.'

'Politician?' Scamarcio asked quickly. He prayed to any god who was listening that he wasn't about to be handed a political case. He had done his time with them.

'No. He's head of drama at Channel One — counts lots of celebs and politicos among his friends, though.'

'Enemies?'

'A few, no doubt. He's a high flier, recently tipped for promotion. Name's Micky Proietti.'

Scamarcio eased back in his chair. 'So we need to establish if it *is* a kidnapping? When did the accident happen?'

'Three hours ago. The window is still open. Like you say, I'd start by contacting emergency services, get the data on the call the stranger made requesting the ambulance.'

'*If* he called them.'

Garramone frowned. 'You think he could have been in on it?'

'Sure. He conveniently appears and offers to make the call ...'

'Hmmm. Our guy wants to keep trawling the smaller hospitals, but instinct tells me he's wasting his time. I'm sending a couple of uniforms down to help him while you make a start on the phones.'

Scamarcio nodded.

Garramone yawned once more. 'Tread carefully. Our guy's connected. We don't want any more trouble for the department.'

These days, it felt like everyone was 'connected'. To get outside of all that, what would Scamarcio need to do? Move to Mars?

3

'I'M LOOKING BACK THROUGH THE LOG NOW—there's no record.'

'Go back an hour,' said Scamarcio.

'I've already checked back to midday,' said the woman at ambulance dispatch.

'Sonofabitch,' said Scamarcio.

'Excuse me?'

'Nothing. So as far as you guys are concerned, that call was never made?'

'No, there's no record. Every call has a record. They must have just pretended to phone us.'

'But an ambulance arrived.'

'Did you see the ambulance?'

'No. But I have a witness who did.'

'Get him to give you a description,' said the woman. 'When ambulances go out of service they are sold off to collectors, charities, prop houses …'

'Do you have any data on where each one ends up?'

'I don't, but there may be someone here who does or who can point you in the right direction. If you give me your details, I'll pass it on.'

Scamarcio reeled off his number and thanked her for her time.

His next call was to the traffic police who patrolled the E45. It took him a few minutes to locate the officers who'd attended. The guy who eventually came on the line had a thick Sicilian accent. 'Yeah, that car had been bashed up pretty bad. It was a miracle nobody died. Thanks to God, the little boy had been on the side that escaped the impact.'

'Did it look like an accident to you?'

'Way the guy tells it, the other car was heading straight for them; the driver definitely meant to take them out. He just kept on going afterwards, and nobody managed to get a look at his plates. Our guy did not provide a useful description, unfortunately.'

'How did Mr Proietti seem to you?'

'Like a coke head.'

Scamarcio took a few moments to absorb this. 'You think his account's reliable?'

'They were targeted, all right; it wasn't a case of paranoia or careless driving. If the rogue driver had taken the bend on the wrong side at speed and then meant to correct, things would have looked different. Luckily for us, there was oil on the road, which allowed us to see that he accelerated *after* the bend — he left tyre residue where he sped up. Besides, if it had all been a mistake, he'd have stopped. You'd definitely stop after a collision like that.'

Scamarcio filled him in on what had happened, or rather hadn't happened afterwards.

'Jesus,' whistled the officer. He shouted to someone in the background. 'Hey, Santoro — that RTA out on the E45 was a kidnap job. Took them all away in a fake ambulance — got the flying squad on the line.'

Scamarcio heard the guy's partner whistle softly. When the officer came back on, Scamarcio said: 'We're not sure it was a kidnapping yet.'

'What else would it be?'

'Did you see the ambulance?'

'No, it had gone before we arrived.'

'What about the stranger who called you?'

'He'd gone, too. That was a pity, because we needed his

statement — can't prosecute without that. He left his details, though, so we could contact him.'

'Have you?'

'I can't seem to get through on the mobile number he left.'

What a surprise, thought Scamarcio. 'Do you have a record of the number he first called you from?'

'Ah. Good idea. I hadn't tried that yet.'

'Can you try it now while I'm on the line?'

The officer sounded surprised for a moment, then said: 'Well, sure, if that's what you want. Hang on.'

After a few seconds he was back. 'That number's not responding either — it's different from the one he left us, though.'

'Did the cokehead say why the stranger had done a runner?'

'Work emergency, apparently.'

Scamarcio could tell that this call wasn't going to get him any further. It was time to pay Micky Proietti a visit. He thanked the officer, and asked him to get in touch if he managed to track down the stranger. But even as he spoke the words, Scamarcio knew they would come to nothing.

4

MICKY PROIETTI WAS HUNCHED UP against the battered wall of the A and E department at the Tiburtina hospital when Scamarcio walked in. Two young officers were eyeing him with a mixture of confusion, exasperation, and just the smallest remnant of sympathy. Clearly, Proietti had not been making the best impression. From a quick glance, Scamarcio decided that he would be arrogant, bossy, impatient, and cold. But he reminded himself that the man had just had his wife and son spirited away from him in plain daylight. That could not be easy to process.

He held out a hand. 'Leone Scamarcio, Flying Squad.'

Proietti accepted the gesture limply, as if he couldn't really be bothered. 'You took your time.'

'I was following up other leads.'

'On this case?'

'Of course.'

'Have you got anywhere?'

Scamarcio scanned the waiting room. There was a Middle Eastern-looking family — mum and dad and two small kids seated up the hall to their right. An elderly man was sitting alone at the bottom of the corridor on the left. He was shaking.

'The ambulance that came to collect your wife and son was a fake. The ambulance service never received the call.'

Proietti shifted on the bench, and then leant forward and hung his head in his hands. He looked like someone trying to recover from a hangover. 'But that makes no sense. I was there when the guy rang them,' he said to the ground.

'I think he was a fake, too.'

'What?' He was looking up at him now, waking up finally.

'There's no record of that call. Either he pretended to call them, or he just rang some other number.'

Proietti was shaking his head, refusing to accept it. 'But that can't be. He phoned the traffic cops, and they arrived.'

'Sure. But the number he called from is no longer in use. I'm sure if they try to visit him at the address he provided, they won't find him there either.'

Proietti was still shaking his head. 'He said he had to rush off — work emergency, or something. I believed him.' He paused for a moment. 'Jesus, I've been a fool.'

Scamarcio sensed that Proietti wasn't one usually prone to self-criticism.

'How were you to know?'

Proietti looked down, and as he did so his expression told Scamarcio that he believed he *should* have known. Scamarcio found that interesting.

Proietti had said he'd prefer to talk at his place rather than at the station. He was worried that a call might come in on the landline and that he would miss it. Scamarcio told him that they were already monitoring the line in case of this eventuality, but he assented to the request. He wanted to get a feel for this man and his family.

Proietti lived in a splendid art deco block on one of Parioli's most attractive streets. Scamarcio reckoned the apartment was near on 200 metres square. It opened onto a huge living room with massive white-leather sofas and sumptuous cream rugs strewn across gleaming parquet. Modernist mirrors lined the walls, making the space feel even larger. Arranged on oak tables and cabinets were small clusters of framed family photos interspersed with trophies of various shapes and sizes. There were several gold and silver figurines of movie reels and cameras on tripods, and when Scamarcio bent down to examine one he saw it was from the Television Society of Italy. He studied the small bronze photo frame next to the trophy. Proietti was laughing into the camera, a beautiful blonde woman beside him, a cute little boy in his lap. The three of them looked like celebrities from a magazine spread.

Scamarcio held up the photo. 'Your wife and son?'

Proietti nodded absently.

'How old is your boy?'

'Nine.' Something dark crossed Proietti's features, and he slumped down onto the sofa. 'He's only nine.'

'Your wife?'

'Thirty-nine.'

'Is this a picture we could use for the press? Is it recent?'

Proietti got up tiredly from the sofa and picked up a larger photo in a sterling-silver frame. 'Use this. It was taken a month ago.'

Scamarcio studied it. If anything, the woman looked even more beautiful. Her face was all smooth planes and angles, and she reminded him of the actress Charlize Theron. 'Is your wife Italian?' he asked.

'Italian father, Ukrainian mother.'

'And things were good between you?'

Proietti glanced up quickly. 'Why is that relevant?'

'At this stage, everything's relevant.'

He sighed and took the photo from Scamarcio, studying it. 'Yes, things were good, *are* good. Why are we talking about her in the past tense already?'

'How long have you been married?'

Proietti kept looking at the photo. He seemed to be studying it closely, looking for a clue as to why she'd disappeared. 'Ten years now. But we've known each other since our early twenties.'

'University sweethearts?'

'No, we were in the same circle of friends. I always liked her, but she wasn't interested at first.'

Scamarcio was surprised by this. With his perfect square jaw, large, dark eyes, and athletic frame, Proietti was handsome by any standards. What had put her off?

'Did she have a boyfriend back then?' he asked.

Proietti seemed surprised by the question. 'No. She just wasn't interested.'

'Did it take you long to win her round?'

'A couple of years. We were dating for five years before we married.'

Scamarcio nodded. 'A couple of officers will need to confirm some basic details with you—your wife's height, hair colour, etc, and the same for your son and driver. We'll need it for the media release.'

'Sure.'

'Do you mind if I sit down?'

Proietti gestured him to a white armchair opposite the sofa. Even the scatter cushions were white. It seemed too much.

'Maybe you should sit as well, Mr Proietti. This might take a while.'

Proietti nodded mutely and did as instructed. Scamarcio sensed that the man was shutting down—that the effects of the coke or whatever it was were finally wearing off.

'Mr Proietti, do you have any enemies?'

Proietti looked at him as if he'd just asked him to count the blades of grass on the manicured lawn outside.

'I'm head of drama on the nation's most popular channel. I've made my name by cutting costs and pushing the talent to the limit. I'm sure I've put quite a few noses out of joint, but if you're asking me if they'd go so far as to kidnap my family—well, frankly, the idea is ridiculous.'

23

'What about outside your work?'

'There is no outside my work. My life is my work and my family. That's it—there's no room for anything else.'

'Can you think of anyone who might be jealous of you, of your success?'

Proietti was shaking his head again. 'I'm sure there are quite a few who are envious. I've climbed the ladder fast; I'm paid well for a job I love. But again, would they kidnap my family out of jealousy? Forgive me, Detective, but it feels like you're clutching at straws.'

Scamarcio ignored him and pushed on. 'What about your chauffeur? Do you trust him?'

Proietti blinked. 'I don't know him. I couldn't even tell you his name. The channel uses an agency, and the drivers change daily.'

Scamarcio made a note. 'Do you know the name of this agency?'

'No. but my secretary would have it.'

Scamarcio fell silent for a few moments and then asked: 'What about you? Your background? Are your parents involved in anything that might invite recrimination? Your wife, for that matter?'

Proietti narrowed his eyes. 'Neither my wife nor my mother work, and my father's not a Mafioso, if that's what you're getting at.'

The thought hadn't crossed Scamarcio's mind. He wondered why Proietti had jumped on this. Then he wondered if he'd already read up on Scamarcio's past, and that's why he'd made the reference. He pushed the question to the back of his mind, trying to focus.

'What does your father do for a living?'

'He was CFO of Enel for the last twenty years before he retired. My mother fills her time with charity lunches, that kind of thing. She's your typical Parioli housewife.'

'They live near here?'

'One floor down. You can pay them a visit on your way out.'

'Do they know what's happened?'

'No. My father and I aren't on speaking terms at the moment.'

'Why's that?'

Proietti raised his eyes to the heavens and exhaled. 'Again, how is this relevant?'

'Mr Proietti, if you want me to find your wife and son, I need to be the judge of what is relevant.'

Proietti sighed and cast his gaze to the swaying palm fronds outside. Scamarcio looked up and saw dark clouds beyond the rooftops. A cooler, charged breeze was sweeping into the room.

'We argued about some stocks he's holding in my name. I want to sell; he doesn't.'

'Why do you need the money?'

'I don't. I just think that the company is heading for trouble, and it's time to bail.' Scamarcio watched his eyes as he spoke. They way they evaded him, shifting once more to the darkening skies beyond the window, told him that Proietti was lying.

5

PROIETTI HAD SAID THAT his secretary would provide Scamarcio with a list of the people he did business with, although Proietti seriously doubted they'd be able to help with the whereabouts of his family. Garramone had dispatched a team to keep watch on Proietti and his home, and had organised a second unit back at base to deal with any potential sightings that came in. Scamarcio had passed by Proietti's parents' place on his way out the previous evening, but they hadn't been in. He decided to head back later, once he'd visited Proietti's office.

The secretary was pretty close to what Scamarcio had expected: bottle blonde, fake tanned, legs to her armpits, collagen lips. *This might be Proietti's bit of rough, quite different from the natural beauty of the wife.*

Scamarcio guessed that this woman didn't expect to remain a secretary for long. And, as she held out a hand to greet him, something in her eyes told him that she was screwing the boss. Had this helpful little message been intentional? Scamarcio wondered. If so, he needed to understand why.

'Micky said you needed a list of his contacts — the production houses he does business with.'

She motioned him to a chair opposite her desk. The office was impressive — sparkling white walls, modernist white furniture. What was it with Proietti's obsession with white? Was it even a colour? Wasn't it just a nothingness, an absence? Scamarcio seemed to remember reading that there was in fact no colour in the universe. The world was black and white, but the human brain had created colour in order to make better sense of the objects around us.

'The people Micky does business with change according to the projects we have on the slate,' she continued. 'There are, however, a few teams we use frequently. I can give you their details.'

'Good,' said Scamarcio. 'If there are any new people he's worked with recently, throw those in as well.'

She narrowed her eyes. 'That will be a lot of names to get through.'

'It's OK; we have a lot of manpower.'

She didn't seem particularly reassured by this, but began delicately tapping at her keyboard, her eyes scrolling down the computer screen. After a few moments, the printer whirred to life.

'And I'll need the details of the chauffeur agency you use.'

She nodded, opened a drawer, and handed him a business card. He saw the name 'Executive Cars' embossed in gold letters. Two Rome telephone numbers were listed, along with an address out near Fiumincino.

'Do you like working for Micky?' he asked, pocketing the card.

Her cheeks flushed, and she looked down at her desk for a moment. 'Very much, yes.'

'How long have you been sleeping with him?'

'Excuse me?' She was trying to do outrage, but it wasn't quite working. If she wanted to be an actress, she wasn't going to make it, thought Scamarcio tiredly.

'I asked you how long you've been sleeping with him.'

She said nothing. She just stared at him and then quickly glanced away. After a few seconds, she looked back, defiant. 'There's nothing going on between us—you've got it wrong.'

'If you want me to arrest you for obstructing a major police inquiry, then let's go. Otherwise we can stay put, and you can tell me the truth. A coffee wouldn't go amiss either.'

She threw him a look of undiluted hatred, then got up and

headed for the espresso machine. 'Sugar?' she hissed with all the charm of a master poisoner.

'No, thank you.'

She quickly handed over the espresso, her eyes refusing to meet his. He smiled, and knocked it back in one sip. It was much better than the coffee they had in his office. Something about this infuriated him.

'So, you were saying …'

She sighed and ran a hand through the fake blonde mane. 'I only arrived here a couple of months ago.'

'When did you start sleeping with him?'

She chewed on her bottom lip and said nothing, then: 'A couple of months ago.'

'Did he promise you anything in return?'

She inclined her head. 'I want to make it onto *The Inheritance*.'

'Fun show—I catch it from time to time.'

She exhaled sharply and slouched back against her chair. Scamarcio sensed that she couldn't be bothered to put on the glamorous-secretary act anymore. Her features seemed to slacken, and her face became even less remarkable.

'Listen, Detective. I won't waste your time and, in return, I'd be grateful if you didn't waste mine.'

Even her voice had changed. It was lower and stronger now, and her eyes conveyed a deeper intelligence. 'I'm sorry to hear that Micky's wife and son have gone missing, really I am. But I had nothing to do with it. You need to understand that I've worked my way up through the school of hard knocks, and I'm a realist. I wasn't harbouring any illusions that Micky was going to leave his family for me.' She stopped for a moment and looked into her lap. 'Micky is just a means to an end. I'm not in love with him and, if you asked him, I'm sure he'd say the same.'

Scamarcio was impressed by the cynicism, by the cold-hearted rationality of it all.

'What happened?'

'What?'

'In the school of hard knocks?'

She began toying with the papers on her desk. 'Children's home followed by foster home, and all that that entails …'

She threw him a guarded look, and he felt something dark pass between them, something better left unsaid.

'I gave up waiting for my knight in shining armour a long time ago.'

He nodded and smiled, trying to convey a little warmth this time. This woman was being straight with him; he wasn't going to push her. 'OK,' he said eventually. 'I won't take up any more of your time. Good luck, Lola.'

Micky had told him her name. Somehow, Scamarcio felt sure it was an invention, just like the rest of her work persona. He rose, and tossed the tiny plastic cup into the trash before picking up the small stack of A4 with the names she'd printed off for him.

As he was heading for the door, she said: 'Start with Giacometti.'

'Giacometti?'

He turned, and she gestured to the paper in his hand.

'He runs the biggest film and TV production house in Rome — a heavy hitter.' She had seemed about to say more, but fell silent.

He decided to let it go. 'Thanks. He'll be my next stop.'

As he was heading for Paolo Giacometti's office, Scamarcio dialled the number for Executive Cars. A harassed-sounding woman answered.

'Sorry, who did you say you were?'

Scamarcio repeated his introduction, trying not to sound irritated.

'Are you calling about Piero?'

'Piero?'

'Piero Cogo, our driver who was assaulted.'

'You've had an assault there?'

'Piero was on his way to a client when some bastard coshed him over the head. They nicked his wallet, phone, and car keys.' She paused. 'That's not what you were calling about then?'

Scamarcio stopped walking and took a seat on a broken wall. He rubbed a hand across his eyes. 'Out of interest, who was Mr Cogo scheduled to drive?'

'One second.' He heard papers being shuffled, and a pen falling to the floor. 'I know it was somewhere around Parioli. Hang on … Oh yes, here we are: it was an executive at Channel One, a Mr Proietti.'

Scamarcio didn't like it. As kidnappers went, they were starting to seem pretty organised. 'Where exactly did this happen?'

'A few streets away from the client's house, I believe.'

'Where was the car?'

'At the client's. We provide the drivers, but our customers often prefer to use their own cars.'

Scamarcio made a mental note to send a colleague to look for street cameras near Proietti's place and to talk to the driver, but he wasn't hopeful.

Paolo Giacometti, the producer, had his legs up on his desk and seemed to be watching something intently on his laptop when Scamarcio arrived. Every so often, Giacometti would lean forward and scrawl a quick note on a pad of paper, his eyes locked on the screen as he did so.

'Why don't you just press pause?' asked Scamarcio from the doorway.

Giacometti didn't look up. 'You don't get the same effect. You need to watch the whole show uninterrupted to get a true sense of it.'

Scamarcio found it odd that Giacometti hadn't asked who he was and what he wanted. Instead his attention remained focused on the screen, his pen still moving. From the laptop, Scamarcio heard shouting then a flourish of piano music.

'Come and take a seat, Detective. You can watch it with me. It's always good to get a second opinion.'

Giacometti swung the computer around so they could both see the screen from either side of his desk. Scamarcio noted that he was well built, but perhaps not tall. He had wavy, unruly salt-and-pepper hair, and was wearing heavy glasses with fashionable black frames. He'd put him at around fifty.

'You watch much TV, Detective?'

'Not really.' Scamarcio wanted to ask how Giacometti knew who he was, then figured that Proietti's secretary might have called ahead. Why would she do that? Good relations perhaps, her eye on the bigger picture, the long-term game?

On the screen a woman was crying. A man was seated next to her, his hand on her shoulder. After several moments of what, Scamarcio guessed, was intended as dramatic silence, the piano resumed, and the screen turned black.

'You see, Detective,' said Giacometti, finally laying down his pen. 'What some people in this business still fail to comprehend is that we are not in America. We are in Italia.' He tapped out the syllables with his index finger. 'These channel executives go to the trade fairs, the swanky conventions, rub shoulders with the big guys from LA, then come back thinking they have to do everything like them. But as Herman Melville once said: 'It is better to fail in originality than to succeed in imitation.' In my business, imitation is the road to ruin; it's idiocy, it's craziness, and, more importantly, it's a huge waste of money.'

'Why?' asked Scamarcio, wondering if Giacometti was just a little bit crazy himself.

'Because things are different here; our demographic is different for a start. This *is* a country of old men. And, more importantly, old women: old women who pray to Padre Pio, who worship the pope, who are superstitious, romantic, narrow-minded, hopeful, vengeful, jealous, traditional, prudish.' He swept an arm across the room. 'And what do these old women want?' He didn't allow Scamarcio time to respond. 'They want old-fashioned love stories. And what do they want in those love stories?'

Again, he didn't stop to let Scamarcio speak. 'They want hope, then the crushing of all hope; they want betrayal, followed by devastation, followed by rebirth, renewal, and reconciliation.' He punched his hand on the table with each 're'. 'And what do they want accompanying all this?'

Scamarcio shook his head again.

'Piano music! That's what they want.'

'I'm sorry …'

'Micky is a cretin. He doesn't get it. He's trying to make shows for people like him. But most Italians *aren't* like him — they're not metropolitan metrosexuals. They live in crumbling old villages, they live with their 90-year-old mothers — they live cut off from the 21st century, they've never been abroad. They want what they *know*, what's familiar. My director understood this perfectly.' He shook his head. 'And now Micky wants him fired. Proietti doesn't get the business; he doesn't understand his audience.'

'I heard he was doing pretty well.'

'Ah, don't believe the hype.' He pointed a finger. 'You start asking around, and you'll get a very different picture.'

'You heard about his wife and son?'

'Yeah,' said Giacometti, as if he was surprised Scamarcio had changed the subject. 'Yeah,' he repeated, staring him straight in the eye now. 'It's weird.' He almost whispered the word.

Yeah, he's just a little bit crazy, thought Scamarcio. There was something of the mad genius about Giacometti.

Scamarcio had expected him to ask if the police knew any more, but Giacometti seemed totally uninterested in what had happened to Micky's family. This was a man who never did as expected, who was probably incapable of conducting a normal conversation.

'Are you surprised to hear about what's happened to Proietti's wife and son?'

Giacometti frowned, then shrugged. 'Nothing in this world surprises me.'

'And why's that?'

'That, Detective, is a very long story, and irrelevant to your investigation.' He had returned his attention to the screen, and was now fiddling with the mouse.

'Do you know of anyone who might have a grievance with Micky Proietti?'

Giacometti kept his eyes on the laptop. 'Detective, if I wrote you a list of all the people who have a grievance with Micky Proietti, you wouldn't be able to carry the 10-tonne brick of paper out with you.'

'Why does he have so many enemies?'

Giacometti yawned loudly, not bothering to cover his mouth. 'He's an arsehole; possibly a sociopath. He has no consideration for people or their feelings. Now, if I'm honest, neither do I, but at least I make an attempt to hide it, to play the game. Micky doesn't bother. Add to that the fact that he'll pay you as little as he can get away with, and he'll pay you late. Then add to that that he's probably slept with your wife, mother, daughter — God knows, maybe your pet poodle ...'

'Has he slept with *your* wife?'

'I'm a homosexual.'

Scamarcio's mind went blank for a moment. 'Your boyfriend?'

'Not as far as I'm aware. My partner has good taste.'

'Do you think any of the people with grudges against Micky would kidnap his family?'

Giacometti leant back in his chair and studied Scamarcio closely for the first time. 'I doubt it. But, of course, I can't be sure. I believe he owes some people money.'

'Who?'

'One or two production houses in Rome. Matrix is one of

them. It's run by a guy from Catanzaro, and I've heard he doesn't take no for an answer.'

Catanzaro—Scamarcio's neck of the woods.

'And the other production company?'

'I don't know who they are. It's just a rumour—I haven't heard any names.'

Scamarcio wasn't sure he believed him. 'Does he owe *you* money?'

'He wouldn't dare. I run the most successful production house in the country, and he relies on our collaboration.'

'And you had nothing to do with the kidnapping of Proietti's family?'

Giacometti sighed. 'Detective, do I look like I'd bother?'

Observing Giacometti now, the piles of DVDs on his desk, the next hit show cued up to play, Scamarcio had to admit that it seemed unlikely.

'So if you were me, what would be your next port of call?'

Giacometti surprised him by smiling. 'I'd pay Francesco Bruno at Matrix a visit. But I'd also try Fiammetta di Bondi.'

'Fiammetta di Bondi? The showgirl?'

Giacometti seemed to enjoy his confusion. 'Of course.'

'And why is she relevant?'

'From what I've heard, her boyfriend isn't happy about Micky Proietti.'

'She was sleeping with him?'

Giacometti pouted, as if to say *Don't be so slow*.

'Isn't she with the Roma footballer, Aconi?'

'Yeah,' said Giacometti, his tone strangely cool and distant. 'But it's the secret boyfriend you need to keep an eye on.'

He winked, and pressed play on his laptop. Scamarcio heard the same dreadful piano music start up again.

'What's the wink for?'

Giacometti raised a hand. 'That's all you're getting, Detective. You ask around, I'm sure you'll find the answer.'

6

'YEAH, THAT FUCKER OWES ME MONEY, but he won't owe me for long, if you know what I mean.'

Francesco Bruno was your typical Catanzaro meathead: heavy-set, with a wide, tanned face and a thick, dark brush of hair. He would have looked more at home beating up debtors in a dark alley than running a TV company.

'No, I *don't* know,' said Scamarcio, eyeing him closely. He wondered if they were connected somehow; whether Bruno had friends in the same dark places as Scamarcio — friends Scamarcio was still doing his best to shake off.

Bruno frowned and looked away. 'All I'm saying is that I've made it pretty clear to Micky that I'm not doing any more work for him until that money comes through.'

Scamarcio guessed that had not been the gist of it. No doubt Proietti could pick and choose the companies he did business with. Judging from the size of the place and the shabby décor, Matrix did not appear to be in the same league as Giacometti's outfit.

'Was Proietti happy with the work he commissioned from you?'

'Yeah, he loved it. Our shows rated really well. Just last week he told me he was going to hire us for a new series. That's when I raised the point about the money.'

'So Micky's wife and son …?'

Bruno shook his head, and actually looked downcast. 'That's terrible. I couldn't believe it when I heard; made me feel as if I was back down south.'

'Any ideas?'

'About who's behind it?'

Scamarcio nodded.

Bruno frowned again and scratched beneath his nose. 'I'm sure he's got a lot of enemies, but I can't imagine anyone in the trade doing anything like that. You've got to remember that work is scarce right now. You wouldn't cut off the hand that feeds you.'

'Besides Proietti, is there much business with the other channels?'

Bruno shook his head and pouted. 'Practically nothing, and they pay peanuts anyway. Micky controls the lion's share of the money that's being spent around this town. For people like me, he's Numero Uno.'

'But if you felt like you had nothing to lose?'

Bruno shrugged. 'I dunno. Who feels like that? We're all manoeuvring for the next deal, reshuffling our decks.'

Scamarcio's phone rang, and he raised a hand in apology. He stepped outside the tiny office to take the call.

'Scamarcio — it's Detective Caporaso — from the team watching Micky Proietti.'

'Yes, go ahead, Detective.'

'Mr Proietti has just received a package. When we opened it, it was found to contain a tooth: the tooth of a child. We've just sent it to the lab for DNA testing. We suspect it could belong to the son.'

Scamarcio took a breath. Bruno was right. This did not seem like the work of a bunch of disgruntled media types. It felt like the game had suddenly got a whole lot dirtier.

'How is Mr Proietti responding?' he asked

'If you had the time to come down here and talk to him, I think it might help.'

'Give me an hour.'

Scamarcio cut the call and stepped back into Bruno's office.

He tried to compose his expression; he didn't want him picking up on any change in his demeanour.

'Sorry, you were saying that you can't imagine any of your colleagues being desperate enough to pull a stunt like this.'

Bruno was eyeing him carefully, as if he *had* noticed a change.

'Yes, it wouldn't make sense. I think you're looking in the wrong place. You probably need to focus more on Micky's love life. From what I hear, that's a very tangled web, and I imagine there could be people there who might have scores to settle.' He smiled thinly, and said nothing, as if there was nothing else to add. 'I'd give you more if I could, but that's all I know. I'm not in his trusted circle.' He smiled again, and extended a hand. 'Sorry not to have been of more help.'

From where Scamarcio was standing, he didn't look too sorry at all.

Micky Proietti was pacing up and down his magnificent parquet when Scamarcio walked in. Seated at either side of the enormous white sofa were a distinguished-looking man of about seventy and an equally distinguished looking woman of a similar age. Both of them bore the contorted expressions of anguish, hope, and despair Scamarcio had seen on the faces of others whose loved ones had been taken. *These must be the parents*, he figured. He wondered why they were seated so far apart, like strangers. Why was their anxiety dividing them, rather than bringing them together?

Proietti turned when he saw him. 'Do you have them?'

'Sorry?'

'The DNA results on the tooth. Are they back?' Proietti eyes were burning with rage. He looked as if he was about to punch him.

'They'll be another few hours probably. Can we sit down? There's something I want to discuss.' He nodded to the parents. The old man rose carefully from the sofa and shook his hand.

The mother just smiled wanly.

Proietti threw himself down into an armchair like a reluctant five-year-old.

'I understand that this situation must be extremely stressful for all of you.' Scamarcio turned to Proietti. 'It seems like someone has gone to a lot of trouble to stage this kidnapping. We've found out that the guy who was supposed to chauffeur you was attacked, which means that whoever drove you into that crash was an imposter.'

He watched Proietti turn pale. 'In the light of this and what's just come in the post, I need to ask: have you ever crossed paths with organised crime?'

Proietti Snr jerked suddenly on the sofa as if he had received an electric shock. 'What on earth!'

'It's a fair question,' said Scamarcio. 'It's not uncommon in mafia kidnappings for body parts to be sent. The parcel casts this investigation in a new light.'

He switched his gaze to the mother. She remained strangely silent, her face impassive. It was as if she didn't want to betray herself with the slightest gesture.

Micky Proietti sniffed loudly. Scamarcio wondered if he'd just snorted a line of coke. 'Listen, Detective, I understand where you're trying to go with this — at the end of the day you're just doing your job — but, no, I can assure you that neither I nor my father have mafia contacts — never have done, and never will.'

Scamarcio tried to read his eyes, but he'd turned to his right and was looking at his mother for some reason.

'Do you owe anyone money?'

Scamarcio felt the air in the room change. He sensed the Proiettis still holding themselves in, trying to inhibit the smallest movement.

'No, of course not.'

'Why "of course not"? It's not uncommon to have debts.'

'Look around you, Detective,' said Proietti, sweeping an arm across the room. 'Do I look like I have money troubles? I earn well at Channel One, and I've been fortunate in coming from a well-to-do family.'

'Even rich boys can overstretch themselves.'

Proietti Snr crossed his legs and smoothed down his trousers. Scamarcio noticed fine blue silk socks and expensive brown brogues.

The old man coughed. 'Detective, I made a lot of money in my career and, I'm proud to say, that money was made cleanly. Likewise my son has risen through the ranks without the need to grease palms. We have always been hard workers in the Proietti family, honest men.'

Proietti Snr's wife toyed with the hair at the back of her neck. The gesture was slow and slight, but Scamarcio noticed it all the same.

'Then you are to be congratulated. Unfortunately, none of this brings me any closer to finding your grandson. Do you have any thoughts on who might be responsible?'

Proietti Snr took a deep breath. 'Right now, we are thinking that it may be someone connected to Michele's work.'

His son snorted with contempt. 'That bunch of bottom feeders. None of them would have the balls. It has to be something else.'

'What then?' asked Scamarcio.

Proietti sprung up from the chair as if something had bitten him. 'If I knew, don't you think I would have told you by now?'

Again Proietti looked ready to punch him. Scamarcio felt certain now that he had taken coke. He was too aggressive, too wired.

Proietti's gaze flitted to the door as one of Scamarcio's colleagues from the squadroom, Sartori, hurried in. The large envelope in his hand told Scamarcio that the DNA results were back.

'Here,' said Sartori, handing over the documents. 'Garramone put a rush on it.'

Scamarcio nodded. The room seemed to hold its collective breath as he unfolded the single sheet of paper. He read in silence for several seconds and then looked up at Micky Proietti. 'The tooth is from your son, sir. I'm sorry.'

Proietti just stood there, open-mouthed. He looked like a prizefighter frozen in stone; his fists were still balled, and his feet were set wide apart. What little colour remained in his face was draining away fast. However, the overriding message Scamarcio read from his expression was *reaction* rather than emotion; *surprise* rather than grief. Proietti had the look of a man who thought he was heading for A, but then discovered he was on the road to B; it was the look of a man whose plans had gone awry. The grief came later, *after* the surprise.

A piercing cry interrupted Scamarcio's train of thought. Proietti's mother was lunging towards her husband, slapping him hard across the face. 'You bastard,' she screamed. 'You selfish, fucking bastard.'

Proietti Snr's face had turned puce. Proietti Jnr had sprung up from the armchair, and was now behind his mother, trying to pull her off: 'Mother, mother, come on. Calm down. Get a grip.'

'I will never forgive you for this,' she screamed at her husband as her son tried to lead her away. 'Never.'

'Mother,' hissed Proietti, as he tried to pin her arms to her sides and point her towards the door.

'You're a murderer, a bloody murderer,' she yelled behind her as they left.

7

'WILL YOU GIVE ME A MOMENT? I need to check on my wife. This whole thing is taking a serious toll,' said Proietti Snr as he rose from the sofa, his bird legs shaking. He looked like a vulnerable old man now, rather than a retired executive.

'Of course,' said Scamarcio, glad of the chance to collect his thoughts.

'What the hell was that?' asked Sartori, once the old man had left.

Scamarcio sank back into the armchair. 'God knows. But whatever it is, we need to get to the bottom of it. Fast.'

'I can't believe they pulled out his tooth,' said Sartori. 'Poor little mite.'

Scamarcio rubbed at his neck. 'Proietti told me that he'd asked his father if he could sell some shares held in his name, but the old man said no. I'm wondering if that's relevant. Perhaps Proietti was in debt, and needed the money to bail himself out. When he couldn't pay up, they took his family as a warning. Now Proietti's mother sees her husband as responsible — if he'd given his son the money, her grandson would not have been taken.'

Sartori shrugged, noncommittal. 'But why would he have debts?'

'He's got a serious coke habit, for starters.'

'Yeah, but his salary would easily fund that.'

'Yes, but coke often leads to other things, other vices. Maybe there are certain aspects of Micky's life we don't yet know about.' Scamarcio looked up from his notepad. 'You on this, or did Garramone just send you as messenger?'

41

'No, I'm yours. I've just come off the Falaguerra thing.'

'Great,' said Scamarcio, tearing out a page from his notebook and scribbling on it. 'Despite his claims he doesn't have one, I want you to dig up what you can on Micky Proietti's social life — the places he hangs out, the people he hangs with. Go and have a chat with his friendly secretary, for starters. And we need to pay a visit to the chauffeur who was assaulted.'

'Madness, that. These guys don't mess about.'

'Can you talk to him and see if he caught a glimpse of his attacker? Find out exactly where it happened. Obviously, we could do with CCTV, but it's probably a long shot.' Scamarcio handed across the business card that the secretary had given him.

Sartori studied it quickly, then asked: 'What will you be doing? Visiting the other production companies?'

'No, there's another team on that.'

'Getting anywhere?'

Scamarcio shook his head and frowned. 'While you take care of the background, I'm going to talk to Micky's girlfriend.'

Sartori raised an eyebrow. 'Not so happily married then?'

'Ah, Sartori, we do things differently here. Maybe up in Rimini you stick to the straight and narrow, but down south a man can have a mistress and still be *very* happily married.'

Sartori rolled his eyes. 'Yeah, well, good luck with that. You'll all burn in hell, I'm sure.'

Scamarcio smiled, and handed over the piece of paper. 'Knock yourself out.'

'Hmm,' said Sartori, throwing him a sarcastic salute as he left.

Fiammetta di Bondi, the showgirl, lived in a small apartment in Trastevere. It was nicely decorated but extremely messy, filthy even. The coffee table was covered with lipstick-smeared glasses, some of which contained tarry pools of cigarette stubs. Dirty clothing littered the floor, and a pair of black lacy underpants had landed where they'd been thrown against the back of a chair. Scamarcio noticed a small stack of unwashed plates on the dusty parquet, greasy cutlery alongside it. Maybe she'd just had a party, he thought. But that wouldn't explain the clothes. Or would it?

'Have you had guests?' he asked.

'No, why?'

'Oh, nothing,' he said, scratching his forehead. He hoped she wouldn't ask him to sit down. He was worried he might catch something.

'Do sit down, Detective.'

'Right, yeah, thanks.'

He opted for a chair where, as far as he could tell, there was nothing but a few old newspaper supplements.

'So,' he said, pushing the magazines aside and noticing a used paper tissue underneath. 'Have you heard about Micky Proietti?'

In stark contrast to her apartment, Fiammenti di Bondi was immaculately turned out. She was wearing pristine white jeans with a shimmery grey top, a long silver pendant hanging from her neck. Her nails were painted a pale coral pink, and her dark eye make-up looked as if it had been expertly applied. Scamarcio couldn't square it. In his experience, if your place was messy, you were messy.

'What about Micky?' asked di Bondi, sweeping her mane of blonde hair behind her shoulder. Her hair was so thick and straight that Scamarcio wondered if she had ironed it.

'You might want to sit down, Miss di Bondi.'

She looked taken aback, but not overly worried. He quickly sensed that she was not in love with Micky Proietti.

When he had finished filling her in about the fake accident, di Bondi rifled through the detritus lining her coffee table and retrieved a dented pack of Camel Lights. She opened the crumpled box and extracted a lighter with a leopard-skin design. She lit up slowly and took a long first drag, surveying Scamarcio languidly

43

through the smoke, her eyes narrowing like those of a cat getting comfortable.

'Wow,' was her only comment. Scamarcio couldn't see any sympathy there, any real concern for Proietti's plight.

'Do you have any ideas about who might be responsible?'

She took another drag and blew the smoke clear of the table. Then she tucked her hair behind her ear and began smoothing out the tips with her fingers.

'No idea, sorry.'

Scamarcio couldn't read anything from her eyes. She might as well have been wearing sunglasses.

'You were seeing Micky, right?'

'Right.'

'So …'

'So, what?'

'So, from where I'm sitting, you might be responsible for what's happened.'

She started laughing—a deep, guttural laugh that didn't quite suit her. He had expected something delicate and glassy. She took another drag on the Camel. 'Really, is that the best you can do? I thought you flying squad guys were supposed to be shit-hot.'

The swearing didn't suit her either.

'It's a legitimate question.'

She leant towards him, her cigarette hand against her knee now. 'Micky and I were sleeping together, but that's as far as it went. I wasn't in love with him. I suspect, however, that he was falling in love with me.'

'Why's that?'

'A woman has a sense for these things.'

'How did you feel about it?'

'Irritated, mainly. He was getting all clingy, calling me all the time, wanting to know where I was, what I was up to. That kind of behaviour can fast put you off a man.'

Scamarcio knew where she was coming from. 'Were you going to do anything about it?'

She brought the cigarette to her lips once more, but didn't inhale. 'Actually, I was. I called him yesterday to end it, but he never got back to me.'

'So your affections lie elsewhere?'

She took a quick drag and then looked away to a picture-less wall. 'No.'

'That's not what I heard.'

Her gaze remained fixed on the wall. 'Well, whatever you heard is bullshit.'

'That's a strong word.'

She turned to face him now. 'Look, I've given you all I can. I think we're done.'

'I decide when we're finished.'

She sighed, her lips forming a child-like pout. How old was she? he wondered. Early twenties?

He pushed on: 'I hear you like to hang out with VIPs, politicos.'

'So what? That's the scene down here, isn't it? You go to any VIP party, and you'll see a bunch of balding old men rubbing up against twenty-year-old girls stoned on coke and mojitos.'

'You sound like you don't enjoy all that very much.'

'It's a whole world of shit.'

'So why are you doing it?'

'Because if you look like me that's the route you take. No young girl aspires to be anything decent anymore, because there's no money in it.'

'That's a bleak analysis.'

'You ask any teenager what she wants to become, and she'll tell you a showgirl or a reality-TV star. They all dream of getting on *Big Brother* or *The Island of the Famous* — that's the only place where the cash is.'

'Would you prefer to be doing something else then?'

'I wanted to be a physicist, specialising in astrophysics. I've been obsessed with space ever since I was small. I want to be reading about all that, opening my mind, not stuck down here in Rome sucking up to arrogant arseholes.'

'So why don't you leave?'

'Oh, it's that simple, is it? To study, you need money. My parents don't have any.'

'Surely you've made a fair bit by now.'

'A fair bit, but not enough. I have a target. I need sufficient to provide me with an insurance policy, a cushion. When I've reached that, *then* I'll leave.'

'Are you far off?'

'I'll be here for another year at least, barring some sort of miracle.'

Scamarcio frowned. This beautiful girl was telling the prostitute's tale. The disquieting thing was that he sensed it wasn't her fault; once again, the state had failed to provide.

'So why were you with Micky?'

'Us girls kind of get passed around. Someone suggested Micky would be a good person to know — head of drama, loads of contacts in TV. I thought, why not?'

'Who was this someone?'

'One of the old codgers.'

'The politicos?'

'May have been, I can't remember.'

'Are you sleeping with any politicians?'

'I can't see the relevance.'

'I decide the relevance.'

She scratched beneath her left eye, careful not to smudge the perfect make-up.

There was a noise behind her, and a short, small-boned young man with peroxide blond hair came hurrying into the room. He was wielding a large silver case. He took a quick look around the room and then slapped a palm across his mouth.

'Fiammetta, you said you were going to clear up! They'll be here in ten minutes. You can't let them see the place like this!'

'What's wrong with it?'

'Jesus, it's a brothel. We need to get moving — maybe your friend can help?'

Scamarcio rose from the sofa and introduced himself. When he extended a hand, the young man blushed and held his fingers to his lips in a pantomime gesture.

'Oh, I'm so sorry, *Detective*, I had no idea! Has Fiammetta been a bad girl again?'

Scamarcio smiled weakly. 'Do you have guests arriving?'

'*People* magazine! We can't let them see this chaos.'

'Fiammetta herself looks perfect, though,' said Scamarcio, wondering where the strange man-boy fitted into the picture.

'Doesn't she?' He extracted a card from his very tight jean pockets and handed it over. Scamarcio read: '*Fabio Bonzo — make-up artist and life coach.*'

'Do feel free to call me *anytime*.' Bonzo turned to the coffee table and began collecting glasses.

Di Bondi muttered something about needing a coffee, and retreated to the kitchen. Once she was out of earshot, Scamarcio lowered his voice.

'Fiammetta was just telling me about her politician boyfriend.'

'Oh, Gianluca Manfredi?'

Scamarcio stopped for a beat. He hadn't expected it to be so easy. 'Yes, the culture minister. What's he like?'

The man-boy glanced over his shoulder quickly and then said: 'Jealous. A pain in the butt.'

'How so?'

'He's obsessed with Fiammetta. It's driving her crazy.'

'Well, she's very beautiful, it's hardly surprising.'

'Yeah, but there are different levels of obsession, aren't there?'

The man-boy swept a stack of cigarette butts into a black bin-liner, and tutted.

'I don't quite follow,' said Scamarcio.

'I don't think I've ever known a more disgusting slob.'

Scamarcio took him gently by the elbow, and he looked up from his tidying in surprise. 'I'm sorry, but I'm conducting a very important inquiry. I need you to explain exactly what you mean about Mr Manfredi.'

The man-boy set down the bin bag and took a seat reluctantly on the sofa, checking behind him yet again that di Bondi wasn't listening.

'So you were saying that Mr Manfredi is obsessed?' Scamarcio tried.

The man-boy crossed his legs and leant forward, his chin in his hands. He lowered his voice to a whisper. 'Well, I'm not sure how much it will help you, but Fiammetta told *me* that Manfredi had told *her* that he'd kill for her. It's a bit OTT, don't you think? Frankly, I think the man's a little mad.'

8

SCAMARCIO WAS ON HIS WAY down to the parliament when his mobile rang. He didn't recognise the number.

'Detective Scamarcio?'

'Yes …'

He'd barely been able to get out a reply before the caller snapped: 'Max Romano.'

Scamarcio was impressed. He'd read that the government's chief spin doctor liked to be on top of his ministers' private lives, but this seemed fast, even for him.

'Do you have time to come by my office this morning?' said Romano.

'You at the Palazzo?'

'Room 614. I'm in all morning.'

'I'll be there in twenty minutes. I was heading that way anyway.'

'I thought so.' Romano cut the call — no goodbye, no 'Thanks for your time.'

When Scamarcio entered Room 614, the first thing he saw was a plain, middle-aged woman behind a large oak desk. To her left was a slightly smaller desk where a bookish young man in his early thirties was cradling the telephone.

'No,' the young man was saying, his exasperation plain. 'Borbera put words into his mouth and then, as usual, the press pack repeated it as gospel. Do you guys ever do any original research?'

He sighed, and ran a hand through his dark, wavy hair before readjusting his spectacles. 'Well, if you do, it will be a lie.'

'Can I help you?' the woman asked, her eyes a frown.

Scamarcio had hoped to hear more of the conversation. He introduced himself, and she buzzed through to Romano. 'He says to go straight in.' She pointed towards an oak-panelled door behind her.

Scamarcio knocked twice before the clipped, confident voice of the man they called Doctor Death shouted, 'Come.'

The chief spin doctor was seated behind a desk so vast that it made the ones outside look miniature. His paperwork appeared to be meticulously ordered in colour-coded piles on which rested a series of marble and silver paperweights shaped like eggs. A gold letter-knife, inkpot, and fountain pen took pride of place at the head of the desk.

Romano was dressed in a blue suit with a crisp, white shirt and a silk silver-grey tie. His dark hair was cut fashionably short, and he was smooth-shaven. He was almost handsome, but not quite: his dark eyes were too small, too close set, somehow.

Scamarcio followed Romano's gaze to a widescreen TV mounted on the wall. Sky TG24 was playing. There was another small set on the desk in front of Romano, and as Scamarcio drew closer he noticed it was showing the parliament channel with the sound muted.

Romano tore his eyes away from the news for a moment and extended a hand. 'Detective, thanks for coming. Please take a seat.' It was more an order than an invitation.

Scamarcio sat down in a wide, studded leather armchair. How many famous names had occupied the same spot, he wondered. How many had been given their marching orders while seated in this chair? It was well known that Romano decided who would sink or swim, whose star was in the ascendant. The analysts said that the party danced to *his* tune; that he had the power to unseat the premier if he so wished; the premier had confidence issues that Romano had managed to manipulate to the best of his Machiavellian abilities. Some commentators even went so far as to argue that Romano could have taught Machiavelli a thing or two.

'So, you wanted to see me?' said Scamarcio. He tried to make himself comfortable in the uncomfortable chair. He wondered whether Romano had chosen it deliberately to ensure his visitors didn't linger.

Romano leaned back and steepled his fingers beneath his chin. 'You said you were heading down here anyway …'

So it was to be a game of cat and mouse. *Hardly surprising*, thought Scamarcio resignedly.

'I was on my way to see the culture minister.'

'Yes, that's what I heard.'

Scamarcio figured that Fiammetta di Bondi had probably phoned Manfredi in a panic once she realised that her friend had said too much.

'Shall we call him in, then?' said Scamarcio. 'I need to ask him about his relationship with Fiammetta di Bondi.'

'What relationship?'

Scamarcio sighed, and patted his pocket for his cigarettes. He'd given up for a whole month a while back, but then Aurelia had left for Munich, and his resolve had crumbled. 'Do you mind?'

Romano waved the thought away. 'I'll join you.'

Scamarcio handed the packet across, then lit up for him.

'I always find the day starts better this way,' said the spin doctor.

They sank back into a semi-companionable smoker's silence before Scamarcio said: 'I'll cut to the chase. I'm not the press. You can't spin me a line. I'm conducting a police investigation into a kidnapping that we're hoping is not about to become a double murder. I know Manfredi was having a relationship with Fiammetta di Bondi. And I also know that di Bondi was seeing Micky Proietti. There's a connection. And I need to understand

51

if that connection might have any bearing on the kidnapping of Proietti's wife and child.'

Romano took a long pull on the cigarette and then pushed a small pile of blue papers carefully to the right, evening out the edges as he did so.

His eyes narrowed through the smoke. He had the look of an emperor who was still trying to decide whether one of his subjects should be executed at dawn.

'Before we involve Manfredi, I need to bring you up to speed: the culture minister's days are probably numbered.'

'*Probably?*'

'He's not popular with voters, he's not a great communicator, and he's said some foolish things to the press on more than one occasion. I've been thinking of ditching him. I need to know whether I should act sooner rather than later.'

'You're asking me to tell you what I've got on him?'

Romano nodded quickly. His blank expression seemed to suggest that such a request was perfectly reasonable.

'Mr Romano, you must know that police inquiries are confidential.'

Romano dismissed the thought with a small shrug. 'Come on, Detective, you know the game.'

Scamarcio wasn't sure he did. 'Right now, I have a connection, nothing more.'

Romano steepled his fingers again, bringing them to his lips this time. 'Manfredi and Proietti,' he said, looking off into the middle distance.

The voicing of those two names together flicked some kind of switch for Scamarcio. The direct connection was Manfredi and Fiammetta. Why had Romano jumped straight to Proietti?

'Obviously, Micky Proietti is an interesting character,' said Scamarcio, tentatively.

Romano took another puff on his cigarette, and loosened

his tie. It was hot. It was only April, but Scamarcio had smelt the first mellow scents of summer from the honeysuckle lining the walk to parliament.

Romano coughed, and set down his cigarette in a bulky glass ashtray. 'The whole bonking-a-showgirl thing is fair enough, as far it goes. I mean, they're all doing it. If I had to sack every one of them who had a bit on the side, then I wouldn't have a cabinet left. Italy wouldn't have a government.'

Scamarcio nodded and tried to look understanding. He sensed a 'but' coming.

'But it's the freemason thing that's the issue.'

'Hmm,' mumbled Scamarcio, covering his mouth with a fist. For some reason, he wanted to smile. 'I thought that might be the nub of it.'

'A member of one of the country's most prestigious lodges has his wife and child kidnapped, and then it emerges that one of his fellow lodge members is screwing the same showgirl. The public don't mind a bit of sex on the side, but they don't trust freemasons. They think they're all up to no good. If it comes out that Manfredi was a mason, then everyone is going to think the rest of the cabinet are as well.'

'Are they?' asked Scamarcio.

Romano frowned with distaste and said nothing. Then he leant forward and pressed a button on his telephone console.

'Gloria, get Manfredi on the line, will you? ASAP.'

Scamarcio felt a spike of irritation. He'd have preferred more time to talk to Romano.

'Let's see what Manfredi has to say. It's only fair to hear him out,' said the spin doctor.

Scamarcio thought this odd, given Romano's earlier comments.

The buzzer on Romano's desk lit up, and the secretary came on again. 'Manfredi's in parliament, but he says he's in a meeting and can't be disturbed.'

'Tell him if he's not here in five minutes, he's fired.'

The line went dead once more.

'Detective, would you mind if I answered a few emails?'

'Be my guest,' said Scamarcio, suddenly glad of having a few moments to think. So Proietti was a freemason? Where did that leave the kidnap inquiry? And, more importantly, why had Romano decided to share this?

It seemed no more than a couple of minutes before the culture secretary bustled in. He was red-faced, and several wisps of his thin, grey hair were standing on end. Scamarcio noticed a small envelope of paunch protruding over his well-cut suit trousers. Manfredi was an unremarkable-looking man. The thought of him with di Bondi was somehow unsettling.

'Ah, Gianluca, so glad you could join us,' said Romano, glancing up from his laptop, and stubbing out his cigarette.

Manfredi said nothing. He was looking at Scamarcio, waiting for some kind of explanation.

'Detective Scamarcio here is part of the team investigating Micky Proietti's wife and son. He wanted to have a quick chat.'

Manfredi nodded, and shook Scamarcio's hand before collapsing into the other chair. 'I understand the rush now. Terrible business. I've got children myself. Micky must be going through hell.'

The words seemed genuine, and Scamarcio decided that Manfredi was perhaps not quite as much of an arsehole as he'd first imagined. 'You know Micky well?' he asked.

'Just in passing. We attend the same parties, move in similar circles,' said Manfredi, patting down his hair.

'You're members of the same lodge, I gather?'

Scamarcio watched the colour slowly rise in Manfredi's already red cheeks. 'How is that relevant?' The geniality of before vanished in an instant. The minister was surveying Romano with contempt now.

'I'm not saying it is.'

Manfredi coughed, but kept his eyes on Romano. The spin doctor just stared him out and said nothing. They reminded Scamarcio of two dogs sizing each other up for a fight.

'You also share another connection, I believe,' tried Scamarcio.

Manfredi rubbed his nose and adjusted his right cufflink. It was a gold stud with an emerald inlay.

After several seconds of silence, Scamarcio wondered if Manfredi was ever going to respond, but eventually Romano said, 'Come on, Gianluca. He already knows about Fiammetta. You might as well tell him the rest.'

Manfredi finally tore his gaze away from the spin doctor. Scamarcio wondered what 'the rest' was, then wondered how good Manfredi was at controlling his rages.

The culture secretary rubbed his round chin and turned to face Scamarcio. Scamarcio had expected some kind of preamble, but Manfredi cut straight to it. 'Fiammetta and I are in love. I'm about to leave my wife, and Fiammetta *was* about to finish things with Micky. She didn't think he'd take it too well. As it happens, she never had a chance to tell him, because he never rang her back before the kidnapping. She hasn't the heart to break it to him now, given all he's going through. She's just waiting for things to resolve.'

Scamarcio looked at Romano. The fact that Manfredi and Fiammetta were 'in love' actually seemed to have taken the spin doctor by surprise. His forehead was pocked with disbelief or confusion—perhaps both.

'*If* they get resolved,' said Scamarcio.

'Indeed.' Manfredi's expression became solemn, and he glanced into his lap for a moment.

'Do you have any idea who could have been behind the kidnapping? Could it have any connection to your lodge?'

The mention of his lodge seemed to stir the rage in Manfredi once more. Scamarcio watched a bunched fist turn red in his lap.

After a few seconds, Manfredi said tightly: 'I doubt it. We don't have any disputes going on, any arguments I can think of. It's a happy ship.'

In Scamarcio's experience, there was no such thing. Human beings weren't made to get along. There was something naïve and childlike about Manfredi, he realised. Even his face was slightly babyish, with his round cheeks and wide-set blue eyes. Manfredi was a man who needed to believe that everything would turn out fine because he wasn't equipped to deal with the alternative; life had always been kind to him. Scamarcio imagined him growing up to rich, doting parents — the spoiled only son, perhaps. Did Manfredi have any inkling that Fiammetta was leading him a dance? Would the thought even enter his mind? How would he cope if he lost her *and* his job?

'Obviously, you're on my initial list of suspects,' said Scamarcio, trying to regain focus.

Manfredi shrugged. 'Like I say, Fiammetta and I were about to move in together. I had no grudge with Micky. If anything, he's the aggrieved party here.'

Scamarcio thought he detected a note of pride. He'd have to check back with di Bondi as to whether she'd really led Manfredi to believe they had a future.

'What about the footballer?' asked Scamarcio.

'What footballer?' asked Manfredi.

'The one Fiammetta is supposed to be seeing.'

'Aconi?' asked Romano, a smile playing on his lips.

He exchanged amused glances with Manfredi, and the tension between them seemed to dissipate for a moment.

'You mean you don't know?' asked Romano, chuckling now.

'Know what?' asked Scamarcio, peeved.

Manfredi rested an elbow on his seatback and crossed a leg. The mention of Aconi seemed to have relaxed him considerably;

Scamarcio sensed that Manfredi felt they'd moved to safer ground, that they'd avoided triggering the mines. *Why?* Scamarcio wondered. What had he missed?

'Aconi plays for the other side,' said Romano.

'What? He's with Roma, isn't he?'

Manfredi and Romano started laughing. When he'd regained his composure, Manfredi said: 'No, Detective. "The other *side*."' He inclined his eyes to the right, to an imaginary spot beyond Scamarcio's chair.

Scamarcio rubbed at his eyes. He felt tired again. 'You mean he's gay?'

'Completely. Fiammetta has an arrangement with his manager. She gets paid for being his "cover". She and Aconi get on, though—she says he's a nice guy.'

'Why's he hiding it?' As soon as Scamarcio asked the question, he knew the answer. Italians would accept homosexuality in the worlds of fashion and art, but the country still wasn't ready for a gay footballer. The soccer culture remained pure macho, the testosterone undiluted. He couldn't imagine the diehard Napoli or Catania fans welcoming a gay player, however much of a star striker he might prove to be. Would the environment ever evolve, Scamarcio wondered? Something more pertinent was bothering him now, though.

'But if you and Fiammetta move in together, what's going to happen to Aconi?'

'Oh, his agent will just find him another girl, and say that he and Fiammetta broke up.'

'And your wife?'

'I'm getting a divorce.'

Again, the news seemed to come as something of a surprise to the spin doctor. He shifted in his seat and studied Manfredi with concern, much like a shrink observing a problem patient.

'What's the name of your lodge?' asked Scamarcio.

Manfredi turned in surprise. He clearly wasn't expecting the conversation to come back around to this.

'Why?'

'I want to pay them a visit.'

Manfredi pinched his nose. 'The Sword and the Serpent. But I'm sure Micky will tell you it's a worthless line of inquiry.'

'It's not for Mr Proietti to make value judgements about my investigation.' Scamarcio wanted to wind things up. He had enough to be getting on with, and he didn't want to rattle Manfredi any further. He rose from the seat. 'Thank you, gentlemen, for your time.'

Manfredi was too slow to disguise the relief in his eyes.

'Good luck with your inquiry,' said Romano. 'I hope you find them quickly.'

Scamarcio thought he actually detected a hint of empathy there, but when he scanned the desk he couldn't find any family pictures. Would a workaholic like Romano waste time reproducing?

Scamarcio shook hands with the pair of them, and made his way out. But once he was the other side of the door, he waited for a few seconds, avoiding the secretary's prissy stare for as long as he could.

'You fucking bastard,' hissed Manfredi, just as Scamarcio knew he would.

'Oh come on, what could I do? They're the police.'

'Yeah, but it's bloody convenient, isn't it? I bet they had no idea about the lodge.'

The spin doctor said nothing.

'You just couldn't resist hammering another nail into my coffin.'

'Manfredi, you've been digging your own grave for months. And all that shit about Fiammetta being in love with you? My God, man, you're pathetic; you're a liability.'

'We *are* in love.'

Romano sighed. 'It's like talking to a teenager.'

'I wasn't born yesterday; I know what I'm doing.'

Romano sighed again. 'Whatever. You're yesterday's man, Manfredi.'

'What?'

'You heard me.'

The secretary had risen from her desk now, and had a hand on Scamarcio's arm. 'Can I help you?'

'No, I'm finished here,' said Scamarcio.

9

SCAMARCIO WAS FEELING QUITE pleased with himself as he walked away from the parliament, even though he knew that Romano had thrown him the freemason tip deliberately.

It didn't matter, though — it was another line of inquiry, and one he wanted to follow up as soon as possible. He decided that Aconi the footballer could be put on the back burner, although he'd need to corroborate the claims about his sexuality.

Scamarcio's phone rang, and he hoped it would be Sartori with new leads from his probe into Proietti's social life or the team investigating the other TV companies, but instead he was greeted with Piocosta's growl. Scamarcio's mood switched in an instant.

'You're a hard man to get hold of,' said the old man.

'I'm working a case — the first forty-eight hours are crucial.'

'A kidnapping?'

Scamarcio sighed. You couldn't get anything past Piocosta.

'I guess you know why I'm ringing.'

'Sure,' said Scamarcio, feeling the need to sit down, to throw himself into the Tiber and quietly drown. 'Can you call me back?'

It was their code for *Ring me back on the other phone*. Scamarcio had recently purchased a pay-as-you-go to deal with the new troublesome development in his relationship with Piocosta. His father's old lieutenant was still digging his claws in, still trying to get Scamarcio to work for him, to become his agent inside the force.

The line went dead, and then the little blue Nokia in Scamarcio's jacket pocket began to buzz. He held it at a distance for a moment, flipping it open with the tip of his index finger, barely wanting to touch it.

'So you said it was Detective Negri?' said Piocosta.

'He's the one heading up the inquiry.'

'And that's confirmed now, is it?'

'Yeah.'

'And how's the prosecutor feeling?'

'Confident.'

'Motherfuckers,' spat Piocosta.

Scamarcio said nothing.

'Where's the footage?'

'Where they keep all the evidence — in the store at HQ. I wouldn't suggest you try to break in.' As soon as Scamarcio said the words, he felt a slick of pool of acid forming in his stomach.

'*We're* not going to be the ones doing the break-in,' said Piocosta.

Scamarcio closed his eyes and bit his bottom lip. When Piocosta said no more, he hung up.

The head of Rome's Sword and Serpent lodge had asked to meet in a café near the Spanish Steps. Scamarcio would have preferred to visit the villa where the meetings were held, but he hadn't pushed the point. It would be a case of little by little with these guys and, besides, he didn't have the energy for a fight. Ever since his call from Piocosta, the anxiety had been building. He imagined he looked quite beaten, and the beads of sweat across his forehead would not do much to create an impression of competence and command before the lodge's Grand Master.

Matteo Monaci was extremely tall, at least 6 ft 3. He had close-cropped grey hair, a tanned complexion, and piercing grey-green eyes. He was immaculately turned out in a light-grey suit and pink tie. A beige Burberry raincoat was folded across one arm, exactly as he'd told Scamarcio it would be.

Scamarcio raised a weary hand in his direction.

'Good morning, Detective,' said Monaci as he approached. 'Beautiful April weather today.' The man was the personification of vim and vigour. 'Spry' was the word for a man like Monaci, thought Scamarcio.

He took his hand. 'Thanks for agreeing to meet me at such short notice.'

'But of course. A family goes missing? One does what one can.' Monaci seemed quite the smooth operator. He took a seat, draping his raincoat across his lap. He ordered a cappuccino from the waitress, and Scamarcio settled for a glass of water, deciding that it was probably the only thing his acid stomach could handle.

When the waitress had gone, Monaci asked: 'So do you have any idea where the kidnappers might be holding them?'

'We think we've picked up the ambulance on CCTV heading out towards the coast near Sperlonga. But we still can't be sure we've got the right vehicle. Unfortunately, that stretch of road is not well covered by cameras.'

'Needle in a haystack then,' said Monaci drily.

'Pretty much at this stage,' conceded Scamarcio, deciding to grant him some sense of superiority.

'And you want to talk to me in case there's some connection to the lodge.'

'Yes.'

Monaci sniffed and eased back in his chair, his arms folded, his legs crossed. He seemed perfectly relaxed.

'Micky has been a member for about ten years now. He's one of those people you either love or loathe.'

Scamarcio was surprised that Monaci was being so open so early. 'Why's that?'

'He doesn't suffer fools; he doesn't bother with social niceties. If he doesn't like you, he'll make it plain.'

Scamarcio frowned. 'Isn't that rather an impediment to networking?'

'Actually, I think some people rather appreciate it — it's a breath of fresh air.'

'With an attitude like that, I'm surprised Proietti has managed to rise so high.'

Monaci held up a finger to stop him. 'Ah, but that's where you're wrong, Detective. You can say what you like about nepotism in this country, but in my opinion Proietti has made his way up on merit alone. He's highly intelligent, and his bosses tell me that he has a real nose for what will make a hit. They say he has cast-iron intuition and an astounding ability to get the best.' Monaci took a sip of the coffee the waitress had placed before him.

'You know his bosses?'

'Yes, Paolo Ricolfi is an old schoolfriend of mine.'

'And Ricolfi is?'

'Head of television at Micky's network. Paolo tells me Micky has a superb knack for keeping budgets low and quality high. He says he's got no idea how he does it sometimes — you can't see the savings on screen.'

'Proietti must be a real asset.'

'Oh, he is,' said Monaci, smoothing down his trousers. 'Paolo says it's rare they find someone like him.'

'So getting back to the lodge, you were saying that some people hate Proietti.'

'Well, it's the rudeness really. Often he doesn't bother to pay other members the time of day — it's like he's in his own world. Or if you say something he disagrees with, he'll call you a cretin to your face. Obviously, some people don't know how to handle that.'

Scamarcio rubbed his hand across his mouth. 'Has he always been this way?'

'Always, ever since I've known him, at least.'

'What do you make of it?'

'Well, I was discussing it with my wife once after a dinner party at which Micky had badly upset another guest. My wife and I were talking about how brilliant people say Micky is. And he *is* brilliant—I've seen him do the cryptic crossword in under five minutes. But my wife made the point that perhaps Micky is slightly autistic. You know that combination you see in people who are highly intelligent, but can't read social cues? Ever since my wife suggested it, I've always wondered.'

It was an interesting thought, but Scamarcio wasn't sure it brought him any further.

'Has he ever *badly* upset any of your members?'

Monaci shook his head. 'No, I don't think there was anyone who really held a grudge. I mean that's Micky, you know—sure, people dislike him, but they've decided to live with their dislike.'

Scamarcio was having difficulty making sense of it. 'Your lodge seems an odd place for someone like Micky Proietti. If you say he was doing well on his own merit, if he didn't thrive in social situations …'

Monaci interrupted him. 'You're astute. The lodge wasn't and isn't the right place for Proietti. I'd actually quite like him to leave. He certainly doesn't need us, and I'm not sure we really need him. But it was his brother-in-law who got him into it, and he's a stubborn son of a b—'

'I didn't know he had a brother-in-law.'

Monaci raised an eyebrow. 'His wife's brother—Davide Stasio? Runs a TV company here in Rome.'

Why hadn't Scamarcio heard about Davide Stasio? 'And he's one of your members?'

Monaci wrinkled his nose in distaste. 'I'm being very indiscreet, but Stasio is a bit of a rough neck—worth a fortune, but most definitely arriviste. He's more polite than Micky, but there's an air about him I don't much like.' He inclined his head. 'Grew up on the wrong side of the tracks, I suspect. From down south, Calabria.'

Scamarcio's mouth turned dry. 'Mafioso?'

'Your words, not mine, Detective.'

Why had nobody mentioned Davide Stasio? Scamarcio had visited two major production houses and Proietti's secretary, but Stasio's name had never come up. Neither had any of Scamarcio's colleagues come across him in their trawl of the other companies Proietti did business with. That had to be significant.

Sartori rang as he was heading for Proietti's office.

'You getting anywhere?' Scamarcio asked.

'That driver who was assaulted doesn't remember shit and, like you thought, there's no CCTV for miles.'

'Great.'

'I've been round a couple of bars in Trastevere that Proietti likes to frequent, but they didn't really give me anything.'

'Anyone mentioned the name Davide Stasio to you?'

'No, why?'

'He's Micky's brother-in-law, runs a production company here in Rome, but everyone's being strangely tight-lipped about him.'

'I'll ask around.'

'Where are you now?'

'Base. Listen, I'm calling because we think we've ID'd the ambulance. The tech guys have grabbed a still lifted from a camera on the SS637, where it joins the coast road.'

'What makes them think it's the right vehicle?'

'The timing matches, and it's got a wide scrape down one side. You don't usually see working ambulances with unrepaired scrapes.'

'Can they read the plates?'

'Yeah.'

'That's nice work.'

'Yeah, if they haven't switched them by now.'

'Will you have someone email me the still and the plate ID?'

'Sure.'

'Next steps?'

'One of the barmen at Eclipse on Via della Pelliccia where Micky likes to hang has suggested I come back later. Another guy is due back on shift who knows Micky better.'

'Remember to ask about Davide Stasio.'

'Will do.'

Scamarcio hung up. As soon as he received the email with the picture of the ambulance, he'd be back on to dispatch to ask them for the contact who dealt with out-of-service vehicles.

His taxi drew up outside the Channel One offices in Saxa Rubra, and he hunted around in his jacket pockets trying to find his wallet. That Proietti's office was completely the other side of town from Police HQ was beginning to grate. Scamarcio hoped he wouldn't be in and that he could question the secretary in peace. He was in luck.

'Any news?' she asked warily.

'Not much. You spoken to Micky?'

'Only to pass on messages. He sounds really stressed.' She bit down on her bottom lip. 'Obviously.'

Scamarcio put a hand on her desk. 'You didn't mention Davide Stasio to me.'

'Davide who?'

If she was acting, she was doing a much better job of it today.

'Micky's brother-in-law.'

'He's never mentioned him.'

'Any ideas who might know more about him?'

She shrugged, then frowned. 'Micky?'

'Besides Micky?'

She shook her head. 'No, I'm sorry.'

Scamarcio sighed, then said: 'Remember, I can always haul you in …'

'For obstructing a police inquiry,' she snapped. 'I know, and I'm telling you I've never heard of Davide Stasio.'

Unfortunately, he believed her.

By the time he made his way back outside, the sun had emerged from behind the clouds. It felt like 25 degrees already. *Who would have background on Stasio?* he asked himself. His thoughts quickly came to rest on the Calabrian producer Francesco Bruno — it takes one to know one.

When he arrived at the Matrix offices, Bruno was holding a meeting. Scamarcio spied him through a glass partition addressing a small group who looked half his age, bar one man covered in tattoos and piercings who seemed at least fifty. Scamarcio took a seat on a sofa in reception, and ran another Google search for 'Davide Stasio TV production', but yet again got nothing. Strange. When he tried 'Davide Stasio company Rome', the results ranged from plumbers to hairdressers; but, again, there was no mention of TV.

After a few minutes he heard chairs scraping and the chatter of voices, and when he looked up, Bruno was standing in the hallway, looking down at him. 'Detective, I'm surprised to see you again so soon.'

'Can we pop into your office?'

Bruno checked his watch. 'I've got a meeting on Via dei Gracchi in half an hour. But yes, if it's quick.'

When they were seated, Scamarcio said: 'Have you heard of someone called Davide Stasio?'

'The porn producer?'

'What?'

Bruno just stared at him, confused. Scamarcio tried to unscramble his brain. 'Proietti's brother-in-law?'

Bruno leaned forward across his desk. It was his turn to be

surprised. 'What? Is he?'

Scamarcio tried to take stock. Were they even talking about the same man? Some instinct told him they were. 'This Davide Stasio, the porn producer — what do you know about him?'

'He's not someone you'd want to mess with — he's well connected.'

'Who to?'

'People from my part of the country.' Bruno coughed. 'And yours, perhaps?'

Scamarcio chose not to confirm it. 'Ndrangheta?'

Bruno nodded, and Scamarcio felt something die inside him. Was he doomed to forever remain the trapped fly, always trying to find a break in the web?

'So Stasio's doing business with them?'

'That's what I heard,' said Bruno, rubbing his nose. 'I can't believe he's Proietti's brother-in-law. You couldn't get two more different types.'

'So you've met him?'

'Just the once. He's a yob — pretty much what you'd expect.'

'Is he successful?'

'He's one of the biggest players in the porn industry. He's branching out now into TV — trying his hand at one of those reality shows on the lives of the porn stars. Total rubbish, but they rate well for the satellite networks. I met him at a drinks do for the Party! channel. We'd been doing some work for them.'

'It seems strange that nobody knows about the connection to Proietti.'

Bruno shrugged. 'Maybe Micky told him to keep it quiet. Who can blame him? You wouldn't want that getting around.'

Did Micky's bosses at Channel One know? Scamarcio wondered. *Did Monaci at the lodge even realise the true nature of Stasio's work?*

'What kind of porn are we talking about?' asked Scamarcio.

Bruno started rubbing his chin. 'As far as I know, just the usual run-of-the-mill stuff for online and TV. Nothing weird, if that's what you're asking.'

Scamarcio nodded, his mind still turning.

Bruno looked at his watch once more. 'Is that all, Detective? I really need to get to that meeting.'

Bruno had told him that Stasio's company was called Sizzle and that they were based on an industrial estate to the west of the city. When he eventually found the place, Scamarcio saw that Stasio seemed to run his business out of a large warehouse that Scamarcio guessed probably housed a studio. He buzzed the entry panel, and a female voice with a strong Calabrian accent told him to take the stairs to the third floor.

After he'd made the climb, Scamarcio pressed another buzzer to the right of two wide glass doors, above some rather tired-looking pot plants. The place could have passed for an accountancy or legal practice; there was nothing to suggest that this was the heart of a porn empire. The effect continued on the inside. A rather plain-looking woman wearing spectacles and a mud-brown cardigan sat behind a computer, the faded red Sizzle logo mounted tiredly on the wall behind her.

'How can I help you?' she asked. Scamarcio noted the slight Catanzaro twang. He felt sure she must be a relative of Stasio. No doubt he was following tradition, and keeping it all in the family.

Scamarcio showed her his badge. 'I'm here in connection with the disappearance of Davide Stasio's sister and nephew.'

The woman slapped a hand across her heart, taking Scamarcio by surprise. 'What? Has something happened to Maia and Antonio?'

'You weren't aware?'

The woman's hand was trembling. 'No. My God. Why didn't someone tell us?'

'Do you know Maia?'

'She's my cousin. What the hell happened? Where are they?'

Scamarcio filled her in on the fake ambulance, watching for her reaction. All he saw was shock. After he was finished, she opened her eyes wide and said: 'But does Davide even realise? I don't think he does—he would have mentioned it.'

'Is he here?'

'No, he's away on holiday down south. But I spoke to him just half an hour ago. He sounded chipper—he can't know. Why the hell hasn't someone told him?'

Indeed, thought Scamarcio. *What was Micky Proietti playing at?*

'Listen,' said Scamarcio. 'I'm trying to find out all I can about Maia's background, her family, her life. Could I have a quick look around? It might help me get a handle on things.'

The woman nodded and got up from behind her computer. She led him through another set of glass doors into a wide open-plan office. Scamarcio saw about ten young people tapping away at computers or talking on the phone. There were quite a few empty desks between them.

'I need a truck and three Harleys,' one was saying. 'For one day's shooting on the 22nd.' He waited for the answer, then whistled softly. 'Seems steep.'

The wall was covered with various posters that Scamarcio guessed were blown-up DVD covers from Stasio's films. All of them had the word *hot* in the title—hot teachers, hot biker babes, hot holiday. All of the women were predictably tanned and predictably blonde.

'This is the main production office,' said the secretary, 'where we organise the shoots. Davide has his office through there.' She pointed to a cabin at the back, a small glass window to its left.

'Where do you do the filming?'

'There's a studio here on the complex. We use that most of the time—Davide owns it, but he rents it out to other companies sometimes.'

Scamarcio nodded. 'How's business?'

The woman seemed distracted, impatient. 'You'd have to ask Davide — I don't have the details, but I know that we have a lot of new contracts coming through.'

Her attention drifted to a TV playing on the desk in front of them. Sky News was on, and they were showing the picture of Proietti's wife and son that Scamarcio had taken from the apartment. The image cut to footage of the stretch of motorway where the family had gone missing. The secretary placed her hand across her heart once more, and whispered something Scamarcio couldn't quite comprehend. She crossed herself and took a breath.

The ringing of a nearby phone broke her concentration. A smart young man a few metres away answered. He was dressed in a blue-checked shirt, chinos, and brogues, and wore serious-looking, thin-framed spectacles. To Scamarcio, he seemed like the very last person you'd expect to find in a porn production office.

The young man's expression became solemn, and he nodded a few times, saying nothing, then started tapping his right knee nervously with his free hand. After a few more moments of silence, he cradled the phone in both hands and turned to where Scamarcio was standing with the secretary. 'Giovanna, Micky wants to talk to you.' He replaced the phone and punched a button. The secretary scratched at the back of her ear nervously before picking up the phone nearest to them.

She said nothing for a few moments, then the colour rose in her cheeks once more. Eventually she muttered: 'Of course, Micky, right away.' She handed the phone to Scamarcio. 'Mr Proietti wants a word.'

Scamarcio took the phone, his expression neutral. 'Mr Proietti.'

'Why didn't you come to me about Davide? Why are you creeping around behind my back, wasting your time on matters that aren't relevant?'

'I couldn't get hold of you,' Scamarcio lied.

71

'You should have tried harder. I don't want you going around asking my suppliers about Davide.' Proietti's voice was shaky with panic. He was trying to disguise it, but he wasn't quite managing. The pitch rose with every word.

'Why's that?'

'I haven't got time for this,' hissed Proietti. 'You want to know about Davide, you come to me.' The line went dead.

Scamarcio carefully replaced the phone. He pinched his nose and thought for a moment.

'What does that guy over there do?' He pointed to the young man in the checked shirt, who was now hunched over his computer, typing out an email.

'That's Sandro, the chief accountant,' said the secretary.

Interesting that Proietti had called him first, thought Scamarcio.

10

ONLY THE THINNEST WISP of red remained in the sky as Scamarcio made his way back to Parioli and Micky Proietti's apartment. The guy who dealt with selling old ambulances had called, saying that the ID on the ambulance captured by CCTV matched one they'd sold to a film and TV prop house two years before. Scamarcio had deemed the TV connection interesting, until the guy told him that 80 per cent of their vehicles got sold on to prop houses.

Unfortunately, when Scamarcio had called Garramone, he'd learnt that they'd lost all trace of the vehicle after a last sighting from a camera on the main dual carriageway to Sperlonga. Garramone figured the kidnappers had changed the plates and repainted the scrape. Or switched vehicles. The freemason Monaci had it right — they were now looking for a needle in a haystack. Last-known triangulations for the mobile phones belonging to Proietti's wife and son matched the area of the kidnapping — the kidnappers must have switched off the phones as soon as they were inside the ambulance. Scamarcio knew that none of this was going to improve Proietti's mood.

When Scamarcio walked in, Proietti was sprawled across one of his huge white armchairs, his eyes fixed on Sky News, a cut-glass tumbler of what looked like whisky swinging precariously in his hand. The TV was showing the same stretch of motorway Scamarcio had seen on the news earlier.

'You shouldn't watch that,' Scamarcio said. 'It will just add to your anxiety. You'll get the most up-to-date information from us, not them.'

'What have you got for me then?' asked Proietti, his gaze still fixed on the screen.

Scamarcio talked him through the latest dead ends. When he was done, Proietti muttered: 'Brilliant.'

Scamarcio took a seat on the sofa and tried to make eye contact. 'Listen, we're doing all we can. But you need to be straight with me — how can I find your family if you keep me in the dark?'

'You talking about Stasio now?' Proietti still wasn't looking at him.

'Among other things.'

Proietti sighed and took a large swig of his whisky. 'I didn't tell you about Davide because it didn't even enter my mind. He has no connection to this.'

Scamarcio watched as Proietti tightened his jaw, and felt doubly sure the man was lying.

'If that's the case, why were you so spooked when I visited his offices then?'

Proietti shook his head slowly, as if he couldn't believe he had to deal with such a simpleton. 'It's not that. I just don't want word getting around about my connection to him.'

'But you're members of the same lodge. Your bosses must know already.'

Proietti sighed again. 'They don't really understand Davide at the lodge. They think he makes wildlife documentaries.'

Scamarcio frowned. 'I find that hard to believe. Francesco Bruno at Matrix knows,' he said, hoping to unsettle him.

Micky shrugged, his eyes glassy. 'I have no idea how. Davide wouldn't have told him.'

'Why's that?'

'He knows to keep it quiet.'

Scamarcio cupped his chin in his hand. 'Why did you call Stasio's chief accountant before you asked to be put through to me?'

74

'What?' Proietti looked up, surprised.

'You heard me.'

Proietti scratched behind an ear, recrossed his legs, and took another gulp of the whisky. Eventually, he said: 'Detective, stop reaching.'

'You haven't answered my question.'

Proietti rubbed his nose and sniffed, then blinked a few times. He was taking too long to come up with an answer, and he knew it. 'I've commissioned a drama from Davide. It's a bio on the life of La Cicciolina. I thought he'd be a good person to make it. I was discussing some budget issues with the accountant.'

'You don't have someone to do that for you?'

'No, I like to be on top of the line items myself.'

'Has Stasio ever made dramas?'

'No, but I think he would have brought a new touch that I wouldn't have got from anyone else.'

'Would you excuse me for a moment?' asked Scamarcio, rising from the sofa.

Proietti nodded absently and returned his attention to the TV. Scamarcio used the opportunity to swipe Proietti's mobile from the table as he passed.

When he was in the kitchen, he scrolled through the contacts and came across a number for Sizzle. He dialled it, hoping that the secretary was still in.

She sounded breathless when she picked up. 'I was just leaving, Detective.'

'You on top of all the recent commissions?'

She said nothing for a beat, then: 'Sure, I need to be across all the stuff that's coming in.'

'Are you guys making a drama on La Cicciolina?' He decided not to mention that it was for Micky — that would shut her up.

'Er, no, I've never heard about that. We don't do drama.'

'Is there anyone there you can ask, just to be sure?'

'Well, I'd definitely know, but hang on.' He heard the phone hit the desk, and then the sound of her shuffling away. After a minute or so, she was back.

'I've spoken to a few people, including our chief accountant— he deals with all the contracts coming in, and he hasn't heard about it, either. Who told you this?'

'No matter,' said Scamarcio. 'Just someone who had their wires crossed.'

He hung up before she had a chance to reply.

Back in his flat, Scamarcio pondered his progress. He had the feeling that nobody in this inquiry was being straight with him. What was the big secret here? Why did he have the sense that the truth was right in front of him, if only he could recognise it for what it was? He wondered if he was losing his touch.

His second mobile buzzed on the kitchen table: Piocosta again. He took a breath. It was starting to feel like harassment.

'Get your things, and be ready to leave in ten,' growled the old man.

'I'm not going anywhere tonight.'

'It's not a choice, it's an order.'

Scamarcio swallowed. 'I can't free myself from a kidnap inquiry. We're working round the clock.'

'Well, find some excuse.'

'No excuse. Not tonight.'

He killed the call and took a long gulp of his Nero D'Avola. Seconds later, the mobile buzzed again with a text. 'Don't be a stupid cunt. Cappadona will locate Aurelia soon enough. If we pull out, she's finished.'

Scamarcio downed his glass. There was nothing subtle about Piocosta. It was carrot or stick every time. But he felt sure that the old man wouldn't lift the protection he was providing for Aurelia quite yet. He still needed to get Scamarcio where he wanted him:

namely in the evidence store at Police HQ, eliminating the tapes that would form the foundation for the prosecution case against Piocosta's loan-sharking operation.

But what Piocosta didn't understand or *chose* not to understand was that it would take very little for Scamarcio's colleagues to work out that he was the one who had lifted the footage. The cage was wired with CCTV, there was a logbook that detailed entries and exits, and Scamarcio was still being closely monitored, despite what Garramone would have him believe.

Scamarcio pushed a palm across his cheek, rubbed at his eyes. This thing with Piocosta was becoming untenable. Night after night, he'd spun through alternative solutions in his mind. One was to tell Piocosta that he was no longer required and to arrange private security for Aurelia. But the cost would be high, and Scamarcio's money wouldn't last forever. The Cappadona had long memories, and it was unlikely that they would forgive and forget Aurelia's devastating assault on their boss. After the Cappadonna had kidnapped her in connection with one of Scamarcio's cases, Aurelia had managed to free herself by stabbing Donato Cappadona repeatedly. But her attack had confined the mob boss to a wheelchair, leaving him to run his organisation with a tilt of the head, a tap on a screen. Scamarcio knew that for a man like Donato, the sense of humiliation and impotence would be extreme. Recently, his worries about this had led Scamarcio to consider going to Cappadona direct, trying to arrange some kind of amnesty. But how? And what could he offer him in return? Piocosta, he'd wondered? Could he rid himself of the old man forever, and kill two birds with one stone? It was a crazy, high-risk strategy, and just the thought of it made him sweat.

The third scenario he'd come up with was a hybrid of the first two. He needed to find a way to get Piocosta off his case and a way to make Cappadona let go. Could he offer Donato Cappadona a cut of some kind of business? Could he promise that the police would turn a blind eye? But here he'd simply be falling back into the same trap he'd made for himself with Piocosta. Scamarcio closed his eyes and leant back against the sofa. He was stuck in a febrile nightmare. But he knew that somewhere out in the darkness lay a solution; he just needed to think harder, to bring it into focus.

The buzzer on his door sounded, and he jolted upright. When he lifted the entry phone, he heard heavy breathing on the line.

'Scamarcio, you there?'

Sartori.

'What's wrong?'

'I've got news. I was in your neck of the woods, so thought I'd deliver it in person.'

'Come up, fourth floor.'

When Sartori emerged from the elevator, he was knocking back a can of Coke. His thinning hair was all over the place, and large sweat patches were visible beneath the arms of his shirt.

'What happened?' asked Scamarcio.

Sartori frowned, then patted down his hair. 'Oh, nothing, I'm just a bit out of shape. Not used to walking lately.'

When they were inside, Scamarcio asked: 'So this news?'

Sartori looked around the room approvingly. 'Nice place. Mind if I sit down?'

'Sure.' Scamarcio hoped he wouldn't stay long. He wanted to get back to his wine and his thoughts.

Sartori leant forward on the sofa, fumbling for his notebook in his pocket while depositing the Coke can unceremoniously on the floor. When he'd finally located his pad, he flicked through a few pages and then stopped to wipe his forehead with a soiled paper napkin. Scamarcio thought he spotted the Burger King logo.

'So I spoke to that barman—you know—the one I said I was waiting to come on shift.'

'Sure.'

'He told me that he's seen a lot of Micky Proietti over the years—that he'd come in at least three times a week.'

So much for not having a social life, thought Scamarcio. He nodded, hoping Sartori would cut to it.

'This barman claims that, until last autumn, Proietti would be at a back table with Monica Brandelli.'

'*The* Monica Brandelli?'

'The very same. She'd been in a lot of his dramas. The barman thought it might have been a professional thing to start with, but then it soon became obvious they were having a relationship.'

'Right, but I don't get the significance—we know Proietti sleeps around.'

'Wait.' Sartori held up a finger. 'Our barman overheard an argument one night. One word in particular made him prick up his ears.'

'What word?'

'Abortion.'

Scamarcio fell silent for a moment, trying to take it in.

'They were in again the next night, says the barman. And it was a night he'll never forget.'

'And why's that?'

'Cos Proietti was beaten to a pulp. This huge guy comes in, looks to be in his early sixties. He pulls Micky up by the collar and kicks the living shit out of him, blood everywhere, teeth missing—you get the picture. It was so bad the barman had to call an ambulance. Then the huge guy leaves with Monica Brandelli.'

'Who was he, this guy?'

'Our barman didn't know at the time, but after the bust-up he googled Brandelli, and recognised the guy in a few pictures. He was Pietro Brandelli, her father.'

'Do you have anything on him?'

'He's a big cheese — runs a load of gambling websites. Worth a fair bit.'

'So he wasn't too happy his daughter had to have an abortion?'

'Brandelli is very devout — a big church fundraiser.'

'How does that tally with being a gambling magnate?'

Sartori shrugged and opened his palms, as if to say, 'You tell me.' Then he smiled and said: 'I've saved the best to last. You read *People* magazine, by any chance?'

Scamarcio frowned. 'Do I look like I read *People*?'

Sartori shrugged again. 'You never know — maybe on the toilet?'

Scamarcio sighed. 'Sartori, spit it out.'

'Well, if you *did* read *People*, you'd know that Monica Brandelli just gave birth to a bouncing baby boy. Got his daddy's eyes, I'd say.'

11

MONICA BRANDELLI LIVED IN A large apartment in Parioli, just a few streets away from Proietti. *Did he buy it for her?* Scamarcio wondered.

He was greeted at the door by a Filipino maid. A baby's cries were coming from a room further down the long, polished hallway.

He showed the maid his badge. 'Police,' he said.

She looked at him, wide-eyed. 'For the lady?'

'Yes.'

'She busy with baby.'

'It won't take long.'

She nodded nervously. 'One minute.'

She turned and retreated down the corridor, heading for a room at the very end. Scamarcio heard raised voices, and after a minute or so she was back, a confused Monica Brandelli trailing behind. Brandelli looked nothing like the woman who had graced countless magazine covers. Her blonde hair was greasy and matted, and there were deep grey rings beneath her blue eyes. Her usually tanned skin looked palid and mottled, and her lips were cracked.

'What is it?' she asked imperiously, clearly irritated to be seen like this.

'This won't take a minute. Is there somewhere we could talk?'

She sagged her shoulders and sighed 'For God's sake', before shuffling into the living room and dismissing the maid with a sharp flick of the wrist.

'What's so important?' She collapsed onto a huge green floral sofa and glared at him. The room was decorated in duck-egg blue with the occasional splash of white thrown in. Scamarcio decided that it worked somehow.

The baby seemed to have stopped crying now. He figured there must be a nanny back there with him.

'You heard about Micky Proietti?' he asked.

It was like he'd mentioned the devil. Brandelli's face became even paler, and the light left her eyes.

'What about him?' she spat.

'His family has been kidnapped.'

She rubbed at her eyes, tried to smooth out the bags beneath. 'What?'

'Taken away in a fake ambulance, two days ago.'

She was shaking her head in disbelief now. 'I don't get it.'

'Neither do we. I was hoping you could help.'

She raised her eyebrows. 'What?'

'I know Proietti is the father of your child. It seems to me that you have good reason to hate him and his family.'

'What?' She almost shouted the word. 'I've just given birth, for Christ's sake. Eighteen hours of pure hell. You think I had time to organise a fucking kidnapping?'

'Your father perhaps?'

She just looked at him, astounded, then began shaking her head. 'I won't lie to you. Yes, that baby is Proietti's; yes, my father is furious with him, as am I. But neither of us would even *think* about touching his family. We hate him, not his wife and kid. If anything, I feel sorry for that woman—she's married to the most unfaithful man in Rome, if not the country. Frankly, I'm hoping for better for myself.'

'I heard your father beat up Proietti pretty bad.'

She shrugged. 'Wouldn't you if it was your daughter?'

Scamarcio didn't know, but guessed that perhaps he would—it would no doubt stir something primal in him.

'I find it surprising that you didn't already know about all this, Miss Brandelli.'

'Like I said, I was in labour for 18 hours — there wasn't much time to watch TV, and there hasn't been since.'

'How can I get hold of your father?'

She shook her head again, exasperated now. 'You'd be wasting your time.'

'I'll be the judge of that.'

She sighed and rolled her eyes. 'I'll get you his number.'

Scamarcio hadn't needed to travel to Prati to find Brandelli's father as he'd met him on the stairs coming down. Well, he'd guessed it was him. The huge 6 ft 4 fellow with the enormous chest and tiny immaculate china doll of a wife had the same strong features as his daughter. Besides that, he was holding a massive bouquet of flowers, a huge blue rosette for the front door, and several supermarket shopping bags.

'Mr Brandelli?' Scamarcio asked.

The giant narrowed his eyes, tilted his head to one side. He looked like the archetypal gangster made good. 'Who wants to know?'

Scamarcio showed him his badge.

'This about that Micky Proietti business?'

Scamarcio nodded.

'You haven't been to see Monica, have you?' His flinty eyes narrowed.

'I've just come from her place.'

Brandelli set down the shopping bags. 'I didn't want her to know. We didn't want to stress her.'

Scamarcio opened his palms. 'I'm sorry, but I'm running a police inquiry. We do what we have to. There's a little boy's life at stake.'

Brandelli looked down for a moment. Then he glanced up and met Scamarcio's eye. 'Sure, I get that.'

'Do you get why I'm here?'

'Someone told you about the baby, obviously. There are no secrets in this town.'

Scamarcio couldn't think of anything further from the truth.

'I hear you were pretty angry.'

Brandelli jutted his chin forward. 'Of course. It's a father's worst nightmare. That man is a total arsehole.' The china-doll wife looked down at the floor.

'I'm guessing you're still pretty angry.'

'I hate Proietti's guts, but listen, Detective: you've got a job to do, and an important one. Don't waste your time on me.'

An interesting choice of phrase, thought Scamarcio. 'Who *should* I spend my time on then?'

Brandelli's eyes were boring into him. Somehow they connected, Scamarcio didn't know why. Maybe they were both made of the same stuff, came from the same place.

'Proietti is the golden boy — delivers great shows on meagre budgets. His bosses couldn't wish for more ...'

'So?'

'So why can't anyone else deliver the same quality on the same money?'

Scamarcio frowned, unsure where this was heading.

'Micky's in a class of his own for one reason, and one reason only. It's not talent, it's not genius — it's simply because he bends the rules. If you had access to such a huge stash of money that nobody would notice if you borrowed a bit, what would *you* do? Most normal people would pocket it and buy themselves a nice holiday or a Ferrari, but not that freak. His ego is so vast that he uses it to turn himself into the miracle worker.'

'You're saying ...'

'I'm saying that he isn't the genius everyone thinks he is. He tops up his own budgets with money from elsewhere, and has done for years.'

'But what money, from where?'

Brandelli tapped the side of his nose and then lifted the shopping bags once more. 'That, Detective, is for you to find out.'

Scamarcio had pressed Brandelli for more, but he insisted he didn't know about the source of the money. He was just passing on what he'd heard 'on the grapevine'. He also claimed Micky had mentioned 'the secret stash' to his daughter on more than one occasion.

Scamarcio took a sip of his cappuccino and wondered if Brandelli was throwing him a red herring in an attempt to damage Proietti's reputation. It was possible, but Scamarcio felt sure that the secret money was an avenue he needed to investigate. Proietti's call to Stasio's accountant, and his argument with his father about selling the shares, suggested that there was a financial background to this inquiry that Scamarcio needed to understand before he could deem it relevant or otherwise. Given that the squad's visits to the other companies Proietti did business with had failed to bear fruit, the financial angle was starting to emerge as the strongest contender.

Sky TG24 was playing on the TV in the shabby bar where Scamarcio had stopped for breakfast. They were now showing the exterior of Proietti's apartment block in Parioli. Garramone had discussed with Proietti the options of recording a media appeal, but he had said he wanted to think it over before deciding. What was there to think over? Scamarcio wondered. The clock was ticking: they'd just passed the 48-hour mark, after which the chances of finding a missing person became considerably slimmer. Did Proietti even *want* to find his family?

Scamarcio asked the barman for another cappuccino and then helped himself to a second chocolate brioche from the cabinet. He was about to take a bite when he stopped, the brioche suspended in mid-air. Sky was now showing pictures of the culture secretary, Gianluca Manfredi. Scamarcio asked the barman to turn the sound up.

'Manfredi had been a leading light in the Democratic Party for many years,' said the announcer.

Hardly a leading light, thought Scamarcio. Perhaps they were just being kind. The past tense suggested that Romano had wasted little time in firing Manfredi. Scamarcio was reminded of the emperor Tiberius and how he had executed his subjects by having them thrown from a cliff into the sea while he watched.

The news switched to an interview with Alberto di Pietro, the education secretary. 'It's devastating news. I just can't believe it, it hasn't really sunk in yet.'

As a response it seemed a bit over the top, thought Scamarcio. Maybe everyone just felt terribly sorry for Manfredi.

'My thoughts go out to Gianluca's family,' added the minister.

Scamarcio set down the brioche, carefully placing it on a napkin. He swallowed, and rubbed a tired palm across his mouth. 'What the fuck?' he whispered, prompting the old gent next to him to turn and frown.

The report switched back to the plastic blonde announcer in the studio. 'At this stage, the police aren't treating the death as suspicious.'

Scamarcio pulled out his mobile and dialled Garramone.

'You heard about Gianluca Manfredi?'

'Yeah.'

'Suicide?'

'Hung himself in his bathroom.'

'We're sure? No signs of foul play?'

'Not that I've heard. Why?'

Scamarcio filled him in on the connection to Micky Proietti.

Garramone clicked his tongue and said: 'Maybe it was the shock of being sacked. Some people can't take it.'

'Hmm,' said Scamarcio. 'I hope it's just that.'

'If I hear any more, I'll let you know.'

'Sure.' Scamarcio's mind was turning on where to take this thing next. He rang Sartori. 'Where are you?' he asked.

'I had a brainwave. I'm at the offices of *People* magazine.'

'Why?'

'Well, we want to get all the dirt on Micky Proietti, don't we?'

'Yes …'

'Well, I figured that if anyone would know, it would be them.'

Scamarcio smiled. 'Don't promise them too much in return, though.'

'OK …'

'Anything so far?'

'I've only just sat down with the editor.'

'Ask him about Fiammetta di Bondi and Gianluca Manfredi as well.'

'Received.'

Scamarcio cut the call. Had Manfredi killed himself because of his ruined career, or because of Fiammetta? He sensed that the answer to this question might provide the answer to a whole lot of things.

12

FIAMMETTA DI BONDI'S APARTMENT looked as if it had been torn apart by a team of ten blind burglars: numerous greasy pizza boxes littered the floor; the oily contents of an overturned ashtray lay strewn across the coffee table next to a stack of dirty plates, a ripped map of Rome, and one muddy running shoe. Beneath the table, a wicker wastebasket had also overturned, spilling out crumpled envelopes, used blister packs of pills, a broken purple lipstick, and a huge quantity of metallic chocolate wrappers in every colour of the rainbow. High-heeled shoes, bras, and shimmery dresses lay where they'd been tossed on the sofa. Di Bondi herself was far from immaculate this time: she was still in her dressing gown, and her blonde hair hung limply and lifelessly around her unmade-up face. Her eyes were red and swollen, and there were lines across her forehead. Despite all this, Scamarcio still found her remarkably beautiful.

'You heard about Manfredi?'

'Sure,' she said, tucking her legs up beneath her as she took a seat on the sofa and lit up.

'How are you feeling?'

She rubbed at an eyebrow and closed her eyes as she drew the smoke in. 'What are you, my therapist?'

Scamarcio said nothing and sat down on the sofa opposite.

'That little idiot should never have told you about Manfredi.'

'We'd have found out eventually,' said Scamarcio.

'But now Manfredi's dead.'

Scamarcio blinked. Why was she making a connection between

the fact he knew about Manfredi and the fact he was dead?

'But that had nothing to do with us.'

'Hmmm …'

'Go on.'

She seemed to be about to speak, but then stopped. After a beat, she said: 'Well, if you hadn't gone to that bastard Max Romano, Manfredi wouldn't have lost his job.'

Scamarcio felt sure this was not the answer she'd first intended to give. 'I had the impression Max Romano had been thinking about firing him for a while. Romano seemed worried about your decision to move in together.'

'What decision to move in together?'

'Manfredi said you and he were planning to get a place — that he was about to leave his wife.'

Di Bondi's eyes widened. 'What? That's ridiculous.'

'You'd never discussed it?'

She grimaced; it seemed a cold gesture, given the turn of events. 'He'd raised it a couple of times, and I'd said something like, you know, *Maybe one day*, but I'd never said we were definitely going to do it.'

'You didn't want to?'

'Of course not.'

'You weren't in love with him?'

'Of course not.'

'You seem quite upset though.'

'How do you mean?'

'Your eyes are red. You look like you've been crying.'

She touched below her right eye as if she'd forgotten it was there. 'Oh,' she said, apparently remembering something. 'I have conjunctivitis.'

Scamarcio frowned.

She stared at him, and for a moment her face looked as if it was made of marble.

'So you're not troubled by his death?'

She continued to stare, lifeless like a statue. 'Of course I find it upsetting. It's a shame for his family.'

To Scamarcio it seemed as if she was expressing emotions she knew she was supposed to feel, but didn't. There was something missing in this girl, thought Scamarcio, something human.

His mobile buzzed in his pocket, and he fished it out. 'Excuse me,' he said.

'My *People* idea was a blinder,' said Sartori, out of breath again.

'Tell me,' said Scamarcio, rising from the sofa and mouthing an apology to di Bondi as he put some distance between them.

'That editor is a treasure trove. He has a whole load of dirt on a whole load of VIPs, but chooses to publish just a small proportion.'

Scamarcio knew why: *leverage*. The man was a viper.

'So, according to Beppe, the editor, Micky Proietti has one big problem.'

'I'd say he's got several.'

'No, but this one's the mother lode.'

'Sartori, cut to it. This is a kidnap inquiry, and there's a kid involved.'

'Proietti has a gambling habit.'

Scamarcio fell silent. 'Gambling?' he repeated, letting it sink in.

'He's just lost a fortune. In debt up to his eyeballs.'

'You serious?'

'Would I joke? He's a regular visitor to the illegal dens, as well as to the casino in Venice. Apparently he's a sucker for roulette and the slots. Until now, lady luck has been pretty forgiving, but a few months back it all turned to shit.'

'What kind of amounts are we talking?'

'My guy from *People* says it's running past a million and a half. Proietti's at risk of losing his house, his family — the whole shebang.'

'What?'

'You deaf or something?'

'Shit,' said Scamarcio.

'Puts everything in a new light, doesn't it?'

'Perhaps.'

Scamarcio had been about to ask him for more detail when Sartori said: 'You were right to ask about di Bondi. Apparently she's sleeping with a whole load of people.'

Scamarcio glanced behind him. Di Bondi was still on the sofa, sucking on her cigarette, staring into nothing. 'That I already know.'

'Yeah, but did you know that she's only got eyes for one of them?'

'Manfredi?'

Sartori snorted. 'No, she's not blind. Aconi, of course.'

'No, you've got that wrong. Aconi is gay.'

'Na, nah, nah,' said Sartori like a man who knows he's holding the killer deck. 'He's what they call "bi curious" — keeps the guy side of things quiet, though, cos he doesn't want to damage his football career. He definitely likes his women, according to Beppe.'

Scamarcio pinched his nose. He felt as if he was struggling to keep up. After a moment, he asked: 'How does Aconi feel about di Bondi?'

'They're very much in love, apparently.'

Scamarcio wanted to sit down. It was as if he'd been dragged right back to the beginning.

13

SCAMARCIO HAD BEEN ON HIS WAY to Micky Proietti's apartment when his phone rang. It was Detective Caporaso, calling from the unit at Proietti's home. Scamarcio knew that the detective wouldn't be ringing unless there'd been a development. Scamarcio felt his chest tighten; some instinct was telling him that this inquiry was about to take a major turn, and that they'd soon all be running to catch up.

'We've received a video,' said Caporaso, his tone grave.

'From the kidnappers?'

'Who else? They've filmed Proietti's wife.'

Scamarcio swallowed and let him continue.

'She's in a bad way. It looks as if she's been beaten up—black eyes, torn clothes. She's on the verge of hysteria. She's begging Micky to give these guys what they want—says the little boy is in agony, that they still haven't treated him for the tooth, that there's a problem with his arm.'

'And what *do* the kidnappers want from Proietti?'

'They're going to call with their demands in half an hour.'

Scamarcio upped his pace. 'I was on my way to you anyway.'

When Scamarcio arrived, the envelope containing the USB key with the video was being packaged up for analysis.

'How was it delivered?' he asked Caporaso.

'Courier company. They say it was handed to them outside Termini by a guy in motorbike gear—they couldn't see his face.'

'Did he have to sign anything?'

'Yeah, but we've drawn a blank on the name.'

'Paid cash?'

Caporaso shrugged and said: 'Of course,' as if Scamarcio was living in cloud-cuckoo land to hope for anything different.

'Come on, I'll show you.' He led Scamarcio to a laptop open on the kitchen table. Where was Proietti, Scamarcio wondered. But he was too keen to see the film to ask.

Caporaso pressed play, and a head-and-shoulders image of Maia Proietti came into view. She looked nothing like the woman in the photo Scamarcio had taken from the Proietti's living room. Her make-up had gone, and there was a large black bruise beneath her right eye. The top of her dress was torn, revealing a large portion of her pale chest and shoulder, and when she raised her hand to rub her eyes he saw that she was shaking.

'Please, Micky,' she was saying. 'Just do what they ask — if not for me, then for Antonio. He's in a bad way. His tooth and arm are killing him, they won't get us medical help; he can't sleep; he can't eat. I'm so worried.' She broke down in sobs. 'I don't think he'll ever be the same,' she murmured through the tears. 'They've ruined his childhood.'

There was a buzzing in Scamarcio's head. Something was bothering him, but he couldn't put his finger on it. He bit down onto his lip in frustration, and tasted blood. *Focus*, he told himself, *just focus*. But he wasn't getting it; it was still out of reach.

'They'll call you at 5.00 pm on the landline. Make sure you're by the phone. They'll tell you everything then,' continued Maia Proietti.

'Where is Proietti?' asked Scamarcio, pressing pause.

'Throwing up,' said Caporaso.

'This really got to him?'

'That, or he's been taking a little too much of the hard stuff.'

'There much more to see?' said Scamarcio, pressing play once more.

'No, it stops here.'

When the screen went black, Scamarcio spun back through the film looking for details, trying to work out what was troubling him, but he couldn't get any clarity. How could he, if he didn't even know what he was looking for?

Caporaso and his men took up their positions by the phones. Micky Proietti was resting against the sofa, still in his pyjamas. His face was so white that Scamarcio wondered if he should see a doctor.

Proietti was cradling his usual tumbler of scotch. Scamarcio carefully extracted it from his hand, expecting an outburst, but Proietti remained strangely passive, like a feral dog that had been beaten into submission.

'It might be best if we leave that until after the call, Mr Proietti.'

Proietti just nodded absently. Was the man having some kind of breakdown, Scamarcio wondered. He took a seat next to him and placed a hand on his forearm. He had the sense that Proietti might do something unexpected, that the pressure might prove too much.

Caporaso checked his watch. 'The call should be coming through in the next thirty seconds.'

The room fell silent, the phone team making last-minute adjustments to their laptops and headsets.

Scamarcio counted to thirty in his head. The silence was shattered just as he finished. Even though he knew it was coming, the ringing still startled him.

Proietti leant forward and shakily picked up the receiver, as though he were afraid it might detonate on touch.

'Yes,' he said softly. His voice was raspy, as if he had flu.

'You know who I am?' The words had been deliberately distorted.

Scamarcio noticed one of Caporaso's men tapping at his keyboard, preparing to send the number through to the phone company for tracing. Scamarcio had no idea if the caller was using a mobile phone or a landline, but either way they'd be able to pinpoint a location from it. And, indeed, after several seconds a triangle appeared on Caporaso's screen somewhere to the south-east of the city. Scamarcio was sitting too far away to see properly, but it looked like it might be out near Prenestino. Caporaso was speaking into his mobile, no doubt alerting Garramone to dispatch a team to the location.

What were the chances the kidnappers and their victims would be there when they arrived? Less than zero, Scamarcio told himself. Sometimes he wondered why the squad even bothered with this charade. At times it felt as if they had to go through the motions, tick all the boxes, rather than focus on getting a real result.

'Who are you?' whispered Proietti into the phone, his hand trembling.

'Well, if you're too stupid to work it out, I'm not going to tell you.'

Proietti sighed and looked down into his lap, defeated. 'What do you want?' he asked after a beat.

'Again, if you're too much of a cretin to work …'

'Cut the crap,' screamed Proietti. His entire demeanour seemed to transform in an instant: he sat up bolt upright, his shoulders stiffened, his jaw protruded. The feral dog had returned. 'You do anything to harm my wife and son, you're dead.'

Scamarcio tightened his grip on Proietti's arm. He was not following the advice he'd been given before the call.

'It's too late for that, Micky boy.'

'Just tell me where to bring the bloody money, you cunt.'

Scamarcio rubbed his forehead, and forgot to breathe.

'I'm not the cunt here. You don't understand any of this, do

95

you? You're a long way from the genius everyone thinks you are, Micky.'

'Tell me where to bring it!' hollered Proietti.

'Fuck you!' shouted the caller before the line went dead.

Scamarcio finally remembered to exhale. *Why hadn't Proietti asked how much they wanted?* was his first thought. His second was why the caller seemed so emotional. In his experience, most kidnappers displayed more *sangfroid*.

'Money, money, money,' mumbled Scamarcio under his breath. Could it be that this case had nothing do with it?

14

JUST AS SCAMARCIO HAD EXPECTED, when they reached the location near Prenestino, there was no sign of the kidnappers or Proietti's family. Proietti had insisted on coming along, and Scamarcio was glad, because from the moment they entered the warehouse complex, Proietti seemed to relax considerably. Scamarcio watched as his shoulders dropped, his forehead softened, and his hands ceased shaking. Finally, his breathing evened out, and he sank back against the leather of the backseat and closed his eyes.

'You OK, Mr Proietti?' Scamarcio asked, expecting some kind of explanation for the change.

'Yes.'

'Does this place mean anything to you?'

'No.' Proietti didn't bother to open his eyes.

Scamarcio suddenly wanted to punch his perfect jaw. If he knew something more, if he felt like the threat had passed, or that the danger wasn't as great as he'd first feared, why the hell couldn't he just come out with it?

'Mr Proietti,' Scamarcio said, struggling to remain calm. 'I get the sense that you've been here before, that this place holds some kind of significance. You seem considerably less on edge than an hour ago, and I need to know why.'

'You're mistaken,' said Proietti, almost whispering the words, his eyes still shut.

Scamarcio sighed and turned his gaze to the window. They were pulling up outside a line of small warehouses, each marked with a number on the roller door. The series appeared to rise to twenty. To the left of the warehouses was a sentry box, a man in uniform hunched inside. Scamarcio stepped out of the car and approached the sentry, his badge at the ready. He tapped on the window. 'What is this place used for?'

The guard clocked the badge and nodded in the direction of the warehouses. 'Studios mainly. They're hired out for magazine shoots or TV and film work.' He pointed to the end of the lot. 'But the last three over there are rented by a fashion company and an artisan bakers'.'

Scamarcio frowned. 'You keep a logbook?'

'Sure.' The security guard pointed to a large tome in front of him.

'Can I take a look?'

The man pulled up his window to let it through, and Scamarcio scanned down the day's arrivals. There were only ten names on the list, and of course none of them meant anything to him.

'Where are these people from?'

'They're the regulars from the fashion company and the bakers', plus a small crew of four who were using one of the studios. It's been a quiet day.'

'A film crew?'

The man nodded.

'They still here?'

The man swung the book around and glanced down. 'No — they left about an hour ago.'

An hour ago. That was when the kidnapper had hung up on Proietti.

'Can you describe them?'

The man's face was a blank. He rubbed his cheek. 'I'm sorry — if I'm honest, I don't remember anything about them.'

Scamarcio wanted to say 'Call yourself a security guard?', but instead he glanced inside the small booth and asked: 'You guys got CCTV?'

'Sure.'

'Have you got a camera on the entry gate?'

'Sure.'

'Can we spool back to when the film crew arrived?'

The man looked down at the logbook once more, searching for the timings with his finger.

'You'd better come round the other side.'

When Scamarcio was seated in front of the small TV, Detective Caporaso knocked on the door of the cabin.

'We could have something,' said Scamarcio. 'I'll come get Proietti once we cue it up — he might recognise them.'

Caporaso nodded. 'He's fallen asleep, would you believe?'

'Drink?'

'God knows.' Caporaso tossed his Marlboro into the trash and headed back to the car.

The security guard leant forward and fiddled with a small joystick on a console. It took a minute or so before he said: 'Here they are.'

Scamarcio peered in closer. He saw a series of young people taking turns to sign the logbook. The first was female; the others, male. They seemed to be in their late twenties, early thirties. They were all reasonably good-looking, apart from the last to sign, who, with his unfashionable glasses and balding pate, appeared to be the geek of the group. Scamarcio didn't recognise any of them.

'Can you freeze it there? I just need to get someone.'

The guard nodded.

Proietti cried out when Scamarcio woke him. He appeared to be in the middle of a nightmare. Scamarcio put a hand on his arm in an attempt to calm him down. 'I need you to come with me.'

Proietti just looked confused, but then, with the easy compliance of a sleepwalker, he stepped carefully from the car and followed Scamarcio towards the cabin.

When he was finally positioned in front of the small TV,

Proietti pushed up his lower lip and said: 'I've never seen any of them before.'

'You sure?' asked Scamarcio, trying to read his eyes, trying to understand whether he was lying again.

'Yes,' said Proietti, his gaze fixed on the screen, his eyes desperately tracking the faces, the expressions, the movements.

Scamarcio watched him hunched over the TV, his forehead a scowl of confusion and disappointment, his finger in his mouth like a troubled child. Proietti was telling the truth. Any vague doubts Scamarcio might have had about Proietti really wanting to find his family disappeared in that instant.

Back home in his flat, Scamarcio ended his call to Forensics. He'd ordered them to conduct a DNA search of the studio used by the TV people Proietti hadn't been able to recognise. Scamarcio didn't really expect to find anything, but he wanted the location sealed and inspected before anyone else could use it.

He pondered the change in Proietti's demeanour when they were out at the industrial park. He'd felt sure that as soon as they entered that place something clicked for him, something that had made him feel that his family weren't in serious danger. The park was used regularly by TV people. Was it this connection that had reassured Proietti? Had he originally believed someone else to be behind the kidnapping—someone far more dangerous? Had it therefore been a relief to discover that there could be a more benign explanation?

Scamarcio sighed, and ran a hand across his face. If that was the case, why couldn't Proietti just be open with them? Surely he didn't want them pursuing the wrong leads, if he already knew better? Scamarcio shook his head. *He doesn't know*, he said to himself. *He thinks he might know, but he's not sure. And it's that little bit of doubt that scares him*. As long as an element of doubt remained, Proietti had to make sure the police tried all avenues.

That doubt, Scamarcio realised, had to relate to something very big and very dangerous for Proietti to risk exposing his secrets.

Scamarcio thought of Davide Stasio and the Calabrian connection, and something stirred in him — something toxic. His mind flashed on parasites: ripe, bloated, visceral. When was Stasio coming back? Where was he? Scamarcio sensed that Stasio had been keeping his head down, that he didn't want their paths to cross.

It was time to meet this ghost, time to make him real.

15

SCAMARCIO DREW UP OUTSIDE the offices of Sizzle. It was a cold, misty morning, and the early promise of summer seemed to have disappeared. The soulless, pale buildings against the slate-grey sky made him feel newly down, and he wondered yet again about Aurelia and how she was doing. Had she already met someone? Was she moving on? He imagined that she'd attract a lot of attention from the other researchers at the lab, that she wouldn't have trouble creating a new life for herself. He stopped himself: if he really cared about her, that was what he should be hoping; after everything, she needed to be able to put what had happened last year behind her. Why couldn't he just want the best for her? It was the very least he could do, given the disaster he had brought upon her.

He thought of Piocosta's threat. Could he risk enraging the old man? If he didn't do what he wanted, how far would Piocosta go? Would it just be a case of him lifting Aurelia's protection, or would he strike harder? Would he throw her to the lions himself?

Scamarcio pinched his nose and looked up into the grey sky. He would be a fool to trust Piocosta on any level. And now, this Calabrian connection on the Micky Proietti case just sharpened his anxiety. He sensed that he was being dragged back under; that however fast he swam, the riptide would suck him back down, again and again. He took a long, silent breath: he needed to stay near the shore for as long as he could.

Stasio's secretary did not look pleased to see him when he walked in.

'Davide's not here,' she said before Scamarcio could get the question out.

'When is he coming back?'

'I don't know,' she snapped, looking away, as if Stasio's absence was a personal affront.

'Where can I find him?'

She sniffed. 'Well, if you feel like making a daytrip to Catanzaro, you might get lucky.'

Piocosta's stamping ground.

'I might?'

'Look, I just told you, I don't know where Davide is. I think he's still down south, but I'm not sure.'

'Didn't you ask?'

'It's not my business,' she hissed, turning her attention to her computer screen. Scamarcio noticed that her nails were bitten to the quick. He thought he saw dried blood on one.

'Can you give me Mr Stasio's telephone number and address in Catanzaro? And for his place in Rome?'

She sighed, and pulled out a block notepad. She started scribbling the details, her pale face set in anger.

'You know what I don't understand in all this is that you'd think that Maia Proietti's relatives would be doing all they could to help the police find her and her son. But all I've had from the start is lies and obstruction. It makes me think I've stumbled into a nest of vipers.'

She looked up, open-mouthed now, but he just snatched the piece of paper from her hand and left.

The secretary's quip about a daytrip to Catanzaro riled him. It was a ten-hour drive there and back, which meant Scamarcio had no choice but to start with Stasio's place in Rome. On the one hand, he very much doubted he'd find him there; on the other, he wondered if Stasio would feel the need to be near the scene of the crime. If his sister and nephew had been kidnapped, he couldn't imagine him sweating it out down in Catanzaro, waiting for news. Why hadn't he been round Proietti's place, offering a shoulder to cry on, then? The quick picture Scamarcio had formed of Stasio was of a mover and shaker, a doer. He imagined that he'd want to be on top of things; that he'd want to know how the police were proceeding — what their next moves would be. His absence made no sense.

It seemed that Stasio lived on a very respectable street just five minutes from the Piazza Venezia. Scamarcio figured that he must have a lot of high-profile politicians for neighbours. The man had certainly done well for himself, but how he'd managed it was the million-dollar question. Scamarcio didn't know much about the porn business, but he wondered if Stasio's wealth could be attributed to that alone.

When the maid brought Scamarcio into a vast living room with sumptuous oriental rugs, glinting chandeliers, gold mirrors, and chesterfield leather sofas, he wondered again. The place had the stamp of the southern boy made good: ostentation, opulence, and colour-blind chaos. The room was an orgy of different styles and patterns, the frenzied accumulation of wealth evident in every hideous bauble and trinket, every gold-tassled cushion.

He followed the maid through the living room into another smaller lounge. A huge projector screen was mounted on one wall, a vast grey leather sofa opposite. Scamarcio noticed little speakers and compartments built into the arms. When he drew closer, he saw that they contained bottles of beer and white wine — little fridges, he realised.

The maid stopped, and knocked on the outside of a gold-studded door. A soft voice mumbled a response, and she walked in.

'The police are here.'

Scamarcio couldn't believe it was this easy. Stasio had been at home in Rome all this time.

A small man with a grey beard was seated behind the desk. He was the absolute antithesis of what Scamarcio had expected—he could have passed for a classics teacher or a librarian.

Scamarcio extended a hand and introduced himself.

'Renato Guidice,' said the man, smiling.

Scamarcio frowned. 'I was hoping to speak with Davide Stasio.'

'Do take a seat,' said the man, still smiling as he gestured to a wide leather armchair in front of the desk. The décor was more sober in here.

'Where can I find Stasio?' snapped Scamarcio, not wanting to waste any time sitting down.

'Mr Stasio is out of town. I'm his lawyer. You were lucky to find me—I just popped in to deal with some paperwork.'

'Have you heard about Stasio's sister and nephew?'

The lawyer nodded, his expression giving nothing away. 'Mr Stasio is with his mother now. She's very ill—heart trouble—he doesn't want her to find out about what's happened. He's down there to make sure nobody tells her.'

How convenient, thought Scamarcio. 'When are you expecting him back?'

The lawyer shrugged. 'How long is a piece of string? I suppose when all this is over, when the police have tracked them down.'

'It seems odd to me that Stasio isn't in Rome. He could be assisting us with our inquiries.'

The lawyer's thin mouth turned down at the corners. 'Mr Stasio is very much a family man. There is nothing he wouldn't do for his mother. But you could reach him by telephone or, if you were prepared to travel down to Catanzaro, I'm sure he'd be happy to help in any way he could.'

Why did Scamarcio have the sense that the lawyer had been expecting him—that he'd been wheeled in precisely to deal with the problem of the bothersome detective?

'OK,' he said, rising to his feet. 'I'll give him a call. Unfortunately, a trip down to Catanzaro is a bit difficult right now.'

The lawyer nodded understandingly. Scamarcio knew this was the answer he'd been hoping for.

If he had to, Scamarcio would make the sodding trip to Catanzaro, as much as that god-forsaken hellhole made his stomach churn and his mouth dry, but first he wanted to check out a hunch. The feeling that he was being led a dance was growing by the day, and he couldn't help thinking that Catanzaro was a part of it; that Stasio was still in the capital, keeping out of his way. Scamarcio figured that if he was vigilant he could soon find out where.

'How's Proietti doing?' he asked Detective Caporaso when he called him after leaving Stasio's pad.

'The usual. Drinking too much, sitting in that chair all day waiting for the phone to ring.'

'Nothing more then?'

'No.'

'You think he pissed the kidnappers off?'

'Nah. They're testing him, making him sweat. There'll be another call.'

Scamarcio had reached the same conclusion.

'So he never goes out?'

'He takes a walk in the evening at about nine — always nine. He's usually gone for half an hour or so — doesn't want protection.'

'Do you see where he goes?'

'Well, we followed him the first time, and he just went round the block, sat in a park for a bit, watched the birds — nothing out of the ordinary.'

'Did you follow him again?'

'No, just the once.' Caporaso paused. 'Should we have? Has there been a fuck-up?'

'No. I was just curious, that's all.'

Caporaso exhaled. 'The pressure's on. Garramone's on our case cos there's no progress to show the media.'

'There's so fucking little to go on, though. These guys have it down pat. They don't seem like yokels.'

'Yeah, but I keep asking myself why they bothered with the phone call. That's a risk.'

'They knew they could get away with it, and—like you say—they wanted to make Proietti sweat.'

'He's sweating, all right.'

Scamarcio yawned and said: 'Well, ring me if there's any news. I'm heading back to the squadroom.'

When he was back at his desk, Scamarcio called Manetti about the DNA search of the studio.

'Zero,' said the chief CSI breezily. 'Nothing from the mum, and nothing from the son. No matches to any crims on the database.'

Scamarcio stifled a sigh. 'Well, I wasn't expecting to find anything. Just going through the motions, really.'

'I guess the kidnappers might have rung from that studio, but they'd never have taken the victims there if they knew you could trace the call.'

'That's it, Manetti, a waste of time basically.' Scamarcio thanked him and hung up. Then he dialled the numbers he had been given for Davide Stasio, but they both rang out. He was about to try again when a thought occurred to him. Maybe it would be best to wait until after tonight. There was a strong chance Micky Proietti *was* taking a quiet constitutional every evening, but Scamarcio wondered if he should check it out. If there was any significance to these evening strolls, it might be useful to understand that before dealing with Stasio.

Scamarcio's thoughts turned to the new steer from Sartori. The news that Italy's leading footballer was in love with Fiammetta di Bondi couldn't be ignored. She'd not really allowed herself to be drawn on the matter — so now, at least, Scamarcio had to pay Aconi a visit, get a sense of whether he might hold some kind of grudge against Proietti. But going as far as to organise a kidnapping? A celebrity of Aconi's stature had way too much to lose. Scamarcio chewed on the top of his pen, and the cap came loose. He spat it on the desk in frustration, tasting ink. It came back to the same thing: the box had to be ticked; the man had to be questioned. He thought about sending Sartori, but quickly decided that he didn't have the confidence to delegate this. Besides, if he was honest, he couldn't help but feel a little excited at the prospect of meeting the country's star striker.

He ran a web search for Aconi's representation, and was put through to an officious-sounding woman. When he explained what he wanted, her tone softened slightly.

'You'll find him at the training ground out at Trigoria. He'll be there for the next couple of hours — after that, I don't know. He has an event on Via Settembre later this evening, but that might not be the best place for a talk.'

'Sure. I'll head out to the ground now.'

The woman cleared her throat. 'Is this anything we should be worried about? Mr Aconi has a legal team. If they need …'

'I can assure you that this is just a casual chat. Right now, he's not a person of interest. I was just hoping he could provide some background.'

'Are you close to finding them, that man's wife and son?'

Scamarcio paused to craft a response. 'We're confident, yes.'

'Glad to hear that. Well, let me know if you need anything else.'

He thanked her, and cut the call.

Scamarcio realised that when women described Aconi as a Greek god they perhaps had a point. Standing at 6 foot, with curly blonde hair and large blue eyes, the man was a tight knot of tanned muscle and sinew. When Scamarcio walked in, he was emerging from the shower, rubbing his enormous shoulders with a blue-and-white Inter towel. Scamarcio thought it must have been given to him as a joke. The rest of the team appeared to be several stages ahead, and were already dressed and gathering up their kit. Scamarcio took in a few famous faces, and was surprised at how short a couple of them were. On TV they seemed so much taller. As they bustled past, he pulled out his badge and headed to the bench where Aconi was patting himself dry. Scamarcio gave him a few seconds to put on his boxers and then made his approach.

'Can I take a few moments of your time, Sir,' he said, holding the badge up for him to read.

Aconi studied it, his expression switching from confusion to discomfort.

'Is this one of those candid-camera stunts? Are you from Channel 5?'

'No, like the badge says, I'm Detective Scamarcio of the Flying Squad. I'm investigating the disappearance of Micky Proietti's wife and son.'

Aconi frowned, and pulled on a tight white T-shirt, followed by a pair of baggy designer denims. He carefully took a seat on a dry patch of bench, not bothering with shoes. 'Yeah, I heard about that,' he said running a huge hand through his wet hair. 'It's been all over the news.'

Scamarcio took a seat opposite. He didn't want to be standing over him.

'You and Fiammetta di Bondi have been seeing each other, I hear.'

Aconi looked across at him, not following. 'Sure, but …'

'I'm guessing you knew she was seeing Micky Proietti—

otherwise you would have asked me why I'm here.'

Aconi rubbed his nose and studded his bare feet against the tiles. He must have been at least a size 48. That would explain his magnificent record as a striker, Scamarcio figured.

'Yes,' said Aconi slowly. 'I did know that she'd had a thing with Proietti, but Fiammetta was about to end it. She'd been trying to call him to tell him, but then the kidnapping happened, and the timing no longer felt right.'

Scamarcio took a silent breath and blinked. These were almost exactly the same words he'd heard from the culture minister, Manfredi. Had Fiammetta been spinning them *all* a line? Had she told Proietti the exact same thing?

'Can you describe your relationship with Miss di Bondi?'

Aconi looked down at his feet once more and said nothing for a few moments, then:. 'I guess you could say that I have very strong feelings for her. She's a remarkable person — highly intelligent. We can talk about all sorts of things.'

Scamarcio wanted to ask *what* they talked about, but stopped himself.

'I suppose you're wondering if I wanted to get at Proietti, if I was jealous,' said Aconi.

'Well, obviously it's something we need to consider.'

'I admit that there was some of that, yes. I'd seen him on the party circuit over the years, and never liked him. He's arrogant and rude. But I know he's very bright, very educated, and I imagined that that would appeal to Fiammetta. I could see why the two of them would hit it off. Fiammetta can also be pretty obtuse when she wants to be. She's not really one for social niceties either. I guess I was worried that she'd maybe found a soul mate in Micky.'

Scamarcio was taken aback by the man's lack of confidence. He was stunningly good-looking, he was the country's star striker and a household name, but he didn't deem himself good enough for Fiammetta di Bondi.

'You know I got a 108 in my Laurea,' said Aconi, almost under his breath.

The comment came from nowhere, and Scamarcio had no time to disguise his surprise. The fact that Aconi had a degree was a revelation; the fact that he'd scored so highly was astounding, given his long-cemented reputation for keeping his brains in his feet.

'What did you read?'

'Philosophy.'

Scamarcio blinked again. He was struggling to come up with a response.

'You're wondering why nobody talks about it?'

The man was a mind reader as well as a genius. 'Yes, to be honest.'

'My agent doesn't think it's good for the image.'

'Why?'

The footballer shrugged. 'I dunno — she thinks it would be too alien from the core fan base, that it might risk some sponsorship deals.'

Scamarcio pondered this for a moment, then tried to drag his mind back to the interview.

'So you were jealous of Micky Proietti?'

'Yes, slightly I guess, but I would never go around harming his family — that's not the kind of person I am. Besides, even if I did want to do something appalling like that, if I ever got found out, it would be game over. Literally.'

'And Fiammetta was going to leave him anyway …'

Aconi shrugged once more and opened his palms. 'Things were going my way. I had no reason to harm Proietti, did I?' He paused. 'The strange thing is that I've actually got Micky to thank for introducing me to Fiammetta.'

'How do you mean?'

'We were drunk at a party one night — well, he was drunk, and I wasn't, because I was in training — and he said *I must introduce you to this girl, you'll love her.'*

'So he wanted to hook the two of you up?'

'He was pissed, and I think he wanted to do me some kind of favour — maybe he wanted something in return. Anyway, he introduced us there and then, and kind of gave me a nudge and a wink.'

Scamarcio nodded, just willing him to keep talking.

'But I could tell that the next day he regretted it. He called me, and asked me all about it, what I thought of her, what she said to me, etc etc. He seemed quite panicked. I got the feeling he wanted me to back off.'

'What did you tell him?'

'I really liked her; I wanted a shot with her, so I kind of behaved like I wasn't that bothered one way or another. I just wanted him to leave me in peace, quit worrying.'

'And did he?'

'No. He started putting the pressure on Fiammetta. She told me that he wouldn't stop calling, texting, started dropping by at all hours. I admit the whole thing did make me jealous, but, like I say, I'd never have done anything to hurt Micky's family. That would have been crazy.'

That was exactly what Manfredi had said. But what if Aconi or Manfredi grew to suspect di Bondi had just been spinning them a line, playing them for fools? What then?

Scamarcio coughed. 'Did you know Fiammetta was also seeing Gianluca Manfredi, the politician who just died?'

Aconi nodded somberly. 'I did know about that, but it finished some time ago.'

'I met with Mr Manfredi the day before he died, and he was under the impression that Fiammetta was about to move in with him.'

'What?' Aconi leaned forward, his face tightening with fury. 'No way!'

'That's what he told me. He may have misunderstood her, of course.'

The footballer got up from the bench and hurriedly started pulling on his shoes. Where were his socks? Scamarcio wondered. He noticed that Aconi's bottom lip was quivering, his mouth a tight line of anger. The huge blue eyes had become dark slits. He was reaching for his holdall already.

'Where are you going?' Scamarcio asked.

'None of your fucking business.' Aconi grabbed the bag from the bench, and smashed it hard against the wall as he left. Scamarcio thought he heard something break inside.

16

SMALL SHARDS OF ELECTRIC BLUE punctured the darkening sky as Scamarcio approached Proietti's street. His high-flier neighbours were returning from work, dismounting tiredly from their mopeds, struggling with heavy shopping bags and briefcases.

Scamarcio's problem was that he didn't want to be spotted by any of his police colleagues. He preferred to follow his semi-hunch alone, to see where it took him. He pulled out a plastic chair at a pavement bar opposite Proietti's block and lowered his baseball cap. He checked his watch. It was ten minutes to nine. He unfolded the edition of *La Repubblica* he had just bought, and turned to the sport. But there was no time to pretend to read — because out of the corner of his eye, he spotted Proietti emerging from the doorway, making a swift left down the street. He was early.

Scamarcio slid the paper under his arm and crossed the road, keeping an eye out for any officers coming or going. He fell into step behind Proietti, who was moving surprising swiftly for someone who seemed to spend most of his day in an alcoholic haze. Proietti strolled quickly up the road, then took a left into a smaller street of equally desirable properties. Sprays of purple wisteria emerged every so often between a hodgepodge of art deco and liberty buildings. Scamarcio noticed palms, orange trees, and white roses jostling for space in their immaculate gardens.

There was a small intersection up ahead, and he felt sure that Proietti was about to turn again, heading for the park, but instead he came to an abrupt stop outside a large cream villa with green shutters. Scamarcio immediately ducked into a garden to his left, certain that Proietti would now check behind him to see if he was being followed. Indeed, Proietti scanned the street several times, then, satisfied he wasn't being observed, walked up to the front door and rang the bell. Scamarcio carefully detached his jacket sleeve from a rose bush, then stepped back onto the street in the hope he could see who had answered the door. Proietti was now some metres away, but still close enough for Scamarcio to observe a heavy-set middle-aged man pushing him inside. Somehow he felt sure this was Davide Stasio.

Back in the squadroom the next morning, Scamarcio gave Garramone the details of the property. He hadn't wanted to head straight back to Proietti's apartment last night, because he knew that sharing his discovery with the team would change the atmosphere there and risk spooking Proietti that something was amiss. Garramone had agreed that they'd try to find out if Stasio was living in the building. One they'd established that, they'd wire the place to kingdom come.

Scamarcio leant back in his chair and surveyed Via San Vitale. There was still no sight of the stray. *It must be dead*, he told himself. *It wouldn't just disappear*. He felt low again, and resolved not to spend too much time back at base. The depression seemed to lift when he was out on the road. There was something about being at his desk that sucked him back into the void, consumed him.

After a few moments, he sensed someone looking at him, and glanced up. The tableau before him was both banal and apocalyptic, innocent and devastating. The image of a whale on a beach came into his mind. It was logical that the whale might end up there, but the sight of it was so very wrong. The same applied to this scene: Piero Piocosta, his father's old lieutenant, was standing in the middle of the squad room next to the desk sergeant. The sergeant was saying something, but there was a ringing in Scamarcio's ears, and the sergeant's voice was disembodied, as if coming from a distant shore.

Scamarcio closed his eyes, trying to breathe. He exhaled slowly, then counted to five in his head. 'Sorry, Sergeant—I didn't quite catch that.'

The desk sergeant was eyeing him with concern. 'I was saying that this gentleman here needs a quick word. Are you feeling all right, Sir? You look very pale.'

Scamarcio sat up straighter in his seat, forcing his mouth into a smile. 'No, I'm fine, just tired.' He motioned Piocosta over to his desk. He couldn't get up; his legs were jelly.

'Thanks, Sergeant. I'll take it from here.'

The man nodded and left. Scamarcio scanned the room, but there were only two detectives in, and they were over on the other side. Scamarcio thanked a God he didn't believe in.

Piocosta pulled out a seat, leant back, and stretched out his short legs in front of him.

'What are you doing here?' whispered Scamarcio.

'Seemed like the only way to get your attention. You need to learn to answer your phone, Leo.'

Scamarcio swallowed, and tried to put himself somewhere calm. 'I need you to leave right now; we'll talk about this later.'

'Yes, we will,' said Piocosta. 'When you answer your phone. I'll be calling at eight tonight.' The old man's eyes were mean cracks of light, his mouth a dark gash. 'Understood?'

'Understood,' hissed Scamarcio. 'Now get out.'

'Is that any way to treat your father's best friend?'

Scamarcio grabbed his cigarettes and turned his eyes to the street.

He had intended to use the rest of the morning to try to root out the illegal gambling dens frequented by Micky Proietti, but Piocosta's visit had scrambled his brain and left him unable to concentrate. All Scamarcio felt capable of was staring at the complicated web of cracks lining his desk and wishing that he might disappear inside. But then his landline rang, forcing him back to reality.

'We've had another video,' said Detective Caporaso darkly.

'What are they saying?'

'It's the little boy. He's very quiet, subdued.'

'What fucker would use a kid?' asked Scamarcio.

'Whoever they are, they've really got it in for Proietti. They're torturing him.'

'What's the son telling us?'

'He says he's OK, but that he's worried about his mum. He doesn't know where she is, and he wants to see her.'

He doesn't know where she is, Scamarcio repeated to himself. They'd separated them; the situation was degenerating. Surely seeing his son like this would finally persuade Proietti to open up, to share what he knew or at least suspected.

'What's Proietti's reaction?'

Caporaso sighed. 'He's just gone back to the bottle. He's clammed up—he's barely speaking.'

Scamarcio drummed a finger against a tooth. In what situation would a father, seeing his family suffer, choose to remain silent? Why would he not tell the police what he knew? Micky Proietti was an arsehole, but from what Scamarcio had seen so far, he was not a monster. The man was clearly extremely worried. So why wasn't he talking?

Scamarcio's thoughts switched to Piocosta, and in that exact moment he finally understood Micky Proietti. The kidnappers already had Proietti over a barrel. They'd already set out their terms in a deal the police had not been privy to. Proietti was being blackmailed, and right now he was sitting it out, playing for time while he worked out his next move. Scamarcio's mind flashed to the man in the doorway, and he wondered yet again whether Davide Stasio was Proietti's friend or foe.

17

SURVEILLANCE HAD TOLD THEM two things: the first was that the middle-aged man who had answered the door to Micky Proietti was living on the third floor of the villa; the second was that he was indeed Davide Stasio. Establishing this had not been easy, as they had been unable to trace any passport or ID card records. It had taken numerous attempts at a photograph before Scamarcio had an image clear enough to show the Calabrian TV producer Francesco Bruno.

'Yep, that's him. He's put on a fair bit of weight, though. He used to keep himself in better shape.' Bruno paused, then asked, 'Why the surveillance shot?'

'Long story,' Scamarcio had replied, hurrying for the door.

Garramone had ordered Stasio's place wired 'to kingdom come' as promised. They'd had to wait seven hours until Stasio finally went out and they could send in a team of six to install listening devices in all the rooms. Normally, this kind of job would have been done by a crew of three, but Garramone sensed the squad had very little time to play with and needed to finish as quickly as possible. He'd been right — after just forty minutes, Stasio was spotted approaching the house, and they'd had to hot-foot it out of there. Unfortunately, the first hours' recordings offered meagre pickings. Stasio spoke only to a cleaner who delivered some shopping. He made no telephone calls and received no visitors. Scamarcio wondered if he had them sussed already. If that were the case, though, Stasio would have abandoned the villa and moved on elsewhere, surely? Scamarcio hoped they'd get lucky when Proietti called by for his evening chat, but his instincts were beginning to tell him otherwise. Davide Stasio already seemed one step ahead.

As there were several hours to kill before Proietti's next stroll, Scamarcio decided to head back to Stasio's production company and wait for the accountant to leave for the day. It was time for a full and frank discussion.

He realised with dismay that he'd have to drive, as there'd be nowhere to sit it out otherwise. The area was a wasteland, and he hadn't noticed any bars nearby on his last visit. He reckoned the journey across town would take him the best part of an hour.

This turned out to be an optimistic estimate. It seemed that nearly every road in the city had been ripped open for urgent maintenance. After an hour and a half stuck in one dusty traffic jam after the other, Scamarcio finally pulled up outside the industrial estate, sweating and furious. He hoped that the accountant wouldn't emerge just yet, because he couldn't trust himself not to lose it. He counted to ten slowly in his head, and watched his chest move in and out as he did so. He tried to imagine himself on a beach, tropical breezes whispering through the palms.

Inevitably, Piocosta interrupted his thoughts yet again. He would be calling in two hours. Scamarcio's back was against the wall. There was no room left for manoeuvre. He sighed, and wiped the sweat from his forehead with a monogrammed handkerchief that had once belonged to his father. What would he have made of all this? How would he have felt about his old friend now?

When he opened his eyes, Scamarcio saw the secretary exit the building and make for a red Fiat Punto. He edged down lower in the seat and covered his face with *La Gazetta dello Sport*. He heard the Punto's engine fire up and, a few seconds later, the little car passed his.

From behind the newspaper, he saw a few other people emerge. He recognised several faces from his visit to the office the day before, but he couldn't spot the accountant in the group. He heard central locking being released, doors slamming, a blast of 'I'm a Barbie Girl'. A fly kept throwing itself against his windscreen, its exhausted buzzing slowly winding down like the dying battery on a child's toy. A couple of cars passed him, and, when their engines had finally melted away, he peered out from behind the newspaper once more. The accountant was exiting the building, making purposefully for a blue Lancia parked up the kerb on the right. He was wearing another checked shirt — green and white, this time — and appeared to be in a hurry. He was walking so fast he seemed about to break into a run. It was now or never.

Scamarcio stepped out the car and headed straight for him. 'Sir, may I have a minute?'

The guy turned fast, and for a moment it looked as if he was about to bolt. Scamarcio recognised the look of the hunted in his eyes. But then the man just stopped dead as if he'd been stunned by some kind of weapon. Scamarcio watched as he blinked rapidly, his brain turning over, trying to calculate his best move.

As Scamarcio drew closer, he noticed him wipe the sweat from his forehead with the cuff of his shirt. For a fellow so neatly turned out, it seemed an incongruous gesture. He was clearly in a panic.

Scamarcio extended a hand. 'I passed by the office the other day. I saw you hard at work.'

The accountant wiped a palm against his trousers and accepted the handshake. 'Yes, Detective. How can I help you?'

Scamarcio thought he detected a slight tremor in his voice. 'As you know, we're investigating the disappearance of Davide Stasio's sister and nephew.'

'Yes. How are you getting on?' He glanced away when he asked this, checking to make sure he wasn't being observed.

'I believe there's a financial aspect to this crime, and I was hoping I could ask you a few questions.'

The accountant scratched behind his ear, and looked at him for a few seconds before averting his gaze once more. 'I think you may have been misled. We don't really have any dealings with Micky Proietti.'

Scamarcio lowered his eyebrows. 'Come on, I was there when he asked to be put through to you.'

He seemed surprised. 'Oh, right. That was just about a favour we were doing for him.'

'What kind of favour?'

Scamarcio could see him struggling once more, desperately trying to come up with something, anything.

'Er ...'

'Yes?'

'It was, erm ...'

Scamarcio hadn't got the time. 'I know there's something going on between Micky Proietti and Davide Stasio, and you need to tell me what *you* know, fast. Otherwise I'll have you in front of the magistrates' quicker than you can say Rebibbia.'

The man finally looked at him properly now, and Scamarcio observed his resolve gradually crumble. After a few moments, the accountant's shoulders sagged, and he laid down his briefcase gently on the pavement, plomping himself down beside it, as if his legs would no longer carry him. With his sweat-stained shirt and tousled hair, he suddenly looked like a rough sleeper, exhausted from a day's begging.

Scamarcio took a position alongside him on the kerb, pulled out his cigarettes, and offered the box across. The accountant had been about to wave it away, but then seemed to change his mind, his hand shaking as he reached in for a smoke. Scamarcio lit up for him, and the guy took a few greedy drags before leaning back and closing his eyes.

'You a smoker?' Scamarcio asked, knowing the answer already.

'No, gave up years ago.'

'It's a tough habit to quit.'

The man nodded, his eyes still closed.

'So why did Proietti want a word?'

The accountant took another drag and breathed out slowly. 'I don't know.'

'Come on, man, I wasn't joking about the magistrates'.'

The accountant sighed. After a few moments, he said: 'I don't know what I'm involved in, but I know it's not good.'

'Tell me. Let's try to piece it all together.'

The man opened his eyes and turned to him, his forehead a frown. 'Listen, Detective, I fell into this by accident. Jobs are few and far between at the moment, so you end up in places that you never imagined you'd see. I always thought I'd be with a top-notch firm, earning six figures, not working for some low-life porn producer. This job was just meant to be a bridge, a temporary solution until I found something better. That something better hasn't come along.' He stopped and flicked some ash into the gutter. 'You need to understand that I never got into all this knowingly. I want you to promise me that I won't be prosecuted for what I'm about to tell you, because it's only recently that I began to realise what I was dealing with, and even now I still don't quite understand it.'

Scamarcio laid a hand on his arm. 'There'll be no consequences for you.'

'You'll guarantee it?'

Scamarcio pulled out his notepad and pen from his jacket pocket, tore off a piece of paper, and started writing. 'What's your name?'

'Alessandro Benedetto.'

'I guarantee that Alessandro Benedetto will not be subject to criminal investigation for the information he provided to the police on the business dealings of Davide Stasio and Micky Proietti,' said Scamarcio, the pen lid moving at the side of his mouth. He dated and signed the piece of paper, then handed it over.

The accountant scanned it suspiciously, then placed it in his top pocket. He blinked a few times then flicked away more ash, imaginary this time. Scamarcio was wondering if the man was ever going to speak until he said: 'A large amount of money comes in from Micky Proietti each month.'

'How large?'

'It can be up to 20k a time.'

'Does it come from him personally?'

'Sometimes, but from his department at the channel as well.'

'Is there a reason why it comes in?'

The accountant bit down on a nail and looked around him yet again. 'That's the strange part. I've been told to mark it up as payment for projects Proietti has commissioned from us. If a particularly large amount comes in, I have to write it in as contingency for specialist-equipment hire or star talent.'

Scamarcio guessed what was coming next.

'The thing is that Micky hasn't commissioned any projects from us. We make porn, Detective, not dramas for prime-time TV.'

'Has anyone given you an explanation for the money?'

'When I questioned it, I was told that Micky was quietly investing in the company, but he preferred to keep things under the radar. It was made clear to me that I shouldn't ask again.'

Scamarcio took a long suck on his cigarette. After some seconds had passed, he asked: 'What happens to the money once it's come in?'

'A few days later it goes out again.'

'Where to?'

'A whole load of places—none of them with any immediate connection to Stasio.'

'Give me some examples.'

'Accounts in the Caymans, accounts in New York, a few construction companies around the country — there was even a hospital building project once.'

'Where?'

'Down south. I don't remember where exactly.'

'Could it have been Calabria?'

'Might have been.'

Scamarcio's gut was getting ready to churn; he felt a buzzing between his shoulder blades. 'How long has this been going on?'

'Ever since I've been here — that's getting on for a year now.'

'Were you brought in to replace someone?'

'Yes, the previous accountant left for another job.'

Or scarpered. 'Have you noticed any pattern to the activity?' Scamarcio asked.

'Not really. I mean, there can be busy periods when a whole load of money comes in for a few weeks, and then it dies down again, but I've never noticed a routine to it, no.'

'So when Micky called the other day, what did he want?'

The accountant chewed his thumbnail some more. 'He told me not to talk to you.'

'Where do you think Micky is getting all this money from?'

He shrugged. 'How can I know, but you asked me about Calabria. I mean Stasio's Calabrian, and he's made a lot of money, and putting two and two together ...'

Scamarcio didn't want to put two and two together. He didn't want to go there. How come this case had been handed to him? Was there a fucking hex on him? Had that frightening old crone who used to hang around the family villa set his life on a path to misery? He stubbed out his cigarette and looked up into the darkening sky.

No, it was his father who'd done that.

18

SCAMARCIO DOWNED HIS NERO D'AVOLA in one, and waited for his other mobile to ring. He knew that Piocosta would be punctual.

This time, there was no 'Good evening'; no 'How are you, son?' The old man was clearly losing patience. 'You've got two days,' he barked. 'I want you in there Wednesday night, lifting those tapes.'

'Why Wednesday? The weekend would be safer.'

'Because we're running out of time. If you were any help at all, you'd have told me that they're planning an arrest on Thursday. I shouldn't be fucking left to dig this shit up for myself. If you weren't Lucio's boy, I'd have shopped your girlfriend to the Cappadona by now.'

'She's not my girlfriend anymore,' said Scamarcio, not really sure why he'd bothered to correct him.

'Whatever, you've got until Wednesday. You get in there, you lift that stuff, then you walk down San Vitale, take a right, and we'll be waiting in a black Mercedes SUV. You just hand those tapes across and dust off your fingers. Case closed, debt repaid.' Piocosta coughed. It sounded like he had bronchitis.

'What time will you be there?'

'You tell me. When do you want to go in?'

'After midnight. That night sergeant will be on — the place will be emptier.'

'How long do you need inside?'

Scamarcio had no idea. It could take five minutes; it could

take 50. He had no experience in these things. 'Why don't you circle the area? I'll tell you when to pull up.'

Piocosta coughed again, and Scamarcio heard phlegm being released. 'Leo, you've lived in this shithole of a city long enough to know that's not going to work. We need to be parked and ready.'

'Be there for 1.15 and make it Via Venezia. There's CCTV on Via Genova. I'll meet you where Venezia joins Palermo.'

'OK,' grunted Piocosta before the line went dead.

Scamarcio pinched his nose and took a breath. Was he really going to go through with this? And once he'd done it, would the Proietti inquiry drag him straight back under again? He needed to find out where Micky Proietti was getting his money. And fast.

He decided to call Carleone in Vice. He'd been helpful on another inquiry, and Scamarcio hoped he might come good this time.

'Ah, Scamarcio,' said Carleone when he picked up. 'You pining for your tranny pals?'

Despite the people his job brought him into contact with, Carleone remained steadfastly bigoted. 'Aren't some of them *your* friends by now?' Scamarcio asked.

'No,' replied Carleone, stiffly.

Why does the squad always push the old guard into the jobs that require a fresh perspective? Scamarcio wondered. But instead he said: 'Listen, I've got a case with a guy who likes to lose his cash at illegal gambling dens. But I've got no idea where these joints are. Do they have any kind of vague location?' Scamarcio felt like a fool asking this, but right now it was his only option.

Carleone snorted, just as Scamarcio knew he would. 'That's like asking which hair on my head should I comb first.'

'Yeah, well, I'd guessed that.' Scamarcio paused. 'There's a Calabrian connection,' he added, not sure if he should be limiting his inquiry this early. But there wasn't time to trawl the whole of Rome.

Scamarcio could hear papers being shuffled, a pen tapping a screen. 'The Calabrians are behind a lot of legal slot-machine places now. Often they'll terrorise bar owners into installing rigged machines that never pay out, then they'll keep watch with CCTV 24 hours a day to make sure they get every cent. We know, and the Calabrians *know* we know, that alongside some of these places, they're also running roulette tables, Blackjack, craps ...'

'Alongside?'

'Sometimes literally alongside — out back or in the block opposite. But they're never in the same place for long. They're "pop up" joints — always moving on to a new spot.'

'Who uses them?'

'People with a serious habit. People who need more than a twice-yearly trip to the legal casinos in Campione d'Italia or Venice.'

'So they let anyone in?'

'No, they vet them. Their clients need to be discreet, and they need to be flush.'

''Ndrangheta money was being laundered through the mainstream casinos, wasn't it? Didn't they find them cleaning funds through Sanremo?'

'Yeah, a couple of years back, and the anti-Mafia guys believe it's still happening at other places, too — probably Venice. They don't have all the evidence yet, though.'

'Could the 'ndrangheta be laundering their money through the dens as well?'

'Most certainly.'

'Why don't we just shut them down then?'

'Because they're always one step ahead. When we get there, there's never any evidence. They've already moved on.'

Scamarcio chewed on a broken nail, and tasted blood. 'So people can find themselves in serious debt to these places?'

'Of course.'

'And what happens then?'

'The usual. The 'ndrangheta set them to work on their behalf, squeeze favours from them, intimidate them until they pay up.'

'And if they can't pay?'

Carleone whistled through his teeth. 'Scamarcio, don't take this amiss, but surely you're the last person who needs to be told what these guys are capable of.'

Scamarcio felt a flame of anger rising in his chest, but he pushed it down, trying to stay lucid. 'Do you have anyone on the inside, Carleone? I need to find out what kind of mess my guy was in. I've heard he was in deep. I need to know where it happened, who he holds the debt with.'

The line went silent for a few seconds. 'Again, don't you have contacts, Scamarcio?'

'What's that supposed to mean?'

'Look, all I'm saying is that I reckon you might be better wired-in than I am. I know about these places, but that's about it. I don't have grasses, as much as I try. All I can suggest is that you look at where they control the slot-machines — maybe someone there could point you in the right direction.'

It was clear to Scamarcio that he wasn't going to get any further with Carleone. 'OK,' he said, his tone deliberately off. He wanted Carleone to know that he was narked.

'They have a couple on Via Magdalena: Bar Vegas and Bar Cosmos, I think they're called. We know they've got their claws in there. That might be a place to start,' Carleone added, more placatory now.

Scamarcio could have solved the issue with a quick call to Piocosta. But that would have resulted in two problems: one, the old man would have wondered why he was interested in the gambling op, and word would soon spread; and two, he would create a new debt, which he would then use to manipulate Scamarcio with.

Instead, Scamarcio rang Francesco Moia, a PI he'd used a few times in the past.

'What's cooking?' said Moia, who seemed to be in the middle of dinner. Scamarcio could hear slurping. He imagined a long, greasy strand of spaghetti being sucked up into Moia's gummy mouth. Moia was a good detective, but he didn't take care of himself — he was an alcoholic, and addicted to sugar. Scamarcio had heard that he was in danger of losing his left leg to diabetes.

'Have I disturbed your dinner?'

'Nah, Scamarcio. No worries.'

'You working on anything right now?'

'Times are lean. The men of Rome are too busy worrying about their finances to cheat on their wives.'

'Sorry to hear that.'

'It's a tragedy. How can I help you, Scamarcio?'

'I need to find out about a debt a guy I'm investigating has with the 'ndrangheta. It was run up at their illegal gambling dens in the city. I need to know how badly burned my guy is, and who he holds the debt with.'

Moia whistled. 'That's a lot of man-hours, Scamarcio. I'm not going to have that kind of thing done and dusted in an afternoon.'

Moia was as slippery as an eel.

'I hear you. Money's no object, but time is. I need this fast — I'll pay you a weeks' wages if you solve it for me in 24. You'll be rewarded for the speed of the result.'

'Why the hurry?'

'There's a kidnapping involved — a woman and her son.'

He heard the clang of fork against dish. 'This that Proietti thing?' asked Moia, more alert now.

'Yep.'

'Jesus — is that preppy Proietti wanker in hock to the Calabrians?'

'Smells like it to me, but I'm not certain.'

'I always thought that nothing could surprise me anymore, but this ain't bad.' Moia fell silent for a beat, then asked: 'You couldn't get on the inside track then?'

Scamarcio felt like screaming. He took a breath. 'No, too risky.'

'Understood,' said Moia, sucking up another strand of spaghetti. 'I'll finish my dinner then I'll be straight out.'

'Vice told me to start at some slot-machine joints on Via Magdalena.'

'Hmm,' mumbled Moia, sounding sceptical. 'I'd rather try the ones on Via Regnoli. Lower profile, less busy, less risky.'

Moia never ceased to amaze him with his inside knowledge. He should have called him first, and not bothered with Vice. 'Whatever you think best. Keep me updated.'

'Regular phone?' asked Moia.

'Regular phone.'

19

SCAMARCIO HAD HEARD NOTHING from Moia overnight, but hadn't really expected to. Moia only ever called if he had news. He never liked to be distracted from the hunt.

When Scamarcio arrived at the squadroom, Garramone was perched on his desk waiting for him, looking down miserably at Via San Vitale.

'Everything OK, Sir?'

'We're not getting anywhere with Stasio.'

'What, nothing?'

'Proietti hasn't paid any more visits. Stasio hasn't said anything of interest.'

Scamarcio knew what was coming.

'You sure about this Stasio angle, you sure they're up to no good? Cos I've got a lot of man-hours on this, and I can't keep it up forever. We need to be seen to be getting results. There's too much pressure from the media.'

'At this stage, it's just a hunch, but I'm confident it's going to turn up something.' Scamarcio had already told him about his talk with the accountant, about his suspicions that Proietti might have got himself into debt. He hadn't, however, mentioned the potential 'ndrangheta connection. He wanted to give that one time to play out. For this reason, he hadn't told Garramone he'd hired Moia. He should have run it past the boss, but it seemed wise to keep things simple for as long as possible. That said, there was always the risk Garramone would pose the 'ndrangheta question himself.

'Scamarcio, you have my backing, but we need Stasio to start talking. I can probably scrape together the funds for another day or two, but after that it will be difficult. We have to find this family, bring them home. Right now, we're looking like a bunch of losers.'

Scamarcio ground his teeth. Moia needed to come up with something soon.

Ever since he'd heard about the suicide of Gianluca Manfredi, Scamarcio had been curious about the wife's opinion. Were they looking at the actions of a love-sick fool or a thwarted careerist? Or was the answer more complex? It stressed Scamarcio that he was obliged to investigate the Manfredi angle with so much else going on, but he reminded himself that Manfredi could yet prove important. There were tangible connections to Proietti that could not be dismissed.

Gianlunca Manfredi's flat was surprisingly modest for a cabinet minister's. He didn't live in the parliament district or a luxury villa along the Via Appia, but in a modern 100-square-foot apartment in Aurelio.

The furniture looked as if it had come from IKEA, and the décor was plain — white paint on the walls, very few paintings, a pale-tiled floor, chipped in a few places. Several photos of a boy and girl in graduation gear took pride of place above the fireplace.

Manfredi's wife was dressed conservatively in black, and looked exhausted. She was petite, with short, blonde hair and a slight stoop. She motioned Scamarcio tiredly to a sofa across from the fire. He was surprised to notice that the flame in the pellet stove was alight. It was at least 20 degrees outside.

'I'm very sorry to disturb you in your time of mourning, Mrs Manfedi.'

She waved the apology away. 'It's OK. It's good to have a distraction.'

'I'm investigating the disappearance of Micky Proietti's wife and son.'

She scratched at her forehead. 'I don't understand how that relates to Gianluca.'

'Mrs Manfredi, I'm afraid I have some uncomfortable news.'

She screwed up her face, and sat up straighter on the sofa, folding her hands in her lap. 'What can be more uncomfortable than hearing that your husband of forty years is dead?'

'I take your point. The reason for my visit is that your husband *was* connected to Micky Proietti.'

How to frame this? He stopped, tried to think it through. 'They were both having an affair with the same woman.'

'Fiammetta di Bondi?'

Scamarcio rubbed at the stubble on his chin. 'You knew?'

Mrs Manfredi sighed, and patted the corner of her eyes with a cotton handkerchief. 'I've known for some time. A friend told me she'd heard there was something going on between them.'

'You didn't confront your husband about it?'

She shrugged. 'What was the point? Men will be men. Gianluca was a marvellous father to our children, maybe not such a marvellous husband. So he was having a bit on the side? She shrugged again. 'He had his needs, and I, well … I wasn't really into all that, so I can't really blame him for straying.'

This was the first time Scamarcio had heard a cheated wife speak like this. That it came from someone who looked so twinset-and-pearls conventional as Mrs Manfredi was more surprising still.

'So you weren't angry?'

'A little bit, I guess, but anger is a destructive emotion. I decided to push all that to one side.'

Scamarcio wished he could manage that.

'But I *was* surprised,' added Mrs Manfredi.

'Why?'

'Well, Gianluca was hardly a looker.'

'He was powerful.'

'No, he wasn't. Max Romano had castrated him. He couldn't stand him.'

'Rich then?' Scamarcio tried.

'Do we look rich to you?'

Scamarcio cast his eyes around the room. He didn't want to offend. 'Well, I must confess I'd expected something in a different part ...'

She interrupted him. 'Neither Gianluca nor myself come from money. Gianluca worked his way up through politics the hard way. When he started to earn, most of what he made went on funding our children's' education in the US.'

Scamarcio studied the photos above the fire. 'Were these pictures taken recently?'

She smiled, and the sadness left her eyes for a moment. 'Last year. They're twins. They both graduated from Harvard Law School last summer.'

'You must be very proud.'

She nodded tightly; she seemed scared that she might cry again. 'I am, we were. Before Harvard they attended American high school for three years. We wanted to make sure their English was tip-top, that they stood a fighting chance. All that cost a lot of money. But it was worth every cent.'

'Wouldn't you have preferred to keep them close by?'

'Of course, but what future does this country have? Gianluca was convinced that if they stayed here, they'd stagnate like all the other young people who have no chance of finding work. He knew it would be very hard for us, but we had to do it. The fact that they're the same age was a big help. If we'd had to send one of them alone, that would have been much tougher, it would have been so much more of a worry.'

Scamarcio nodded. 'It's refreshing to meet people who don't adhere to the materialism that the rest of Rome's VIPs seem to.'

'Maybe it's because we've never known what it's like to have money. Perhaps it's easier to do without all those things if you've never had them in the first place.'

There was something solid about this woman that appeared to be lacking in the other people he had encountered on this case, thought Scamarcio. 'So, going back to Fiammetta di Bondi's reasons for being with your husband …'

Mrs Manfredi arched an eyebrow and shook her head. 'I've been mulling it over, and I still can't work it out. Maybe she was misled. Maybe she *thought* he was rich; maybe she thought he could take her places. But the affair went on quite a while, and I can't help wondering why she hung around. Surely, after a time, she'd realise she wasn't going to get anything from him.'

Knowing what he did of di Bondi, it didn't make sense to Scamarcio now, either.

'Your husband told me they were going to move in together.'

She grimaced. 'You think she wanted that?'

'Well, I asked her, and she said no, that she had no intention of moving in with him.'

Mrs Manfred opened her palms as if to say, 'I told you so.'

Scamarcio took a breath and said: 'Mrs Manfredi, I'm sorry to ask such a difficult question, but why do you think your husband killed himself?'

She bit down on her bottom lip and pushed her fringe from her eyes, then said: 'He didn't.'

'I'm sorry …'

'I don't believe for one second that Gianluca killed himself.'

'Why?' Scamarcio leant in closer.

'Because Gianluca was many things, but he certainly wasn't selfish. He would never have done that to me or the children — he would never have left us in the lurch. He was a provider. He modelled himself on his father, who always made sure his family had food on the table, even when he went to bed hungry.'

Scamarcio wondered at how different this picture of Gianluca Manfredi was from the one he had formed in Max Romano's office.

'But if Fiammetta di Bondi had led him to believe they had a life together, but had then let him down ...'

She frowned. 'Oh, please. Gianluca was a 62-year-old man. He wasn't naïve, and he wasn't about to leave his family. He'd just booked us both a holiday to the Bahamas for Christmas. It would have been the first holiday we'd taken for ten years. Why would he do that if he was planning to leave?'

Indeed, why would he? wondered Scamarcio. 'Did you contact the police about your suspicions?'

'It's taken some time for my thoughts to coalesce. It was all too much of a shock for me to think straight. I wanted to give myself some time for the dust to settle, then I was going to go down to the local station myself. You've saved me the trouble.'

Mrs Manfredi had claimed that her husband had never suffered from depression, and that the fact the bathroom window was open when she found him was odd, as they'd been unable to unscrew the lock for the last few weeks and were about to get someone in to fix it. The Manfredis lived on the second floor, so a drop to the ground by an intruder was not out of the question, Scamarcio reasoned.

When he'd spoken to Garramone, he'd said that a separate inquiry would need to be opened into the death of Gianluca Manfredi, but with a constant eye on the connections to Proietti. Scamarcio would be expected to be across both investigations.

As Scamarcio walked to his desk, one image refused to leave him: the gold cufflinks that Manfredi was wearing the day they'd met. Those expensive cufflinks didn't square with the picture Mrs Manfredi had painted of a parsimonious family man, intent on saving every cent for his children's education. He needed to ask

Mrs Manfredi about those cufflinks. He needed to make sense of them.

Out of respect, he'd switched his mobile to silent when he'd been with Mrs Manfredi, and when he pulled it out to reset it, he noticed several missed calls from Moia that had come in over the last few minutes. He rang him back immediately, hoping to God he'd got somewhere.

'Scamarcio, listen up,' said the PI, wheezing down the line.

'You OK? You sound terrible.'

'Just been in a place with dogs. They really set me off.'

'What place with dogs?'

'Believe me, you don't want to know.'

Scamarcio rolled his eyes and started tapping his desk with a biro. 'OK, Moia, spit it out then.'

'So I went down to the slot-machine joints on Via Nago. Hung around for quite a while, lost a fair bit, then got chatting to a helpful lad who told me if I wanted some real fun, they were running a card game above a bakery on Via Don Carlo tonight. When I get there, it's all low stakes, and pretty unexciting. My instincts are telling me it's a dead end; that I need to try elsewhere. So I sit it out, but when the game is finished, I pull a guy aside and say I want to carry on; that I want a bit more chilli in my sauce. Glances are exchanged, then the guy tells me to head for Via Aprica and ask for Gino above the dry cleaners. When I get there, it's all smoke and shadows, just like something out of the movies. I half-expected to see Al Pacino in the corner, sucking on a Havana. There were about ten men at the table, playing for scarily high stakes, and I know I'm in the right place now.' Moia paused to wheeze again. 'By the way, Scamarcio, you're going to have to cover my losses.'

Scamarcio grunted in the affirmative.

'I picked up a few Calabrian accents, but it was impossible to really see the faces, it was too dark. But then I struck lucky, cos there's a TV on in the corner, and it's showing Sky TG24, and I notice that twat Proietti's mugshot — they're running his story yet again. So I think this is a gift from God, and I say: "Poor bastard — must be a nightmare living through that." A few guys turn and look at the TV, and then a voice at the end of the table says, "That cunt got what he deserved" and then the room falls silent. Nobody says a word about it again. We all get on with the game, and I go on to lose one thousand.'

'One thousand?' Scamarcio almost screamed. A few colleagues turned to look at him.

'Scamarcio, it's high stakes. They wouldn't have let me in there if I didn't have cash to burn.'

'Christ, Moia.'

'You wanted a quick result, didn't you?'

'Am I getting one?'

'Be patient, man. So around 7.00 am the game finally winds up, and we all shuffle out onto the street. I've already turned into a side road when I feel a hand on my shoulder. First thought is that they've made me and I'm about to be neutralised right there. Then this voice I recognise from the card table says: "Why did you mention Proietti? You looking for info? You a PI?" I try to deny it all, then I see that the guy is quite young, and doesn't look or sound like a Calabrian heavy. So I say: "What makes you think that?" He says: "You wouldn't have mentioned him otherwise." We stand there for a few seconds, not quite sure what to make of each other, then I ask: "What's it to you?" He says: "I'm trading info for cash." I ask him if he's in deep with the Calabrians, but he doesn't take the bait. "Info for cash," he just keeps saying, like he's simple or something. By this point I've only got 300 left on me, but that seems OK for him, cos he grabs it straight away. Once he's pocketed the dough, he pulls out a mobile phone. He fiddles about with it for a while, then shows me a video. It's of a man in a carpark. He's surrounded by four goons, looks like they're threatening him. At one point, one of them pushes him and he falls onto the ground, and they start kicking him shitless. It looks like it's going to get rough, then they just stop for some reason, shout at him, and leave — I couldn't make out what was being said.'

'This man they're threatening?'

'It's Proietti, no doubt about it.'

'And the other men?'

'The audio is shit, so I don't know about accents, but they look like heavies — southern heavies.'

'I need to see the video, and I need to meet the guy who made it.'

'Thought you'd say that. He wants another 500 for the trouble.'

'Where is he now?'

'Sleeping on my couch. I had to promise him another 200 to stay put till I reached you.'

'OK, Moia. Good work. Where do you want to meet?'

'How about the patisserie on my road, Via Mattonato? They do good fresh cream brioche, get the filling just right — my guy doesn't want to come anywhere near your place.'

'I can understand that.'

'See you there in twenty?'

'See you then.'

Moia already had a cream brioche in his hand when Scamarcio walked in. He noticed another lined up and ready to go on Moia's plate. Sitting across from him was a young guy in a grey hooded sports top. He had shoulder-length, curly dark hair, grey-green eyes, and the palest skin Scamarcio had ever seen. It was almost translucent; he could make out a bluey skein of veins beneath. How could anyone live in Rome and be this pale? If they were casting for a new *Twilight* film, this chap would be a shoo-in for the lead.

'Scamarcio, take a seat,' said Moia, through a mouthful of

pastry. 'Meet Claudio,' he said, keeping his piggy eyes on the second brioche as if he was worried Scamarcio was about to swipe it.

Claudio just managed the faintest of nods. The boy looked exhausted. *Well, they've been up all night*, Scamarcio figured.

Moia quickly finished the first brioche and wiped his fingers with a paper tissue. 'Claudio, tell Scamarcio what you know. He'll be wanting to hear it straight from the horse's mouth.'

The boy tried to stifle a yawn, but failed. He took a sip from a glass of water, but made no sign of being about to speak.

'You took that video?' Scamarcio asked, rapidly losing patience.

The boy nodded.

'When?'

Several moments of silence followed, and Scamarcio wondered if he'd ever hear the boy's voice.

'Three months ago now.' The words barely rose above a whisper.

'Where?'

'Out near Tor di Valle.'

The old racetrack, and soon to be the new Roma training ground. Scamarcio wondered quickly about a connection to the soccer star Aconi, then dismissed it. 'Why did you film it?'

The boy closed his eyes and scratched at an eyelid. 'I owed them money — I was looking for leverage.'

'Who did you owe?'

'It's complicated, but if you're looking for a simple answer: the Calabrians.'

'The 'ndrangheta, the people who run the card games?'

The boy nodded, emotionless.

'Why did you think this would give you leverage?'

'The guy they were threatening has a reputation, prestige. I was hoping to use the video to convince him to help me clear my debts.'

'That's bold.'

'I didn't have many options.'

'Can I see the film now?'

The boy pulled a white Samsung from his pocket and clicked the pad a few times before handing the phone across.

Scamarcio pressed play. A man of average height was pushed up against the fender of a car and was surrounded by a ring of four heavily set thugs. They were all lit by the sodium of the street lamps. When the camera zoomed in, Scamarcio realised that Moia had been right: the cornered man was indeed Micky Proietti. The audio was impossible to decipher, but Scamarcio wondered if someone at the lab could fix that. The camera panned to the right to get a better look at the goons pressuring Proietti, and, as it did so, one of them knocked him to the ground. He fell onto his back and immediately swung his right arm across his face in an attempt to shield himself from blows. Scamarcio watched as the four gorillas started to kick Proietti while he was prone. Proietti jerked and squirmed into a foetal position, but the beating just went on and on. Scamarcio realised with disgust that he was actually enjoying watching this, and it wasn't because he disliked Proietti. He pressed pause.

'I still don't understand why you happened to be in the carpark,' he said, resuming his scrutiny of the deathly pale boy.

'I'd followed them from the card game,' said Claudio.

'How come you were at the game, if you were in debt to them? Why did they let you keep on playing?'

'It was a case of robbing Peter to pay Paul. I'd settled with the Calabrians cos you always settle with them first, but by that point I was in debt to someone else.'

'Who?'

The boy sighed, and it turned into a yawn. 'I'd prefer not to elaborate.'

There was something about this boy that made Scamarcio wonder. 'You a good boy turned bad?' he asked.

Claudio scratched at his nose. 'My parents are wealthy. I was given everything, but I still managed to fuck it all up.'

'You've got a serious habit then?'

'Yep,' said Claudio all matter-of-fact. 'I need help.'

'That explain why you were back playing when you were still in debt?'

'Yep, you know how the gambler's mind works …'

He sounded like he'd just fled therapy, thought Scamarcio. 'Your parents talking to you at the moment?'

'No.'

Scamarcio shook his head. He'd heard it all before. He pressed play on the phone once more, and watched as the kicking continued. One of the thugs seemed to be weighing in with considerably more gusto than the rest. As he turned his smiling mug towards the camera, Scamarcio felt the air leave his lungs.

'You seen a ghost, Scamarcio? You don't look too good,' said Moia. 'I was going to offer you this brioche, but as you're a bit peaky, I'll eat it myself.'

Scamarcio wasn't listening. He recognised the grinning man. He worked for Piocosta.

20

SCAMARCIO HAD WANTED TO HEAD home early and digest what he'd just seen on the video, but a call from Manetti, the chief CSI, had forced him to scrap that idea.

'I was just passing the squadroom, so I decided to deliver my news in person for a change.'

Scamarcio felt an irrational urge to punch him. Why couldn't Manetti just have emailed it through, as he always did?

Manetti reached into his briefcase and pulled out a shiny A4 sheet of photographic paper. When he handed it across, Scamarcio saw the dusty outline of the imprint of a shoe.

'What's this?'

'We found it on the ledge outside Gianluca Manfredi's bathroom window.'

The desire to punch him quickly faded. 'Nice work,' said Scamarcio.

'It's from a size-43 Adidas trainer.'

'Lucky that it's still there after so many days.'

'There hasn't been any rain for nearly two weeks now.'

Manetti reached into the briefcase once more, and handed over another couple of photos. They were a wide shot and a close-up of Manfredi's corpse on the autopsy table.

'Mrs Manfredi had delayed the funeral, so the body was still at the funeral home. It had been nicely embalmed, but that didn't present Dr Giangrande with too many problems. You'll see from the photo that Manfredi has an inverted-V bruise around his neck where the noose made contact with the skin.'

'Isn't that what we're supposed to see? Isn't an inverted V the sign that he did in fact hang himself?'

'Yes. We're not seeing the straight-line bruising we'd normally have in a murder. Giangrande also found the customary small bleeding sites on the lips, inside the mouth and on the eyelids.'

'Manetti, I don't get it. You seem to be telling me that Manfredi did hang himself.'

Manetti nodded. 'Manfredi hung, all right, but the question is, did he hang *himself*?' He smiled, clearly enjoying the game. 'It is my belief that he was pushed off a chair and made to hang.'

'Yeah, Manetti, but you know as well as I do that pinning down that shit in court is like trying to prove the existence of God.'

'Wrong, Scamarcio. In this case, I've got evidence. I found the same shoeprint on a chair in the Manfredi's kitchen, and I've got DNA in the bathroom and on the chair that does not belong to Mrs Manfredi, her husband, her twins, or the cleaner who comes once a week. Apart from those people, Mrs Manfredi tells me that nobody else has visited the flat in a long time. Luckily for us, the Manfredis don't like to entertain.'

'Is this substantial DNA?'

'Hair and skin.'

'Any hits?'

'This is where it gets weird. We got a partial match to a Calabrian low-life who died five years ago.'

'Name?'

'Raimondo Stasio.'

Armed with the breakthrough from Manetti, Scamarcio knocked on Garramone's door.

When he had finished talking the boss through Manetti's findings, Garramone smiled and said: 'This might help my case with the penny pinchers.'

'So we can maintain the surveillance on Stasio a while longer?'

'Yes, but if the man's committed murder, I'm not going to let this one play out. We need to bring him in soon.'

Scamarcio nodded, expecting as much.

'So how do we think this feeds into the Proietti kidnapping?' asked Garramone.

Scamarcio rubbed his nose. It was time to come clean on the 'ndrangheta angle: 'I'm still not sure, but I do have firm evidence that Proietti had run up a significant gambling debt with the Calabrians. What side of the fence Stasio sits on is as yet unclear.'

'So the Calabrians may have taken the Proietti family as a warning?'

'I think so, yes.'

'And the money coming in and out of Stasio's business?'

'My guess is that he was cleaning up 'ndrangheta cash. But whether this arrangement was in place before or after Proietti ran up his debts, I don't yet know for sure.'

Garramone became pensive, and a silence descended between them. 'All this must be pretty uncomfortable for you,' he said.

'How do you mean?' Scamario fired back, too defensively by far.

'Well, I think I'm right in saying that you've never had a case before that touches so directly on your father's old stamping ground.'

Scamarcio shrugged. 'Maybe not, but perhaps this is my chance to finally prove to everyone that I'm clean.' God, why had he said that? Was he out of his fucking mind?

Garramone shook his head and said: 'You don't need to prove that to me.'

Scamarcio suddenly wanted to tell Garramone everything: about the mess he was in with Piocosta; about how he couldn't find a way out; about how every which way he turned he ran up against a wall. He wanted to unload it all, have the boss take care of everything. But instead all he said was: 'Thank you, Sir.'

21

Scamarcio poured himself a large glass of Glenfiddich and finally sat down to think. So, one of Piocosta's boys had been involved in roughing up Micky Proietti. This was significant because it told Scamarcio that Piocosta was across the 'ndrangheta's gambling ops in the capital, on top of his other interests such as loan sharking and extortion. Up until now, Scamarcio had never really thought too hard about Piocosta's current role in the organisation. He had always viewed him through the framework of the past: when Scamarcio's father was *capo,* Piocosta had been his general, his *capo crimine,* and had been responsible for running the locale's criminal activities. In some ways he was like a minister of war or a minister of defence. When Piocosta had showed up in Rome, it meant that he had moved higher up the ranks, but Scamarcio had still tended to see him as a San Alberto native made good, dispatched to oversee aspects of the clan's business interests in the capital. But Piocosta was across far too many things lately. He seemed to be travelling a lot between Rome and Calabria's regional capital, Catanzaro. He'd also mentioned recently that he had been 'abroad', and that he had had to take an early-morning flight to get back to Rome. There were a few places he might have been, but Scamarcio's guess would be Germany. He knew that the locale Piocosta and his father had run had sown its influence through a series of small towns in Baden Würtemburg, thanks to other family members who had emigrated there and set up front businesses, such as pizzerias and bars, ideal for disguising the far more lucrative trade of drug dealing and money laundering.

All this travel of Piocosta's was making Scamarcio wonder quite how influential he had become. Rather than being responsible for one aspect of the clan's dealings in the capital, was Piocosta in fact responsible for all of it? Had he scrambled his way to the very top? When Scamarcio's father had been gunned down on the steps of his villa twenty years ago, a new *capo bastone* had stepped in, and Piocosta had been pushed aside because he did not enjoy the same close relationship with the new boss. As a result, Scamarcio had presumed that Piocosta had remained somewhat in the shadows until he had resurfaced almost twenty years later and worked hard to convince Scamarcio to return to his roots. Until now, Scamarcio had been too absorbed considering his own position. But now, understanding exactly how Piocosta fitted in to the 'ndrangheta matrix seemed of urgent importance. If Piocosta had risen up through the ranks and was now running the show in Rome, Scamarcio was in fatal trouble. If Piocosta presided over the usual web of contacts of a big-time boss, that could quickly prove catastrophic. Scamarcio thought about Piocosta's constant commute between Rome and Catanzaro; about the huge river of public money that flowed that course; about the powerful politicians the 'ndrangheta held in their pockets. Scamarcio knew now that he had been blind and perhaps suicidally stupid. If he was as powerful as Scamarcio now suspected, Piocosta could end his police career with a snap of the fingers.

Scamarcio took a Marlboro from a fresh packet on the table, and lit up. He needed to find out exactly what Piocosta had become. But this wasn't the kind of information he could get on the street; neither was it the sort of question he wanted to raise with the Anti-Mafia squad. With his history, it was wise to stay below the radar. A realisation was starting to dawn, but it was troubling and deeply unwelcome: if he analysed his situation coldly, stripping away all emotion, it seemed as if there was only one real option left: he would need to travel south, back to the heart of the beast. He would need to visit people he hadn't spoken to for years, people he'd hoped never to see again.

Scamarcio was the black sheep, the one who had been bold enough or crazy enough to reject his inherited position. Unlike his cousins who, suited and booted, had taken the business across borders, witnessing the murder of his father had made him want to take a different path, and, while she was alive, his mother had done all she could to make sure he kept to it. Scamarcio thought of her and the debt he owed her. He needed to finally shake himself free of Piocosta; he needed to start building the kind of life his mother had tried so hard to give him.

He was about to turn in for the night when Garramone called. 'We've got something from Stasio,' was his opener.

'What kind of something?'

'Want to come and listen?'

When Scamarcio arrived at the squadroom, Garramone was the only one there.

'Things kicking off?' Scamarcio asked.

'I've got every man out,' said the boss, taking a large slug of coffee. 'And I don't have enough to cover all that's coming in. The budget tightening is going to turn parts of Rome into no-go areas.'

Certain suburbs are already there, thought Scamarcio. 'I thought you were off that stuff,' he said, motioning to the cup in Garramone's hand.

'I told the wife to forget it.'

Scamarcio had a feeling she probably didn't know. 'So, Stasio?'

Garramone leaned over his computer monitor and fiddled with the mouse. 'This audio has just arrived,' he said. 'I think you'll agree that it's a nice piece of work.'

Garramone clicked the mouse a few times, and a strong Calabrian accent came through. The recording was crystal-clear.

'I'm doing all I can to contain this mess,' the Calabrian was

148

saying. 'But you need to accept that you've fucked up.'

'What do you expect? They've got my wife and son — your sister and nephew, in case you've forgotten.' It was Proietti. His voice was hoarse, as if he had been shouting moments before.

'But why didn't you come to me? That would have been the logical thing to do.'

'Christ, Davide, we've been through this a million times. They'd bloody run us off the road, and my boy had broken his arm. Then when I get to the hospital, they weren't there. What the hell would you have done in my position?'

'I'd have stopped and thought, Micky. Where I come from, you think first and act later. And you *don't* get the pigs involved.'

Proietti said nothing.

'You've turned a small problem into one huge fucking problem.'

Scamarcio heard Stasio suck in air, then exhale loudly. Smoking, probably.

'A small problem?' You call the kidnapping of my family a small problem?'

Stasio was breathing more heavily now, and seemed to step closer to the mike. 'Micky, I've got a good mind to resolve this once and for all.'

'What the hell is that supposed to mean?' Then, after a beat: 'You don't scare me, Davide; you never have.' Proietti sounded as if he'd been drinking again. 'That approach might work for you down south, but you can lose it up here. This is where civilisation begins, in case you hadn't realised, you illiterate cunt.'

Scamarcio grimaced and exchanged glances with Garramone. Did Proietti have a deathwish? He continued with the kamikaze insults: 'You're nothing but a hulking ape. Your fists almost scrape the pavement. How you and Maia can be related, I have no idea. I wish I'd never met you. You've brought me nothing but misery, you filthy peasant.'

Scamarcio felt a wave of heat push up along his thorax. He didn't like Proietti, but he didn't want to hear him die. But Garramone would have told him if that had happened, surely …

Stasio had fallen silent. When he did finally respond, he sounded disquietingly calm. 'You know what, Micky, I'm sick of running behind you all the time, cleaning up your shit. I wash my hands of you. Maia was a fool. She should have stayed with her real family, where there were people who would have taken proper care of her. As for the Manfredi fuck-up, you're on your own.'

It was Proietti's turn to fall silent. 'What Manfredi fuck-up?' he asked eventually, his voice suddenly small and quiet. For the first time, Scamarcio heard real fear.

'You'd screwed up, as usual.'

'He owed me money!'

'You should have just let it go.'

'How could I?'

'But couldn't you have thought it through? If you back a bastard like that into the corner, he's going to use whatever he has on you. You needed to think first, *think*.' Stasio fell silent, and Scamarcio imagined him drumming his temple.

'But Manfredi killed himself …' Proietti's voice sounded even more fragile now. It was a child's voice — a child who had never properly become a man, thought Scamarcio.

'Manfredi killed himself …' Stasio mimicked, exaggeratedly high. 'Your parents might have made sure you never had to grow a backbone, but you sure as hell need one now. You're about to be eaten alive, Micky.'

'I never asked you to do anything about Manfredi,' Proietti said slowly. He was working it out now, seeing it in all its horror.

'You'd been whingeing about him for weeks.'

'What are you saying?'

'I'm not saying anything. But from where I come from, it

doesn't always work to just stroll over there for a friendly chat; to ask someone to be a gentleman and just forget an entire conversation. Especially when you have no money to offer them because your fuck-up of a brother-in-law has made it all disappear.'

Was Stasio admitting to killing Manfredi? And what was that about the money? Scamarcio wondered. Was he saying that Proietti had gambled it all away, or was Stasio referring to something else? Scamarcio glanced at Garramone, but the boss was staring at the wall, apparently deep in thought.

For a few moments, all Scamarcio could hear on the recording was faint static, then Stasio finally spoke. 'Micky,' he said, his tone more conciliatory now. 'Take a breath, keep your head; stay clear of the police.'

'How can I stay clear of them? They're in my apartment 24 hours a day.'

'Just don't tell them anything, Micky,' Stasio sighed. 'I have this under control. We'll get Maia and Antonio back. I've got people on the ground who'll make sure of it.'

'Yeah, but what can we give them in return?'

'I've got a plan, Micky,' said Stasio. 'But because I can't trust you not to open your mouth, I won't be sharing it.'

'Davide, for God's sake!'

'Shut the fuck up, Micky,' screamed Stasio, his rage spilling out of the computer and filling the room.

Garramone leaned forward and clicked the mouse.

'Is Proietti still alive?' Scamarcio asked. 'Stasio sounds like he's about to kill him.'

'Don't all Calabrians sound like that?'

When Scamarcio failed to reply, Garramone confirmed: 'Yes, he's back in the flat.'

'So, what now? It looks like Stasio killed the culture secretary.'

'Yes, but that audio could be interpreted either way. We could haul him in on suspicion, but that's a long shot. The alternative is to let it evolve a while longer.'

'But we've got the DNA partial.'

'The prosecutor thinks we could do with a bit more.'

'Jesus, what do they want—a signed confession?'

'You know what they're like. So do we let it play out?'

Scamarcio sighed. 'I guess. We've got nothing from CCTV that helps us locate that family. I suppose that if we bring Stasio in, we're going to shut our only window into Proietti's life, because Proietti sure as hell ain't talking. We need to know what Stasio knows, and the only way to do that is to keep him on the outside.'

'I thought you'd say that.'

'I know men like Stasio, and, fine, you can arrest him, bring him in for interrogation, train the guns on him, but he won't talk. These guys never do—they've taken the poison oath. The culture of silence infuses them, makes them who they are. If one of their relatives is murdered and the police come to investigate, they'll slam the door in their faces. That's what's going on here—*omertà*.'

'Yes, but we *are* in Rome.'

'But Stasio doesn't think he's fighting a Rome war. For him, this is a Calabrian matter: the taking of Proietti's family was the settling of a score or a warning of some kind. Stasio's Calabrian connection makes me think he's got Micky into something. Perhaps it was a business opportunity that Micky fucked up. Did Micky gamble away 'ndrangheta funds? That would be my guess. Stasio had got his old friends to pump some money Micky's way, but Micky lost control of it. I heard he liked to bolster his production budgets with cash from elsewhere. I reckon Micky was dipping his finger in the pie too many times, and it got way out of hand. Now he and Stasio are in deep shit.'

'Hmmm,' said Garramone. 'So Stasio's trying to sort it on his own terms—but obviously we can't let him do that. There's a child's life at stake.'

'We have to allow it to play out, but we can't let it go too far.'

'It will be a tricky one to call.'

Scamarcio smiled tiredly. 'Isn't it always?'

On his way home, Scamarcio's thoughts turned to Fiammetta di Bondi. What had she seen in Manfredi? Why had she stuck it out? He found Manfredi's wife's confusion on this point interesting. Her doubts were significant, and he shouldn't lose sight of them. He reminded himself not to leave it too long before revisiting di Bondi.

As he turned his key in the lock, he asked himself, yet again, if he was really going to go ahead with lifting those tapes for Piocosta. If he was going to survive in the force, the answer had to be no—he would never get away with it. What was he going to do? Rip out all the CCTV in the corridors, wear a disguise; hold up the night guard at gunpoint? And even if, by some miracle, he got his hands on the footage, it would only be a matter of time before suspicion fell upon him—his card was still too marked. He had no choice: he had to get down to Calabria; he had to get a handle on Piocosta; he had to find some leverage. He dialled Garramone's number, his hand trembling.

'I'm sorry to bother you again so late, Sir,' he said.

'No worries. What's up?'

'I need to go to Calabria.' He knew he was rushing the words, but he pushed on anyway. 'I've been thinking it through, and it's the only real way to learn more about Stasio, who he's connected to, what he and Proietti might be involved in. I'm not going to find the answers up here in Rome.'

The chief said nothing, and Scamarcio's heart began to race. Had he pushed it too far this time?

'How exactly are you proposing to come by that kind of information?' asked Garramone eventually. But he sounded more exhausted than suspicious.

'Legwork—I've still got contacts.'

The chief fell silent again for a moment. 'After the mess of last year, I thought we all decided that the best thing for you was to stay well clear.'

'What would you have me do?' he asked, probably sounding too impatient. 'We need to resolve this fast. We can hang on for Stasio to say more, but you know as well as I do that we may well have had the best of it.'

'But it's the same old risk, isn't it — that you overstretch yourself with the wrong people? I don't want you beholden. And if for any reason word of your little trip gets back to Chief Mancino, we're fucked — same goes for Stasio. Wouldn't it be safer to contact the Anti-Mafia guys down in Reggio or Catanzaro? To go the usual route?'

'The usual route will lead to a dead end. Those guys aren't on the inside. I'll find the people with the *real* information. And it'll mean I can be back in Rome within 48 hours.'

Garramone said nothing for a long time. Scamarcio heard the second hand on his watch completing its circuit, heard his heartbeat in his ears. Eventually, Garramone sighed and said: 'OK, I hear you. But be discreet — we can't afford any more trouble. You fuck this up, and Mancino will fire you.'

'Goes without saying,' Scamarcio heard himself murmur.

'I didn't want to tell you, but he's still watching.'

'I won't put a foot wrong, trust me.'

22

SCAMARCIO HAD DECIDED NOT TO fly into Catanzaro. He didn't want
to be spotted by any of Piocosta's people. His face was known
down there ever since the national papers had run pieces on how
he was Italy's big bright hope. Far from being a beacon of honesty
and progress, the way Scamarcio's cousins and uncles saw it, he
was the worst traitor to have ever been born into their *locale*. That
one of their number might actually *join* the police, rise through
the ranks, and make it to detective in the Flying Squad was so
far beyond their field of reference that Scamarcio might as well
have revealed himself as a Martian, put on earth to monitor the
behaviour of humankind. How these cousins and uncles might
react to him now, twenty years after he'd left, was difficult to
predict. In certain villages, he perhaps risked being shot at first
sight. That was why he'd made a decision to avoid direct family,
and approach only a few of his father's old associates, all of whom
were probably very old and very infirm by now. He needed to
leave the rank and file right out of it.

The ageing Alitalia MD80 descended rapidly above the Strait
of Messina. Sicily's Mount Etna rose up on the right as the plane
banked left towards the Aspromonte Mountains and then sharply
left again towards the southern suburbs of Reggio Calabria.
Scamarcio's unease grew. Sure, he could do his best to avoid the
Scamarcio clan; but, by coming back here after so long, he was
still walking straight into the lion's den.

He picked up his hire car from the airport and swung right at
the exit and then right again onto the Via Ravagnese that fed onto

the southernmost point of the country's motorway network. He fiddled with the radio, trying to find a station that wasn't playing 1980s trash. He finally gave up when he spotted the exit leading to Croce Valanidi. A darkness settled on him, wrapping him in a tight cloak, but he knew he had to turn off, that he had to make this pilgrimage; Valanidi had determined so much of what happened in his life.

He spun the car up the shabby three-mile stretch from the motorway, reliving the war that once raged here. This godforsaken track had been the scene of one of Calabria's most bloody 'Ndrangheta conflicts in which countless young men, little older than Scamarcio at the time, had lost their lives. It was a war that had exercised both his father and Piocosta for years, a war that had seen them huddled with their footsoldiers into the early hours while they studied maps and checked their bombs, bazookas, and Kalashnikovs for the hundredth time. Scamarcio had only been a teenager, but when his father had started driving around in an armour-plated car, even he knew that it was the beginning of the end.

Scamarcio pulled up alongside the Valanidi River. It was as if some other force was guiding him, willing him to be here. He turned off the engine, lowered the window, and just sat. There was a strange air to this place — too much suffering, too many trapped souls. He looked out at the waste-strewn channel running along the river valley. Beyond the worn tyres, broken refrigerators, stained mattresses, and mounds of brick and plaster he could just make out orderly groves of dark-green bergamot trees, the sun forming luminous pools beneath their branches. He closed his eyes and tried to clear his mind. He needed to get beyond the squalid; he needed to reach those trees whose powerful fragrance masked even the vilest smells. He opened his eyes and fired up the engine. He'd seen enough; he'd leave Valanidi to its ghosts.

As Scamarcio passed the outskirts of Reggio Calabria, he was struck anew by the ugliness of the place. Reggio had been destroyed by earthquakes twice, and then pounded by World War II bombers, so that almost nothing remained of the city Lear had once described as one of the most beautiful places on earth. The poet had found gardens of orange, lemons, and bergamot, but now all Scamarcio could see was concrete, barbed wire, and garbage dumps. There was no trace of green, no hint of nature here.

He pushed on north, glad to leave the city behind. The motorway was climbing steeply now, its carriageways soaring on towering viaducts suspended above deep ravines. He recognised the small town of Scilla where, according to Homer's Odyssey, a six-headed monster had snatched oarsmen from Odysseus's boat. Close by on the Sicillian side of the strait, a whirlpool called Charybdis had threatened to suck Odysseus and his band into oblivion.

Scamarcio reflected on his years growing up in this land. Murder had been a daily event. Probably everyone living here had seen at least one dead body in the street during the wars of the 1980s. By the time he turned sixteen, Scamarcio had seen half a dozen, although his father always preferred to keep the killing as far away from the family villa as possible. Scamarcio had always thought it ironic that Lucio Scamarcio had been killed outside his pristine home, the marble steps that had cost a fortune soiled by his own blood.

After a few minutes, Scamarcio took the turn off for San Alberto. Soon he was on a narrow road winding its way through the dense groves of the Sinopolesi — their thick, wizened branches creating dark, sinister hiding places, ideal for discarding a corpse or staging an ambush. Just the sight of these shadowy groves after so many years made Scamarcio sweat.

He had no idea whether Annunzio Morabito, his father's former chief financial officer, was still alive. But if he was,

Scamarcio felt sure that San Alberto was where he'd find him. The old guard always came home to die, and Scamarcio reckoned that Annunzio could not be far off — he would be nearing ninety now.

Scamarcio swung the hirecar onto a paved street leading up to a small park where the town looked out over the valley. He took a left and drove across the main square, the white expanse of the church giving back the light of the sun. He took in the view for a moment, then cut across the piazza and turned into an alleyway running down the hill. He didn't want to leave his car in the piazza. Some might call him paranoid, but he knew a sniper would have a clearer aim from there. Would any of them recognise him after twenty years, he wondered. No doubt, like Piocosta, they'd been following his progress in the capital.

He locked the car and walked back up the alley, and then along the edge of the square, heading for the tobacconist to the left of the church. He passed Mario's bar, and wondered if the old goat was still alive. He lowered his head and hurried on. He could have gone in and asked for directions, but that would have been tantamount to standing on a podium and announcing his arrival with a loudhailer. He pushed through the plastic fly strips hanging from the doorway of the tobacconists, and immediately recognised the familiar smells of dust, caramel, and furniture polish, unchanged since he'd come in as a boy to buy football cards. The sudden assault on his senses made him feel as if he'd slipped back in time to rejoin his twelve-year-old self, as if his adult life had been little more than a hallucination.

There was a young lad sitting behind the counter, reading a magazine. He looked to be around sixteen. Chances were good that he'd have no idea who Scamarcio was.

He asked for a pack of Marlboro and, as he was paying, said: 'I'm looking for Annunzio Morabito. Do you know where he lives?'

The boy glanced up from his football magazine, more

interested now. Scamarcio felt his heart quicken.

'Annunzio, married to the Swedish model?'

Scamarcio had been about to say 'No, not that Annunzio,' but something stopped him. Morabito had always been a ladies' man. Not only had he had the looks and physique of a matinee idol, he'd also had the silver tongue to go with it. Scamarcio remembered his father once remarking that he'd never known a woman to say no to Morabito. Word was that he'd enjoyed over a thousand conquests. Had the old bastard still got it, Scamarcio asked himself. At ninety, had he hooked a Swedish model? Something told Scamarcio that when he found Morabito he'd probably be in much better shape than he had anticipated.

He tore open the plastic on the Marlboro packet and said: 'Yes, that might be him.'

'He lives at the end of the road behind the church, where it becomes a track. His house is at the very end.'

Scamarcio thanked him, and stepped back into the glare of the sun. It was a different sun here: harsher, relentless, unforgiving. It was at least 4 degrees warmer than Rome, and he could taste the citrus of the lemon trees on the breeze. They gave off a sharp, heady aroma that unleashed yet another tide of memories and emotions— all of them ambiguous, all of them contradictory and confusing.

Scamarcio passed the white church, and thought of the old priest Carlotto who'd been around when he was a boy. Carlotto had always reminded him of a tortoise, his tiny bespectacled bulb of a head threatening to disappear inside his clerical collar at any moment. The old priest had been living proof that *omertà* didn't stop at the gates to the House of God. He'd been the embodiment of 'See no evil, hear no evil', but that was how most southern priests survived back then. The situation had improved slightly over the years, but not enough, in Scamarcio's opinion. The Church was still scared into silence far too often; far too many of its shepherds still looked the other way.

He emerged from the cool shadows of the alleyway and made his way towards the track. He had the feeling this might have been the same place Morabito had been living all those years back. He remembered hearing that he'd built himself a magnificent villa somewhere, and indeed when Scamarcio rounded the bend he was confronted with a huge pink-stucco confection, so totally out of keeping with the crumbling concrete decay in evidence all around that if it was not the house of the *capo*, it had to be that of his right-hand man.

After Scamarcio's father had been gunned down, Morabito had stayed on as chief financial officer to the new boss Don Pecoraro. They said Morabito had worked hard to shore up his position, to make sure that he wasn't pushed aside like Piocosta. Morabito had always been a pragmatist, whereas the hothead Piocosta had often been led astray by his ego.

Scamarcio approached the house, his heart hammering now. Through the bars of the iron fence, he took in an immaculate lawn, a sparkling, tiled fountain, and tumbling bougainvillea, already dense and plentiful. Another smaller fountain stood beneath the shade of some orange trees, its gentle murmur creating a sense of peace and wellbeing. Scamarcio froze as he noticed a sudden movement beneath the branches: a small figure was sitting hunched in a wheelchair, a red blanket draped across its knees. Scamarcio felt a spike of heat shoot up his spine, and fought a sudden urge to turn and run. But he knew he couldn't. He'd come too far this time: this was his last chance, his one card left to play.

He pressed the buzzer on the gate, his heart pounding in his ears, his stomach liquid.

The figure in the wheelchair stirred again, then after a few seconds the wooden front door of the villa swung wide open. A tall, blonde woman stood blinking out into the sunshine, shielding her eyes.

Scamarcio held up a shaky hand, and she started down the

steps towards him. As she approached, he saw that the woman was handsome, with a wide, kindly face. She was tall and lithe, and her long, sinewy legs emerged from tight white shorts. She was nearly at the gate now, and despite the athletic body, he realised that she must be in her fifties. Scamarcio tried to remember whether Morabito had been married before. Several times, he seemed to recall. There'd been some joke about how certain jobs were being done just to replenish his alimony fund.

Scamarcio took a breath and tried to think of what to say, how best to frame it. But before he could get the words out, the figure in the wheelchair was spinning towards him at a startling pace, dark brows set in a thick line of determination. Morabito's small grey eyes were blinking rapidly, and his mouth was forming a large O. As he drew closer to the gate, he began crossing himself and whispering. Scamarcio suddenly wondered if the old man had dementia. He hadn't considered this.

'As God is my witness, I never thought I'd see this day,' said Morabito, still making the cross. 'Why have you come back to haunt me after all these years?' He was smacking his lips together, moving his fluffy white head from side to side. 'I was always loyal, I never did wrong by you. Never.'

Morabito's wife reached gently for his hand in an attempt to stop the frenzied signing. 'Annunzio, what's going on?' she asked in the strangest Calabrian accent Scamarcio had ever heard.

'It's my old capo, back to seek vengeance.'

The woman placed her other hand on his arm. 'Darling, I don't think this man is a ghost. He seems very real to me.' She reached out and touched Scamarcio's shoulder through the gate. 'See — he's quite solid.' She looked into Scamarcio's eyes, and her gaze was colder than he would have expected. 'How can we help you?' she asked.

'Your husband is half-right. I'm Leone Scamarcio, *son* of his former capo.'

Morabito's mouth fell wide open now, and Scamarcio watched a thin trickle of saliva dribble down his chin. Morabito just kept staring at him, his rheumy eyes prised open like mussels from their shell. Seconds passed, but Scamarcio didn't see him blink.

'My God,' the old man rasped eventually. 'This, I never thought I'd see.'

'Can I come in? I really need a word,' said Scamarcio, wiping his palms on his jeans. His mouth was dry.

Morabito laid a trembling hand on his heart. 'Boy, I may be old, but I'm not stupid. You're with the police.'

'I'm not here on police business. This is a personal matter.'

Motabito's tiny eyes narrowed even further, and his mouth pushed up into a frown. But then he stroked his nose a few times, and Scamarcio sensed he was wavering. Curiosity was getting the better of him.

Morabito surprised him by rising shakily in his wheelchair and releasing the lock on the gate himself, his wife looking on with concern.

'Come in then, Leo. Let's get you a drink.' He turned to his wife. 'I've known this lad since he was in nappies. I first saw him when he was just two days old.'

She smiled nervously.

'Get him a juice then—snap to it.' He clicked his fingers, and she shook her head at him before retreating inside the house. Scamarcio sensed that the act was for his benefit; it was the wife who was the boss now.

Morabito wheeled back quickly towards his spot under the orange trees. There was a little marble table by the fountain, and he picked up a pair of glasses with ridiculously wide lenses and put them on. He motioned Scamarcio to a stone chair.

'You're the spitting image of your father,' he said, leaning forward and squinting at him once the glasses were on. 'I can't see your mother in you at all.' Scamarcio thought he detected a note of disappointment. 'So what's this personal business? I would have thought you'd want to stay well away from here.'

'I'm in trouble,' said Scamarcio. 'You're one of the few people who can help.'

Morabito just frowned and continued to stare.

'You have much to do with Piero Piocosta these days?'

Morabito snorted. 'As little as I can manage. Why?'

His wife returned with a jug of iced water and some orange juice. She laid the drinks on the table, and had been about to sit down when Morabito said: 'Listen, Margot, can you give us a minute?' She sighed and rolled her eyes, then turned back towards the house.

Scamarcio wondered how much she knew about Morabito's old life. But instead he asked: 'Why do you avoid Piocosta?'

'I wouldn't say I avoid him — I just don't go out of my way to maintain contact. You didn't answer my question. Why the interest?'

'He's been making things uncomfortable for me up in Rome.'

Morabito chuckled. It quickly became a cough. When he finally had control of it, he said: 'That doesn't surprise me. Piero was always an opportunist. You must seem like the prize picking — his best friend's boy risen so high.'

'I don't trust him.'

'Well, of course not.'

'I thought that, being Lucio's boy, he'd look out for me …'

'Don't be ridiculous. You're an asset, that's all; there's never any special treatment. Piero isn't sentimental; he doesn't let anything get in his way.'

Scamarcio fell silent. This was what he'd suspected, but to have it so readily confirmed did not make it any easier to digest. 'He was always around when I was a kid, but I realise now that I know so little about him.'

Morabito shifted in his wheelchair so he could sit up straighter.

163

'They were thick as thieves, Piero and your father; you couldn't put a blade of grass between them. I remember I raised doubts about Piero once, and your father just wouldn't have it, just didn't want to hear. After that, I gave up.'

'Why did you have doubts?'

'I thought some money had gone astray and that Piero knew where it was.'

'Just the once?'

Morabito sighed, and rearranged the red blanket on his knees. 'Several times, actually.'

'Did you have any thoughts on why he was stealing?'

'Greed, I suppose. Why else do people steal?'

'He seems to be based up in Rome now. I get the feeling that he's climbed to the top …'

Morabito raised an eyebrow. Scamarcio noticed that the skin on his forehead was dry and flaking.

'You know, after your father died, Piocosta didn't hit it off with the new capo. Pecoraro didn't trust him, and pushed him aside. But then, about five years later, when Pecaro died in that car accident, Piocosta found himself back as minister of war to Angelo Calabrese, and from there on in, he just rose and rose. While a lot of the old guys decided to call it a day, he just kept going. Last I heard was that he was working out of Catanzaro, but handling certain interests up in Rome.'

'Certain interests?'

'You forgot the lingo now?'

'Government money?'

'Government money.' Morabito poured a tall glass of orange juice with a trembling hand, and pushed it across to Scamarcio. 'Have a drink, boy, it's hot.'

Scamarcio nodded his thanks. 'So when he went to work for Calabrese, where were you?'

'Oh, I was with Calabrese, too. But I didn't stay long. We didn't

164

really see eye to eye—I thought he was too much of a risk-taker. And I wasn't that happy about having Piocosta back in the fold. I just told them I wanted to wind down. I'd just met Margot, and I wanted some peace finally. Those years took it out of me.'

Scamarcio understood. The wars of the 1980s had taken their toll on everyone, one way or the other.

'So besides the fact that Piocosta works between Catanzaro and Rome, you don't know much more about his life now?'

Morabito took a breath. 'I know he's powerful. I know you should tread carefully. You were bold in coming here. How did you know I wasn't still in up to my neck with him? You took a risk.'

'I had to—I'm out of options.'

Morabito leant forward in the wheelchair and wagged a gnarly finger at him. 'Listen. Whatever he's got on you or got you into, I don't want to know, but you need to understand one thing. Your dad and he were close for a time, but I don't think it was always the case.'

'What do you mean?'

'I don't think that things were that good between them in the weeks before your dad died.'

A gust of wind whistled through the garden, and the branches of the orange trees began to stir, releasing another troubling mix of memories and emotions.

'How so?' asked Scamarcio, feeling confused, feeling that he was finally home, but that he had to get away as soon as possible.

'They were arguing. About what I don't know, but I walked in on rows several times. As soon as I entered, they stopped.'

'Was there any particular issue at the time that might explain it?'

He shook his head. 'No, but I guess you need to remember that Piocosta's sole goal was the accumulation of power. That's what drove him.'

Scamarcio's chest felt hollow.

'I don't know anything,' said Morabito. 'All I'm saying is that Piocosta was always out for himself.' He folded his hands in his lap. 'Why don't you talk to Gaetano Foti? He was well in with Piocosta, but he's safe for you now because they fell out badly. Gaetano might have more of a handle on what he's become.' He pinched his nose and sniffed. 'What are you really hoping to achieve with all this?'

'I dunno,' said Scamarcio. 'I guess I'm just trying to understand Piocosta better so I can work out how to solve my problem with him.'

'There's only one way to solve that kind of problem.'

'That option isn't open to me.'

'You sure?'

'Yes.'

'Well, let me know if you change your mind.'

A silence descended between them. Scamarcio suddenly found the peace of the fountain troubling. It was taunting him, reminding him of that elusive something he could never attain.

'Why did you decide to go into the police, son? It was such a strange move. None of us could ever get our heads around it.'

'I'd seen enough killing by the time I was eighteen.'

'You'd see more in the police.'

'It's not the same.'

'I think you take after your mother. She was a good soul, pure. She wanted Lucio out; she'd been begging him for years. This was no place for a woman like her.' He smiled, and Scamarcio noticed his sharp little teeth for the first time. 'I'm sure she'd be very proud to see you now.'

Scamarcio just nodded. He felt a deep remorse.

'Don't fuck it up, son,' said Morabito. 'You've come too far.'

Morabito had told Scamarcio that Gaetano Foti lived on the road between San Alberto and Locri in a large sand-coloured villa set in a grove of Cyprus trees. It took Scamarcio half an hour of back and forth before he finally found the turn-off and pulled up in front of the tall wrought-iron gates. He noticed a video camera mounted on a post to the right of the gate. A small TV monitor was built into the wall. When he pressed the buzzer, the screen remained blank, but a young man's voice answered.

'He's at the bar in Polisto,' said the boy. Scamarcio was surprised he gave up the information so readily. Shouldn't someone like Foti be more careful about revealing his whereabouts? Maybe he considered himself untouchable.

'There's just one bar there?'

'You'll be wanting Bar Rita.'

'How do I find Polisto?' Scamarcio had forgotten the geography after so many years.

'It's another five minutes further down the road on your right. The bar's on the square.'

Scamarcio thanked him, and considered his options. Did he really want to stride into a busy mafia drinking-hole at lunchtime? Sure, he was half an hour from San Alberto now, but news travelled fast down here. The alternative was to sit it out at Foti's place, but that could take all day. He needed to speak to him, and he didn't want to hang around waiting for the opportunity.

Scamarcio found the village of Polisto easily enough. A group of old men were sitting outside the bar arguing, all dapper in pinstriped shirts and fedoras. He guessed that the bar had become their office now. One of the old guys was fanning himself with a newspaper, surveying Scamarcio beneath hooded lids.

'I'm looking for Gaetano Foti,' he said to the group as he approached. For some reason, he was feeling slightly less nervous than when he'd arrived at Morabito's.

'Who wants to know?' came a loud voice from the end of the line. A small, fat man with a thick brush of grey hair, a large hooked nose, and enormous ears was squinting at him, his mouth turned down in suspicion. As Scamarcio drew nearer, the suspicion seemed to give way to confusion. 'Don't I know you?' said Foti.

'Is there somewhere we can talk?' said Scamarcio.

A murmur rippled through the group, and Foti leant forward, shielding his eyes with a veiny, pudgy hand. 'Who are you?' he asked again.

'If you find us a quiet place to chat, I'll tell you.'

The old man grunted, and reluctantly shifted his bulk free of the plastic chair. He tapped his trouser pocket at the old guys, indicating that he was carrying. His comrades exchanged dark glances as Foti headed inside the bar. Scamarcio followed, the eyes of Foti's guard dogs burning into his back.

Inside, the bar was thankfully empty.

'Gino, give me the keys to the back room,' said Foti to the haggard-looking barman who was busy drying glasses with a filthy dishcloth. His face betrayed no emotion as he handed over a thick bunch of keys, a tiny plastic skeleton swinging from the fob. He gave Scamarcio the briefest of nods.

Foti led him into a small, windowless room painted a strange electric-blue. The plaster was coming away in places, and Scamarcio suddenly wondered whether this was where Foti used to do his enforcing. Despite his girth, he noticed that Foti moved with surprising alacrity. Who knew if he was still active? Depended on whether his kids allowed him to be, Scamarcio reasoned.

'So,' said Foti, pulling out a battered plastic chair bleached by the sun. He placed his huge hands on a greasy table, where a bluebottle was worrying over a solitary grain of rice. 'Who are you, and what do you want?'

Scamarcio took a seat on an equally filthy-looking chair, and removed his jacket. 'Remember Lucio Scamarcio?'

Foti began waving his finger at him. 'That's it. That's who you remind me of!'

'I'm his son, Leone.'

Foti's mouth fell open, much like Morabito's had. 'But I'd heard you were in the police.'

'I am.'

Foti's mouth stayed open, but then he seemed to remember to close it, and said: 'You really look like him, you know. But I see your mother in you, too.' He closed his eyes for a moment. 'God, she was a looker, your mother, a true beauty.' Then he opened his eyes and snapped: 'You here on anti-Mafia business? If so, I've got nothing to say. I'm old and I'm tired — you're sniffing around the wrong corpse.'

Scamarcio held up a placatory hand. 'I'm here on personal business.'

'What business would that be, after all these years?' Foti produced a neatly pressed white-cotton handkerchief from his top pocket, and emptied his nose into it loudly. 'I smell a rat,' he said when he was done.

'No rat. I wanted to ask you some questions about Piero Piocosta, that's all.'

Foti's eyes narrowed. 'That wily fucker — I haven't spoken to him in years.'

This was precisely the response Scamarcio had been hoping for.

'But I've heard you used to know him well.'

Foti moved his tongue around inside his cheek, then said: 'He's my second cousin and, yeah, we used to be tight, and now we ain't. That's it.'

'What happened?'

'What business is it of yours?'

'Please, Mr Foti. I need your help. I know I'm a stranger to you, and I'm not sure how you felt about my dad, but if you had any

169

respect for him, please lend me a hand. I'm desperate.'

Foti's eyes bore into him, tracking every word. Scamarcio watched his mind moving behind them, calculating and recalculating, totting up risk against benefit, favour against reprisal. Eventually, he said: 'Look, Piocosta and I don't see eye to eye, but I'm not going to shop him to the pigs. I don't have a death wish.'

'Like I said, this is personal. Piocosta has been giving me grief, and I need to put a stop to it. I just want to move on with my life, like my mum wanted.'

The mention of Scamarcio's mother seemed to unlock something in Foti. 'She had class, your mother,' he sighed.

'I just want to understand Piocosta a bit better, to work out how I can get him off my back,' said Scamarcio.

'All you need to understand about Piero Piocosta is that he's out for himself. Sure, he was your dad's number two, but he was a loner. It was always about what would get *him* further, what would get *him* noticed by the big guns.'

'Someone else said that.'

'Who?'

'Doesn't matter. When did you last see him?'

'About five years ago now, and that was by chance. I ran into him in San Alberto.'

The mention of San Alberto made Scamarcio nervous. 'Did he go back there much?'

'I wouldn't know. I try my best to avoid the place.'

'I've heard Piocosta has risen pretty high in Rome.'

Foti barred his tattooed arms across his huge chest and frowned. 'Look, lad, what is it in particular you're trying to find out?'

'Piocosta has got me in a bind. I'm trying to work out how to free myself.'

'Is he trying to squeeze you after all these years?'

'He tracked me down, and now I can't shake him off.'

Foti shook his head. 'He's bold, I'll give him that.' He paused for a moment. 'So there was nothing specific about him and your dad?' He threw Scamarcio an odd, sideways glance. Why had he come back around to that, Scamarcio wondered.

'No, but if I've missed …'

Foti jumped in. 'No, nothing.' Then: 'It was all just rumour anyway.'

Scamarcio leant forward: 'What? What was just rumour?'

Foti waved the question away. 'Look, lad, it doesn't matter. Last I heard, Piocosta was running with the big dogs up in Catanzaro. He'd made some useful contacts, so they put him up in Rome. But that was a few years back now. Word was he'd been tipped to replace Don De Rose when the time came.'

'Don De Rose?'

'You should have done your homework before sniffing around down here. Don De Rose calls the shots here now.'

'I thought that was Esposito.'

'Until six months ago — until he got himself killed in Hamburg.'

Scamarcio made a mental note to avoid *La Gazzetta dello Sport* and to read the proper papers more often. 'So Piocosta's being lined up for the top spot?' He couldn't disguise the despair in his voice.

Foti picked up on it and said: 'Doesn't mean he's going to get it, though.'

'Why not?'

'Might be that someone else wants it.'

Scamarcio's heart beat louder. 'Who?'

Infuriatingly, Foti chose this moment to rise from his seat and make towards the door. 'If we're going to finish this chat, I need a drink.'

'Let me,' said Scamarcio, scraping back his chair.

'Mine's a house red,' said Foti, holding the door open for him.

'Get Gianni to prepare a plate of his appetisers as well. On second thoughts, you might as well make it two plates.'

When Scamarcio was back with the food and drink, Foti said: 'You remember the olives from round here?'

'Of course.'

'You should take some boxes back. I'll sort that for you.'

Scamarcio thanked him, wondering about the diversion. He set the food on the table and sat down. 'So, this person who doesn't want Piocosta to get promoted?'

Foti took a surprisingly dainty sip of his wine and said: 'Dante Greco, based in Catanzaro now. They call him the little Greek because he's 6 foot 4. He and Piocosta hate each other's guts. They're cut from the same cloth, those two, which is probably why they want to kill each other. The little Greek knows that if Piocosta takes over, he'll be shoved aside like a bikini at Christmas, perhaps worse.'

'How serious is he about taking Piocosta on?'

Foti helped himself to a large forkful of octopus vinaigrette. 'Very,' he said after a few chews. 'If you accept the old adage, "My enemy's enemy is my friend," then you and Greco are a match made in heaven.'

'How do I find him?'

'How long are you here?'

'Just a couple of days.'

'It'll take me a bit of time to track him down. Leave it with me, and take a stroll around town.'

'That safe?'

'You'll be OK,' said Foti, in the tone of a man who still had it all under control.

Why was Foti helping him, he wondered. Could he be trusted? He looked at him shovelling more seafood into his mouth, and sensed that he was enjoying their encounter. What was in it for him? Did he detest Piocosta that much that he hoped to play a part in his downfall?

'What did he do to you?' asked Scamarcio.

'Who?'

'Piocosta.'

The line of Foti's mouth dropped, and he swallowed the last bites slowly, smoothing a hand around his neck as he did so. It was a strange gesture. It was almost as if he was thinking about strangling himself.

His lips moved, but Scamarcio didn't catch the words. 'Sorry, Mr Foti, could you repeat that?' he asked.

Foti's lips moved again, and this time Scamarcio thought he heard him say: 'Killed my boy.' The words were barely above a whisper, and Scamarcio immediately felt sure he must have misunderstood. 'Sorry ...'

Foti let out a slow, painful sigh. 'It was back during the wars. Piocosta was pushing it. It was a tinderbox down here, but he wouldn't step back, wouldn't tone it down. Even your dad tried to rein him in at one point, but he just wouldn't listen. We started asking ourselves who was actually running the show — whether Lucio Scamarcio had control of his man.'

Foti began speaking faster, a new fragility in his voice. 'Angelo Talarico was driving my boy to his piano lesson out in Santa Magdalena. My wife had this bee in her bonnet about Taddeo being "accomplished" — that was the word she used to use. Angelo drove straight into an ambush that day.' Foti paused for a moment to clear his throat. 'Piocosta had raised the stakes, and the Macris wanted revenge — didn't really matter who.'

He took a breath. It sounded like he was sucking in the air around him. Scamarcio was reminded of the last breaths of a drowning man.

'They had to bring my son home in pieces,' said Foti. 'The boys wouldn't let me go to the place where it happened; they wouldn't

173

let me see him. Even though I kicked and screamed, they wouldn't let me.' He wiped his huge nose with the back of his hand.

'The Macris wouldn't have staged that ambush if Piocosta hadn't been baiting them, daring them, pushing them to their limit. He cranked the whole thing up to a level where it didn't need to be.' He sniffed. 'No general should sacrifice his men for his own personal advancement. It's the first rule of warfare. As far as I'm concerned, Piero Piocosta should have been punished for what he did. I lost respect for your father after that. He'd lost control of his lieutenant.' Foti sighed and closed his eyes. 'I'd be happy to see Piocosta pay his dues. And you, of all people, have good cause.'

Scamarcio's mouth felt dry. He needed to swallow, but his throat caught. There was too much emotion in the room. He wanted to open a window, let some of the grief out. Foti was staring intently at Scamarcio now, trying to convey some meaning, some secret message, that Scamarcio could tell Foti couldn't bring himself to articulate.

'My boy would have been about your age now, a little younger maybe. And there you are, all the way up in Rome, trying to do good work.' He paused. '*Are* you doing good work, son, or has Piocosta properly got his claws in?'

'I'm OK—for the moment.'

'You know,' said Foti, his voice shaky. 'You should do your best to keep it that way. Down here, it's nothing but shit and suffering. There's no rhyme or reason to it anymore. This isn't the way; it doesn't serve any of us. If my boy was still alive, I would have wanted him to get out, just like you did.' He got up from the chair, the scraping sound sending Scamarcio's nerves rattling.

'Don't tell anyone I said that—those old fuckers will think I've gone soft. Now you just go take a stroll, and I'll be back with your info in an hour.' And with that, Foti left the room.

Scamarcio had wanted to ask what he'd meant by 'you, of all

people', but the timing felt wrong. It was clear that Foti wanted to be left alone with his grief now.

Gaetano Foti never returned to the bar. Instead, a small boy showed up with a large crate of sinopolesi olives. Scamarcio noticed a small scrap of paper taped to the inside. 'You Scamarcio?' asked the boy.

When Scamarcio nodded, the boy pushed the box across to him and ran off. Scamarcio found himself hoping that he was a grandchild; that Foti had had other children. Then he wondered why he was feeling so sorry for an ageing mafioso who had probably dispatched hundreds to an early grave. The answer was quick to come: he and Foti had shared a similar fate; they'd both been caught up in a madness that was bigger than them. Back then, there had been no other options; there still weren't. If it hadn't been for his mother, how many lives would Scamarcio have taken by now? He sighed and turned away from the bar. He cast his eyes around the empty square; the shops had shut, and the old men had left. It was time he did the same — this was not a place to linger.

23

THE SCRAP OF PAPER FOTI HAD TAPED to the olive carton told Scamarcio that the little Greek could be found by asking for Mirco in a bar in Germaneto, Catanzaro's southern suburb. But Scamarcio knew that the motorway from Polisto would soon pass by Rocca, the village where Scamarcio had lived when his father had been gunned down. He asked himself yet again if he wanted to visit the family villa. Did he really want to drive up the gravel driveway, with phantoms murmuring through the cypresses, and nightmares becoming real? Did he really want to stand at the base of those steps that had been splintered and stained by his father's blood?

The turn for Rocca appeared on his right. He swallowed, and gripped the wheel tighter. He felt hot, then cold, and the back of his shirt grew sticky with sweat. In the distance, a crow's orphan cry echoed out across the hills — lonely, forgotten, abandoned to its fate. He ignored the turn and drove on.

Scamarcio switched on the radio and lost himself in Fabrizio De André for a while. He thought it over: could he really expect to use a man like the little Greek and then step away unscathed? He tried to work through the alternatives. But, yet again, he couldn't find any.

'Andrea is lost, he's lost and doesn't know how to get home,' sang De André.

Scamarcio knew that he had been shown a way out of the well. If he didn't take it, there might not be another.

The individual who called himself Mirco was a huge tank of a man. He was at least 6 foot five, and his enormous tatooed biceps strained through his *Mad Max* T-shirt. His neck was thicker than that of any rugby player Scamarcio had seen, and with his sunbed tan and coarse, dark hair shaved to a buzz cut, he fitted every archetype of the big-time enforcer. As he drew closer, Scamarcio's attention was drawn to a red-and-green tattoo on the inside of the thug's left forearm. He'd expected to read a woman's name — something like 'Maria' or 'Sara' — so was surprised when he finally made out the word 'Jesus'.

'Who wants to know?' barked Mirco once the barman had pointed Scamarcio in his direction.

Scamarcio held out a hand, which Mirco didn't take. 'I'm the son of Lucio Scamarcio. Gaetano Foti suggested I speak with your boss. It's about a matter regarding Piero Piocosta.'

At the mention of Piocosta's name, Mirco's rat eyes narrowed, and he adjusted the waistband on his baggy Nike sweatpants. 'What?' he hissed.

'I have a business proposition for Mr Greco. I just need ten minutes of his time.'

Mirco raised his chin and studied Scamarcio slowly from his shoes, to his cords, to his cotton shirt and leather jacket, until he stopped at eye level. His expression said, *You are a preppy twat*. His lips said: 'Why would he bother? I've never heard of you.'

'Listen,' said Scamarcio, 'could you just pass the message on? I can give you my number, so you can call if Mr Greco wants to speak to me.'

Mirco scratched at the back of his neck and frowned. 'No need. Wait here.'

He nodded at the guy behind the bar, then turned sharply, his pristine white trainers squeaking on the floor tiles. He stopped, and looked back at Scamarcio for a moment before making his way through a side door. Scamarcio swallowed, and approached the not-so-friendly barman. His nerves were on fire, and the back of his shirt was damp again, but he managed to cough out enough words to order an espresso.

He'd only just finished the coffee, the black eyes of the barman on him all the while, when Mirco was back.

'Follow me,' he snapped.

Scamarcio scrabbled for cash in his pocket to pay, but the grunt just dragged him away, muttering: 'Leave it, doesn't matter.'

Scamarcio followed him through the side door into a narrow alleyway that smelt of rotting vegetables and summer drains. Mirco seemed to be making his way towards a dim light at the end. As the light grew stronger, they emerged into a carpark, Mirco striding past the rows of cars at a brisk pace. Beyond was a small residential street lined with nondescript apartment blocks. They crossed the road, and Mirco headed for a mud-brown building, impatiently holding the glass door open for Scamarcio. They took the tiled steps up to a large, carpeted lobby, where Mirco swung a right and approached a door built into the panelwork. It was made from the same wood as the paneling, and was barely visible. He rang a buzzer, and a heavy who looked much like Mirco opened the door from the inside. They stepped into a large room, where around ten well-built men were playing cards or watching the football on TV. None of them looked up when the two of them passed by. Mirco carried on walking until he stopped outside a second door and knocked. Scamarcio thought he saw a flicker of anxiety cloud his features.

'Come in,' said a soft, surprisingly small, voice.

Mirco pushed the door open, and they entered a dimly lit room. There was plush burgundy carpet underfoot, and an aroma of sandalwood in the air. A tall, long-limbed man sat perfectly upright behind an ornate oak desk, its thick round legs banded with gold. His face was extremely lean, his cheeks almost sunken. He had penetrating, bluey-grey eyes and a long beak of a nose.

As Scamarcio approached, he noticed his expensively tailored tweed jacket and finely polished brogues. A quick scan of the walls revealed a series of framed portraits of racehorses. There was something about their faces that reminded Scamarcio of the man behind the desk.

'So, Leone Scamarcio, son of Lucio, what a pleasure,' said the man, rising from his chair and extending a hand.

Scamarcio didn't detect any sarcasm. He shook the hand of the man he now presumed to be Dante Greco, and took a seat opposite him.

'Can I offer you a coffee, some tea, perhaps?'

'No. Thank you.' Scamarcio wasn't sure how to play this. He'd been expecting hostility. After a moment, he said: 'I hadn't realised you knew my father.'

Greco leaned back against his leather chair, his long, bony hands resting neatly on his lap, and studied Scamarcio. 'We met several times. I had a lot of respect for him, actually. Your father was a decent man.'

This was the first time Scamarcio had heard that said about him; but, given the speaker, he couldn't take the comment too seriously.

'Leone, I know you're in the police, and I'm sure you're aware of who I am and what I do. No doubt you wouldn't be calling on me unless you felt that you had nothing to lose, so I'm very curious as to why you're here.'

'Why do you think I have nothing to lose?'

'I read desperation in your eyes. And why else would a high-profile policeman make a public visit to one of the 'ndrangheta's most powerful bosses?'

Scamarcio nodded. He was surprised by Greco's directness. 'My father and Piero Piocosta were always close.'

Greco snorted, but said nothing.

'Piocosta seems to think this closeness should extend to his relationship with me. But I'm trying to make a clean breast of things up in Rome. I don't want Piocosta on my back.'

'How did you allow him to get there in the first place?'

'I thought I could call on him for certain pieces of information.'

'You grew up in the life, Leone. You should have known that he would never just leave it at that.'

'I underestimated him.'

'Then you've been foolish.'

That was the polite way of putting it. 'I've spent the last day visiting some of my father's old associates. They suggested that you might be interested in helping me solve my problem with Piocosta.'

Dante Greco suddenly threw back his head and laughed. It was a thick, guttural laugh, too deep for his lean frame somehow. Mirco joined in for a moment, then something in Greco's expression made him stop.

When Greco had recovered his composure, he said: 'Do they think I have a deathwish? That I've lost my marbles? That rabble down in San Alberto may have all gone senile, but I haven't.'

Scamarcio no longer knew how to read the atmosphere. He couldn't tell whether Greco was angry or genuinely amused; whether he was about to have Mirco beat him to a pulp, or invite him over for dinner. Scamarcio chose to remain silent and to allow Greco to explain himself.

The little Greek studied him for several moments, then said: 'There are certain things we long for in life, but going as far as to make them happen … Wisdom is knowing when something is out of reach; when the cost of pursuing it is too high.'

Scamarcio felt as if he were being played. 'That's a surprisingly defeatist attitude from someone like yourself.'

Greco raised an eyebrow. 'How dare you judge me.'

Scamarcio felt the molecules shift around him, felt them change their charge. He shrugged, and tried to keep his tone neutral. 'I assumed that we might find common ground.'

'Well, you assumed wrong,' said Greco, staring at him hard.

'I'm sorry to have wasted your time.'

Scamarcio rose slowly from the chair, but, as he did so, Mirco pulled out a handgun. In the semi-darkness, Scamarcio couldn't tell what kind of weapon it was, and this troubled him.

'Calm down, Mirco,' said Greco testily.

Mirco just looked confused and stood there, still levelling the gun at Scamarcio.

Greco sighed as if all this weighed on him personally. 'I feel sorry for you, Leone. I know you witnessed your father's death, and no boy should have to live with that. I understand why you went into the police; it makes perfect sense to me. I'm sure if your father was still alive or had died an easier death, you would have stayed put down here and taken the path that had been carved out for you. But fate prods us and pushes us, and steers us off into uncharted waters.' He sighed again and tapped the edge of the desk a few times, seeming to think something through. 'What I fail to understand, though, is your readiness to take me for a fool. All this bullshit about wanting Piocosta off your back—why not just come out with it and give me the real reason? Everyone down here understands why you'd want him gone. We don't need a lie.'

Scamarcio's face must have been a mask of confusion, because Greco pushed back from the desk, his cold, blue eyes narrowing, his hard face contorting into a frown. 'They say revenge is a dish best served cold, but twenty years is a long time to let it cool.'

'But I'm not out for revenge. I …'

Greco didn't let him finish. 'What are you so ashamed of? We invented the concept!'

'But why revenge? Revenge for what?'

Greco shrugged. 'For your father's murder, of course.'

Scamarcio felt dizzy, and for a moment he couldn't breathe. It was as if the walls of the room were falling away; as if he was being spirited somewhere else, to a place completely removed from everything he'd always known. Low cheers were coming from the card game outside, followed by the distant fragments of a far-off conversation. Then, suddenly, he was back in the room again, where Greco was staring at him with a strange mixture of concern and suspicion.

Of course, realised Scamarcio, this was where it had all been heading: the oblique comments from Morabito, the hints from Foti. This was where they'd wanted to lead him. His mind flashed on Piocosta, and for a moment he struggled to believe it could be true. But then as quickly as he'd doubted it, he understood that it was possible. This murdering, filthy dog of a man had ordered the hit on his father, had had him executed in front of his wife and son. Then he'd tracked the son to Rome, tried to exploit him, tried to ruin him—tried to destroy him, like he'd destroyed the father. Piocosta was a monster; he was disgusting, subhuman. Scamarcio saw that now. He wanted to lash out and hit someone: Mirco— no, Greco—for delivering this news.

Dante Greco was still studying him closely. Scamarcio was vaguely surprised to read what looked like alarm in the old man's eyes.

'I thought you weren't being straight with me.' Greco paused, and looked down into his lap as if it held the answer to a complex puzzle. 'How can you call yourself a detective and not know?' He was shaking his head. 'It beggars belief.'

'I never came back. This is the first time in twenty years.'

'But surely someone would have told you? Your mother?'

'Why would she know?'

Greco frowned, but said nothing.

'Why did Piocosta do it?' asked Scamarcio, half-guessing the answer.

Greco rose from the desk and poured himself a coffee from a cafetiere on the sideboard. 'The word was that they had some kind of deal, that your father would step aside at an agreed time and allow Piocosta to take the helm. But then your father had second thoughts. He no longer wanted Piocosta at the top — he was unreliable, a loose cannon. Piocosta, of course, decided to take matters into his own hands at that point.' He gestured to the cafetiere in his hand. 'You sure you don't want a coffee?'

Scamarcio just wanted to get away. He needed to feel the wind on his skin; he needed a whisky, not a coffee. He turned to leave. 'Thanks for setting me straight. I appreciate it.'

Greco looked troubled. 'I'm sorry you had to hear it from me. And I'm sorry I can't help you further.'

'It doesn't matter,' said Scamarcio. 'Way I'm feeling, I'd prefer to sort this on my own now anyway.'

Greco seemed to have returned to the puzzle in his head. 'Look, lad, don't forget how it works. Don't do anything stupid.'

'Nothing stupid.' Scamarcio considered the words.

Greco stood with his gold-ringed coffee cup poised in mid-air. He had the look of someone who had finally found the solution to his conundrum, but who didn't like the answer that had presented itself.

'God be with you,' he whispered.

24

SCAMARCIO SLAMMED HIS HAND AGAINST the steering wheel. The traffic was backed up for miles. He was desperate to reach the airport and get on a flight back to Rome. He was desperate to get his hands on Piocosta, to watch him plead for mercy; to smell his blood, to hear him take his final breaths, to watch as the light left his eyes.

Scamarcio knew he should be trying to get a grip, but he couldn't. That man had singlehandedly ruined his life: he'd stolen his father at a time when Scamarcio had most needed him; he'd pushed his mother into a spiral of depression and alcoholism from which she'd never recovered. Piocosta had to die — before there was any time for Scamarcio to reflect.

After an hour stuck in traffic, Scamarcio finally reached the airport and dropped off the hirecar, his hands still shaking. He made his way quickly towards the departures hall, desperately looking about for a bar. He had to have a drink before he got on the plane. He soon spotted a dingy place next to the toilets, pulled out his wallet, and took a seat at the bar next to an elderly woman in a blonde wig who might have been a faded 1960s siren. Her thick, dark eyeliner was smudged, and she was drinking morosely from a large glass of white wine.

He ordered a double whisky from the barman. The guy was back with his drink in seconds, but before Scamarcio even had a chance to bring the tumbler to his lips, he felt a painful grip on his bicep. He turned, too angry to be alarmed. Mirco was standing there, dressed in a dark suit and tie, and looking quite different from the muscle-bound meathead of a few hours before.

'Not so fast,' he said, but the tone was surprisingly unaggressive.

'What do you want, Mirco? Missing me already?'

'Mr Greco needs a word.'

'Why?'

Mirco said nothing; he just stood there, his huge feet spaced wide apart as if he owned the place. Perhaps he did, Scamarcio reasoned. 'You can tell him that the offer is off the table,' he said, turning back to his whisky.

Mirco grabbed the glass with his other hand so Scamarcio couldn't take it.

'That stuff won't do you any favours. Mr Greco understands why you want to settle this alone, but he's thought it over, and he thinks you're making a mistake. If you try to take out Piero Piocosta without backup, you'll die. Not only will you lose your life, but you'll lose your reputation. Mr Greco says that's no way for an honourable man to go.'

'Thanks, but no thanks.'

'Mr Greco doesn't take no for an answer.'

'There's always a first time.'

The grip on his shoulder tightened. 'No. You're coming with me.'

'Or what?'

'I'll have to kill you.'

'Are you crazy? What does it concern you whether I go after Piocosta? If anything, Greco should be grateful.'

A strange expression crossed Mirco's face.

Scamarcio sighed. 'Oh, I get it. Mr Greco's worried he's been indiscreet. He doesn't want Piocosta finding out he was the one to tell me.'

Mirco said nothing, and Scamarcio knew he'd guessed correctly. 'Then the little Greek has no balls. But tell him he can stop

185

peeing his pants. That information could have come from any number of people.'

Mirco shook his head firmly. 'No, Scamarcio, you're coming with me. Do I have to kick the shit out of you?'

Scamarcio studied him for several seconds, and knew he was serious. They were robbing him of the fight. There was no longer an outlet for the tide of anger coursing through him. He felt an almost uncontrollable desire to dislocate Mirco's jaw, break his arm, but then he stopped, took a breath, and let the reality sink in. Mirco would flatten him in a second, and anyway, what was the point? Scamarcio was suddenly overwhelmed by an all-consuming, exhausting grief; it was as if his father had died that very afternoon. He closed his eyes and allowed himself to be led away.

Dante Greco was in an armchair reading a book when Scamarcio was marched back in. When he drew closer, Scamarcio saw that it was *Men are from Mars, Women are from Venus*.

What the fuck? In other circumstances, Scamarcio might have found it amusing, but now it was just disconcerting. Mirco seemed to notice him observing the title, and quickly looked away, embarrassed perhaps.

Greco sighed and set down the book. 'What a load of shit,' he said after a few moments. Scamarcio wasn't sure whether he was referring to the book or the matter with Piocosta.

'Take a seat, Leone — you look tired.'

Scamarcio did as instructed. He was so spent now, he was willing to allow other people to make decisions for him.

'You're a hothead, just like your father.'

'If you'd just discovered the identity of the man who'd ruined your life, wouldn't you want to kill him?'

Greco scratched beneath an eye. 'Of course. You need to be careful, though, when you say he ruined your life.'

'You're defending him now?'

186

'Certainly not.' He eased back in the armchair. 'I just wonder what would have happened to you had Piocosta *not* killed your father …'

'Look, Greco, I don't have time for this bullshit.'

Greco slammed a palm on the desk, but it was a gentle slap, not that forceful. 'What would you have become, Leone, if your father was still alive? Would you have still gone to Rome and joined the police, or would you have stayed down here with us vermin, and taken the helm of the family business?'

Scamarcio stopped for a moment. Greco was framing the question in a new way. Scamarcio had never considered it in these terms before. It was true; it was the murder that had changed Scamarcio, that had pushed him north, that had made him take a new path. Without that tragedy, would he have still listened to his mother, and left? Would she have even pushed him to go? He swallowed. Who was he? Who was he, *really*?

Even the indistinct outline of the answer was too much to contemplate.

Greco tapped his upper lip with a finger and watched him.

Scamarcio realised he had a headache. It had come on suddenly — a piercing, burning dagger behind his right eye. He rubbed a palm across his forehead. 'Greco, what do you want?'

Dante Greco smiled. He got up from the desk and came around to the other side, perching on the corner so he was just a foot or so away now. Scamarcio noticed that his skin was far less lined than he would have imagined. He found this youthfulness unnatural and disconcerting.

'I'm willing to cooperate with you on the matter of Piero Piocosta. It's clearly in our mutual interest, and I believe we'll work better together than apart.'

Scamarcio wanted to say something about Greco being a coward, about him needing to think before he spoke, but he remained silent. He took in this man with his perfect posture

187

and immaculate suit, his smooth hands and neatly combed hair. There was too much of the Dark Lord about him, too much of the serpent.

'I want you to find a way to get Piocosta to Catanzaro. I want him down here on home turf. And I don't want him surrounded by muscle. Do you think you can make that happen?'

There was something hypnotic about the tone and timbre of Greco's voice. The headache was properly fierce now, and Scamarcio felt faint, but he heard himself say: 'Perhaps.'

'You don't sound convinced.'

Scamarcio took a breath. 'I'll try.'

25

DESPITE THE THREE SCOTCHES he'd knocked back at the hotel bar, Scamarcio's fingers were unsteady as he dialled Piocosta's number.

'Hmm,' grunted the old man when he picked up.

'Can you meet me?' asked Scamarcio.

'You got a problem with tomorrow night?'

'I need to talk — a few things have come up. I don't want to discuss them over the phone.'

'The usual place? I can be there in an hour.' The tone was more reasonable now.

'No. I've left the capital. Better that way.'

'Shit,' said Piocosta, immediately picking up Scamarcio's hint that he was being monitored.

'I'm in Catanzaro.'

'What the fuck are you doing down there?'

'I'm here as part of the investigation I'm on. I thought it would be a good place for us to talk.'

The line fell silent. Scamarcio could almost hear Piocosta's brain whirring. He was either wondering what inquiry Scamarcio was working on, or he already knew and was curious about how much progress was being made.

Eventually, Piocosta said: 'I can't just up and leave. I've got meetings.'

'What about tomorrow? They won't keep me down here long — they've always got one eye on the budget.'

Piocosta sighed and said: 'I'll take the train in the morning. I'll text you the time. You can meet me at the station.'

Scamarcio wanted to tell him to come alone, but he knew there was no way to say this without arousing suspicion.

'OK,' he said. 'See you then.'

Dante Greco poured him another glass of Amarone. It was from his private cellar, and was one of the finest Scamarcio had sampled. Greco seemed happy to stick to his Italian roots when it came to wine, but as far as the food was concerned he displayed distinctly Anglophile leanings. They'd had smoked salmon for a first course, roast beef and roast potatoes for an entrée, followed by apple pie for desert. A maid was now in the process of carving off a couple of slices of Stilton and laying them alongside two plates of grapes.

Scamarcio hadn't wanted to meet Greco for dinner, but Mirco had made it plain that no wasn't an option. When Scamarcio had left his hotel he'd had little appetite, but he'd surprised himself by how much he'd ending up enjoying the food, given the circumstances. At times he'd felt as if he was acting out a feverish hallucination; answering Greco's questions, nodding his head when appropriate, smiling at his jokes, all in the pursuit of some increasingly indistinct, but deeply troubling, purpose.

'This is the best Stilton money can buy,' said Greco. 'It's from a small village in Nottinghamshire. Nothing beats it. Have you ever been to the UK?'

'Just as a teenager,' said Scamarcio. 'I didn't really like it.'

'You probably saw the wrong places.'

'Probably.'

Although Mirco had collected Scamarcio from his hotel, he had asked him to wear a blindfold for the last ten minutes of their journey to Greco's villa. When he'd been helped from the car, still blind, Scamarcio had immediately noticed the silence and the evening musk of a familiar spring blossom — cherry perhaps. He'd wondered if they'd left Catanzaro, but then reminded himself that Greco could probably afford a sizeable chunk of city land on which to construct a mansion. Scamarcio hadn't seen the outside of the house, but from the exposed stone walls and wood panelling inside, he imagined that Greco's tastes would probably extend to a mock-Tudor facade.

Greco leant forward across the dining table, brushing some crumbs into the palm of his hand and then depositing them carefully into a thick cotton napkin.

'Once you've met him at the station, take Piocosta around the corner to Trattoria Georgia. I'll have my men there — Mirco will show you where it is on the map.'

'Won't Piocosta know that's one of your places?'

'It's not. I'm just renting it for the afternoon.'

'And if he suggests somewhere else? Piocosta sees Catanzaro as home turf; he'll want to take the lead.'

'Tell him you were there yesterday, and that the Black Pig 'Nduja is really good. Piocosta loves Black Pig 'Nduja.'

'How do you know that?'

Greco's face remained a mask of stone. It was as if Scamarcio hadn't asked the question.

'When did you two last work together?' he pushed.

Greco sat back and undid the top button of his waistcoat. 'Never, really. We were always on parallel trajectories, but heading for the same destination. It pained me to see him arrive first.'

'So your problem with him is that he took your spot?'

'It's not just that. I don't like how he operates. Piocosta will sell his own grandmother to get ahead. There's no loyalty there, no appreciation or esteem for years of collaboration. He's the definition of a psychopath.'

'The whole system down here is psychopathic.'

Greco shook his head sharply. 'If you think that, then you don't understand the South.'

Scamarcio cleared his throat. He thought about saying nothing, but in the end he couldn't help himself. 'You all countenance murder after murder, blood feuds escalate, killings double, triple, quadruple in a year … none of you ever say *Stop, enough is enough.*'

'How can we? No businessman can allow himself to be walked over, to be squeezed out. That's the road to famine.'

'But if you all sat down together, if you let reason prevail for once, maybe you could come up with a plan?'

Greco looked at him as if he were mad. 'A plan? A *plan*? What kind of plan would you suggest to resolve centuries of banditry, resentment, poverty, and desperation? And don't tell me the government is capable of coming up with something, because those pigs will never leave the trough. They have no interest in bringing wealth here.'

'In some places, people are starting to fight back …'

Greco slammed his hand hard on the table, sending silver cutlery rattling. 'That's just bullshit for the papers! What you have here in Calabria is a modus vivendi: there's no money or investment, so we fill the gap. Some of us grow rich doing so; the rest are just comfortable. The state puts up with us, because they know there are no alternatives and because half of them are in bed with us anyway.'

'The state doesn't put up with it. The Anti-Mafia Commission is hardly putting up with …'

'The AMC is a fig leaf.'

Scamarcio was about to say that he didn't buy it, that he truly believed that some forces within the state were doing all they could to bring about the demise of men like Greco and Piocosta. Yet he suspected that Greco was half-right; that it was the men at the *very* top who lacked the will. There weren't enough pure hearts leading the charge.

He was about to try to wind up their discussion when Greco said: 'Piocosta is the worst kind of criminal; he has no compass.'

So they'd come back around to that. The man was obsessed.

But there was an unsettling look in Greco's eyes that made Scamarcio reluctant to interrupt.

'Most men have rules, boundaries. Piocosta has none,' Greco continued, staring off into the middle distance.

Scamarcio sensed that he wasn't just talking about the murder of his father now.

'You need to know what you're dealing with. Before Piocosta steals your life, that man will take your heart, your soul, your sanity—piece by piece, fibre by fibre. He's the devil in a blue beret.'

Why the hard sell? Scamarcio wondered. He didn't need to be convinced about the man who'd killed his father.

Greco tapped his wine glass with his index finger, then took a long slug of Amarone. 'There was an old well near your father's villa.'

Scamarcio blinked.

'For a while they hid children there.'

The comment had come from nowhere. Greco fell silent as he watched Scamarcio try to make sense of it, process it.

'Children?' Scamarcio whispered eventually.

'When they were into kidnapping for ransom,' said Greco, all matter-of-fact.

'Kidnapping for ransom?'

'You seem surprised.'

Scamarcio just stared at him. Eventually he asked: 'Both of them, they were both involved?'

Greco nodded.

Scamarcio swallowed. His tongue felt dry, too bulky. 'I didn't know they were ever into that.'

'No?'

'I can't imagine my father ...'

Greco held a finger up to stop him. 'From what I heard, it was Piocosta's idea.'

'Why did my dad let him do it?'

'I think he tried to stop him, but Piocosta just carried on behind his back.'

'So Dad wasn't aware?'

'That would be a generous analysis.'

'Well, which is it?'

'I don't know; no one ever did.'

The doubt was a new dark presence, another evil spirit in the room.

'You ever heard of The Priest?' asked Greco, gently pushing the bottle of Amarone across to Scamarcio.

That was it, the small worm of anxiety that had been threading its way along his spine, burrowing down into his skin; a question so troubling and unwelcome that he'd pushed it to the depths of his mind a long time ago.

'I met him,' said Scamarcio after he'd drained his glass and refilled it.

'You met The Priest?' asked Greco, seemingly wrong-footed for once.

'It wasn't as a child; it was last year, when I was conducting an investigation on the island of Elba.'

'Did he realise who you were?'

'He told me he knew my father.'

Greco smiled tiredly. 'There you go — we can forget the generous analysis.'

'What happened?' asked Scamarcio. He didn't know if he could handle the truth, but every fibre of his being willed him to ask.

Greco took another drink. 'Piocosta needed some favour from The Priest to do with a land deal. The Priest held some kind of influence over one of the interested parties. In return for him swinging it, Piocosta gave him access to the well — the kids.' Greco pursed his lips in disgust.

Scamarcio wanted to vomit. He noticed that even Greco looked pale.

'Jesus,' Scamarcio whispered.

'I suppose just because The Priest said he knew him doesn't mean Lucio was involved. They could have met socially, something like that.'

Scamarcio wasn't really listening. He was thinking back to that summer's day on the Tiber when he'd asked Piocosta about The Priest; he recalled Piocosta's heartfelt denials, so passionate, so convincing.

'So?' asked Greco, the tone still soft and unobtrusive.

Scamarcio just looked at him.

A door suddenly swung open and a blast of cooler air rushed in. An extremely tall, stunningly beautiful brunette entered, her blue eyes and pale skin definingly un-Italian. She took a seat next to Greco and cupped her perfect chin in her hand while she studied Scamarcio, her gaze direct and unabashed. He sensed danger, but didn't care. His stomach was churning, his mind still trying to process the story of the well.

'Who is this man, Dante?' she asked in a thick Russian accent, her cobalt eyes pinning Scamarcio with a stare.

'This is a business matter,' said Greco, his tone neutral.

'You're not going to introduce me?' Her eyes were intelligent and alive, unforgiving.

Greco remained motionless for a moment, then said: 'Vladlena, can you leave us?'

'Don't patronise me, Dante.'

Greco rose from the table slowly and placed a gentle hand on her elbow. 'Come with me.' He led her out of the dining room, and as they left she threw Scamarcio a fiery look. He wasn't sure what that look was supposed to convey; whether it was anger or interest, or something else.

He had expected to hear raised voices, but no sound came. His mind caught on the image of a seal pup being silently slaughtered, its blood slowly pooling on the ice.

After a couple of minutes, Greco was back. There was a flush of red running up his neck, but his demeanour was unchanged.

'So,' he said, 'I need Piocosta to enter that restaurant alone.'

Scamarcio knew he was properly part of this now; there was no going back, and he didn't want to. 'I'm not sure how to ask him to drop his protection, without putting him on his guard,' he said.

'What if you tell him that you need to talk in private — that it's personal?'

'I doubt he'd buy that.'

'Tell him you've found out something about him and your mother.'

'My mother?'

'Piocosta betrayed your father in *every* way.'

After the revelation about The Priest, this felt like nothing. Anyway, Scamarcio had always suspected something along these lines since he'd walked in on his mother and Piocosta shortly before his father died. There had been nothing immediately wrong with the scene: his mother had been sitting on the sofa, a book open in her lap; Piocosta had been pouring himself a vodka from the bar. However, it was the atmosphere that had troubled the young Scamarcio; it was too charged, too tense, too far from daily mundanity. After his father had died, he'd tried to ask his mother about it, but she'd just left the house and driven off, not returning until several hours later.

'Right,' said Scamarcio. He was starting to resent having his strings pulled.

'When this is all over,' said Greco soothingly, 'we can go our separate ways. You head back to Rome and get on with being a policeman. I'll go about my business down here, unfettered.'

It seemed an odd choice of word, and it had been delivered with an unnecessary emphasis. Scamarcio had wanted to say that there was nothing he could do about whether Greco's business went uninterrupted or not. But he felt that even the act of articulating this would create some kind of precedent, some kind of understanding. It was better left unsaid. He thought of Aurelia; about her protection in Munich. Once Piocosta had gone, there'd be no more help; no more safe haven from the Cappadona clan. Scamarcio resolved to fund her security himself from now on: he didn't know how long he could maintain it, but he did know that he couldn't be beholden to Greco.

Scamarcio took in the powerful man in front of him, noticing the coldness of his stare, the plasticity of his skin: 'I'll try the personal line. I'll text you Piocosta's arrival time. All being well, I'll see you at the restaurant.'

Greco nodded and took a small sip of wine. 'Sleep tight, Leone.'

26

GARRAMONE CALLED AT ELEVEN the next morning. 'Any progress?' he asked testily.

Scamarcio had almost forgotten that he was supposed to be finding out more about Davide Stasio.

'Yes, but I can't talk now. Could I ring you back later?'

Garramone huffed and puffed like the big bad wolf, then muttered: 'Make sure you do.'

Scamarcio pocketed the phone and waited for Piocosta's train to roll in. It was supposed to be the high-speed service, but, as usual, it was running late. Several more minutes passed, and Scamarcio's anxiety grew.

When the train finally pulled up to the platform, Scamarcio scanned the faces of the passengers spilling out, tired and harried, excited and beaten, but he couldn't find the old man. The anxiety was now a burning sensation between his shoulder blades. He pinched his nose and tried to breathe. Piocosta was always the gentleman; maybe he'd been polite and let a few people pass in front of him. Scamarcio checked his watch, then looked up once more. He tracked the battered, care-worn faces—the nuns, the salesmen, the whores, the grandfathers—but still he couldn't locate Piocosta. He felt a primal warmth at the back of his neck, and turned to look behind him. But he couldn't spot anyone who seemed to be paying him particular attention. As he returned his gaze to the passengers, the disposable mobile he used for Piocosta rang.

'Change of plan,' said the old man chirpily. 'I decided to take the car.'

'Why didn't you tell me before? I'm at the station.'

'A couple of my boys are outside. They're going to drive you to a place where we can talk.'

'Where?' Scamarcio knew it was a pointless question.

'Don't worry about that.'

Scamarcio figured that the worst thing he could do now was tell Greco that plans had changed. He needed to get the measure of Piocosta first; work out what he knew or at least suspected. He would only contact Greco once he'd got a handle on that.

'Where are your crew?' Scamarcio asked, trying to sound calm.

'In a grey Dacha Duster outside the main entrance. They know you — they'll spot you first.'

It sounded like a threat.

One of Piocosta's meatheads was waiting for him by the car. When he saw Scamarcio, he raised a palm, his face expressionless. Scamarcio recognised him. When he'd had some trouble with an investigation last year, Piocosta had brought this man along to help clean up.

'Morning, Scamarcio,' he said, opening the back door for him. 'How's it going?'

'Not bad,' said Scamarcio, scanning the car to see who else was inside and what weapons they might be carrying. There was just one other, the driver. As only the back of his head was visible and he didn't turn to greet him, Scamarcio couldn't tell whether they'd met before.

The meathead jumped in the passenger seat, and they sped away from the station and joined the mid-morning traffic. After they'd swung a left, he turned and said: 'Sorry, Scamarcio, but the old man wants you lying down for the rest.'

'What?'

'You know what he's like. Don't shoot the messenger.'

'He doesn't trust *me*?'

'Piocosta doesn't trust anyone.'

'OK,' sighed Scamarcio. 'I guess I could do with a nap.'

The meathead grunted and turned on the radio. The news was reporting another boatload of migrants from Libya who had drowned off the island of Lampedusa. Women and children had been among the many dead.

'Dreadful business,' tut-tutted the meathead. Scamarcio opened his eyes.

'Don't be soft,' said the driver. 'They're ruining this country. We should bomb those boats before they have a chance to dock.'

'You've got a wife and kids. How would you feel if they drowned?'

'It's not the same.'

'Yes, it is.'

'No, it isn't.'

Scamarcio closed his eyes again. More and more, he felt as if he was inhabiting a surreal dream, drifting aimlessly from one incongruity to the next.

'Way I see it, there isn't anything left in this country to ruin,' continued the meathead.

'Oh for fuck's sake! All the way down from Rome we've had to listen to this shit.'

Scamarcio wondered why Piocosta wasn't with them — why he'd gone ahead to the location.

The driver turned up the radio, and the conversation died. Scamarcio felt the sun burning through his eyelids, and smelt the chemical musk of hot plastic. He wished he could just drift off to sleep and forget — wipe the disc clean and reset to 'normal'.

After ten minutes or so, the car slowed, and he heard the tyres beneath him crunch over gravel. The guy in the passenger seat started whispering something that Scamarcio couldn't make out, and then the car came to a stop. But, for some reason, the driver waited a few seconds before killing the engine. Scamarcio could hear birds high up in the trees now, and the impatient hum of cicadas. In the distance, a church bell marked out midday.

He lay quite still and waited. His blood was pounding in his ears, mocking the rhythm of his heart with a taunting, merciless tattoo. He waited for the doors to open, but no movement came. The two men ahead just sat in silence like guard dogs turned to stone. There was a new tension in the car, and he sensed it wasn't down to the argument of before.

More minutes passed, and then Scamarcio heard boots on gravel. The car shook slightly as the trunk behind him sprung open. Someone shouted, there was laughter — Piocosta's laugh. Then the voices retreated and the footfalls died away. The two men in front remained motionless. For a crazy moment, he wondered if they'd been shot.

'Can I get up now?' he asked.

'No, just sit tight,' whispered the driver. He sounded on edge.

Scamarcio counted to ten in his head. Burning tendrils of panic were spreading through his chest, reaching out and encircling his heart. He knew that if he didn't get ahold of the fear, he was lost. He wondered whether to call Greco now, and sound the alarm. But how could he do that with these two listening in?

Suddenly the door behind him opened, and a blast of hot air hit him. He inhaled jasmine, wet roses, the metallic heat of the bonnet baking in the midday sun.

'OK, you can come out,' said a voice he didn't recognise.

Strong arms helped him to his feet, and he smelt expensive cologne. They were outside a modern white villa. Dense bougainvillea framed the wide front door, where two men with Kalashnikovs were standing guard. *Piocosta's Catanzaro home*, he figured.

He looked up at the man holding him. He was well muscled, but he didn't look like one of Piocosta's typical foot soldiers.

He was wearing a dark suit, and had the air of a lawyer or accountant about him.

'This way,' he said, leading Scamarcio up to the house.

He suddenly wanted to bolt, to make a run for it. Every instinct told him that Piocosta had discovered the truth, and that he was about to pay for it. Scamarcio took in the armed men at the doorway, the two men behind him. He knew he'd die trying. In that instant, he saw himself from a great distance, a tiny speck shuffling off this mortal coil, following his father down and down, deeper and deeper. He had grown up believing he was free, but he wasn't. All his efforts, all his principles, had been worthless, pointless; a ridiculous nothing.

He took the stone steps, timing his exhalations with each tread. He counted ten breaths.

They entered a luminous lobby tiled with pale granite slabs, and passed through a wide oak doorway into the lounge. Piocosta was sitting on a long tan-leather sofa, his legs crossed, watching TV. Scamarcio scanned the room for his men, but it seemed that he was alone.

'Thanks, Stefano. I'll take it from here,' said Piocosta, not looking up.

The man escorting Scamarcio nodded and left the room, closing the doors behind him.

'Leo, sorry about the change of plan,' said Piocosta, his eyes still on the TV.

'Don't be.'

'Take a seat. You want a coffee?' He motioned him to an armchair next to the sofa and finally looked at him. Scamarcio couldn't read anything from his eyes.

'I'm good, thanks.'

'So what did you want to talk to me about?'

He hadn't practised this scenario in his mind. He'd figured that Greco's boys would have saved him the trouble. *How stupid.*

'This job you want done,' he said, recalculating. 'We need to discuss details. I'll need more backup; I'll need help with a couple of things on the inside.'

Piocosta nodded, his expression neutral. After a moment, he said: 'So you brought me all the way down here for that?'

'Like I said, I was feeling nervous up in Rome.'

Piocosta leant towards the coffee table and picked up a lit cigar from a silver ashtray. He eased back slowly against the sofa and took a long drag, rolling the smoke around in his mouth for a while. He stared at Scamarcio through the haze, unblinking.

After what seemed like an eternity, Scamarcio said: 'Would you be able to provide me with a couple of men then, for help on the inside?'

Piocosta just carried on staring, the back of his non-cigar hand against his mouth now. He said nothing, the dark pinpricks of his eyes sucking in all the light. The game was up, Scamarcio realised, a cold blade of fear pricking his spine.

'You idiot,' hissed Piocosta.

'What?'

'You think you can come down here and stir up a hornet's nest, and that word's not going to get back? Shit, you're even more of a fool than your father.'

Scamarcio sprang to his feet. 'Don't you fucking dare! I could have you inside on a murder charge in two seconds.'

Piocosta's laugh was cold and cruel. 'With what evidence? Hearsay? The senile ramblings of a few old duffers? Give me a break, Leo.'

Scamarcio wanted his gun. He wanted to tear a hole through Piocosta's chest. He wanted to see the sky through it.

Piocosta leant towards the coffee table and pressed a button on a small console. Scamarcio heard a flurry of footfalls, then a cluster of Piocosta's heavies scrambled into the room. The tight knot of men pulled Scamarcio to his feet. He smelt sweat and breath mints, and felt his legs go weak.

'Take him to the shed. I need to know what kind of shit he's been stirring.'

They nodded, and pushed Scamarcio towards the door. They made him think of Siamese quadruplets, joined at the hip, sharing a brain.

As they approached the doorway, he suddenly felt feverish, and couldn't work out if he was really getting sick or whether the stress had tripped some kind of switch in his nervous system. Was 'shed' a euphemism? Would they be taking him elsewhere? A nearby scrap yard or warehouse? Piocosta probably owned a heap of business interests that he used as and when required. Scamarcio knew that Piocosta was pernickety, fastidious. He wouldn't want the blood spilled in his own backyard. If they had to travel, there was hope, thought Scamarcio; there still existed the smallest chance of …

All at once, there was an explosion behind him. He heard a huge quantity of glass cracking and splintering, shattering to the floor. He turned to see the massive window to Piocosta's left dissolve into a million tiny fragments. Next to Piocosta on the sofa was a small smoking canister. After a couple of dazed moments, Piocosta started to cough — short, dry coughs to start with, which soon became desperate, heaving rasps. Scamarcio tried to run for the front door, but his eyes were burning and his chest felt tight. He stumbled, and as he tried to get up he was overcome by dizziness, and vomited. His vision was failing, and he could no longer make out the contours of the room. He was trying to stand, trying to find the wall, when he felt legs push past him, and arms shove him aside. It felt like they were running towards the smoke, rather than running away. But he'd lost his bearings and couldn't be sure.

Then all at once the air around him erupted into gunfire — a terrifying, relentless bombardment that shook the walls and rattled the doors. Volley after volley, it came; salvo after salvo. He lay flat, trying to shield his head with his arms, trying to protect his ears. The floor beneath him was trembling, pictures and ornaments tumbling and shattering. He counted to ten, twenty, thirty, but still the firing continued, louder and louder, growing in intensity. Past fifty, he thought his sanity might desert him, but then at seventy the noise suddenly ceased. There was no coughing, no begging for mercy, no croupish last breaths. It was a total, all-encompassing silence, dark and conclusive, chilling in its finality. He twisted his head to the side, and the stench of sulfur, iron, and excrement hit him. He wanted to retch again, but then he felt arms beneath him pulling him to his feet, propping him against a wall.

'Can you walk?' someone was asking.

His voice had left him.

'Let's get him outside. Take his legs.'

As they emerged into the sunlight, he gasped at the fresh air, trying to suck it in, to drink it down, his lungs burning with every breath.

'Sit him on the step, get him water,' said a voice that Scamarcio recognised but couldn't place.

'Pour water in his eyes — more, more. That's it, keep going.'

The voice drew nearer. 'You're going to be all right. Stay calm. It will soon pass.'

Slowly, Scamarcio's vision began to return, and he started to make out the blurry outlines of two men removing gas masks. As the scene came into focus, he noticed rounds of ammunition on their belts, semi-automatics at their feet. Their faces were pale, their eyes scared and excited like dogs at a fight. A middle-aged blonde woman was standing on the step below them, quickly loading rifles into a holdall. She could have been a soccer mum, packing up her kids' kit.

Scamarcio rubbed at his eyes. As he moved his head to his

right, his stomach lurched, and he felt that he might vomit once more. Dante Greco had entered his field of vision, a beige cashmere coat draped across his shoulders.

Dante's expression was sombre; there was no smile of triumph. 'Now you can get back to Rome and forget all about it,' he said quietly.

Scamarcio looked at him standing there, lord of all he surveyed, his men filthy and exhausted all around him.

Greco tilted his head to one side and studied him back, his eyes two pools of ice.

'No need for thank yous; I thought you might fuck it up, so I had a contingency plan. Always have a contingency, Scamarcio.'

Scamarcio nodded. His throat was too sore to speak.

Greco turned and began descending the steps. Scamarcio saw a silver Bentley waiting in the turning circle, its engine idling. Greco was about to get in the car when he stopped and looked back at Scamarcio. 'And good luck sorting that American business.'

'What?' said Scamarcio, barely managing a whisper.

'You know that mess from last year — that put Cappadona in a wheelchair?'

Scamarcio tried to swallow again, his tonsils a painful lump.

Greco smiled thinly and raised a hand in salute before sliding into the passenger seat of the Bentley, a chauffeur gently closing the door behind him.

Scamarcio felt a rush of heat to his belly, and suddenly tasted bile. Had he made a fatal miscalculation? He wiped the sweat from his eyes and took a long, shaky breath. As the car disappeared down the driveway, he thought of devils, and whether it was wiser to do business with the ones you already knew.

27

THERE WAS SOMETHING REASSURING about the mess in Fiammetta di Bondi's apartment. Scamarcio found some comfort in returning to a situation that was predictable, that had remained unchanged. He didn't know if he'd just struck out for survival in Calabria or whether he'd signed his own death warrant, but in the midst of this fresh hell, the one thing he could be sure of was that di Bondi's place would be a pigsty.

'You don't look too good, Detective,' she said, handing him a cup of coffee he hadn't asked for. The cup was chipped, and there was a faded lipstick stain on the other side of the rim.

'There's a flu going around. I think I might have the beginnings of it.'

She frowned. Her eyes seemed to say that she didn't quite believe him. Although it was four in the afternoon and warm outside, she was wearing a heavy, pink towelling dressing gown with a ketchup stain on the sleeve. There was nothing of the femme fatale about it.

'I'm here because we're trying to tie up some loose ends regarding the death of Manfredi,' said Scamarcio, pulling out his notebook.

'I thought you were focussed on the disappearance of Micky's family.'

'We are, but to make progress with that, we need to understand the Manfredi connection.'

'There is no connection.'

'You know that's not true.'

She tossed her hair behind her ears and took a seat on the sofa, leaning forward to retrieve her cigarettes from the table. Once she'd lit up, she sat up straighter and crossed her legs beneath her, rearranging the dressing gown across her knees. She studied him through the smoke. From where Scamarcio was sitting, it did not look like a positive appraisal.

'How long have you been a detective?' she asked.

'Almost eight years. Now, Miss di Bondi …'

'Do you enjoy your job?'

'For the most part, yes.'

'Why do you always look so miserable then?'

He sighed. 'Do I? I hadn't realised.'

'It's like you're dragging some huge weight around.'

'I didn't come here to talk about me.'

'What does it matter? We've got plenty of time — I don't have any work today.'

'I do. We need to find Proietti's wife and son as quickly as possible. I need you to answer my questions.'

She scratched beneath her nose. 'Here's the deal, Scamarcio. I'll tell you about me and Manfredi if you take the time to tell me a little bit about yourself.'

He wanted to scream. Garramone had asked him to be in the squad room in an hour. As he had nothing new on Davide Stasio to offer, Scamarcio had decided to drop by di Bondi's first, so at least he could perhaps deliver the boss something more on the Manfredi angle.

'OK then. You go first,' he said through gritted teeth.

'How do I know you'll honour your side of the bargain?' She rearranged her dressing gown yet again.

'I'm an honourable man.'

He realised distractedly that she might be flirting with him, but he was too tired and strung out after Catanzaro to work out how he felt about this.

She nodded. 'The thing between me and Manfredi was never love.'

'You told me that already.'

'Stasio, Micky's associate,' she hesitated for a moment, took a quick drag of the cigarette, and scratched at the corner of an eye. 'Well, Stasio wanted me to hang around Manfredi for a while.'

'Why?'

'He wanted to know what he was up to.'

'Why?'

'Manfredi had some dirt on Micky, and Stasio was afraid he was going to use it.'

'What would make him do that?'

'He owed Micky money, but he couldn't pay up. He was looking for a bargaining chip.'

'What did Manfredi know?'

'Stasio never told me, but he wanted me to keep an eye on Manfredi—he wanted to know whether he ever spoke to anyone about Micky.'

'And you did this?'

'Yes.'

'Why?'

'Favours in return. Micky is big in TV—I need work in TV.' She shrugged as if to say *Don't be slow*.

'And did you find out anything?'

She fell silent and took another long drag on her cigarette. Eventually she said: 'Manfredi told me one night when he was a bit tipsy that he was about to ruin Proietti. Those were his words. He said he had evidence that could prove he was a criminal.'

'And you told Stasio?'

'Yes.'

'When was this?'

She fell silent again and studied the floor. After several seconds had passed, she said, 'The night before Manfredi died.' Then, almost as an afterthought: 'Like I told you, it's a whole world of shit.'

For the first time, he thought he heard some genuine emotion there.

She looked up and smoothed her fringe away from her forehead. 'Now you need to keep your side of the bargain.'

'Sorry?'

'Tell me something about yourself.'

Scamarcio shrugged. 'What's to tell?'

'Come on. That's not what we agreed.'

Scamarcio wanted to get up and leave, but he willed himself to remain civil. He couldn't afford to alienate a witness. He took a few moments to gather his thoughts, then started speaking. But it was as if his voice was coming from afar, as if someone else was doing the talking: 'You may have read that I grew up in the South, down in Calabria,' he heard himself say. 'My father was a godfather in the 'ndrangheta. When I was a teenager I decided that I didn't want the life, *his* life, so after university I came to Rome and joined the police.'

'What made you decide you didn't want the life?' asked di Bondi calmly.

'My father was shot. I saw it happen. After that it felt like time for a change.'

'Did he die?'

'Yes.'

'Was it quick?'

'Was what quick?'

'His death.'

Jesus, what is it with this woman? He wanted to tell her to go hang, but instead he heard himself reply: 'Actually, it took around ten minutes.'

'Did he say anything to you?'

210

'When?'

'While he was dying.'

Scamarcio stopped breathing. This was something that he *never* spoke about. How dare she? Who the hell did she think she was? Did she think he was just another sad fuck she could manipulate any which way she wanted? Yet at the same time it was as if she *knew*; as if she'd somehow caught a glimpse of the maelstrom inside his head; as if she realised that he needed to release some of the grief.

'He told me that he loved me and that he wanted me to be happy. That I should do whatever it took to be happy. Rules and traditions were meaningless.' Scamarcio heard his voice catch. He swallowed, trying to push the grief back down. This woman couldn't be allowed any kind of victory over him. He got up to leave.

Di Bondi said nothing for a moment, then: 'I feel like an idiot. If you can make it in this world, then I certainly can.'

Scamarcio shrugged, not wanting to pass judgement. He coughed, trying to steady his words. 'If you remember anything else, Miss di Bondi, let me know.'

'Please, call me Fiammetta.'

She rose from the sofa and accompanied him to the door. As he was heading out into the corridor, she reached out and brushed his cheek with the back of her hand. 'Maybe we could try to be there for one another, give each other some support.' Her eyes were burning with intensity, uncompromising, and he was surprised to feel something undeniably honest pass between them. There was an electric connection that he hadn't seen coming. For a second, it floored him; the next moment, he just wanted to act on it, do something about it. But he couldn't — it would cost him his job. He tried to summon every ounce of willpower to get himself out of the flat and across the threshold before the whole situation spiralled away from him. He inhaled and held his breath until he was safely at the top of the stairs. 'I'll be in touch,' he said, his mouth dry.

She smiled and swung the door shut gently.

As Scamarcio made his way to the squadroom, the spring sunshine burning through his damp shirt, he spun back through the conversation in his head. Could he really take her words at face value? Was she interested in *him*, or was she just trying to use him, like she used everyone else? Wasn't he simply another means to an end? He stopped at a bar and ordered a cappuccino in the hope of settling his thoughts. As he drained the cup, he realised that he really didn't know what to make of Fiammetta di Bondi. She confused him, but now he couldn't stop thinking about her.

28

'SEARCH HIS HOUSE AGAIN, search the parliament. We need Manfredi's evidence, whatever it is,' said Garramone, as if Scamarcio was unable to work this out for himself.

'Stasio is tight-lipped. He's been around the block too many times to say anything incriminating.'

Garramone took a breath and fixed him with a stare. 'So you were really unable to find out any more about him? You were so confident.' He sounded more disappointed than angry.

'I didn't expect to have every door slam in my face. People seem really scared.'

'That's worrying.'

'And Proietti?'

'The team at his place thinks he'll be in hospital with cirrhosis of the liver before this inquiry is out. The man's falling apart before our eyes. We need to sort this, and sort it quickly.'

'And no more communications from the kidnappers?'

'Nada.'

Scamarcio said nothing for a moment, mulling it over. 'On the wiretap you played me, Stasio said he had a plan. Do you think he's put it into action, and that's why we've heard nothing more? Perhaps he's made contact with the kidnappers, made them some kind of offer?'

'OK, but then why is Proietti falling apart?'

'Because he doesn't know. Stasio said he wasn't going to share the plan—he doesn't trust Proietti not to tell us.'

Garramone nodded and took a sip from a large cup of coffee.

'I've got a bad feeling about this,' he said eventually.

'Why's that?' asked Scamarcio, although he already knew exactly what he meant.

'Because it feels like we're working in the dark, as if the power has been taken from us. And whenever that happens in a kidnapping, it never ends well.'

On his way to the Manfredis, Scamarcio thought about what Garramone had said. Stasio, too, was labouring in the dark, perhaps dealing with forces well beyond his control. But could events down in Calabria have an impact on this inquiry? Now Piocosta had been assassinated, where would this leave the Rome operation? Would his footsoldiers give up every last spit and cough to Greco? Was it possible that, in the confusion of the transition of power, Proietti's debt might be wiped—that the kidnapping could be forgotten? Scamarcio did not know enough about how Greco ran his operations to understand whether this was probable. For a moment, he felt tempted to call him and discuss the case, to ask him to stand down Piocosta's former team and bring home the Proiettis. Yet, another part of him knew that this was the road to ruin. He'd simply be repeating the mistakes of the past, mistakes that had brought him to Greco's door. No, they had to go their separate ways. Piocosta's slaying had to be the beginning and the end of their contact.

Scamarcio pulled up outside Manfredi's apartment and killed the engine. He sat staring into space for several moments before closing his eyes and leaning back against the headrest. Events in Catanzaro had unsettled him—had left a rip in his heart and acid in his stomach. Now he just wanted to forget, to kill the memory and put an end to the exhausting churning in his mind. He sighed and reached for the door handle. It was a relief to be here on this nondescript street, to have work to do. He needed the distraction.

He'd decided to start with a search of Manfredi's place first, because he couldn't face a head-to-head with Max Romano at the parliament, and only wanted to fight that battle when there were no alternatives.

'Did your husband ever work from home? Did he have an office?' he asked Mrs Manfredi once they'd exchanged pleasantries.

'He has a small study next to the kitchen — *had* a small study.' She looked down at the floor for a moment. When she looked up, she asked: 'Do you think you'll have a case for murder? Is there enough?'

Scamarcio felt guilty that he hadn't called her to bring her up to speed. 'I think you were right. There are signs of third-party involvement, and it's enough to rule out suicide. The reason I'm here is that I'm looking for evidence that might help confirm the identity of the killer and explain his motives.'

'Can you give me any ideas about who is behind this, Detective?'

He was about to answer when a tall young woman entered the hallway from a side room. She was wearing striped pyjamas, and one of those airline eye masks was pushed back on the top of her long blonde hair. The daughter, figured Scamarcio, although she looked quite different from the earlier photos he'd seen. She laid a hand across her mother's shoulder and studied him with concern.

'If I'm honest, I'd prefer to do that once I'm sure. Is that OK with you?' he said.

Mrs Manfredi nodded, and the daughter looked even more worried. Scamarcio introduced himself and gave his condolences. She smiled tiredly, but said nothing.

'I'll take you to his study,' said Mrs Manfredi, leading him by the elbow.

When she'd shut the door and left him to it, Scamarcio began pulling out the thin drawers of Manfredi's antique desk. It was the only antique item in the room — everything else looked as if it came from Ikea or Savings World. He removed one drawer after the next, laying them next to each other on the ground, but he couldn't find anything of interest — it was all household bills, tax forms, and energy contracts. He scanned the room for a filing cabinet but, besides the desk, there wasn't any other storage furniture. He noticed a couple of Polaroid photographs pinned to the wall of Manfredi's twins when they were small.

Scamarcio carefully replaced all the drawers, his heart sinking with the realisation that he'd probably have to extend the search to Manfredi's office at the ministry. Max Romano would no doubt relish every moment of making life as difficult as possible for him. Would he make him come back with a warrant? No doubt. Would he instruct Manfredi's staff not to speak to him? Of course.

Scamarcio rose from the floor and headed back to Mrs Manfredi, refusing to give up quite yet.

'Would you mind if I checked your husband's …' Scamarcio stopped dead as he entered the kitchen, his brain struggling to process the scene before him. It was as if he'd been winded. Mrs Manfredi appeared to be locked in what could only be described as a romantic embrace with her daughter. *What the hell?* he whispered. Up until now, he'd deemed the Manfredis the most normal of the people he'd encountered in the course of his investigation.

'Er, Mrs Manfredi?' He tried to keep his tone light.

'There's no need to fret,' said Mrs Manfredi, pulling away primly and rearranging her blouse. 'She's not my daughter. You've got the wrong end of the stick.'

'Er, who is she then?' asked Scamarcio, hoping to hell that he didn't need to turn this investigation on its head. There just wasn't the time.

'She's a friend.' Mrs Manfredi sniffed, and walked over to the work surface, where she took a shaky sip of coffee. The other woman surveyed Scamarcio with a look that bordered on contempt now.

'I, well, well, like I told you, Gianluca and I, our lives diverged at some point, and they never really found their way back together again.'

Scamarcio couldn't think of a response. The best he could come up with was: 'I see.'

She frowned. 'I know what you're thinking, but don't worry, you don't need to factor this in. I just needed some comfort. It has no bearing on my husband's murder.'

'But hadn't you and Mr Manfredi just booked a holiday together? It sounded like you were trying to make a go of it.'

The other woman looked surprised by this news, and turned to Mrs Manfredi for explanation.

Mrs Manfredi reddened. 'That was for our children's benefit. But, like I say, don't let this confuse you. Things remain the same. I had no motive for killing my husband, Detective.'

Although he couldn't permit himself to take her word for it, Scamarcio believed her.

He sighed and said: 'Can you show me your husband's closet? I need to take a look inside.'

She nodded and hurried from the kitchen, the other woman's eyes tracking her. 'Follow me.'

As Scamarcio began pulling Manfredi's shoes from the drawers beneath his wardrobe, he ran through the conversation he'd have to have with Mrs Manfredi. How long had she been seeing this woman? Had she been thinking about leaving her husband? Was she considering divorce, etc etc …? It was as if this investigation was adding new layers by the day, making it harder and harder for the light to penetrate.

Scamarcio laid out the shoes in front of him. Manfredi's tastes were conservative; there was very little colour on display, but they all looked surprisingly new and expensive. When Scamarcio checked inside, the labels confirmed it: there were a pair of brown brogues from Tods, black evening shoes from Ferragamo, tan deck shoes from Hogan.

'Mrs Manfredi,' he shouted.

After a few moments, she peered around the door. It looked as if she'd been crying.

'I'm sorry to disturb you again,' said Scamarcio. 'It's just …' He held up one of the brogues. 'These shoes all seem quite new and rather pricey. I'm a little surprised, given what you told me about Mr Manfredi's attitude to money. I rather got the impression that most of it went on your children—that he didn't spend much on himself.'

She nodded sadly and took a seat on the edge of the bed.

'You're right to ask. It all changed a bit—a few months ago now. I think it must have coincided with when he started seeing the showgirl.'

'He started spending on himself?'

'Yes. I found some things in his closet—new shirts, a couple of new suits. When I asked him about it, he became quite defensive. At first I thought it was some kind of midlife crisis. Then, when I found out about di Bondi, it all started to make sense.'

'How much new stuff did he buy?'

'Well, a lot at first, then, after I challenged him, that seemed to be the end of it. I didn't find any new purchases after that.'

Scamarcio scratched his head. 'I saw him wearing some very expensive-looking gold and emerald cufflinks when I met him at the parliament.'

Mrs Manfredi's mouth turned down. 'Did you? I don't think he has any like that.'

She rose from the bed tiredly and crossed to the other side, where she pulled out a drawer on the bedside table. She took out a series of small jewellery boxes, and opened them. 'These are his cufflinks,' she said.

Scamarcio got up from the floor and walked around to take a

look. The cufflinks he'd seen on Manfredi that day weren't there.

How strange, he thought. In the next instant, he wondered if Manfredi had been keeping his spending spree from his wife — whether he'd been hiding his shopping in his office at the ministry.

'You know,' said Mrs Manfredi. 'My daughter told me the other day that Gianluca had asked her if she was in a position to lend him some money. She's just started a new job with a law firm in New York, but rents are exorbitant, and she doesn't have much spare. She'd told him she couldn't help just yet, but that she would do as soon as it became possible. He'd sworn her to secrecy; he didn't want me to know.'

Scamarcio wondered if this was significant, or whether he was just looking at the symptoms of a middle-aged man's obsession with a woman half his age.

Mrs Manfredi seemed to read his confusion. 'I don't think the money's a big deal, Detective. It was tight when he died; we were still paying off the twins' education. I think Gianluca just overstretched himself trying to impress that girl.' She tilted her head to one side and shrugged. 'Who can blame him? All those years never spending on yourself; it's hardly surprising that at some point you're going to want to kick back, indulge yourself a bit.'

Scamarcio nodded, again wondering at the calm acceptance of Mrs Manfredi.

'Shall I leave you to it then?' she asked.

'Yes, thank you, Mrs Manfredi.'

She shut the door gently, and he remained perched on the end of the bed, staring at Manfredi's shoes as if they held the key to everything. Scamarcio reflected on how nothing in this case was what it seemed. He wished he could just smash through all the layers and pull out the truth. He was tired, and he wanted this over with.

He reached back into the closet to check that he hadn't missed anything, and took out a pair of Adidas running shoes he'd overlooked the first time. He laid them on the floor and felt around inside. He stopped. His hand had come up against something hard and smooth. He fished it out and held it up to the light. It was a white, rectangular object with a cap—a standard USB key. He turned it over in his palm a few times, examining it. Then he reached for his jacket and took out the keys to his car.

'I've left something downstairs. I won't be a moment,' he shouted to Mrs Manfredi as he passed the kitchen.

'Ok, you can let yourself out—the door's unlocked.'

Once he was safely in his car, he lifted his tablet from the glove box. He waited a few moments for it to boot up, and then inserted the USB key. He'd been expecting documents or photographs, but after a few seconds the video icon appeared, offering him the option to press play.

He glanced around him a couple of times, but the street was empty. He started the film.

It looked as if the video had been shot inside parliament— the place had a similar feel to Max Romano's study. Manfredi was seated behind a desk, and Proietti was across from him. Both had thin crystal glasses of what looked like prosecco in front of them. Scamarcio heard distant laughter, and wondered if the film had been taken at a government bash. From the angle, his guess was that Manfredi had pre-positioned his laptop on a side table to capture any conversation.

'You've got the world at your feet, Micky,' Manfredi was saying. 'You're quite the star.' His tone was friendly and warm—it didn't sound as if there was any tension there.

The laptop camera was only capturing Proietti's right profile, and he was several metres away, but Scamarcio thought he looked downcast.

'Thing is, Gianluca, I've got myself in a bit of a scrape.'

Manfredi's forehead bunched with concern, but to Scamarcio it looked staged.

'Sorry to hear that. Anything I can do to help?' asked the culture secretary, amiably enough.

'You know that money …'

Manfredi leant back in his chair as if he suddenly wanted to put as much distance as possible between himself and Proietti. He steepled his hands before his chest, but said nothing for a moment. Then: 'I can't do it Micky, not yet. You need to give me more time—I'm still paying for the twins' university.'

'There's no time left, Gianluca. I've run out.'

Proietti's voice was shaky; he sounded like a man on the verge of collapse. Scamarcio noticed that his right foot was jiggling up and down.

Manfredi ran a nervous hand through his hair. 'I don't know what to tell you, Micky. I don't have it. I can't just click my fingers and make it appear.'

Proietti leant forward. There was a sharpness to the set of his features now. 'Manfredi, if you don't pay up, I'll be forced to make things extremely difficult for you.'

'What's that supposed to mean?'

Proietti sat back in his chair, but said nothing.

'Listen, if you tell me what your problem is, I'll try to work out how we can sort it,' said Manfredi quickly. 'I'll try to come up with something.'

Proietti stroked down his trouser leg; his foot stopped moving finally. 'That's more like it, Gianluca.'

'So, this scrape?'

'I owe money to some people—the kind of people who don't take no for an answer. The kind it's usually best to avoid.'

'What, Stasio's kind?'

Proietti nodded.

'He's bad news, Micky.'

'I know.'

'How come you owe them?'

'One of my vices ran away with me.'

'You've been hitting the tables?'

Proietti hung his head slightly. 'Yeah.'

Manfredi sighed. 'Oh God, Micky, you need to get a grip on that.'

'Yeah.'

'And Stasio can't help?'

Proietti reached forward for his prosecco and downed it in one. 'You got any more of this?'

Manfredi rose from behind the desk and left the frame for a moment. Then he was back with a silver-necked bottle. He refilled Proietti's glass, and he drained it immediately.

'Stasio's associates were giving us money they needed ...' He paused for a moment. 'Well, how can I put it, money they needed *legitimised*,' said Proietti, slurring slightly now. 'I creamed a little off the top, started using it for the tables, to smooth out a few problems at work ...'

'Work—how the hell does work come into it?' asked Manfredi, returning to his seat.

'Like you say, I'm the golden boy; it's hard to maintain that. Sometimes you need a bit of ...' He stopped for a moment, reaching for the word again: '*extra padding*.'

'Don't tell me you used their cash for your shows, Micky. That would be fucking madness.' Manfredi was trying to sound incredulous, but Scamarcio had the feeling he already knew; that he was just hoping to get Proietti to commit it all to record.

'Well, I guess I am mad, aren't I?' The slur in Proietti's voice was becoming more marked. 'That's what you all say.'

'We call you the mad genius, Micky. That's quite different from being outright crazy, with a deathwish to boot.' Manfredi paused, then said: 'Fuck, I can't believe you were gambling away their cash in front of them. You're on the road to hell this time. Does Stasio know?'

'Some of it, but not the full extent.'

Manfredi bit down on his bottom lip. 'Jesus, I worry for you, Micky, I really do.'

'Then get me that money.' Proietti leant forward, placing his glass precariously close to the edge of the table. 'Way I see it, you're obliged to help me.'

'I'm thinking, I'm thinking.' Manfredi got up from his chair and started pacing, a fist at his mouth. He walked nearer to the laptop — careful, though, not to obscure its view of Proietti. 'What do you reckon they'll do, these associates of Stasio? If you don't pay up, I mean?'

Proietti rubbed a shaky thumb across his lips. 'I don't want to think about it.'

'Hmm,' said Manfredi.

'So, do you have any ideas — any ideas about how I'm going to come out of this with both legs intact?'

'Perhaps,' said Manfredi, quickly. 'But I'll need a couple of days.'

With that, Manfredi moved slowly towards the laptop and eased it shut, his eyes on Proietti all the while.

As he drove, Scamarcio started to dial Garramone, high on his discovery. But before the call could connect, the display on his phone came to life, and the squadroom number flashed up.

'We've got a body,' said Garramone quietly.

Scamarcio blinked. He wondered if he'd misheard. 'Sorry, boss, can you repeat that?'

'We've got a fucking body, Scamarcio.' The words were too loud, and Scamarcio had to hold the phone away from his ear for a moment. He had rarely heard Garramone lose his composure like this.

'Where?'

'Outside Proietti's. It's the wife — she's been shot through the lung.'

Scamarcio took a breath. This made no sense; it was so far from what they'd been expecting, it simply wasn't possible. 'What the fuck?' he whispered. Then: 'Is she alive?'

'No.'

'They killed her?' He couldn't process it.

'We've fucked up.'

'I'm heading to Proietti's now.'

'I'll see you there.'

There were at least twenty officers and around ten CSIs on the thin strip of grass outside Proietti's apartment block. A junior officer was erecting a cordon to prevent the tight knot of neighbours from pushing in any closer and trampling the scene.

Scamarcio spied the chief CSI, Manetti, stooped over a twisted form at the edge of the lawn. The body's right arm was extended, while the left was bent strangely at the elbow. The wrongness of the angle turned Scamarcio's stomach. As he drew nearer, he saw that Maia Proietti's eyes were closed. Apart from the beginnings of a blueish tinge to her skin and the disquieting lie of her limbs, she could easily have been sleeping. With her long, blonde hair fanned out beneath her, her delicate, arched eyebrows, and sharp cheekbones, she reminded him of a fairytale queen in repose. He pictured her ghostly face trapped beneath a sheet of ice, its ephemeral beauty finally captured, frozen in time.

'She was thrown from a moving vehicle,' said Manetti by way of hello. 'This bruising on the arms is post-mortem.'

He pulled up the sleeves of the man's coat that Maia Proietti was wearing, and showed Scamarcio the bluey-grey patches of skin.

'Garramone said she was shot.'

'Yeah, single bullet through the lung. Strange choice. I don't know why they didn't just go for the heart.'

'Maybe it wasn't an expert shot.'

'Or they didn't mean to shoot her,' said Manetti, looking up at him, his eyes full of meaning.

'You think it could have been a mistake?' asked Scamarcio.

'Might have been — I can't see any other kind of wounding, and it's only one shot. If they'd wanted to kill her and only got the lung, they'd try again, surely?'

'Good point.' Scamarcio thought it through for a moment. 'Couldn't she have survived a shot through the lung?'

'Yeah, if she'd received medical attention quickly enough. From a first look, I'd say she bled out. But I'll let you know for sure in a few hours.'

Scamarcio nodded. 'Why didn't they take her to hospital, I wonder?'

'Perhaps they were too scared.'

'Yeah, but they could have just dumped her outside A and E. These two things don't add up — not meaning to shoot her, but then not doing anything about it.'

'Well, we don't know for certain that it wasn't intentional — I'll need some time with it.'

'When did this happen?'

'Scamarcio, hold your horses.' Manetti sighed. 'I need to get her on the table for that.'

'No, I mean when was the body thrown here?'

'About forty minutes ago, but your boys will be able to give you the spit and cough.'

Scamarcio thanked him and turned to look for Garramone. Then, after a beat, he swung back around. 'Can you see if you can lift any prints off the coat she's wearing?'

'Of course,' said Manetti in a *Don't teach your grandmother to suck eggs* tone.

What was eating him, Scamarcio wondered. Perhaps this death had got to him. Probably, given there was also a little boy involved.

He felt a grip on his arm. Garramone had come up alongside him. 'Proietti is a jibbering wreck,' he said. 'He's convinced the son will be next.'

'I guess that's what we're all thinking,' said Scamarcio.

'Chief Mancino is heading down here now.'

'Way I see it, Stasio decided to take matters into his own hands, and it all went tits up. Is he still at the villa?'

'We lost him.'

'What the fuck.' Scamarcio kicked at a piece of rubble on the grass, which set other stones tumbling.

'Careful,' said Manetti, helpfully. 'Could be evidence.'

'The tap went dead, and when we went to investigate, there was nobody inside. Our guys on the outside didn't see him leave,' said Garramone.

'Shit.'

'He's gone to ground. I reckon he sees himself as the lone warrior now.'

Garramone spotted something to his right and grimaced. When Scamarcio followed his gaze, he saw a white satellite truck pulling up at the kerb, marked with the Sky TG24 logo. A young man jumped out and walked around the back to open the doors. After a moment, numerous silver boxes began appearing on the pavement.

'How did they find out so fast?' hissed Garramone.

'This area is full of media professionals.'

'Great,' sighed Garramone, his eyes moving off to the right once more. 'It just gets better.'

Chief Mancino's Panther was pulling up behind the truck. After half a minute, the boss of bosses emerged, trying hard to keep his long grey overcoat clear of the drains.

'Come with me,' said Garramone, striding towards the car.

Scamarcio took a breath and followed.

Chief Mancino, ever the political operator, had already

spotted the TV crew. Scamarcio watched him recompose his initially furious expression into something more measured, observed him tame an unruly eyebrow and smooth down his thick, dark hair.

'Garramone,' hissed the chief under his breath. 'This is a mess. How the hell did we get here?'

'We believe this is the result of the victim's brother trying to take matters into his own hands.'

'And how on earth was he able to do that?'

'We had him under surveillance,' Garramone paused. 'But we lost him, Sir.'

'That's not acceptable.'

Garramone said nothing.

'We can't have another murder.' Mancino's blue eyes had shrivelled to nothing.

'I understand.'

'So—next steps?'

'We're doing our very best to locate the brother.'

'And the kidnappers?'

'We're following up some final leads.'

'Still nothing from the motorway CCTV?'

'Nothing.'

'That's impossible. We must have missed something. Go through your final sightings again. Check and double check.'

Scamarcio saw Garramone's shoulders sag beneath his jacket. He knew he would have done this already. But the mention of the CCTV was triggering something for Scamarcio: he thought back to the video of Maia Proietti, and remembered that it had bothered him, but that he wasn't sure why. He still didn't understand the significance of his doubts, but instinct was telling him that the TV angle couldn't be ignored: that it could be foolish to write off this kidnapping as a purely Calabrian matter now.

He cleared his throat. 'Actually, there is something, Sir, but until now we haven't pursued it, due to the legwork required.'

'Tell me,' barked Mancino.

'There *is* CCTV footage of four people claiming to be a TV crew who used some studios at the location where we traced a call from the kidnappers. Proietti claimed not to know them, so we didn't follow it up. When Stasio's Calabrian connections came to the fore, we concentrated on those, but it may now be time to return our attention to Proietti's television work. I'd like to send some officers around to the television companies Proietti does business with, and try to identify the four people from the CCTV.'

'But if you traced the call to the studios, they should have been investigated immediately.'

'As I say, our focus was the Calabrian connection. There were a number of people using the location that day, and the call could have been made by any one of them. It could also have been made by someone who had simply pulled up outside and never entered the lot. It felt like too much of a long shot.'

'Well, it seems as if long shots are all we have left to work with. Do it — I'll give you what you need.'

'Scamarcio, how can we rule out the Calabrian angle, given the wiretaps we have of Stasio?' asked Garramone. 'It sounds like Proietti had run up debts; we have video evidence of him confessing as much to Manfredi.'

'What I'm saying, Sir, is that it's possible that there are two explanations for this kidnapping, and that they may well co-exist.'

'Meaning?'

'I don't have the finer details yet, but I really think we need to go back to that CCTV and track down those four people.'

Mancino was studying him carefully. 'Just get me a result. I need something to throw to the lions.' He cast a furious eye towards a blonde TV reporter who was now standing next to the cordon, adjusting a wire behind her ear. 'Up until now these kidnappers have run rings around us. We need to start hitting back. We need to stop looking like a bunch of fuckwits.'

29

'RIGHT, HERE YOU GO,' panted Sartori, shuffling towards him with a stack of photographic paper. 'I'm about to distribute them to the officers. I'll need your list.'

Scamarcio handed over several sheets of paper detailing the names and addresses of the production companies Proietti did business with.

'You can cross GD Films off that,' said Scamarcio, taking a printout of the CCTV picture. 'I've already met the mad Mr Giacometti who runs it, and I feel like paying him another visit. It'll provide some light relief.' He rubbed a tired hand across his mouth. 'We're clear on our officers going in at the same time? We don't want any of these places tipping each other off.'

'It will all be synched. They will be entering at 11.00 am on the dot.'

'That's when I'll be paying Giacometti a visit then.'

Sartori jabbed a thumb through the doorway, towards Micky Proietti hunched up in his armchair. It looked as if Proietti was trying to return to the foetal position. 'Did you get anywhere?'

Scamarcio shook his head. 'Nothing. He claims to have no idea about who might have killed his wife.'

'Do you think he's telling the truth?'

'I dunno. On the Stasio wiretap, it sounds like he believes the Calabrians have taken his family. But weirdly, when I was with him last night, I got the impression that he really isn't that sure anymore.'

'Hmm … What *about* Stasio? What's our friend saying on that?'

'He just won't go there. Same goes for the conversation with Manfredi on the USB.'

'But doesn't Proietti realise that all this could help us find his son?'

'He's scared, I think, like a rabbit caught in headlights. Even if he's no longer sure about the Calabrians being involved, he's still shitting himself.'

'What could be scarier than the Calabrians?'

'God knows. But these doubts of his are wearing him down, confusing him.'

'So how do we get past all that? Can't we haul him in? Charge him with obstruction or something?'

Scamarcio shook his head. 'Garramone thinks that'll be counter-productive, and I tend to agree. We need to break Proietti, make him realise that it's time to let go, time to let us handle it. But if the death of his wife isn't enough to convince him of that, God knows …'

Scamarcio glanced at Proietti once more. He was sitting up now, trying to pour himself a scotch from a decanter. His hands were shaking, and he was spilling a vast quantity of whisky down the front of his jeans.

Sartori tutted at the sorry spectacle. 'Will he be OK?'

'Not until he gets his son back. The man's guilt-ridden. Says it's time to change his life, devote himself to his kid.'

'He could start by being straight with us.'

'I tried that. All he said was that if his boy comes home, he'll be taking him abroad. He wants to get out of Rome, leave it all behind.'

'Hmm … can't see his debtors agreeing to that one.'

A thought resurfaced in Scamarcio's mind. It was the second time today. But he pushed it aside and checked his watch. 'Right, off we go then — we've got two hours to distribute the pictures and get across town. I'm going to grab some breakfast first.'

'Lucky you,' said Sartori.

'I didn't sleep last night. While you were comfortably tucked up in bed, I was playing nursemaid to Proietti.'

Sartori raised both palms. 'All right, calm down. No one's going to snitch on you.'

Scamarcio wondered how Giacometti would react to him searching his premises for potential kidnappers. Knowing how off-centre the man appeared to be, it was possible that he might actually enjoy it.

Scamarcio glanced at the picture of the TV crew again, and continued his climb of the stairs leading to the offices of GD Films. The elevator was out of order, which was precisely what he didn't need after being up all night with Proietti sobbing into his shoulder.

Uninvited, an image of Fiammetta di Bondi came up to his mind. Yet again, he asked himself if she was just a troubled girl desperate to accumulate wealth, or whether there was genuinely more to her. The way she told it, she was trapped by her circumstances, but working hard to free herself and build a career she cared about. If this version of her life was true, what was so very wrong with it? If she'd found a way to get where she wanted, who could sit in judgement? He tried to push these thoughts aside, but then felt a fresh stab of guilt as he pictured Aurelia and her new life in Munich. He'd tried to contact her to explain the switch in security, but it seemed that she was still avoiding him. The way she saw it, he'd ruined her life, and the last thing she wanted was to hear from him.

Scamarcio sighed and tried to drag his thoughts back to the investigation. He continued the endless climb — it felt as if Giacometti's block had the longest staircase in Rome. He was rounding yet another corner when a young, dark-haired woman wearing thick-framed spectacles almost mowed him down. 'Sorry,' she mumbled, bounding down the stairs two at a time.

'Watch it,' he shouted behind him, anger flaring.

He climbed a few more steps, then stopped and turned. Jesus, he was a fucking idiot. He knew that girl — he'd seen her before, and recently at that. He hadn't made the connection because of the glasses.

He swung around and sprinted back down the stairs. 'Hey, you, stop!'

Several floors below him, he heard the heavy front door release and then swing back shut with a thud. He reached the ground floor in seconds, jamming the buzzer and prising the door back open. He scanned right and left down the busy street — once, twice, three times — but he couldn't find the girl anywhere in the crowd. It was as if she'd evaporated into nothing.

He reached for his mobile and called base, reeling off a description and requesting that all units in the area keep an eye out, although he knew the chances of finding her were slim. Would she just show up again at work? Could he count on that? Somehow he doubted it.

He began his long climb of the stairs once more, cursing himself for being so slow, so spectacularly unobservant for a detective. When he finally made it to Giacometti's floor, he shoved the glass door angrily, looking around for someone to shout at. A young man was hurrying past, clutching a white iPhone.

'Excuse me,' said Scamarcio, grabbing him by the arm, probably harder than was necessary.

The boy swung around, alarmed. 'Yes?' he said, hesitantly.

'Is Giacometti in?'

'No, he's on a shoot up in Trieste. He'll be away until Monday.' The boy looked down at his arm, and Scamarcio released his grip slightly.

Scamarcio was infuriated by Giacometti's absence, but in the next instant he wondered whether the fact that he was away was actually no bad thing. He drew out the sheet of photographic paper and showed it to the boy. 'Do you know this girl?'

The boy took the photo and studied it, his lips forming a thin frown. 'Er, yes, of course. That's Chiara.'

'Chiara?'

'Chiara Bellagamba — she works here.' The boy frowned some more. 'And you are?'

Scamarcio pulled out his badge. The boy took a quick look and said: 'Is Chiara OK? Has something happened to her? She only just left …'

'No, she's all right. Is there a place we can talk?'

'I think I should get one of the execs in — I'm quite junior and …'

Scamarcio placed a firm hand on his shoulder. 'I'd really rather talk to you for now. We'll bring in the bosses afterwards.'

The boy nodded nervously, and led Scamarcio towards a long meeting room with opaque glass windows. They stepped inside, and Scamarcio saw that the far wall was lined with various framed posters and publicity campaigns for what he presumed were Giacometti's shows. He drew out a seat at a plastic table.

'Can I get you a coffee, Detective, water?'

'No, I'm fine. So, Chiara?'

The boy seemed on edge, but Scamarcio sensed this was more because he was worried about upsetting the management. The lad kept scanning the corridor outside, and rose hurriedly to his feet a couple of times before sitting back down again.

'She works here, you say?'

'She's a researcher, like me. We started on the same day — we've both been here a year now.'

'What's she like?'

'Chiara? Well, she's good, very good, very ambitious, one of the most ambitious people I know, actually. The bosses really like her.' He paused for a moment. 'Word is, she'll make producer soon.' He didn't sound that happy about it.

'What kind of projects does she work on?'

'She's been up in Trieste with Giacometti a lot on the *Autumn of our Lives* series.'

'*Autumn of our Lives*? Who's that for?'

'Channel One. It will be the centrepiece of their autumn schedule.' The young man cleared his throat. 'Detective, can I get one of the bosses in now? I don't want to ...'

'What's going on here?' said a gravelly female voice from somewhere out in the corridor.

Scamarcio turned to see a handsome woman in her fifties standing in the doorway, one hand resting proprietarily on the doorframe. She had perfectly coifed highlighted hair and sinewy, tanned calves. She was immaculately dressed in a beige skirt and jacket, with a cream bow blouse on which was resting a long string of pearls. A pair of bright red-and-orange glasses were perched on the top of her head, pinning back her luxuriant hair. All Scamarcio could think of at this precise moment was that her glasses didn't quite match her suit.

He rose to shake her hand. 'I'm Detective Leone Scamarcio from the flying squad. I was asking your researcher some questions in relation to an inquiry. This young man kept insisting I talk to you first, so don't hold it against him.'

'So why didn't you?'

'Why didn't I what?'

'Talk to me first.'

'I needed a quick answer to a quick question.'

The woman's hardened gaze seemed to relax slightly. She smiled thinly at the boy. 'I could never be annoyed with Simo. He's one of my best.'

The boy looked down into his lap, a flush of red making its way up his neck.

'So can I ask what this is about?' she said, pinning Scamarcio with a stare. He had the feeling that she was the dealmaker of this company, and a consummate ballbreaker.

'It's the Proietti inquiry.'

'Really?' Her face became a furrow. 'But how can Simo help with that? I don't think he's ever met Micky.' She turned to the boy. 'Have you met Micky?'

The boy shook his head quickly.

'But *you* have, I imagine?' asked Scamarcio.

'Of course. Me and Micky go back a long way.'

A doubt surfaced in Scamarcio's mind. 'Did Mr Giacometti mention that I'd visited him?'

'No. When was this?'

'A few days ago now.'

'No.' She paused for a moment. 'He didn't.' She seemed to be thinking something through. 'Paolo's been very busy lately. I guess it must have slipped his mind.' Even she didn't sound convinced.

Scamarcio was beginning to detect the faintest outline of something; a form was starting to emerge, but its contours remained unclear. He told himself to stay alert.

'OK, thanks, you can go now,' he said to the boy.

The boy rose hurriedly to his feet and scurried out, seemingly desperate to get away.

The woman took a seat in a leather chair next to Scamarcio and carefully crossed her legs, smoothing down her pearls against the bow as she did so. 'My name's Diana Delaney, by the way, but you can call me Didi. I'm Paolo Giacometti's business partner.' She adjusted her hemline. 'So what were you asking Simo?'

'Delaney? That's not an Italian name.'

'English father, Italian mother. I grew up in Rome, though, so I'm Italian through and through.'

Scamarcio nodded, and handed her the picture of the girl. After she'd studied it for a few seconds, she said: 'How does Chiara fit into this?'

He filled her in on the kidnappers' call from the studio and the four people captured on the CCTV. When he'd finished, Delaney said: 'Forgive me, Detective. I'm sure you know how to do your job, and I know you guys must be desperate after what happened to Micky's wife, but it seems to me that you're clutching at straws.'

Scamarcio ignored her. 'Have you and Giacometti worked together long?'

She turned in the chair so her body was angled more tightly towards him. 'We started this company 25 years ago now, although sometimes it feels like 25 days.'

'You're doing very well, from what I hear.'

'We are,' she said breezily. 'We've put in a lot of hard work, but we've also had a fair bit of luck. Of course, you need both for a business to succeed.'

'Do you often make programmes for Micky Proietti?'

'He usually commissions his big projects from us — his centrepiece series.'

'So you have a good relationship?'

He saw a cloud cross her face before she tried to correct it. 'Yes, we do …'

'I sense a "but" …'

She coughed, then said: 'If I'm to be honest, our latest venture has not been going that well. Micky isn't happy with it — he's fired the director, and has brought in his own people.'

'That must be pretty frustrating.'

'It's challenging, but I was sure we'd get through it. I know Micky — I thought he was just having a panic.'

'What does Mr Giacometti say?'

'Oh, Paolo feels the same way. We've learned to put up with Micky over the years, ride out his tantrums. In the end, he always comes back to us.'

'And you and Mr Giacometti are on good terms? You get along?'

'Oh, of course — it wouldn't work otherwise. We're great friends.'

'That must make for a positive working environment.'

'Oh, yes. We have our bad patches, of course. Paolo can throw his toys out of the pram on occasion. He's the creative in the partnership, so I put up with it.'

Scamarcio said nothing for a moment while he cast around for the right phrase. After a beat, he said: 'I must say, I found Mr Giacometti a little eccentric.'

Delaney snorted. 'Paolo does the mad-genius act pretty well, but underneath it all he's a steely operator. Don't be fooled — he might be the creative, but he has an excellent business brain when he wants to.'

'He must have to have helped you make this company such a success.'

'Yes, but we also have Paolo's boyfriend to thank for that. He's our CFO. He's been excellent at ensuring we never grew too quickly, didn't overstretch ourselves. That can be crucial for a business at the beginning.'

'Have they been together long?'

Scamarcio wasn't really sure why he'd asked this, but some instinct was nudging him down this road.

Delaney's forehead bunched in surprise. 'Almost ten years now, but, sadly, they're about to split.'

'Oh?'

She sighed and pushed the strange glasses higher up her head. 'This is of zero relevance to your inquiry, but Paolo doesn't know how to keep it in his pants. It's a crying shame, because his partner is the loveliest man you could hope to meet. I wish *I* could find a man like that.' She looked down, and Scamarcio sensed she'd immediately regretted saying it. He wondered suddenly if she'd been having an affair with Micky Proietti. Chiara Bellagamba, the researcher, worked for her as well as Giacometti, surely?

238

So the lead from the studio lot came back to Delaney, as well as to Giacometti. In theory, it made sense; but looking at Delaney now, he didn't get the sense that she was romantically involved with Micky Proietti. She didn't seem emotionally invested — perhaps in the past, but not now.

'Paolo has met someone else, so it's all very nasty and complicated,' Delaney added quickly. 'The new guy is in the public eye, so that makes it even trickier.'

'Who is he, this new guy?' asked Scamarcio, his instincts about Giacometti still needling him.

She sighed and shook her head. 'In all my years of friendship with Paolo, he's never kept a secret from me, but this time he just won't tell. I can honestly say I have absolutely no idea. Frankly, it's driving me mad.' She fell silent, then said: 'Why all these questions about Paolo? There's no way he could have anything to do with this. I mean, we're talking about a murder now.'

Scamarcio tuned her out. He sat back in his chair and ran his fingers across his forehead. He sensed that there *was* something here: the form was drawing nearer, its outline gaining definition. But he didn't know how to give it breath, bring it to life.

Diana Delaney had claimed that she didn't recognise any of the other faces on the photo from the CCTV. And a tour of Giacometti's offices had confirmed it. Unfortunately, none of the searches at the other production companies had produced a result either. Delaney had assured Scamarcio that if Chiara Bellagamba showed, she'd contact him immediately. She'd provided him with an address for her, but when he'd tried the bell, there was nobody home.

Scamarcio was weighing up the value of a trip to Trieste to speak with Giacometti. But, after brief consideration, he pushed the idea aside, telling himself that he wasn't even certain to find the producer there. When he'd called the crew shooting in the city, they claimed not to have seen Giacometti for 48 hours. His Rome staff might have believed he was up north, but the possibility remained that he'd stayed down in the capital. If there was the smallest chance he was somehow tied up in the business with Proietti, he'd need an excuse for staying away from the office, and Trieste would provide that.

Scamarcio decided that the best thing he could do for the moment was to have a word with Giacometti's soon-to-be ex. On his way to the address in Trastevere, he called Garramone to update him.

'But this vague outline of an idea, as you call it, I don't really follow how it hangs together,' said the boss after he was done.

'The girl on the CCTV from the studios works for Giacometti, so that's the first point of contact, the first link. The second element is that Giacometti is secretly involved with a VIP — that might also prove significant.'

'Or it might not.'

'It's another potential connection to Rome's showbiz set.'

'A flimsy connection.'

'But what else have we got to go on right now? Where are we with Stasio, for starters?'

'Nowhere,' sighed Garramone. 'Fucking nowhere.'

'Exactly — let me chase this one down, see if it brings us any further.'

'Chief Mancino's got the team going back through all the CCTV from the motorway,' said Garramone, sounding as if his heart was breaking at the wasted budget.

'Politics.'

'He wants Forensics to sweep that studio lot again.'

'But Manetti didn't find anything the first time! And God knows who's been in there since.'

'I know.'

'He might just as well have set fire to a huge bundle of cash.'

'Call me if you get anywhere with this hunch of yours,' said Garramone absently, his mind clearly already turning on something else.

The line went dead, and Scamarcio slumped down on a nearby bench. Chief Mancino was right; they were looking like a bunch of chimps, and Scamarcio's failure to come up with anything down in Calabria probably hadn't done him any favours either. He thought of Dante Greco and the fact that he'd heard nothing from him. He needed it to stay that way.

There was a mossy, post-rain musk emanating from the paving stones on Giacometti's street. It seemed that he owned an apartment in one of Trastevere's most desirable medieval buildings, its tiny diamond windowpanes and wandering ivy creating the impression that they were hundreds of kilometres from the capital. Opposite the address was one of the area's more famous restaurants, and Scamarcio wondered if Giacometti ever did any cooking. He could probably afford not to.

Giacometti's soon-to-be ex was a tall, good-looking man with foppish, streaky-blond hair, fashionable turquoise glasses, and a tawny complexion. He showed Scamarcio through to the living room, and politely offered him a coffee.

Scamarcio declined, and took a seat on a wide leather armchair. The place had a minimalist modern feel, with a few designer pieces carefully positioned. He took in angular chrome lamps, asymmetrical bronze mirrors, and multi-coloured Afghan rugs.

Giacometti's partner introduced himself as Sebastiano.

'But I don't understand what Paolo could possibly have to do with the Proietti thing,' he said after Scamarcio had explained the reason for his visit. 'I mean, he isn't mad on Micky, but he respects him. Micky gives the company a lot of work; frankly, we'd be nowhere without him.'

Scamarcio nodded. 'I'm going to need to ask you a few difficult questions, Sebastiano, but I have to explore every angle, especially in the light of what happened yesterday.'

'What happened yesterday?'

Scamarcio glanced up in surprise. 'You haven't seen the news?'

'I don't really watch TV.'

Scamarcio pulled out his notepad. 'Proietti's wife was murdered. They threw her body outside his flat last night.'

Sebastiano placed a hand over his mouth. 'My God.'

'I'd presumed you'd heard.'

'There's absolutely no way Paolo would be involved in *that*.' He took a seat on the sofa and took a few hurried sips from a bulb-shaped tumbler of what looked like water.

'Well, I can't say I see him doing something like that, either, but I do want to find out why one of his staff was at the exact location at the exact same time we traced a call from the kidnappers.'

'Couldn't it have been coincidence?'

'I don't believe in coincidences. Police work soon teaches you that.' Scamarcio paused for a moment. 'Paolo's business partner told me that you guys are splitting up. I'm very sorry to hear that, but I'm afraid that I do need to ask about it. Do you know who Paolo is seeing now? It might be important.'

Sebastiano was shaking his head, looking at the parquet. 'I just don't see why any of this is relevant.'

'I know it seems odd, but bear with me. So, this new guy? Do you know him?'

Sebastiano looked up, rolled his eyes at the ceiling, and sighed. 'No. At first, I thought it was just one of Paolo's fads, a stupid fling, but then I realised that he was really obsessing.'

'Obsessing in what way?'

'Changing his behaviour, his habits.'

Scamarcio was about to steer him back to the identity of the mystery man, but then decided to just let him follow whatever

242

train of thought he was on. 'How did Paolo change?'

'He became interested in his physique, started going to the gym. Paolo has never been into sport. It was all I could do to get him off the sofa sometimes.'

'What else?'

Giacometti's former partner dropped his shoulders, his mouth folding into a frown that made his irritation plain. 'He started reading a lot, but not the usual stuff — he's always been a fan of crime novels, Carrisi, Camilleri, all those guys. But I noticed that he started buying things like *The Odyssey*, *The Iliad*, *The Decameron*. It was as if he was trying to better himself, to reacquaint himself with the classics.'

Scamarcio didn't feel as if he was being brought along any further. 'Anything else?' he asked, trying to disguise his impatience.

Sebastiano barred his arms across his chest. 'No.'

'And this new man?'

'No idea.' The tone was icy now.

'Giacometti's business associate says he's a VIP.'

Sebastiano's expression morphed through surprise, then alarm, and then outright distress. 'Really?' He took another sip of water and then set the glass down slowly. 'News to me.'

Scamarcio felt no sympathy. He wanted to punch something or someone — he was getting nowhere.

30

HE TOOK THE LIST OF TELEPHONE numbers that had been handed to him.

'There are only a few hundred Bellagambas in Rome. One of them must know her,' said the junior officer desperately.

Scamarcio mumbled an unconvincing thank you.

He didn't feel like heading out of the office straight away, so he ran a web search for Giacometti's *Autumn of our Lives* series. There had been a flurry of pre-publicity, and it seemed that there were a handful of big stars involved, the biggest of which were Enzo Fernando, Zac Dandini, and Mario Pepe—all household names. He realised that this was what Giacometti had been watching on his laptop when they'd first met. Scamarcio wondered if these national institutions were all up in Trieste shooting, or whether he might catch any of them down in Rome.

After a few calls to their agents, he learned that the big three were still in Trieste, but Matteo Bini, an up-and-coming young actor, had already completed some filming and was on a four-day pause in Rome to shoot a commercial. If Scamarcio needed to speak to him, he could be found at Cinnecittà, the friendly agent informed him. Scamarcio wondered if she'd misunderstood the nature of his call, so helpful was she, but he quickly jotted down the details, deciding it might be worth a shot.

The prospect of observing a commercial being made was considerably more appealing than a visit to Chiara Bellagamba's parents, who had soon been located in Testaccio, but Scamarcio knew it had to take priority.

As he'd somehow expected, the Bellagambas lived in a drab block just off the main Ostiense arterial.

When Scamarcio told them why he was looking for their daughter, the portly father just looked confused and said: 'But why would Chiara be involved in anything like that?'

'We don't know for sure that she is, but it's something we're looking into.'

'But we haven't seen her for a couple of weeks now. She's been up in Trieste for work.'

'I saw her at her office here in Rome just this morning.'

'Really?' The father turned to the worried, pale-faced mother. 'Did you know she was back?'

She shook her head. 'I haven't heard from her. I did call her yesterday, but she didn't pick up.' She looked up at Scamarcio. 'Should we be concerned?'

'Like I say, I saw her just this morning. I think she may be trying to avoid me. Please let me know if you hear from her.' He handed over his card, and the mother studied it for a moment, mouthing the words.

'Is Chiara happy in her work?' asked Scamarcio.

The father nodded emphatically. 'Oh, yes. She enjoys meeting the actors; she enjoys the technical side. She wants to be a director one day—she's been into films since she was little. She used to have her own little cinecamera, and would shoot anything and everything that moved.' He stopped for a moment. 'In my heart of hearts, I wanted her to have a proper job—you know lawyer, accountant, something solid. But then I told myself, if this is what's she's into, if this is her passion, then maybe she'll make a good fist of it.'

'They really like her there,' the mother chipped in. 'She was told by her boss that she's in line for promotion to producer.'

'This boss—what's his name?'

The mother brought a hand to her mouth. 'Oh, I forget. She

talks about him all the time, what is it now …'

'Paolo Giacometti?'

'Yes, that's it,' she said. 'Chiara thinks he's a genius. Says he's the cleverest person she's ever met.'

Again, Scamarcio felt like he was getting nowhere. He thanked them for their time, and reminded them to call as soon as they heard from their daughter.

Matteo Bini was standing in front of the camera, holding up a bottle of mineral water and grinning gormlessly. His face was covered by a thick layer of foundation, and every few minutes two women with an array of brushes and mirrors swinging from their belts would magically appear and readjust his hair or eyeliner. Scamarcio was quite fascinated by the fact that Bini was wearing eyeliner. He knew that it wouldn't look like it when the commercial aired, and he wondered why that should be the case. After spending far too long contemplating this, he told himself to focus.

They seemed to be shooting the same thing over and over again, and Scamarcio couldn't believe the director wasn't satisfied. A number of times, Scamarcio was tempted to scream 'cut' himself and release Bini from his misery. Yet he had to admit that he was impressed by the actor's professionalism. He seemed able to maintain the same pose and absurd expression minute after minute, and never once complained when the lighting was adjusted or the lenses changed for the fifty-fifth time. No doubt, being paid a small fortune helped.

Eventually, someone shouted 'Break,' and Scamarcio rose quickly from his chair. He felt for his badge and made his way towards the perspiring young star.

'Sorry to bother you at work, Sir,' he said, holding up the ID for Bini to read.

Bini narrowed his eyes as he scanned the badge, the foundation caking into dusty craters around his laughter lines. 'Oh, God, is everything OK?' he said, looking up at Scamarcio. 'Has something happened to my wife?'

'No, no,' said Scamarcio. 'Nothing like that. I'm just here in connection to the Proietti inquiry.'

'Oh, really? God, it's a dreadful business. I couldn't believe it when I heard about Maia.'

There was a level of recognition in Bini's eyes when he said the name that felt slightly off to Scamarcio.

'Did you know her?'

'No, not personally,' Bini ran a hand across his forehead. 'I knew of her. I'd seen her at a few things with Micky.' Bini made towards the edge of the studio and collapsed into a foldout chair. A minion handed him a small bottle of water. Scamarcio noticed that the brand was different from the one the actor was pushing.

'Can we offer you anything, Detective?' said Bini, motioning to the pretty girl who had given him the bottle.

'A water would be good. Watching all that has made me thirsty.'

The girl passed it across and hurried off.

Bini extended his long legs like a spider unfolding, and took a few sips from the bottle. 'So how do you think I can help?'

Scamarcio parked himself on a rickety bench and tried to ignore the make-up caking the man's face. Bini was a handsome guy, but the trowelfuls of foundation made for an unsettling look beneath the harsh studio glare.

'I hear you're working on *The Autumn of our Lives* series.'

'That's right.'

'And you've been shooting up in Trieste.'

'Correct.'

'Has Paolo Giacometti been around much?'

'Er, Paolo was there for a few days when I was filming, then I think he headed back to Rome.'

'When was this?'

'The first half of last week—I think he left on the Wednesday.'

'You sure?'

'Not 100 per cent. It does all tend to blur into one after a while.'

'I bet.' Scamarcio pulled out a notebook and jotted down the dates. 'Have you worked with Paolo before?'

'On a few things. We did a series last year for Channel One again. It was about a family who ran a vineyard in Alto Adige.'

'Oh, yes, I think I caught some of that,' Scamarcio lied. 'Do you get on well with him?'

Bini was starting to look concerned. Scamarcio could see him trying to work out how Giacometti might fit into all this.

'Yes, I mean Paolo's a bit mad, but his heart is in the right place, and he definitely knows the business; his scripts are always rock-solid. I've never had any issues with him.'

'And him and Micky? Do they get on, do you think?'

Bini exhaled. 'Well, you know, Detective — the way our business works — if Paolo had an issue with Micky, he'd never talk to us actors about it. It would be the height of unprofessionalism. He'd keep that kind of thing for off the shoot.'

'OK,' said Scamarcio. 'That makes sense.' He made a pointless note on his pad while he allowed a thought to take shape. 'Given you've worked with Paolo a bit before, can I ask you if you've noticed any change in him recently, anything different?'

Bini frowned and shook his head: 'No, not that I can think of.' Then, after a few moments' silence, he laughed and said: 'Well, apart from the newfound football obsession, of course.'

'What?'

'It's like he suddenly can't get enough of it. When I was up in Trieste, he kept watching matches on his iPad or checking the results on his phone. I mean, he seemed more interested in that than the shoot, half the time! It's hilarious, because he's never been into sport, Paolo. He couldn't have cared less. We've all been making jokes about the transformation; ribbing him that he's having a mid-life crisis!'

Scamarcio's heart was doing double time. This was it — he was starting to see it properly now. 'Has Mr Giacometti declared himself for any one team in particular?'

Bini nodded keenly, still amused by it all. 'Roma, of course! And Aconi is the star striker. He carries the show, according to Paolo. I think he's half in love with him.'

Scamarcio took a long drink of his water. It might as well have been champagne.

He'd nailed it — the missing element.

31

Aconi was lying down, his huge back to the ground, taking it in turns to hug each mammoth knee to his chest. All around him, his teammates were repeating the same exercise. It was a surprisingly cold morning, and Scamarcio could see eleven little clouds of breath suspended in the frosty air.

He approached one of the trainers who appeared to be in deep discussion with a man who looked alarmingly like Franco Zandelli, the Roma manager. Zandelli was renowned for having a terrible temper, and Scamarcio didn't relish the prospect of going head to head with him. He steeled himself and pulled out his badge.

'Excuse me, gentlemen. May I have a minute of your time?'

They turned, and looked first at him and then the badge.

'Detective.' Zandelli seemed to be having trouble making out the rest of the writing on the ID. He patted his pocket for a pair of glasses, but then quickly gave up. 'What do you want?'

'I'm investigating a kidnapping. I need a moment with Aconi.'

'A kidnapping?'

'There's a boy's life at stake. I need to speak to him urgently.'

Zandelli and his trainer just looked at him, shocked.

'Please—just five minutes. It could be crucial.'

Zandelli nodded, confused. 'OK. But take him somewhere else—I don't want the lads distracted. Then, when you've spoken to him, come back and report to me. I need to know if there's a problem in my team.'

Scamarcio felt like one of his stressed-out players, but nodded anyway. He just wanted to get this over with.

Aconi didn't seem that surprised to see him again. 'I thought you'd be back,' he said, glancing up quickly before continuing with his leg presses.

'Is there somewhere we can talk?'

The footballer took a long, controlled breath and said: 'Just let me do ten more.'

Scamarcio waited patiently for him to finish, the eyes of Zandelli boring into him all the while.

After a minute or so, Aconi splayed his huge hands by his sides, then sprang up from the ground with the grace of someone half his weight. 'Let's go to the canteen. I'm hungry,' he said, waving quickly at Zandelli, who was still staring.

When they were seated at a far table in the empty cafeteria, Aconi said: 'So what is it this time?'

'You said you weren't surprised I was back. Why's that?'

'Because Pollett's wife was killed. The whole thing seems to be unravelling, running away from you. You've got to try everything now.'

Scamarcio averted his eyes and took a sip of the espresso in front of him. It was good. Aconi, he noticed, had opted for a fruit tea. Maybe footballers weren't allowed caffeine. Perhaps it did something to the muscles.

Scamarcio took one more sip and then looked hard at the man before him. 'So, Aconi, I've heard you're bisexual, and that, as well as Fiammetta di Bondi, you've also been seeing a TV producer called Paolo Giacometti.'

Aconi just stared back at him, his expression blank.

Scamarcio pulled out his notebook and opened it to a clean page. He smoothed down the page and pushed down the button on his biro. 'Needless to say, nothing you tell me today will make its way to the press. You have my word on that. I hate those bastards as much as you do, perhaps more. I know what it's like to

251

be at the wrong end of their lenses—I know the fear, the panic, the shame. All I want is to solve this inquiry as quickly as possible. That is my only agenda; the sole reason I'm here.'

Scamarcio looked up at him once more and scratched at the corner of his nose, expectant.

Aconi just kept staring at him, his face a blank.

'Come on, man. They've got Proietti's boy and, as you so observantly noted, we're desperate. I need to hone down this angle and move on. And I need to do it in the next ten minutes.'

Aconi took a quick sip of his tea, but when the waitress brought over a plate of scrambled eggs on toast, he immediately pushed it away. He sat back in his chair and barred his arms across his vast chest. To Scamarcio, the gesture seemed born more from self-protection than defiance.

'How *can* I trust you? I start talking to you, and my career could be over by tonight,' said the nation's top striker. Then, as an afterthought: 'I need to call my agent.'

Scamarcio sighed. 'I don't have time for that. You *can* trust me, because not too long ago I found my face splashed all over the papers when they decided to write about what it must be like to be a top policeman and the son of a leading Mafioso. I'm still reaping the consequences, and I'm still trying to shake the shame. So you have my word when I say I'll make sure the same thing doesn't happen to you.'

Aconi nodded slowly, his expression solemn. 'Yes, I thought you seemed familiar.'

Scamarcio exhaled and tapped the biro against the blank page of his notepad. 'OK, so now we've got all that over with, can you tell me about Paolo Giacometti?'

'Paolo,' said Aconi hesitantly, as if he was trying to match a name to a face. 'Paolo and I had a thing for about two months, but I called it off when I met Fiammetta.'

'Why was that?'

'Like I told you, I fell for Fiammetta. By that point, I was beginning to find Paolo rather stifling. He'd become quite intense about the relationship, and I realised he wanted more out of it than I did.'

'Did Micky Proietti know you were seeing Paolo Giacometti?'

'I kept that side of my life very quiet, and I'd never told Micky. But Paolo said once that he suspected Micky knew.'

'Why was that?'

'Micky had made some comment that had got Paolo worried. Paolo believed that Micky could be malicious when he wanted to be — often quite arbitrarily. He was worried that Micky was planning something that would hurt me.'

'What kind of thing?'

'Paolo wasn't sure — he just said he had a bad feeling.'

'And this comment that Micky made?'

'I can't remember the nature of it now.'

'But why would Micky want to get at you? Or Paolo, for that matter? Paolo was one of Micky's top suppliers.'

'Paolo believed that Micky was jealous of him, of his success.'

'Micky's successful.'

'But he's not in the same league financially as Paolo. He hasn't made the millions Paolo has. Paolo has launched a few reality shows that have made him mega bucks. He thinks Micky resented that.'

'It seems so petty.'

'Shit, Detective, then you don't understand these people at all. It's a petty world they inhabit.'

A thought occurred to Scamarcio, stopping him in his tracks for a moment. When he'd brought it into focus, sharpened it, he asked: 'How soon after Paolo Giacometti mentioned his suspicions about Micky did Micky introduce you to Fiammetta?'

Aconi scratched at his neck and frowned. 'Well, now you ask, I'd say pretty soon. It was the same week, I think. We'd been at my house on the Sunday having breakfast when Paolo brought up his worries about Micky knowing something. Then I think it was the Wednesday or Thursday night that I was at the Fendi party with Micky, and he introduced me to her. So, yeah, we're talking three or four days. I'd need to check my diary to be sure, though.'

Aconi inclined his head to the side, and Scamarcio saw the realisation slowly dawn. Aconi may have had a Laurea of 108, but he wasn't being particularly quick on this one.

He turned to Scamarcio, his eyes alive. 'Jesus, do you think Micky introduced me to Fiammetta to make sure I broke up with Paolo?'

'Could be ...'

'But that's mad ...'

'I wonder if Proietti may in fact be slightly mad.' Scamarcio took a breath. 'Did Paolo Giacometti know that Micky introduced you to Fiammetta? Did Paolo Giacometti know that you'd left him for *her*?'

Aconi began to understand where Scamarcio was heading. 'Christ, do you think Paolo has something to do with the kidnap?' He wiped his hand across his forehead. 'Jesus Christ.'

'You haven't answered my question, Mr Aconi.'

'Oh, right. Yes, did he know, did he know? Let me think ...'

He was getting flustered, losing it. The realisation that his connection to the kidnapping might be far tighter than he had imagined seemed to be proving too much to process. Scamarcio waited patiently for him to answer. A fly was attempting to land on the rim of his espresso cup, and he flicked it away with his biro. But it wasn't deterred and kept coming back, its disgusting little legs criss-crossing over where Scamarcio had just placed his mouth. He wanted to swat it dead, but didn't want to distract the footballer.

'Oh shit,' said Aconi, bringing both hands to his lips as if in prayer. 'Yes, of course he knew. He was there, Paolo, at the Fendi party. I remember him watching us when Micky introduced me to Fiammetta. He was watching us from a corner. I remember now that I was thinking I must go and talk to him, get him to stop staring, stop looking so angry. Oh shit …'

Oh shit indeed, thought Scamarcio, swatting the fly away once more. How the hell were they going to track down Giacometti before he let this madness escalate any further? Who the hell knew what else the man was capable of?

32

THE POLICE IN TRIESTE had visited the location for the *Autumn of our Lives* shoot, but there'd been no sign of Paolo Giacometti. He hadn't shown up at his offices either, and his ex, Sebastiano, hadn't seen him. They'd put surveillance on both GD Films and the flat in Trastevere, but so far had nothing. Scamarcio insisted they also maintain their search for Chiara Bellagamba, but when he'd suggested keeping an undercover unit outside her parents' place, Garramone had said, 'That would be one cost too many.'

'What does Mancino want us to do? Just keep wasting money repeating pointless tasks, or actually spend it on something useful?'

'That horse has already bolted.'

'In a case like his, there can be no such thing as too much surveillance. It prevents there being too many murders.'

'You're preaching to the choir, Scamarcio.'

But it seemed that Garramone had quickly changed his mind and had put it to the chief, because just an hour later they had two plainclothes officers posted outside Bellagamba's parents' flat in Testaccio. Davide Stasio hadn't been seen in days, so Garramone had decide to lift his men off that, convinced that they'd been rumbled and that Stasio had gone to ground.

Scamarcio was now sitting with Micky Proietti in his living room, where everything, including Proietti himself, was starting to take on a grimy, faded hue. The cleaner hadn't been in, so the floors were dusty, and smeared with dried-out footprints from countless police boots traipsing in and out. The sofa cushions looked far less pristine than on Scamarcio's first visit, and were now slack and wine-stained in several places. As for Proietti, his hair was hanging in limp, greasy strands, his eyes were bloodshot, and his chin bore the dirty, grey stubble of several days' growth. Yet again, Scamarcio prayed silently to a God he didn't believe in that the investigation would conclude before Proietti had grown a beard.

'Every day I feel like I'm about to wake up, that the nightmare is almost over. But I never do, I never wake up,' said Proietti, taking a sip from a glass that looked like water, but which Scamarcio knew was neat vodka.

'We're close to finding him, we're making progress now.' Scamarcio wasn't lying—he believed it. He always had the same feeling on every case when it turned a corner, when the switch was finally flicked. It was an expectancy, an electric anticipation that the goal was in reach, that they just needed to make the final push.

'I can't believe Paolo would do this. It's just so fucking warped,' said Proietti, cradling the glass.

'Love can make people do all sorts of irrational things — things they'd never normally be capable of,' said Scamarcio.

'But a kidnapping? For fuck's sake!'

'From what I've heard, you baited him a bit ...'

Scamarcio thought he might lash out, tell him to go fuck himself, but the result was quite the opposite. Proietti stewed in silence for a few moments, then said: 'I'm a fucker. I've behaved like a shit — for years. This is my comeuppance, my divine retribution.' He paused and looked down into his lap. 'It's been a long time coming.'

He glanced up and shook his head at Scamarcio, still bewildered by it all. 'Funny thing is that it came from where I least expected.'

'Life's always playing tricks like that,' said Scamarcio.

Fiammetta di Bondi was getting ready to head out when Scamarcio dropped by her place.

'Oh, Scamarcio,' she said, shaking on a brown-leather jacket.

'I've got a photoshoot in Piazza di Spagna. Can it wait?'

He was disappointed that she seemed quite unruffled by his visit. It was as if their last encounter had never happened. He wondered for a moment if she were mentally ill. Perhaps she said things like that to strangers all the time then forgot about it.

'I just wanted to know what the situation is with you and Aconi, the footballer. I'm trying to tie up that line of inquiry.'

He knew deep down that the question was not of central relevance to the investigation, but while they were waiting for Giacometti or his researcher to surface, he deemed it worth a try.

'Walk with me,' she said quickly.

She swung shut her front door behind her, and he was almost relieved that he didn't have to see the inside of her flat. What would it be this time? A rotting chicken carcass on the coffee table? An overturned dustbin in the bath?

'Me and Aconi,' she said, taking the steps two at a time, 'we're having a break. All this business with Manfredi and Micky, it's got to us. They were people we hung around with, came to know. Aconi tells me he wants to take some time out to reassess his life, and I'm taking the opportunity to do the same.' She turned to look at him for a moment, and he felt a small spark of something that might have been hope. Then he wondered if she was telling him that she wanted time out from everything; that she was retreating for a period of reflection.

'Right,' he said lamely.

She pulled open the heavy wooden door to the street and stepped out into the mild warmth of the afternoon. She turned to face him. 'Is that the answer you were looking for, Detective?'

He frowned, confused. 'Perhaps.'

She smiled, then hurried off in the opposite direction, not looking back once.

He wondered at the neatness of it all. Just a few days before, Aconi had claimed he was in love with di Bondi. Then, less than

24 hours ago, di Bondi made a move on Scamarcio. Now she was telling him she was single. It was all too convenient. If he could have stepped outside his body and kicked himself, he would have. He needed to wake up and stay sharp. His emotions had to be left right out of this.

33

PAOLO GIACOMETTI HAD BEEN spotted on CCTV at Trieste station that morning, boarding a train to Rome. Why such a public re-entry? Scamarcio wondered. Could he be coming home to talk, to finally face up to his breathtaking stupidity?

From what little he knew of him so far, Scamarcio decided that Giacometti was someone prone to spectacular madness, but whose rational side would always pull him back down to terra firma eventually. Had he been mulling it over up north—had he decided that he wanted it over with? The police had now talked to too many of his friends and associates. It must have been clear to him that the net was fast closing in.

Scamarcio waited with the team on platform 9 at Termini. They had come prepared for a fight, as they always did, but Scamarcio sensed there wouldn't be one. Giacometti was tired, and would come willingly.

His assessment was correct. The producer appeared dishevelled and exhausted when he descended from the carriage. Scamarcio noticed a large, yellow stain on his jacket that looked like vomit. As Giacometti stepped onto the platform, ten officers surrounded him and brought him to his knees, but there was no need to pull him to the ground, because he quickly held out his hands for the cuffs. Once they were on, he closed his eyes and began whispering. Scamarcio wondered if he was praying. He couldn't tell from any of this if he was surprised to have been captured or had prepared himself. Either way, it wasn't relevant. Scamarcio's sole objective was to get him to the station and make him talk.

There were deep, grey hollows beneath Giacometti's eyes, and his salt-and-pepper hair was matted and awry. One of the lenses of his trendy glasses was chipped, and there was a cut to his upper lip. Scamarcio wanted to know when all of this had happened. Giacometti had the look of a rough sleeper, and Scamarcio wondered if he had been hiding out for a time up in Trieste, avoiding hotels while he tried to find a solution to the mess he'd created. Giacometti's hands were shaking as they tried to grip the paper cup of coffee that had been handed to him. Scamarcio noticed a thin sheen of perspiration on his forehead that he kept trying to wipe away with a soiled paper tissue. He showed none of the self-assurance of their previous meeting.

'Mr Giacometti,' said Scamarcio, pulling out a chair. 'I know all about you and Aconi, how he broke your heart, how you tried to get back at Micky by staging the kidnap. So let's not to do the dance of you trying to pretend otherwise — we've come way too far for that. I'm sure that you, as much as I, want all this over with now. Let's just get that little boy home.'

Giacometti looked dazed. His seemed to stare straight past Scamarcio, to some indefinable point, far far away. There was something disturbing about the emptiness of this gaze, and Scamarcio wondered if he should call Psych. Then he told himself that he should put this off for as long as possible, that he needed to get some sense out of Giacometti before Psych got all proprietorial and starting waving the rule book.

'Giacometti, I understand what love can do to a man, believe me.' Scamarcio stopped, and scratched his head. 'But what I don't get is why you had to kill Maia Proietti. That's a breathtaking step too far.'

'I didn't kill her,' said Giacometti, deadpan, still staring into nothing.

'I don't believe you.'

'Why would I kill her? That would be madness.'

261

'Yeah—like the rest of it makes a whole lot of sense.'

'It was just for show. We were going to bring Maia and the boy back after a couple of days. We just wanted to rattle Micky, make him stop and think for once, teach him a lesson.'

'Well, killing his wife is a pretty clear lesson, I'd say.'

'I didn't kill her.'

Scamarcio wanted to yell in his face, but fought his frustration. 'So if you didn't, who did?'

Giacometti sighed. 'Can I have a cigarette?'

Scamarcio had a fresh pack of Marlboro in his pocket that he had been doing his best not to work through too quickly. He knew that just the act of pulling it out would be enough to smash his resolve. He tore off the wrapping and handed a cigarette across to Giacometti. Then, after the briefest of pauses, he took one for himself and lit up for the pair of them.

'So, Maia?'

'God knows,' said Giacometti after a long drag. 'I hear glass smash, someone screaming, then I start to cough. Then my eyes are burning, and I'm retching and puking. My eyes feel like they're going to melt in my head. I don't know what's up or down, left or right. It's chaos.' He took another drag, his fingers trembling as he brought the cigarette to his lips. 'Then the shooting starts, and on and on it goes. It feels like it will never end. We all fall to the floor, screaming. Then, a few seconds later, someone starts yelling: *'You got Maia, you got Maia.'* They didn't sound too happy about it. Then I hear someone say, *'Get her out, get her out, we need to get her to a hospital.'* I can't see what's happening, my eyes are gummed shut, but I hear a weight being dragged, and I presume it's her body. Then they start shouting: *'The boy, the boy, where's the boy?'* I'm being kicked in the ribs by a boot. They're kicking me for the answer, I realise. I tell them he's at another location—we'd separated them, you see, the boy and Maia. They keep kicking, and I give them the address. But as soon as they're gone, I realise

I gave them the wrong place. That's where we had him yesterday. We'd moved him in the morning, because the boiler had broken at the other place, but in my panic I'd forgotten.'

Scamarcio breathed in and out carefully for several moments, thinking hard, trying to suppress an unexpected disquiet.

'It was a gas canister, I realised after,' added Giacometti.

'What was?'

'What caused the coughing, the burning. They must have thrown it in. I found it when they left.'

The disquiet was now a rising tide of panic. Scamarcio counted to five in his head, reminding himself that Giacometti was in the business of TV drama, and could easily invent such a tale. He told himself that maybe the use of gas canisters was all the rage among the clans of Calabria right now. *Stay on track*, he told himself, *keep your focus*. OK, so Giacometti had come back to Rome because he was scared. He'd tumbled into something far darker than he'd imagined, and right now the police seemed a less intimidating prospect. Scamarcio's mind drew a blank. The image of the gas canister was bubbling up to the surface once more, disrupting his concentration, eating away at his sanity. He suddenly felt cold.

He folded his hands across his notepad, then took the top off his pen and flipped to a fresh page. 'These voices?' he asked, trying to keep his voice steady. 'Were they familiar at all? Did they have accents?'

'Calabrian — definitely Calabrian. One of them was called Davide. They kept referring back to him; he seemed to be the leader.'

So, as they'd suspected, Stasio had decided to take matters into his own hands. But who had been helping him?

'Any other names?' he asked.

Giacometti shook his head. 'No. I mean, I don't know, I can't remember. I just know I heard the name Davide a lot; they kept asking him what to do. He seemed to be the one in control.'

Scamarcio sank back against his chair. He was struggling to get a hold on his panic; the counting wasn't helping now.

He stepped out into the corridor and took a long drag on his Marlboro, tracking the fragile smoke rings as they drifted aimlessly to the ceiling. He noticed watery patches of yellow and brown, a peppering of black mould. Were they all being slowly poisoned by the budget cuts now?

He sucked out the cigarette, then lit another. So Stasio had decided to act, believing the 'ndrangheta were involved. But why the cannisters? That was the million-dollar question. Was it really possible that Stasio had links to Dante Greco? If he knew Piocosta's former men were owed a debt from Proietti, wouldn't Greco have rounded them up and taken control by now? Wouldn't he have put the thumbscrews on Stasio, trying to claw the money back, just as Piocosta's boys had done? Scamarcio felt as if he were back at Piocosta's villa, the poison seeping in. He could no longer be sure of the world around him; he could no longer make out the contours.

A further question was bothering him: why, when they realised they'd made a mistake, didn't Stasio and his men take Maia Proietti to hospital? Perhaps she'd died on the way, and Stasio had panicked. Had he decided to save his skin, and lay the blame at the kidnappers' door?

Scamarcio reminded himself that these were all secondary issues. The priority remained the same: they had to find the boy's location, and find it fast.

Scamarcio stubbed out his cigarette and re-entered the interview room. He was surprised to see that Paolo Giacometti was slumped over the small table as if he had fallen asleep. When Scamarcio walked in, he jerked awake and rubbed a shaky hand across his mouth.

'Keeping you up, are we? Let's cut to the chase so you can

get some shut-eye. Where have you taken Proietti's son?' barked Scamarcio.

Giacometti kept rubbing his hand across his mouth, but his coordination was out; it was like watching a one-year-old trying to master its limbs. There was something very off about the gesture in a fifty-year-old man.

'Come on, I've had enough,' said Scamarcio, thumping the table.

'I don't know where he is,' whispered Giacometti, a thin sliver of saliva working its way down his chin.

'How can you not know?'

'I don't know where they've taken him.'

'Who's "they"?'

'The others.'

'What others?'

'The other ones.'

His speech was starting to slur, and his eyes weren't holding focus. Scamarcio wondered if Giacometti was physically sick, or if this was indeed a mental-health problem.

'We know the driver was a fake. Are there other people involved, besides you and your researcher?'

'Of course,' he murmured. 'We all hate him, we're all sick of his arrogance. But their agenda wasn't quite as personal as …' His head was beginning to loll against the desk once more. Scamarcio shook him by the shoulder. 'Come on, Giacometti, keep up. What's the matter?'

The saliva was still running from Giacometti's mouth, and his eyes were rolling in their sockets, the whites exposed now. When he saw this change, Scamarcio finally understood that something was very wrong. He jabbed at the emergency buzzer, and two uniforms ran in.

'Call an ambulance,' he snapped.

One of the officers darted out again.

Giacometti's breathing was laboured. The officer who had remained lifted his wrist and felt for his pulse. 'It's sky high,' he said after several seconds.

Scamarcio scratched at his hairline. There was heat in his stomach, and he felt jittery. 'Do you think it's a fit, some kind of epilepsy?'

The officer was shaking his head. 'To me, it looks like an overdose.'

'How can that be? We searched him at the station, and he hasn't swallowed anything since I've been with him.' Scamarcio thought about the few minutes when he'd stepped outside. Had it been then? But Giacometti had seemed slightly out of it from the moment he'd arrived.

'Could he have necked it before we cuffed him? Maybe whatever it was took some time to work,' said the officer.

Scamarcio's mind flashed back to events at the station. He wondered if Giacometti could have swallowed something just before he stepped off the train.

'Jesus,' he hissed.

At that moment, Giacometti's breathing became more of a rattle. It was a repugnant, animal sound that made the hairs on Scamarcio's neck stand on end.

'Fuck, is he dying?'

The officer bent down next to Giacometti's mouth. 'Help me get him on his side.'

They manoeuvred him onto the floor and rolled him carefully onto his right side. The rattle was becoming more pronounced, more desperate now.

'What about mouth-to-mouth?' said Scamarcio. Then: 'Where the fuck are the paramedics?'

The officer leaned over Giacometti's chest and began administering CPR. 'I don't think it's going to work, Sir,' he said after a few tries. 'Not if he's overdosed.'

'Just keep going. I don't have a location for the little boy.'

The officer worked on, up and down on the chest, pinching Giacometti's nose, breathing into his mouth, on and on, until Scamarcio felt as if they'd been in the room forever, as if they'd become trapped inside a loop in time. He began to count, higher and higher, past 100, then 200, until finally the paramedics ran in and the young officer slumped aside, exhausted.

Scamarcio could tell by the calm approach, by the careful rhythm with which they progressed through their routine that they knew Giacometti wasn't going to make it.

When he was pronounced dead at 13.14, Scamarcio slid down the wall and buried his head in his hands. They were fucked.

34

'IT'S GOT TO BE THE GIRL BELLAGAMBA,' said Chief Mancino. 'We focus all our efforts on her now. She'll come home eventually; she'll lead us to him.'

'And what if she doesn't?' asked Scamarcio.

'We can't think like that.'

'We must.'

He saw Garramone flinch.

'What would you suggest then, Detective? You failed to prevent our prime suspect from committing suicide on your watch, so you'll understand that I now have serious reservations when it comes to taking your advice.'

Scamarcio pushed on. 'There are others involved. Giacometti told me as much. His exact words were: "They all hate him, but their agenda is not quite as personal." We need to look harder at the TV scene, at the people Proietti does business with.'

Mancino dismissed the thought with a flick of his hand. 'A massive waste of time — we follow the girl, we get the boy.'

Scamarcio shook his head. 'You won't get the girl, and you won't get the boy. When we went back to the CCTV at the studio location, it bore fruit; we need to keep mining this vein — we can't just give up and expect the girl to tie it all up for us.'

'Yes, but you only found the girl. You failed to locate any of the others from the CCTV, so the girl is all we have to work with.' Mancino snapped his large notebook together with a thud. 'We're done here. Go get me a result. I've been waiting long enough.'

When they were out in the corridor, Garramone said: 'If

there are a few people you met first time round who caught your eye, then go back and talk to them. Keep it on the QT, though. Mancino has his spies.'

Scamarcio raised an eyebrow. 'Spies?'

'You didn't hear it from me.'

Scamarcio rode the elevator to the offices of the Matrix TV company. When he arrived, Francesco Bruno, the Calabrian producer, was hovering in the foyer and let him in. 'I saw you come up,' he explained, seemingly embarrassed.

Scamarcio couldn't work out how that would be possible unless there was a camera on the front door, or unless Bruno had been hanging out the window, watching out for him.

Bruno quickly retreated into his office and pulled the door shut behind Scamarcio.

'The rumour mill is buzzing,' said Bruno, moving hastily around his desk and perching on the edge of his swivel chair. 'Word is that you guys have Paolo Giacometti in your sights.'

Scamarcio didn't read any anxiety there, just curiosity. He pulled out a seat opposite and felt in his pocket for his notebook, weighing up quite how much to reveal.

'I can't go into all that,' he murmured.

'Right,' said Bruno, clearly disappointed.

'When we first spoke, you said you couldn't imagine that any of the producers who work for Proietti would do this.'

'I stand by that. For the life of me, if Paolo was involved, I can't understand what he would have been thinking. He'd been getting great business from Micky over the years. He would have had to have lost his mind.'

'Mr Giacometti has suggested to me that others are involved— others from the business.'

The realisation slowly dawned. Bruno had been given confirmation that Giacometti *was* involved. He traded glances with Scamarcio, a momentary triumph in his eyes, then he exhaled sharply and just shook his head. 'He's got to be spinning you a line—I don't buy it.'

Scamarcio leaned in. 'I've been around the block a bit. I know when to spot a faker, and I don't believe I was being lied to.'

Bruno took a deep breath. 'I don't know what to tell you. I have no idea.'

'Really?'

'Really.'

Here they were, right back at the beginning, thought Scamarcio. The worst thing was that he believed him. Bruno was playing it straight.

'Go see some of the others, but I don't think they're going to bring you any further,' he said. 'They'll just tell you the same as me.'

Scamarcio's mood wasn't improved by his most recent encounter with Micky Proietti.

'I have no idea who these people might be,' he slurred. 'Paolo Giacometti knew everyone in the industry, same as me. He could be talking about anyone.'

'But he must have had particular friends, people he hung around with.'

'I wouldn't know, Detective. My relationship with Paolo was professional; I couldn't tell you who his friends were.'

'That's bullshit. You attended the same parties.'

'I don't much like your tone.'

'And I don't much like your attitude. You need to start helping your little boy. This has gone way too far. Start talking, Proietti, before you condemn your son to death.'

Proietti tried to get to his feet, but couldn't quite manage it. He slumped back down in his armchair, a fist balled. 'Don't you fucking talk to me like that,' he spat. 'Get the fuck out of my house. I want to deal with someone else, someone *professional*. I'm sick of the sight of you, you incompetent fuck.' He attempted to stand again and managed to get shakily to his feet this time, but tottered as he tried to swing an arm towards the door. 'Now fuck off back to the mafia hellhole you came from, you son of a whore.'

It had taken five Marlboros to bring Scamarcio down after that. As he was contemplating whether to finish the last cigarette in the box, Sartori shuffled in. He was covered in sweat and trying to eat a Big Mac while checking his phone at the same time. He'd just completed another trawl of Proietti's principal producers, and didn't look that happy about it.

He took a large bite of burger and wiped the fluorescent mayonnaise away with the back of his stubby hand. 'I hate to say it, but we're barking up the wrong tree.'

'There were other people with that girl on the CCTV — other people we still haven't identified. If we haven't found them at Giacometti's, they have to be from one of the other companies.'

'I don't know what to tell you, Scamarcio; we *can't* find them, and we're looking hard.'

'There's got to be something,' said Scamarcio. 'Someone we've overlooked.'

Sartori scratched his head and sighed. 'I think we need to let it go, focus on the missing researcher.'

He sounded like Mancino's pet parrot, thought Scamarcio. As is to confirm Sartori's assessment, Scamarcio's mobile rang, and Detective Lovoti's name appeared on the display. Lovoti was one half of the team stationed on surveillance outside Chiara Bellagamba's parents'.

'Got some movement, Scamarcio,' he grunted. Lovoti was what HR would call 'a team player'. He was always the joker, the prankster of the pack. He would have been the kind of boy Scamarcio would have steered well clear of at school — the kind of boy who was way too sure of himself to have been a friend.

'What kind of movement?'

'Well, it's not the girl per se, but the little brown mouse of a mum has just hurried out the house by the back door, checking all around her that she wasn't being followed. She'd put on a baseball cap and a pair of sunglasses, but it was definitely her. She was carrying two Unes shopping bags — full, by the looks of it.'

'Were you able to get a glance at what was inside?'

'It's definitely food, because at one point one of the handles snapped and she was scrabbling around on the pavement trying to get it all into the other bag. Those bags, for life they give you these days, are shite. You're lucky if they last a month.'

Scamarcio gritted his teeth. 'What kind of food?'

'Well, I saw what looked like a couple of trays of Gran Biscotto, some eggs — I think they broke — milk, bread, cheese, some Fanta. Seemed like the staples, really.'

'Interesting to be taking shopping out of the flat, rather than into it …'

'Quite.'

'Fanta, you say?'

'Yep.'

'That's a kid's drink.'

'That's why we've got a tail on her, Scamarcio.'

'Where's she heading, then?' He heard the crackle of radio comms in the background.

Lovoti stopped to speak to someone for a moment, then was back on the line: 'As we speak, she's going north up Viale Giotto.'

Scamarcio heard more static. He realised his cigarette was almost down to the filter, but he smoked it anyway.

'Now she's turned right into Viale Baccelli.'

'Don't lose her. Are you on the tail, or are you still in situ?'

'In situ.'

'Don't move. I'll meet you there.'

Scamarcio managed to slip on the slick pool of egg whites on the pavement outside the Bellagambas' apartment. The impact with the concrete ripped a tear in the knee of his brown cords, and before he had a chance to get back on his feet and brush himself down, he heard Lovoti and his partner guffawing like two lobotomised apes from the front seat of their grey Corolla.

'For fuck's sake, keep it down,' he hissed as he crawled onto the back seat. There was egg on the sleeve of his leather jacket, he realised.

'Sorry, couldn't help it, boss,' said Lovoti, his shoulders heaving, his pudgy pink hand bunched into a babyish fist against his mouth.

Scamarcio thought that Lovoti was probably the kind of guy who got his rocks off watching *Strip the News* on Channel 5, or one of those endless outtake shows where a fat American dad slips on a banana skin, or a toddler nearly drowns in a paddling pool. Scamarcio had always wondered where the humour was. If the toddler had fallen at a more acute angle, or the dad had gone through a window, they'd both be dead.

'Cunts,' whispered Scamarcio under his breath.

'Sorry, boss?' said Lovoti

'Where's Mrs Bellagamba now?'

'She's heading north-east towards the centre.'

'Still walking?'

'Still walking?'

'Any sign of the dad?'

'No. He left for work at the usual time.'

'Let's head north,' said Scamarcio.

'But we're the only ones outside their place.'

'We'll risk it.'

Lovoti held up his palms. 'If you say so, but you'll have to clear it with Garramone.'

Scamarcio wanted to deck him for that. 'Will do.'

Lovoti's partner, a blond-haired man in his mid-thirties whose name Scamarcio was always forgetting, fired up the ignition, and they slowly pulled away from the kerb, careful not to attract attention. Lovoti punched Mrs Bellagamba's most recent location into the SatNav, then turned in his seat towards Scamarcio.

'You think she's taking that food to her daughter—that it's meant for Proietti's kid?'

'Could be,' said Scamarcio, chewing on his bottom lip.

'Is it true that the prime suspect just offed himself in front of you?'

'Good news travels fast.'

'Shit, what a headfuck.'

Scamarcio couldn't think of how to respond to that.

'Then you fall flat on your face and rip your trousers. It's not your day, is it, boss?'

'It won't be yours, either, if you don't shut the fuck up.'

Lovoti swung back around smirking, and they travelled on in silence. Scamarcio had been thinking lately that he should make more of an effort to do something about his reputation in the squad as a loner. But it was encounters such as these that sapped his resolve.

'Domodossola Ancona Bari, Domodossola, Ancona, Bari ... All units ...'

Lovoti leant forward and snatched the radio from its hook. 'Eight here. Status?'

'Subject has stopped outside an apartment block on Via Valle delle Camene. Number 26, opposite the baker's.'

Scamarcio knew that street. It was in a better part of town, not far from the Villa Celimontana and its gardens.

'Subject has rung the buzzer and is going in.'

Scamarcio leant forward and grabbed the radio from Lovoti. 'Get a man in there.'

'Received. Stay on the line,' said the officer calmly.

They heard talking, raised whispers, a car door being gently closed, light footsteps on the tarmac, the buzz of an entry system. A distant female voice purred: 'Oh, I do beg your pardon, Madam.'

'Stay on the line,' repeated the officer under his breath.

Scamarcio heard the man sniff, then there was a short blast of static, then a whisper out in the ether, and then the female voice again. 'Fourth floor; flat opposite the elevator.'

'Good work,' sighed Scamarcio.

'You got that?' said the officer on Via Valle delle Camene.

'We got it. Wait for us; we'll be there shortly. And radio for backup. We'll be entering the location.'

'OK.'

Lovoti's partner immediately abandoned the cautious act and rammed the accelerator to the floor. Scamarcio had to grudgingly admit that the two of them worked well together, Lovoti providing a fluid, improvised back-of-the hand navigation while his partner manoeuvred expertly around corners, roundabouts, schoolgirls, and strollers. At that speed, anyone else would have collided with the courting Japanese couple or the hippy woman dragging five mangy dogs on a tangle of leads, but not this guy. He took the turn into Via delle Camene at such a speed that, for a moment, Scamarcio thought they would all die. But the correction was so immediate, so swift, so expertly timed and perfectly executed, that he immediately felt ashamed for doubting him.

They drew up outside the apartment block at a gentle pace, and Scamarcio stepped onto the pavement feeling like a sailor who'd been at sea too long.

He soon spotted the uniformed officers parked in their Panther some thirty metres up the street. He made no sign of acknowledging them, and pulled out his mobile.

'Patch me through to the uniform crew on Via Valle delle Camene, please,' he told Control. 'It's Detective Scamarcio.'

'One moment, Detective.'

After a couple of seconds, he saw the officer in the passenger seat reaching forward for his radio.

'Detective?'

'I'm going in alone for the time being. Keep this line open.'

'Received.'

On his way up to the entrance, he noticed the plainclothes duo in a white Fiat Punto, and reckoned this must be the officer he'd spoken to moments before. He recognised him as being one of a few new arrivals in the squad. Scamarcio angled himself away from the car and took the steps to the glass door. He tried a few buzzers, being careful to avoid those for the fourth floor. Eventually, someone let him in and he made his way to the stairs. The block might have been in a decent part of town, but inside the décor was pure 1970s faded elegance. Red-veined marble and plasticky brown panelling lined the walls, and the route to the elevator was dotted with dusty houseplants in fake gold stands.

Scamarcio took the stairs two at a time, first checking that the elevator was clear. By the second floor, he couldn't be sure if his heart was pounding because he was nervous or because he was out of shape. Probably both, he figured. There'd been no time for the gym lately. And for a long time before, he hadn't felt like it.

He made his way up the final steps to the fourth floor and turned to the right. The door to the flat was opposite, just as the female officer had told him it would be. What he hadn't expected, though, was to find it ajar.

He quickly reached beneath his jacket for his Beretta and cocked it. He pondered briefly whether to get the uniforms in. *Give it a few seconds more*, he told himself, *you don't want to blow it*.

He edged his back against the wall and moved slowly over the threshold. The first thing he noticed was that a window was open at the end of the corridor. Its white gauzy curtain had blown through the frame and was being buffeted by the breeze outside.

Scamarcio turned as he heard a low thud of pop music coming

from a room off to the right. The music was interspersed with a series of electronic bleeps and clicks. His mind flipped on the possibility of a bomb, but then a little boy's voice shouted: 'Shit, missed it.'

Scamarcio eased through the doorway, his back still against the wall, his gun held high. A slightly overweight lad of about ten was sitting cross-legged on the living-room carpet. He was surrounded by discarded crisp packets and greasy chocolate foils, a half-empty bottle of Fanta by his side. His left arm was in a sling. Scamarcio scanned the rest of the room and then lowered his gun.

The boy still hadn't noticed him in the doorway. Every so often, he'd lift his hand from the joystick to take a swig of the soda, his eyes still firmly fixed on the video game in front of him. From where Scamarcio was standing, it looked like *Grand Theft Auto*.

'You Antonio Proietti, by any chance?' asked Scamarcio in as soft a voice as he could manage.

The boy turned, his eyes falling instantly to the gun in Scamarcio's hand. But he said nothing, and just turned back to the game, as if this was the sort of thing that happened all the time.

'Where are the ladies who are looking after you?'

'In the kitchen, I think.' The boy was grappling furiously with the joystick again.

Scamarcio felt pretty sure the women were no longer in the kitchen, but he checked anyway. As he'd expected, the kitchen and the rest of the apartment were empty. He leaned through the window and saw that there was a fire escape running down to a small ornamental garden and carpark.

'Send two men to the back of the building,' he said into his mobile. 'Two female suspects on foot, Chiara Bellagamba and her mother, Rita.'

'Received.'

'Send a man up here to me on the fourth floor also.'

Scamarcio pocketed his mobile and returned to the living

room. He sensed that Antonio Proietti had no idea about the death of his mother. He knew something of the world of suffering that awaited the boy, and the thought of it robbed Scamarcio of words for a moment. The idiocy of adults and the pain they inflicted on children never ceased to infuriate him.

When he'd finally found his voice, he said: 'What happened to your arm?'

'It's just a sprain. I did it when we had the car crash. I wanted to take it out of the sling, as it doesn't hurt anymore, but Chiara won't let me. She says it still needs to heal.'

Antonio spoke so fast that Scamarcio was struggling to keep up. 'Do you want to see your dad?' he said after a beat.

Antonio Proietti sprang up from the floor, almost losing his balance for a moment. 'Can I? Really? I can't wait to tell him all about this.'

Micky Proietti wept like a baby when Scamarcio brought his son into the room. Antonio hugged him fiercely, and Scamarcio got the impression that whatever compassion Micky Proietti might have lacked towards his wife or colleagues, he was considerably more wired in when it came to fatherhood.

Scamarcio left the two of them for a moment, wondering when and how Proietti was going to break the news about the boy's mother. He stepped into the corridor and lit a cigarette, realising that he'd probably never quit. This job made it fucking impossible. Frankly, he'd done well not to become a drug addict. He leaned back against the wall and dialled the chief CSI, Manetti, who was now working the scene at the flat where they'd found the boy.

'You guys find anything yet?'

'Ah, so I've been promoted from miracle worker to magician now. We've been here half an hour, Scamarcio!'

Scamarcio rolled his eyes heavenward, although there was no one there to see it.

'So far, we've got a lot of hair samples, some skin and fibres, and a bit of blood in the bathroom.'

'Blood?'

'Yeah, but it's minimal — might be menstrual.'

'You have the Bellagamba DNA yet?'

'Of course not — it will probably arrive this afternoon. Who else are we matching against?'

'Just Paolo Giacometti at the moment. I'd like to go and swab the entire Rome TV industry, but no doubt Chief Mancino would have something to say about that.'

'Yeah, these VIPs are always well connected.'

'Actually, I was thinking more about the budget, but you're probably right.'

'I'll call you if I get any matches, but you'll need to give me some time with it. It's early days and, if you ask me, we've been chasing our tail on this one.'

He wondered if the dig was aimed at him. Manetti's tone seemed neutral, though.

'OK, keep me posted,' he said as he spied Micky Proietti's parents exiting the elevator.

When she saw Scamarcio, Mrs Proietti started running towards him: 'Have you got him, have you got him?' Her cheeks were pink, and her watery eyes were searching his, desperate for any kind of answer. Scamarcio cut the call and slid his phone into his pocket.

'Yes, he's in there with your son.'

'Oh, thank God,' said Mrs Proietti, looking to the ceiling and exhaling sharply. 'Oh, Jesus Maria.' She grabbed Scamarcio by the arm and hurried past. He had the feeling that it was meant as a thank you.

Her husband stopped for a moment, then took Scamarcio's hand. 'Thank you, Detective. We owe you a huge debt.'

'Talking of debt, Sir, I need to ask you: why did your wife call you a murderer when we first met?'

Mr Proietti's eyes shifted away from him. He looked down and took a breath. When he glanced up again, something seemed to have changed in his expression.

'I could lie to you, Detective,' he said quietly. 'I suppose that's what I'd planned on doing, but, given everything that's happened, I rather feel that there's no point. Appearance isn't everything. We're all human in the end: we all go to the bathroom; we all die.'

There were tears in the old man's eyes. Proietti Snr had such a chiselled, polished, steely demeanour that Scamarcio was taken aback.

'I was very fond of my daughter-in-law, and I am deeply sorry that it has ended this way. Frankly, my wife had a point when she called me a murderer. In essence, that's what I am.'

The old man's hands were shaking, and Scamarcio felt an unwelcome buzz of anticipation. He really hoped that he wasn't about to get a confession. This case could not go off on a new tangent; he was too tired and too worn down for that, and there were already too many different angles to consider, too many fires to keep alight.

'I don't quite follow, Mr Proietti ...'

'There's no nice way to put this: despite appearances, my son has been a huge disappointment to me. He's a drug addict and a gambler. He's frittered away everything he had, everything we worked so hard to give him. My wife was angry because I had the power to bail Micky out of his latest problem, but I chose not to. She thinks if I'd helped our son, the kidnapping would never have happened.'

'You had a spare million and a half to give him?'

Mr Proietti blanched. 'A million and a half?'

'That's the figure.'

'No, you must have it wrong.' Mr Proietti's cheeks seemed to have suddenly sunk in on themselves.

'I trust my sources.'

'Jesus Christ.' Mr Proietti rubbed a gnarled hand across his eyes, then looked up at Scamarcio. 'Who does he owe it to?'

'Don't you know?'

He sighed. 'I have my suspicions, but I've never been sure. It was my daughter-in-law's brother, you see, he's a bit of a … Well, how to put it?'

'Don't worry, I know all about Davide Stasio and, yes, I think your suspicions are spot-on.' Scamarcio paused for a moment. 'But I'm certain that even if you had a million-and-a-half euros to give your son, it wouldn't have changed anything.'

Mr Proietti frowned. 'How's that?'

'Because I don't think the Calabrians were involved in this kidnap. The Calabrians were patiently waiting for your son to pay — well, in the way those guys do *patient*, which is regular doses of intimidation, progressing in their intensity. They weren't quite ready to kidnap for the debt, but unfortunately Davide Stasio thought they were. When he decided to take matters into his own hands, the whole situation ran away from him, and his own sister ended up dead — killed in the crossfire. It was people from your son's work who really staged this kidnap; the Calabrians had nothing to do with it.'

Mr Proietti's mouth was agape, and Scamarcio noticed a gold molar.

'Jesus, what a mess,' said Proietti eventually.

'Yeah,' sighed Scamarcio. 'And I've got a feeling it's about to get a whole lot worse.'

35

'So I TALKED TO THE CONCIERGE, and that flat is owned by a Mrs Giacobbe,' said Sartori, slurping noisily on a king-size bottle of Coke. The man was on the fast track to diabetes, and Scamarcio wondered if he should introduce him to Moia, and give him a taste of what awaited him.

'Giacobbe — that's not a common name,' said Scamarcio.

'Yeah, can't find a link to this case, though.'

'Course not,' snapped Scamarcio. Sometimes it felt like Sartori didn't actually want them to get anywhere.

'No need to be like that, Leo. We're all trying our best here.'

Scamarcio sighed and got up from his chair. It was time for a second approach with Chiara Bellagamba. When he'd first spoken to her half an hour ago, she claimed she had no idea who owned the flat where they'd found the boy. Giacometti had just provided her with the address, and told her that the boy would be delivered there and that she should look after him. When it came to who had done the delivering, again she claimed not to have seen them. The boy had arrived alone in the elevator. If this were the case, why hadn't the boy tried to run off, tried to sound the alarm, Scamarcio wondered. Her story had far too many holes in it for his liking.

When he entered the interview room, Chiara Bellagamba was sipping slowly out of a plastic cup from the vending machine. Her eyes were red-rimmed, and when she set down the cup, bright-orange liquid splattered onto the table. Scamarcio thought it looked carcinogenic.

'So let's try this again,' he said. 'Chiara, you need to understand that the more difficult you make this, the less lenient the courts will be.'

'I have no idea who owned that place,' she said. 'I'd tell you if I knew.'

'What were you trying to achieve with all this?'

'I just wanted to please Paolo—he said it was a little skit, that nobody would get hurt.'

'Two people are dead, Chiara.'

She sniffed, and pricked at her eyes with the sharp point of a paper tissue. 'I had no idea,' she murmured, 'no idea that it would end up this way.'

'Neither did Mr Giacometti, but that doesn't mean much now.'

Scamarcio took a slow breath and looked around the spartan interview room, trying to locate some calm, some inspiration. 'Chiara, these are very serious charges. You're a young woman; you had a good career ahead of you. If you cooperate, you'll return to your old life, be able to start again so much sooner. Do you really want to live out your days being bothered in the shower by the dykes at Rebbibia?'

Chiara Bellagamba turned paler. She was a pretty girl, but under the strip lighting she looked washed-out and haggard. He watched her swallow, moving a shaky hand to her temple in search of a memory. Her fingers stroked her forehead as if she were trying to comfort herself, reassure herself that everything would be OK. Scamarcio could tell he was losing her. It would be up to him to pull her mind back into focus, keep it sharp. She was unravelling; soon she'd no longer be capable.

He leaned forward in his chair and rested his arms on the table. 'Chiara, look at me.'

She blinked at him a few times, and her breathing steadied slightly.

'Tell me about the shoot in Trieste. How did Mr Giacometti seem?'

She coughed gently and unballed the paper handkerchief from her fist. 'He was preoccupied.' Then, as an afterthought: 'Obviously.'

'If you had to describe his mood, what words would you choose?'

'Angry, sad … worried.'

'Out of those three descriptions, which do you think best describes his general demeanour over the past weeks?'

'Angry,' she hesitated: 'Then, later on, worried.'

'How was his relationship with the crew?'

She swallowed, and grimaced as she did so. 'He was curt with them. Well, apart from the camera guys. He maintained a good rapport with them—I guess he had to.'

'And the director?'

'There were two directors; they'd replaced Andrea, who we'd had before. Paolo was polite towards them, but I know he didn't like them. They were there because the channel wanted them there.'

'And the actors?'

'Paolo was really tight with a few of the actors; they'd hang out together after we'd wrapped for the day. He called them his old-timers,' she said flatly.

'Why was that?'

She sniffed and wiped her nose once more. 'They'd been in a lot of his successful shows; he'd known them a long time. In some cases, he'd launched their careers, I think.'

'Were you ever there when he hung out with the actors?'

She frowned, the tissue poised in mid air. 'Me? You joking? It was a clique; it was clear that Paolo only wanted certain people to come along—nobody dared gatecrash.'

'What did they do when they hung out together?'

'No idea. Perhaps they played cards, or watched the football. Paolo had recently become a fan.' She shrugged. 'God knows what they did.'

'Drink perhaps?'

'Paolo wasn't into drinking on shoots. It was always an early call-time the next morning; he didn't want the talent hungover.'

Scamarcio scratched at his nose and decided to change tack. 'Why were you on the CCTV at the studios that day? As you know, we traced a kidnap call from that location at the time you were there.'

She nodded slowly and looked into her lap, colour in her cheeks now. 'I made that call. Paolo told me to.'

'And the other people with you?'

She looked up, surprised. 'Oh, they had nothing to do with it. They were a team from Milan who'd come down for a few days' shooting. Paolo asked me to help them out with the location.'

That explained why they hadn't been able to find them when they trawled the Rome production companies.

'So, when did you make the call?'

'After we'd finished filming—when we were on our way out.'

'So, you weren't actually holding Proietti's family there?'

'No.'

'Didn't you ever want to stop? Didn't you want to tell Paolo that it was all a bad idea?'

She sighed, her large brown eyes welling with tears again. 'He was my boss; he'd promised me great things. Besides, you don't argue with Paolo. He kept saying it was just a bit of fun.'

'And you never doubted that?'

'Not at the beginning, no. But when we'd been looking after that boy for more than a couple of days and he kept asking for his mum, I did think it was wrong, that it had gone too far. When Paolo asked me to take the boy to the other place, it was clearly much harder for him; he was too young to be away from her.'

'Why did he separate them?'

'No idea,' she said, shaking her head.

Scamarcio rubbed at his eye; he felt as if he were having some kind of allergic reaction, or was it just stress? He looked down at his notepad and tried to focus on the question mark he'd just scored a dense box around.

'These actors that Giacometti hung out with, can you give me their names?'

'It was Dandini, Fernando, and Pepe — the big guns. The three amigos, we called them.'

Scamarcio tapped his pad, remembering the names from the newspaper piece. He was surprised Bini wasn't in the clique, though. Perhaps he was too young for them, too much the rising star.

There was a sharp knock at the door, and he ground his teeth in frustration. He thought he might have had the beginnings of an idea, but the interruption had made it vanish.

Sartori was standing in the doorway, not looking particularly apologetic. 'Sorry, Scamarcio, but can I have a moment?'

Scamarcio reminded himself that he wouldn't be asking unless it was important. He rose from the table, avoiding eye contact with the girl.

When they were out in the corridor, Sartori handed across a scrap of paper. 'As you know, we traced the ownership of that house to a Mrs Alessandra Giacobbe.'

'Yes …'

'Well, I couldn't see a connection to this case, but then I found out that she's married to that famous orchestra conductor, Stefano Sevegnini.'

'And that's significant because …?'

Sartori ran a hand through his hair and looked nervous for a moment. 'Look, Scamarcio, I don't know if I'm onto something, but Stefano Sevegnini happens to be the half-brother of Zac Dandini, the TV actor who is starring in Giacometti's current series.'

'Why the different surnames?'

'Different fathers. I know it's a long shot, but …'

Scamarcio grabbed him by the forearm. 'It *is* a long shot, but it's good work.'

He snatched the piece of paper and hurried back to Bellagamba.

36

THEY WERE FILMING A SCENE in the main square in Trieste when Scamarcio arrived. Two young actors Scamarcio didn't recognise were walking arm-in-arm through the evening light, a steadicam retreating in front of them. Scamarcio turned away from the harsh lights, and immediately spotted Zac Dandini and Enzo Fernando sitting in two foldout chairs next to the catering truck. They appeared to be deep in conversation.

Scamarcio scratched at the back of his neck as he made his approach. He felt a tightening in his gut. He'd never been one to be intimidated, let alone by a couple of actors, but something felt newly amiss — as if he were about to enter unchartered territory.

He felt his mobile buzz in his pocket, and he reached for it reluctantly. His first impulse was to kill the call, but then he figured it could be important.

'Leone.'

The tightening in Scamarcio's gut became fiercer. It was properly painful now. 'How did you get this number?'

There was a tutting-down the line that sounded like a series of strange clicks. 'Goodness, you do get hung up on the small stuff.'

'What do you want?'

'That's no way to talk to someone who just saved your life.'

'I'm in the middle of an investigation. I don't have time for this.'

'I was calling as a courtesy, but frankly I wish I hadn't bothered.'

'Yeah, me too. Goodbye.'

'Hold your horses, Scamarcio. If I were you, I'd try much harder to be nice.'

'And why the fuck should I do that?'

'Cos I might blow your secret.'

'What, and blow yours at the same time?'

'There's a way of doing these things.'

'You don't scare me. Either cut to the chase or hang up.'

'How is Trieste this time of the year?'

Scamarcio swallowed. What the fuck? Then the rational part of his brain told him to just accept that there were a million ways that someone like Dante Greco could get hold of this kind of information.

'So, what's it to be?' Scamarcio asked, trying to sound calm.

'I thought you might like to know that I've been helping Davide Stasio with a small problem.'

When he thought his voice might sound less fragile, Scamarcio asked: 'What kind of problem would that be?'

'His brother-in-law got into a mess with Piocosta's boys. Frankly, I don't like them, don't want 'em; I need a clean slate, a fresh start, up in Rome, but don't want a splinter group, if you know what I mean. Stasio needed a favour, so it was what the Americans would call a "no-brainer"— the perfect "two birds, one stone" situation. A bit like you and me.'

Scamarcio wanted to scream. 'So, what did you do for Stasio?'

'On an open line, Scamarcio?'

Scamarcio said nothing.

'Let's just say that poor Davide is an amateur — he fights shadows. Piocosta's boys are far too lazy to have come up with that kind of plan. I should have known, trusted my instincts, but there you go. Even at 65, you still live and learn.'

There was a buzzing in Scamarcio's ears. He wanted to run around the square howling.

'Anyway, I won't tell anyone that you and I know each other, or that you're aware of the little slip-up with Maia. I'd imagine that might make life difficult.'

Scamarcio remained silent.

'You know what's so funny in all this? I was planning to rub out Piocosta anyway—I had the whole operation set up and ready to roll. Then you turned up, and it seemed like a gift from God.'

The line went dead, and Scamarcio just stood there, holding his phone as if he'd forgotten its purpose. He took a long breath and told himself to let it go. It came with the territory; it meant nothing. He could survive this.

He must have been standing there for quite some time, because when he looked up, Fernando and Dandini were staring at him. He pocketed his phone and approached the two actors, his blood still humming in his ears.

37

'WE'RE ALL IN DEEP SHOCK HERE,' said Enzo Fernando, sweeping a liver-spotted hand through his mane of shoulder-length grey hair. He was an extraordinary-looking man, like a cross between a lion and an American Indian, thought Scamarcio. His face was extremely wide, with strong, chiselled cheekbones, thick, dark brows, and an elegant but enormous Roman nose. Water had collected in his deep, green-brown eyes, and he made no show of disguising his tears, wiping them away ostentatiously with a white silk handkerchief. 'We'd known Paolo Giacometti for many, many years. I think I speak for all of us when I say we wouldn't be where we are without him.'

Dandini and Pepe nodded and looked solemn. They'd all taken refuge from the sea wind in a small café off the square. Scamarcio was conscious of the eyes of the other customers upon them.

'We're trying to work out what Paolo had got himself into, how he could possibly be connected with this Proietti business,' Fernando went on. He was wearing a light-blue silk scarf around his neck, and he began unwinding it and refolding it, smoothing out the frayed edges against his skin.

'Yes, it does seem odd, I grant you,' said Scamarcio.

'I mean, Micky was one of Paolo's biggest clients. Why would he want to harm him in this way? It makes no sense,' said Dandini, leaning in across the table. Scamarcio noticed that the man looked exhausted. He also noticed something slightly off about his posture, something that he couldn't quite put his finger on.

Scamarcio took a sip of his cappuccino and studied the three men in front of him. They were the foremost actors of their generation. Could they be rallying, pulling out all the stops to deliver one of their best performances?

'Are you sure you've got it right, Detective? I mean, we don't mean to insult you, but might there be another explanation?' asked Dandini, his surprisingly unlined face a picture of innocence, his sparkly, blue eyes hooded in confusion. Scamarcio couldn't shake the sensation that this man didn't truly believe what he said. The words were right, even the delivery was right, but it was as if the soul behind the eyes told a different story. Scamarcio had seen something like this before, and recently. But where? He couldn't quite pin it down; it was like a tune he couldn't place. He dragged his mind back to the conversation and said: 'Well, we kept all avenues open for as long as we possibly could, but in the end it came back around to Giacometti. And when I interviewed him, he confessed.'

Fernando brought a quick hand to his mouth. 'Paolo confessed? I can't believe it.'

Pepe tut-tutted. 'It just does not add up.'

'Another thing that doesn't add up is why Proietti's son was found in an apartment belonging to Mr Dandini's sister-in-law,' said Scamarcio, in as matter-of-fact a way as he could manage. Scamarcio watched Dandini's face fall for the smallest fraction of a second before he recomposed his features.

'What?' blinked Fernando.

'You heard me. So, Mr Dandini can you explain it?'

Dandini shook his head limply. Far from being a polished professional actor, he now looked like a bewildered geriatric. 'I haven't seen my sister-in-law for months. We don't get on.'

Scamarcio sighed and tapped out a cigarette from his pack, and then, as an afterthought, offered the box around.

Fernando shook his head angrily. 'Don't touch 'em—lost my pa to lung cancer.'

Scamarcio took a long drag and eyed him through the smoke. 'Stories like that should get to me, but they don't.'

'Then you're a fool, Detective,' said Fernando, fixing a huge, watery eye on him.

'Fool,' repeated Scamarcio. 'There are a lot of fools in this case. More than I'm used to.'

Pepe shifted in his seat and pinched his nose. Scamarcio saw Fernando frown and angle his head slightly towards him. The lion was seething with anger, but was wrestling with it, trying to get control of it.

A thought occurred to Scamarcio. 'This newfound football obsession of Giacometti's ...'

'What of it?' said Fernando, more surprised than angry now.

'What did you all make of it?'

Fernando shrugged. 'Paolo always reminded me of Toad of Toad Hall. He was into one thing, then he was into another. He had such an appetite for life.' He sniffed, and smoothed down his scarf once more. 'Such a bloody waste.'

'It seems obvious to me that the football obsession was due to Giacometti's relationship with Aconi.'

He watched their three mouths drop open. Finally, here was something real. Nobody, not even these national institutions, could do surprise like that.

None of them said a word for several seconds until Fernando stammered. 'Aconi, the footballer?'

'The very same.'

'Surely not.'

'Why not?'

'Well, the guy's straight, for starters.' Fernando was looking at Scamarcio as if he was simple.

'He's not, he's bisexual. But he keeps that side of things quiet—bad for business, and all that.'

'For Christ's sake.' Dandini expelled a hot blast of air. For a moment, Scamarcio felt his rank breath against his cheek. He noticed that Dandini was blinking rapidly, that he seemed to be really struggling with this news.

Fernando remained one step ahead. 'OK, let's say we make that leap of faith, and it's one bloody big leap — what the hell does that have to do with the Micky Proietti business?'

'Micky broke them up. Paolo Giacometti was in love with Aconi, so Micky introduced Aconi to someone else, knowing he'd lose interest in Paolo.'

'Why would Micky do that?' asked Fernando, but Scamarcio sensed he already knew.

'Because, as many people have told me, and, as I'm sure you're all aware, it seems that Proietti was generally a bit of a bastard. And, more to the point, he was jealous of Giacometti.'

He studied the three men opposite him. They no longer appeared to be following him; their expressions were alternating between surprise, disappointment, regret, and fury. Fernando looked like someone who had just been betrayed in the worst possible way. Scamarcio couldn't understand why he might feel like this; Giacometti had hardly betrayed *him*. Scamarcio considered whether Fernando might be jealous, then remembered seeing all the photo spreads of him and his beautiful young wife. He didn't think it probable that Fernando would have a sexual interest in Giacometti. So what was it then, this sense of betrayal? And what was eating Dandini so badly?

Scamarcio was still missing something, something crucial.

He excused himself and stepped outside the café for a moment on the pretence of making a call. He really just wanted time alone to think. It had started to rain, and the film crew was packing up equipment. He watched a cluster of shabby pigeons descend from the roof of the cathedral to a spot by a bench where someone had discarded a soggy sandwich.

He lit another Marlboro and decided to make the pretence real.

He called Manetti, taking a long smoke while the line rang out.

'You got anything from that house where we found the boy?' he asked when Manetti finally picked up.

'Always wasting time with chit-chat, aren't you, Scamarcio?' he sighed.

'Well, have you?'

'It's like Termini in there.'

'What—rentboys and needles?'

'No. I've got a shitload of DNA from a shitload of people, and so far, none of it matches anything on the database.'

'What if I DHL you three samples from Trieste?'

'What do you mean, what if? What will I do? Dance a jig of joy? Cancel my Friday-night date with the wife at Ditirambo— which, incidentally, is a last-ditch attempt to save my marriage …'

'Is it?'

Manetti's sigh sent a high-pitched shriek down the line. 'Don't make me fucking cancel my dinner date, Scamarcio.'

'Look, if I send them now, they'd be with you by … er, I don't know.'

'They wouldn't be here in time.'

'Would you look at them first thing tomorrow, then? Please, Manetti. Chief Mancino has our balls in a vice. I've got to get a result.'

'You and everyone else.'

'I'm begging you. I'll owe you one.'

'You and everyone else.'

'Oh for God's …'

'I'll look at them when I look at them. That boy's been found. I don't see the urgency.'

The line went dead, and Scamarcio flung his mobile in the gutter. 'Lazy fucker,' he muttered before lighting another Marlboro and bending down to retrieve his phone.

When he stepped back inside the café, the three actors were

talking animatedly, hands arcing through the air, fingers bunched in sharp entreaties. Scamarcio figured that, maybe, being actors, they always spoke to each other like that. But then he noticed Fernando sending furious glares Pepe's way. There was trouble in paradise—no doubt about it. As Scamarcio approached, the three of them fell silent.

'Here's the deal, gentlemen,' he said, placing both palms on the table. 'You give me a strand of your hair, and then I'll let you go. For the time being.'

'Won't an autograph suffice?' said Fernando, rolling his eyes.

'But we don't have anything to do with this,' said Pepe, sounding like a wronged child. He was the youngest of the three, and, with his round cheeks and downy beard, he did come across as the ingénue.

'That's why I need the hair—so I can eliminate you from my inquiries.'

Scamarcio took an evidence pack from his holdall, tore it open, and put on the plastic gloves inside. He then unsealed three plastic bags from their containers and snapped open the cap on a pair of sterile tweezers.

'Bullshit,' said Fernando, ripping several strands from the top of his head and looking for a moment as if he were auditioning to play the Jack Nicholson role in *One Flew over the Cuckoo's Nest*. 'I've done enough police procedurals to know where you're going with this.'

'And where would that be?'

Fernando barred his arms across his huge chest and just glared at Scamarcio. Scamarcio deposited his hair in the bag and sealed it. He wrote Fernando's name carefully on the label.

'And you, gentlemen.' He held a bag open for Dandini, who quickly tore a hair from the crown of his head and then looked away.

Pepe seemed to spend some quite considerable time trying to

decide which patch of hair to plunder until Fernando said: 'For God's sake. It's one hair—nobody's going to notice.'

Scamarcio fell silent as he carefully finished packaging and sealing the evidence. He wished them well for the rest of the shoot, and assured them they'd be hearing from him soon. But even as he said the words, he had a sinking feeling that these three might yet slip away from him.

38

IT WAS LATE ON SATURDAY night when Manetti called. Scamarcio had been toying with the idea of paying Fiammetta di Bondi a visit, but kept rejecting it for a variety of different reasons that had at their root the same core issue: cowardice.

'So what's it to be?' asked Manetti.

'I don't follow.'

'Are you paying for dinner at Ditirambo for me and the wife, or will it be a cash prize, or a voucher for the Thai sauna on Via Pellice?'

'Did you find something?'

'It's not whether I found something,' said Manetti, exasperated. 'It's whether I did the work. I gave up a Friday night *and* a Saturday for you, Scamarcio.'

'For which I'm extremely grateful,' said Scamarcio, not feeling grateful at all. He couldn't feel grateful if there wasn't a result.

'I got a partial match on Dandini.'

Scamarcio scratched at the side of his mouth. 'Well, that doesn't really rock my boat, Manetti. His half-brother is married to the woman who owns the apartment. No doubt, there'll be a partial.'

'Yeah, but I got two partials.'

Scamarcio screwed up his mouth. 'How can you get two partials?'

'I got a partial on male DNA that matched the conductor fellow whose wife owns it.'

'And the other partial?'

'On the little boy, the Proietti boy.'

Scamarcio's mind couldn't catch up; he saw black, and rubbed at his forehead. 'Sorry, tell me again.'

'Jesus, I thought you were supposed to be the department's great white hope. I got a partial match between Dandini and Proietti's boy.'

'So, what does that mean?'

'Scamarcio, did you go through police training?'

Scamarcio still couldn't follow. Manetti seemed to grow tired of waiting, and snapped: 'If I get a partial to Proietti's boy, it means Proietti's boy is not *his* boy. You read me, Scamarcio? You even there?'

'Fuck,' he said, realisation finally dawning. 'Proietti is Dandini's kid?'

'Bingo. Christ, you're off the boil. Was it a late one?'

Scamarcio ignored him. 'Maia Proietti had sex with Dandini and fell pregnant by him …' he said, trying to process it.

'If someone has a kid that generally tends to be what happens first; what sets the whole thing in motion, as it were.'

'Fuck,' Scamarcio repeated.

'Not only smart but eloquent,' muttered Manetti before hanging up.

Scamarcio was leaving the squadroom, heading out for Dandini's place, when he saw the young actor Bini coming up the stairs. There was an expression in his eyes that Scamarcio didn't like.

'Mr Bini. How can I help you?'

'I wanted a word, actually.'

'I'm just going out. I've got a development on the Proietti case I need to follow up.'

Bini looked at him nervously, his eyes shifting away from his gaze. He seemed considerably paler than when they'd met at the commercial shoot, although Scamarcio reminded himself that he had been caked in foundation back then.

'That's why I'm here, Detective. I've got information I think you should have.'

'Is this something you've learned since we spoke?'

Bini looked at the ground, studying his pristine Stan Smiths. 'I wasn't completely straight with you.'

Scamarcio motioned to the two uniforms he'd arranged to take with him to Dandini's. 'Give us ten minutes. I'll see you around the back.'

When Bini was seated on the other side of Scamarcio's untidy desk, he said: 'So, this information of yours?'

'Dandini and I are good friends.'

Scamarcio nodded, saying nothing.

'I think he may have been involved in the Proietti thing.'

'Why's that?'

'Because he and Maia Proietti had been having an affair.' Bini coughed nervously and added: 'For years now.'

Scamarcio frowned. 'That's quite an age gap.'

Bini scratched at his nose and recrossed his legs. 'Love works in mysterious ways.'

Scamarcio allowed it to sink in for a moment. 'But why would Dandini go so far as to stage a kidnapping?'

'They wanted to flee, to run away. I think it could have been part of the plan.'

'How would that have played out? Dandini wouldn't have been able to work again if they'd disappeared.'

'I don't think they'd thought it through that far. I just know they were in love and that they wanted to finally get away from Micky. Be a family.'

'Be a family with Dandini's kid.'

Bini's mouth formed a small 'o' of surprise. 'So you know?'

'Just found out, as it happens.' Scamarcio evened out some crumpled papers on his desk as he allowed a thought to take shape.

'Why are you telling me all this now?'

'I'm worried about Dandini. He's been in pieces since Maia died. He's desperate — I've got a feeling he might try something stupid.'

'Stupid like what?'

'Like trying to snatch the kid again.'

Scamarcio looked up sharply from his notepad. 'You think?'

'He called me after he got back to Rome last night, saying all kinds of weird stuff. He'd been drinking, but he's clearly in a very dark place. I'm worried he's going to drag the kid right down there with him.'

Scamarcio scratched at his temple. *Dot the Is, cross the Ts*, he told himself. 'Where does Paolo Giacometti fit in to all this?'

'I came across him and Dandini chatting one time, after rehearsals. They were talking about "roughing up Maia". When I asked Dandini about it, he said they'd just been discussing a practical joke, that there was nothing to worry about. It was only later, when the news of the kidnapping broke, that I began to put two and two together.'

'Why the hell didn't you come to us earlier?'

'I wanted to put it to Dandini first.'

'You were up in Trieste shooting with him — you had more than enough time to do that.'

Bini said nothing.

'For fuck's sake — there was a kid involved.'

Bini just looked into his lap and swallowed.

Scamarcio gave him a few moments and then asked: 'Why would they do this? Come up with such a bizarre plan?'

Bini sighed. 'There are an awful lot of people who feel like they have scores to settle, who've seen their pay diminish year after year under Proietti. Dandini used to complain that his value had been slashed, despite providing Micky with success after success. I'd heard others say the same.'

'Others like Fernando and Pepe?'

Bini waved a hand away. 'That's not the point. The point is the kid.'

Yeah, now you're finally thinking about him, you hypocritical fucker. Scamarcio wanted to punch the idiot, rearrange his perfect white smile.

Scamarcio took a breath, trying to stay focussed. 'Micky Proietti is surrounded by police officers, we've …' He stopped. If Dandini was hell-bent on snatching the kid, he might yet find a way.

'OK, I hear you, Mr Bini,' said Scamarcio, reaching for his phone. 'Don't go anywhere; I need to make some calls.'

It didn't take long for Dandini to show up outside Proietti's apartment.

When Scamarcio and three officers emerged from the shadows, the actor tried to make a run for it, but he was too slow for the uniforms, and they had him pinned him to the ground within seconds.

'He's ruined my life. He's ruined my bloody life, that bastard. All I want is my boy, let me get my boy,' said Dandini, trying to wrestle himself free. For someone in his late fifties, he seemed remarkably strong.

Scamarcio bent down so his face was level with Dandini's. The actor's eyes were wild, and he was perspiring heavily. 'You know we can't do that, Mr Dandini. These kinds of paternity issues have to pass through the courts. You should have allowed all this to play out normally. Getting involved in this stupid scheme has resulted in nothing but disaster.'

Dandini shook his head violently. 'You don't understand Micky. He's a fucker; a vindictive little shit. He'd never have allowed Maia and me to start a life together. He'd have done something, something terrible.'

301

'More terrible than what's already happened? More terrible than losing the woman you love? Than robbing your boy of his mother?'

At that moment, Dandini started trembling and sobbing. The officers lifted him carefully to his feet and delivered him to the waiting Panther.

As interviews went, it had started out straightforwardly enough. Dandini, burnt out and devastated, had confessed to his involvement in the kidnapping and to the paternity of Proietti's son but, like Giacometti, although he'd spoken about 'others', he'd refused to enter into specifics. Scamarcio concluded that the *omertà* among Rome's acting fraternity was on a par with anything he'd ever experienced down south.

Maia Proietti, Dandini claimed, had been happy enough to play the victim in the ransom video. She knew all about her husband's infidelity, and had no compassion left. It gave her some small satisfaction that he was finally being made to pay. Maia had been a trained actress, but Micky had never allowed her to pursue her career, Dandini lamented. It was at this moment that Scamarcio finally understood what had been bothering him about that video. Maia had given a good performance — it was highly convincing — but, like Dandini in the café, something in her eyes had told a different story. Scamarcio cursed himself for taking so long to understand this.

Dandini claimed that Antonio Proietti had been treated well throughout and had not been made to suffer. His tooth had fallen out of its own accord, and his arm was only sprained. 'He was my boy, I'd never leave him in pain,' Dandini had repeated, over and over. Scamarcio sensed that the actor was now struggling with a massive burden of guilt at the anguish he'd inadvertently caused his son.

'Why did you separate them?' he asked.

'Who?'

'Maia and Antonio.'

'We were going to leave Rome. I thought we'd need to move separately. We were waiting for the right time,' said Dandini, his voice trembling.

'Where's the driver?'

'What do you mean?'

'The fake chauffeur you sent to Micky Proietti.'

'Oh, the stunt guy?'

'What?'

'We had to make sure Antonio and Maia survived the crash.' Dandini fell silent for a moment, then said: 'He flew to Brazil, I think.'

Scamarcio shook his head in disbelief. 'Knocking back pina coladas with the helpful passer-by, no doubt?'

Dandini shrugged, as if to say *Why not?*

'Who was driving the other car?'

'What car?'

'The other bloody car — the car that took out Proietti's Mercedes?'

'Oh,' Dandini sighed. 'That was the stunt guy's brother.' It was as if Scamarcio had asked him where he'd bought his shirt.

'I'll need names.'

'I don't have any.'

'I don't believe you.'

'I'm telling you, I don't know. I left all that to En ...' Dandini just stopped in mid-sentence, and after repeated attempts it was clear to Scamarcio that he was never going to get him to confirm the involvement of Enzo Fernando.

It riled Scamarcio that Fernando was just going to dust himself off and walk away from this unscathed. Scamarcio's instincts told him that Fernando *was* involved; that he'd been a part of it, maybe a key part. But there wasn't a single scrap of evidence to pin on him. Pepe bothered Scamarcio less: perhaps because he was a quieter, less assuming type; perhaps because he wasn't quite as much the star. Scamarcio sensed that if Pepe had been privy to this conspiracy, it would have been to a lesser degree. Fernando was the one Scamarcio really wanted to nail, the huge TV name he needed to make an example of. You couldn't go around kidnapping someone's family just because you didn't like the way they did business. And you couldn't arrogantly assume you'd get away with it.

When Scamarcio had called him to the station, Fernando had suggested that they meet at an up-scale wine cellar in Trastevere instead. At first, Scamarcio had wanted to tell him to go fuck himself and haul his arse down to Via San Vitale, then he had thought it through for a moment and changed his mind. He figured that if they were going to do this in a more casual environment, Fernando wouldn't be bringing his lawyers. And, for the time being, that suited Scamarcio just fine.

When Scamarcio arrived at the wine bar, Fernando seemed to be several rounds ahead. He was resting his massive shoulder against the wall, his eyes drooping. How many Brunellos would it take to bring a prizefighter like this to his knees, Scamarcio wondered.

He drew out a chair opposite. 'So, Maia Proietti and Zac Dandini—did you know?'

'No idea, news to me, nothing to do with it,' muttered Fernando into his wine, as if he were choosing default responses from a checklist.

Scamarcio rubbed at his eyes and sighed. He was dog-tired. On impulse, he decided to toss out the rulebook and order himself a large glass of Amarone. He'd play this one on Fernando's terms. Who knew? It might get him somewhere if he could stay lucid. Fernando studied him with the drunk's lopsided gaze while they waited in silence for the waitress to return. Every so often,

Fernando would shift his eyes from Scamarcio back to his glass, deep in thought. Scamarcio preferred to just let him get on with the drinking, and hopefully give him enough rope to hang himself. When Fernando's attention switched back to his wine yet again, Scamarcio glanced in his pocket to check that the recording light on his mobile was on. Whether anything he captured would hold up in court was another story.

When the waitress was back with the Amarone, Scamarcio took a long drink and waited for the buzz to hit. After a few moments, he felt ready for a second approach.

'So, you really didn't know that Maia Proietti and Dandini had been having a relationship? That seems odd to me—I thought you and Mr Dandini were close.'

'Appearances can be deceptive.'

'So, you don't get on?'

Fernando rolled his eyes. 'I'm not saying that. I'm just saying that I didn't know he was screwing her. Dandini has always been one to keep his cards close to his chest. Unlike me—I wear my heart on my sleeve.'

Scamarcio didn't exactly share this analysis. 'And the Aconi thing?'

'No idea,' said Fernando, rolling his eyes again. Scamarcio wondered if, rather than exasperation, it was the drink taking hold.

'Weird thing is that both Giacometti and Dandini say other people were involved in this kidnapping plot.'

'Very weird,' said Fernando, rubbing beneath his nose. He slowly held up a hand and snapped his fingers, his elbow wobbling on the table. The pretty young waitress hurried back over.

'Hello, my angel, be a love and bring me another bottle of Brunello, will you?'

Scamarcio was irrationally pleased with himself that he'd guessed Fernando's poison.

'Biondi Santi 2008 again, Sir?'

'Of course.'

A bottle of that wouldn't leave you much change from a 100. Scamarcio wished he hadn't ordered the Amarone now.

'Do you see Proietti often? Do your paths cross?' he asked.

Fernando scratched below his ear and narrowed his eyes. He waited a few moments before replying. 'Not much. He's the commissioner at the channel, so he stays in his ivory tower. I've met him at a few awards ceremonies, at the odd party, that kind of thing.' He looked away, appearing to remember something. 'I've never seen him on a shoot, though. Some commissioners do pop down to check how it's going from time to time, but Micky — never. That should tell you something.'

'What should it tell me?'

Fernando just shook his head slowly from side to side, and frowned at Scamarcio as if he were an idiot.

'What do your colleagues think of Proietti — the other big players like yourself?'

Fernando sighed. 'It might surprise you to learn that we don't sit around talking about him all day. We have far more interesting things to discuss.'

Scamarcio was beginning to lose hope. The only result he would come away with from this encounter would be a hangover. He drained his glass and asked: 'What are you working on next?'

A smile began playing on Fernando's lips. Scamarcio realised that the actor was very drunk now; too drunk to be useful, perhaps. He thought about leaving, trying again tomorrow. But he didn't feel quite ready to give up, and, besides, he wanted to try the Brunello.

'My next project?' said Fernando, breaking out into a full smile now, several gold fillings sparkling under the lights. 'Oh, it's a good one.' Then, as an afterthought: 'Would you like to hear the outline?'

Scamarcio had been about to decline, but then some instinct

told him to shut up. 'Sure. Go ahead, Mr Fernando.'

Fernando coughed and sat up straighter. He slowly moved his massive palms through the air in an arc as if he were opening an imaginary stage curtain.

'Scene One: It's a beautiful spring afternoon; a silver Mercedes is racing down the motorway towards Sperlonga. A successful executive is up front, his chauffeur at the wheel. The executive is at the pinnacle of his career: his work is going from strength to strength, and he has a beautiful wife, a lovely young son, and a string of stunning mistresses, to boot. On this particular afternoon, it seems that life just couldn't get any better.'

Suddenly, Fernando smashed both palms on the table, sending wine glasses and cutlery rattling. The bar fell silent, and customers turned and looked. Fernando leant in towards Scamarcio, commanding his attention, spearing him with his stare.

'All at once, a car comes round the bend on the wrong side of the road; it's doing way more than 160, heading straight for them. In an instant, the successful executive knows it's not going to stop, that they're all about to die, that this is it, the end, the end of everything he's worked so hard for.'

Fernando brought his palms together into a loud clap, prompting yet more customers to turn and whisper. Scamarcio noticed a man who might have been the manager hovering near their table. It seemed as if he were wrestling with the question of whether it was wise to ask a VIP of Fernando's magnitude to keep the noise down.

'Kapow! There's a dreadful, dreadful crash, and the car is a wreck. A helpful stranger just *happens* to be passing, and calls an ambulance.'

Scamarcio swallowed and didn't say a word.

Fernando shook his head slowly. 'That was a role I'd have liked to play — the helpful stranger — but I'm too well known.' He sighed. 'The price of fame.'

The waitress arrived with the Brunello. Scamarcio quickly took the bottle from her and refilled their glasses. He took a long sip, rolling the wine around his tongue a few times. Fernando nodded sagely, appreciating Scamarcio's enjoyment.

After he'd emptied his glass, Fernando steepled his hands and dipped his head lower, his voice a whisper now.

'The poor man goes to the hospital, but there's no sign of his family. He tries other places, but there's no sign of them there, either. So begins eleven days of hell; eleven days when this man can finally start to reflect on who might have done this, on who might want revenge, on who he might have hurt on the way up. Finally, he starts to understand what a total shit he's been to those around him; to those who made him soar, to those who brought him so much success.'

Fernando had hunched slightly, and was now tracing patterns with his gold-ringed finger in a small puddle of wine. His mood seemed to have shifted. The exuberance was gone. He was doing melancholy reflection now.

'Micky Proietti *was* a bastard; he was cruel, thoughtless, mean-spirited, and vindictive. We made ratings winners for him year after year. And year after year, the money got tighter and the hours got longer. There was never any gratitude, never any acknowledgement, never any praise.' He took another long drink and closed his eyes. 'Some people just need to be taught a lesson.'

'So that's all this was, the teaching of a lesson? A woman died, for Christ's sake!'

Fernando opened his eyes and looked at Scamarcio, but conveyed no discernible emotion. The actor just heaved his bulk slowly from behind the table and threw down a handful of notes. From where Scamarcio was sitting, they looked like 100-euro bills.

'The Brunello is on me, Detective. Knock yourself out.'

39

'So,' said GARRAMONE, 'Will we ever find the elusive Davide Stasio, so we can charge him for his sister's murder?'

'I doubt it,' said Scamarcio. 'My guess is that he's down south somewhere, and that he's being well hidden.'

Garramone ran the tips of his fingers across his desk. 'By whom? I thought those guys were after him for the money?'

'Allegiances shift,' said Scamarcio, a dull blade of anxiety probing his stomach.

'Do they?' asked Garramone, his eyes narrowing to tiny slits.

'I'm just theorising.'

'Hmm,' said the boss. He tapped his pen on the notepad in front of him. 'In terms of an eventual case against Proietti, do we have a paper trail that shows the money coming in and out?'

'Sartori lifted the files from Proietti's office, but the forensic accountants tell me it's murky. They'll need a lot of time with it, and there's no guarantee they'll be able to paint the picture at the end.'

'That's what we pay them 500 euros an hour for?'

'I'm just the messenger.'

'What about Stasio's files?'

'We're having trouble locating those.'

'What about his friendly accountant?'

'We're having trouble locating him, too.'

'Should we be worried?'

'I don't think so. Word is, he's taken a job in London, that he wanted to get away.'

'Will he testify?'

'I don't know. Let's see what the forensic accountants give us, and then we can let the prosecutor worry about the rest.'

'We have the video that culture secretary Manfredi made, where Proietti talks about his debt,' said Garramone, almost to himself.

'Yeah, but the prosecutor seemed to think that it won't be enough without the paper trail.'

Garramone let out a long breath through his nose. 'What a bizarre case — all these self-obsessed people with their strange little agendas.'

'They might be strange, but they're cunning: it seems that Giacometti didn't tell the others about his real reasons for hurting Proietti. My guess is that Fernando and Pepe thought they were just teaching Proietti a lesson for being a shit, and that the family would be returned. They had no idea that Giacometti and Dandini had their own very personal motives for getting at Proietti. It looked like the sky had fallen in on his world when Enzo Fernando found out about the footballer.'

Garramone smiled tiredly. 'I don't know who I prefer — the politicos or the media types.'

'They're all cut from the same cloth, if you ask me,' said Scamarcio.

'What did the lawyers say about your little recording?'

Scamarcio didn't want to go through it again. It had soured his mood all day. 'They're not that hopeful. Fernando is drunk — we're not at the station — and he chooses his words carefully.'

'It was worth a try. We'll get him down here.'

'Yeah — like that's going to bring a result. His lawyers will only let him open his mouth to confirm his name. I don't see him giving up the others.' He paused. 'But if I can pin down an identity for the fake driver, we could go back through his mobile-phone records. On the few stills we grabbed from motorway CCTV, he's wearing sunglasses, but if we do manage an ID and can link him to Fernando et al, we might be able to demonstrate conspiracy. But it's a big if.'

Garramone sat up straighter in his chair and folded his arms across his chest. Scamarcio found the formality of it unsettling.

'It's very good to see you back on your game, Scamarcio. You've done well on this. Keep it up—I have high hopes.'

The comment took Scamarcio by surprise. It sounded like some kind of promise, and Scamarcio slowly felt something lift in him. As he left the office, he reflected that the boss was right; it *was* good to be back in the game.

As Scamarcio stepped out into the mild April sunshine, the ripe-green haze on the trees and the vivid purples of the window boxes consolidated his mood. He began making his way briskly down Via San Vitale, then stopped and looked behind him: he had the unmistakable sense that he was being observed. He scanned the road, but couldn't see anyone. But then his attention was drawn to the pavement, and he realised that a dusty black-and-grey mongrel was scurrying towards him, his eyes trained on him. The dog soon caught up with him and flopped down tiredly at his feet.

'I wondered what had happened to you,' said Scamarcio, rubbing its ear. The dog allowed itself to be stroked for a few moments, then got up and padded back in the direction it had come. Scamarcio watched it trot off the road and edge its way beneath some bushes opposite headquarters.

Scamarcio smiled and carried on down Via San Vitale. Yet again, he thought about paying Fiammetta di Bondi a visit, asking her if she felt like a walk. Maybe he just needed to bury his cowardice and take a risk. Otherwise, what was waiting for him: an empty flat and an empty weekend? He'd always do his best to protect Aurelia, but it was clear she'd moved on. Perhaps it was time he tried to do the same.

'So, it's all wrapped up?' di Bondi asked, taking a hearty swig from a bottle of beer.

It seemed as if the whole of Rome had come out for a stroll by the Tiber: Scamarcio saw swarms of toddlers, battalions of elderly couples, hordes of tourists posing for photos and losing ice-creams from cones.

'As wrapped up as we can get it for now.'

Scamarcio wondered if di Bondi would make some excuse to leave; whether, with the investigation winding down, whatever reason she may have had for trying to get close to him had now passed. He was curious as to how it would play out. He'd park his emotions elsewhere for the time being, until he'd got a feel for the situation.

Di Bondi sighed and said: 'Poor Micky. I bet this has really pulled the rug out from under him.'

'Maybe that's what he needed.'

'What goes around comes around.'

In his mind's eye, Scamarcio saw Piocosta lying dead in his villa. He smelt the gas, heard the screams, felt the endless ricochet. Then he closed his eyes and tried to push the images away. He turned to the woman sitting next to him. Di Bondi really was the definition of beautiful. Yet there was an ephemeral quality to her beauty, a subtle evanescence, which somehow made it more powerful.

'I heard Micky wants to emigrate,' she said, as she watched a couple of giggling toddlers scampering on the riverbank.

'That's what he says, but there could be a case to answer. He won't be allowed anywhere until that's settled.'

'His poor boy — what a mess.' She ran a hand through her hair and pulled it behind her ear. Scamarcio liked the way her ears stuck out slightly.

He leaned back in his chair, trying to put a safer distance between them. 'What about you in all of this? One minute it's you

312

and Micky, then it's you and Manfredi, then it's you and Aconi—then, suddenly, it's none of it.'

'I told you what that was all about.'

'I don't get why it all came to an end so quickly.'

'Micky's family was kidnapped, Manfredi was murdered, and Aconi had had enough of the whole scene—as had I, by that point. It came to an end because we wanted it to, because *I* wanted it to.'

She folded her arms across her chest and looked peeved.

Scamarcio couldn't think of a response. He wasn't sure he believed her.

'Isn't it time you left all this showbiz shit behind, that you gave your attention to your studies, Fiammetta?' He regretted his tone immediately. He sounded like a patronising uncle.

'Seems like you want me gone.'

He rubbed at his stubble. 'You're frittering your life away with this showgirl crap. If money is the problem, I can help.'

Di Bondi surprised him by going completely still. She looked down into her lap for a long time, and began folding and unfolding her hands. Eventually, she said: 'Back to being the prostitute.'

This was not the reaction Scamarcio had expected. 'I don't need to pay women for sex,' he snapped.

'Feel sorry for me then?'

'For fuck's sake! How many ways are there to say it? I want you to be happy because I like you. Jesus, Fiammetta, you don't make it easy.'

She sniffed and smiled, a sadness in her eyes. Eventually she said: 'Thank you, thank you for your offer.'

He took a long breath and tried to ride out his anger. A small, thickset man was hurrying past, a large green holdall over his shoulder. Scamarcio recognised him as a minor crim he'd booked on more than one occasion. The crim spotted him, and immediately looked the other way.

Scamarcio tracked him for a few seconds then just let it go.

'There are good universities in Rome, Fiammetta; you wouldn't need to leave,' he said tentatively. He'd been thinking it, but hadn't decided to put it into words yet. Why the hell had he just come out with it then?

She looked at him and smiled, and in that moment, Scamarcio felt whatever had been inside him finally break its moorings and drift away. It was as if the past months had been a nothing, an insignificance.

They finished their drinks and left the bar, heading in the vague direction of di Bondi's flat. The ducks were out, and the evening sun had transformed the mud-brown Tiber into molten gold. Above it, the sky was a startling mesh of pinks and electric blues, dense and hyper-real, like distorted video.

As they rounded the corner heading for the bridge, a tall gentlemen in an expensive coat doffed his hat.

'What is it, Leo?' asked Fiammetta. 'You look like you've seen a ghost.'

For a few moments, Scamarcio couldn't speak, couldn't muster a response. He turned and looked behind him, but Greco had vanished.

'It was nothing,' he said.